The Urbana Free Library

To renew materials call
217-367-4057

RAVE REVIEWS FOR RICHARD HELMS'
JOKER POKER
and
VOODOO THAT YOU DO
The first two books in the *PAT GALLEGHER MYSTERY SERIES!*

"…For fans of noir mysteries, this debut offers a hearty concoction of violence, intrigue, sex, and even a little articulate humor."
The Library Journal

"…Helms delivers a hard-boiled homage steeped in humid New Orleans jazz, full of cool one-liners…"
-- *Salem MacKnee, The Charlotte Observer*

"Pat Gallegher is a good old-fashioned gumshoe....if you love the formula of the past masters, it's a hard-hitting good time!"
--*P.J. Nunn, The Charlotte Austin Review.*

"...Author Helms can spin a tale, and he's created some truly intriguing supporting characters here, well worth a return visit..."
--*Kevin Burton Smith, Thrilling Detective e-zine.*

"JOKER POKER by Richard Helms is a small feast to read...Very readable, effective, and enjoyable..."
--*Etienne Borgers, Hard-Boiled Mysteries website.*

"The first chapter grabbed me by the throat and didn't want to let go! I finally had to force myself to put it down after the sixth chapter because it was way past my bedtime and I wanted to be fully awake when I read the rest..."
--*Elizabeth Henze, Murder on the Internet Express*

"Brutal…JOKER POKER paints an intense picture of the dark side... good stuff… A bit like a smack in the face, with reality the weapon…. Powerful."
--*LeAnn "Buzzy" Arndt, Buzz Book Reviews*

"Admirable, smooth, funny, intelligent writing. Helms's a terrific storyteller, reminiscent of his idols Chandler, Hammett, and Spillane."
--*Sandra Ceren, author of PRESCRIPTION FOR TERROR*

"…brace yourself for a breath of New Orleans back alley adventure with Pat Gallegher and friends. You'll be glad you did!"
-*Miles Archer, Author of TOO MANY SPIES SPOIL THE CASE*

"...JOKER POKER is full of atmosphere and harks back to the hard-boiled novels of an earlier era. I feel like I've been to New Orleans. The plot, which starts off simple, becomes more and more complicated with double crossing aplenty....Gallegher himself is an irrepressible, multifaceted character who springs from the page..."
-*Karen Meek*, **OverMyDeadBody** *book reviews.*

"...Helms takes us through the back streets of New Orleans and the backwaters of the Louisiana Bayou. He dips us into the cult of Voudan (Voodoo) and he introduces us to the sometimes-insensitive child custody courts. In one scene, which I think is particularly strong he has a one-on-one confrontation with an investigating officer who just won't stay off his back...VOODOO THAT YOU DO is an excellent read, complete with not just interesting characters and a colorfully painted background, but with a well-constructed story and strong emotional involvement..."
- *Jack Bludis, author of* **THE BIG SWITCH**, *on the Rara Avis list*

"...With VOODOO THAT YOU DO, the second in the Pat Gallegher Mystery series, Richard Helms has become one of my favorite authors. This man really knows how to write. His language, vivid descriptions of people and places, realistic dialogue and intriguing well-paced plot and subplot transport the reader to authentic New Orleans..."
-*Sandra Levy Ceren*

"...In forensic psychologist Richard Helms's (*Joker Poker*) second Pat Gallegher mystery, VOODOO THAT YOU DO, our New Orleans jazz-musician hero witnesses a pal's murder and helps out a 10-year-old girl who's run away from her Vietnamese mob-leader stepfather...can Gallegher, the only one privy to various inside information, head off a gangland war and simultaneously pursue his romantic interest?..."
-*Publishers Weekly Mystery Notes*

"...a good story with an interesting and well drawn protag. .. Treat yourself and read this one folks..."
-*Sylvia Matthews, Ivy Quill*

"...Move aside Martin Hegwood, Tony Dunbar, Mike Stewart, Ace Atkins, Julie Smith, and watch out James Lee Burke here comes Richard Helms and his Pat Gallegher Mystery Series...Helms builds several thousand words into a picture of New Orleans that's pure pleasure to read..."
-*Anthony Dauer, editor, **judas ezine**.*

"…Hot New Orleans nights, hot jazz and hot lead all come together in Richard Helms' new Pat Gallegher mystery, VOODOO THAT YOU DO. This sequel to Helms' JOKER POKER is a worthy follow-up that takes the reader on a hot, fast journey from the gator-infested Atchafalaya basin to the steamy back alleys of the French Quarter. Don't miss this book!!"
-Elizabeth Henze, Murder on the Internet Express

"….Helms has a way of making you feel the rhythms and even smell the smells of the New Orleans French Quarter. I'm not a native, but I've been in South Louisiana for 10 years and am very critical of authors who want to take advantage of the Quarter's reputation without even beginning to understand any part of it. Helms's character Pat Gallegher BELONGS in the French Quarter…"
-Jann Breisacher, Amazon.com and Dorothy L. list

"…This one will put a spell on you…VOODOO THAT YOU DO begins with a bang, and doesn't let up for more than 300 pages...A mesmerizing *tour de force*…I heartily recommend VOODOO THAT YOU DO to hardboiled fans, mystery aficionados, and anyone who appreciates well-wrought prose. And I eagerly look forward to the next installment in the Pat Gallegher series…"
- Jack Ewing, author FREAK OUT and KISSING ASPHALT

"…VOODOO THAT YOU DO is a multi-faceted, hard-boiled gripping mystery set in the famed New Orleans's French Quarter. Rich with the seamy characters occupying both sides of the law inhabiting the Vieux Carre, Pat Gallagher, a face-up guy, manages to blast his way through this maze of rival gangs, mobsters, and jaded law enforcement. There are more threats on Gallagher's life than there are tourists thronging the Big Easy. One-liners abound. Helms, an author of exceptional talent, does not disappoint. I highly recommend VOODOO THAT YOU DO to readers who like their mysteries served up noir…"
-Jonni Rich, Author of DARK LEGACY, DEADLY SWEET SIXTEEN, and WEB OF DECEIT, Ivy Quill Reviews, Dorothy L. list

"…Richard Helms has given us another fast-moving, colorful, brilliantly written hardboiled mystery, set in a torrid New Orleans atmosphere so vivid that you can smell the shrimp on Gallagher's fingers when he eats. I give VOODOO THAT YOU DO four aces, two wild cards, and a joker. A genuine power hand, to be sure…"
-Beth Anderson, author of NIGHT SOUNDS and MURDER ONLINE

JUICY
WATUSI

Other Books by
Richard Helms

JOKER POKER

BOBBY J.

VOODOO THAT YOU DO

THE VALENTINE PROFILE

THE AMADEUS LEGACY

RICHARD HELMS

JUICY WATUSI

BACK ALLEY BOOKS

BACK ALLEY BOOKS

An imprint of

BARBADOES HALL COMMUNICATIONS

a thrilling little publisher

Visit the Barbadoes Hall website at:

http://hometown.aol.com/BarHallCom/main.html

ISBN 0-9710159-1-0

Printed In The United States of America

Acknowledgements

This is the third book in the Pat Gallegher Mystery Series. Accordingly, I would like to thank all the people who helped make the first two books a reality. Special thanks go to Patti Nunn, Salem Macknee, Etienne Borgers, Kevin Burton Smith, Pamela Stone, Sandy Ceren, Elizabeth Henze, Miles Archer, and anyone else who's written a review for either JOKER POKER or VOODOO THAT YOU DO.

Special thanks, as always, go out to Alan and Kate Kaplan, my good friends and most loyal (and patient) fans, for their comments and strong stomachs.

My lovely life-partner Elaine deserves more credit than I can ever repay for her support and guidance, so I'll just stay married to her and give her a copy of the book. The rest of the thanks stays strictly between us.

As ever, I would like to recognize Belva Dare Steele, my tenth grade writing teacher, who saw something encouraging in me, and convinced me that I might actually be able to produce readable prose. Though she has been gone thirty years now, she still stands, looking over my shoulder, as I write.

It's beginning to creep me out a little.

For Elaine

The Best Of Us
Is Still Being Written

JUICY
WATUSI

ONE

They say that the only problem with twenty-twenty hindsight is that you only get it when you no longer need it. Looking back, walking into *Les Jolies Blondes* around four that afternoon was probably a bad idea.

Merlie Comineau, my girlfriend, had thrown me a fiftieth birthday party, several days early, so I would be surprised. Everyone I knew was there, along with at least one person I'd never met. I'd come to this Bourbon Street strip bar to speak with her again.

I didn't like being in there. Strip joints give me the raving heebie-jeebies. Maybe it's my Catholic training from seminary, or maybe deep down I'm just this big fat closet prig. Whatever, there's just something about being in a room filled with naked women flinging their boobs about, trolling for tips, that falls somewhere along the outer fringes of my comfort zone.

"Hey, Gallegher," Shorty had said at the birthday party, tapping me on the shoulder. "I want you to meet someone."

I turned toward him. He was standing with a woman who looked to be in her middle twenties, but at second thought I realized that this was deceptive. Shorty introduced her as Lucy Nivens.

"Lucy and me, we been going out for about a month," he said.

"So," I said, "What do you do, Lucy?"

"Oh," she said, "I'm a dancer."

"Lucy works at Les Jolies Blondes," Shorty said.

The music rattled my eardrums, the air was too smoky by half, and the joint could have stood a decent fumigation for cockroaches. The beer was domestic. It ran four dollars a bottle.

I took a seat at one far end of the bar, since I stood the least chance of being hit on there by one of the dancers. Girls in the pussy clubs make about half their income off tips. The rest they make by shilling drinks out of the customers and giving lap dances. Sit still long enough in one of these places, and sooner or later one of the dancers will sidle up and offer a "private session" in the back, complete with a triple-priced bottle of cheap champagne. It isn't prostitution, exactly, since the come-on is all tease and no squeeze.

I wasn't in the mood.

It wasn't long before Lucy made her entrance. The stage was like a three ring circus. Reynard wanted the customers' attention on the girls, and not on how fast their beers were disappearing. At any one time, there were as many as four dancers on the stage, gyrating and twisting and swinging on the poles.

Lucy had to be thirty-five if she was a day, but she had held up well. Her belly was flat and her breasts were still firm, and she had the legs of a marathoner. I felt sheepish as hell, sitting at the bar and watching my boss's girlfriend thrusting her naked crotch at the guys sitting on the front row, as they stuffed dollar bills into her elastic garters. I felt, somehow, as if I was trespassing on Shorty's turf.

"Lucy works at Les Jolies Blondes," Shorty said.
I think I felt my head tighten a couple of notches.

Les Jolie Blondes was owned and run by Sylvester Reynard, a plegmatic, scheming whale who had tried to have me killed a couple of years earlier. I don't kill easily. He figured that out, and after a while the whole matter blew over and he gave up the notion of squibbing me.

I think.

I drained a couple of beers, and waited for her to come out from the back after her show. I stood next to the door to the back, so she couldn't help but see me when she hit the bar.

She stepped out, wearing this cutoff tee shirt and a pair of jeans shorts cut off just at the top of her thighs. There was a sheen on her face from the exertion of her show. I lifted a hand to get her attention. She froze for a second, and then walked over.

"Man, I could not believe that twist was here," Grover, my redbone pimp friend, had said.

"Lucy?"

"Yeah, Juicy Lucy."

"Tell me more."

"She be a rental, Doc. Guys used to lease her by the hour for parties and shit."

"Any chance she's out of the business, Grove?"

"Sure. Slim and none, and slim done got on the fuckin' bus. How you know that snatch, anyhow?"

"I didn't, before tonight. Shorty brought her."

"What kinda party he be plannin', anyhow?"

"I'm working," she said.

"I'm buying," I said, holding up my beer.

"So buy me one."

"You want a beer?"

"No, a gin and tonic."

Another eight bucks down the drain. I was beginning to think I was in the wrong business, not that anyone would give a nickel to watch me strut my fat fanny on a stage. I bought her the drink.

"Is there someplace we can talk?" I asked.

"We can talk here."

"Someplace private?"

"You want to buy a bottle of champagne and talk back in my dressing room? That's as private as it gets around here."

I sighed and stroked my face. This was getting expensive. It grated on my stingy Irish character.

"Sure," I said.

Lucy leaned over the bar and said something to the bartender, who dumped a warm bottle of Taylor champagne into a plastic bucket of ice and dropped two plastic flutes into it before handing the whole mess over to Lucy.

"Thirty dollars," she said.

I dropped a twenty and a ten on the bar. The bartender glowered at me for not including a tip, so I tossed another five down. Lucy nodded her head in the direction of the door, and I followed her into the back hallway.

Tommy Callahan had pulled up a chair to sit next to me.

"Listen, Gallegher, your bartender's girlfriend...."

All my Spidey-senses started going off. Callahan was deeply immersed in the original Mafia gangs, as a deep-cover operative for the Department of Justice. He had worked his way up the ladder with Lucho Braga's organization, about as far as a mick is ever going to get, before Lucho bit the big one.

"Yeah?"

"Look, maybe this is none of my business..."

"Get to it, Tommy."

"Okay. You remember the night I came in and told you about Braga dying?"

"Yeah."

"And you recall how I told you he stroked out while he was shagging this dancer chick?"

"Uh-huh," I said, even though I could already see where he was going.

"Well, that's the chick he was bangin'," he said, pointing at Lucy Nivens.

Once the door was closed, the music muted a bit. The hall was narrow and high, like so many in the Quarter, and the walls were exposed brick. There was a series of doors, and through the open ones I could see small sitting rooms with cheap recliners and plastic tables. I felt like watching my feet, not knowing what I might step in. Lucy led me to the far end of the hall, and stood at a doorway, waiting for me to go in first.

I sat in a chair, and she set the champagne down on the plastic table. She immediately pulled the tee shirt over her head, and started to take off the shorts.

"With champagne you get me naked," she said.

"No," I said. "That's okay. Do me a favor and keep your clothes on. This is difficult enough as it is."

She stared at me strangely for a moment, as if looking for antennae, and then pulled the shirt back on.

"What's this all about?" she asked.

"A friendly visit. I had some questions. This seemed the best way to get you alone."

"Questions?"

"Some of the people at the party were surprised to see you there. It seems they already knew you. You looked like you knew them, too."

"Yeah?"

"Look, there's no easy way to ask this. Shorty's been a friend of mine for years. Does he know about the hooking?"

Her eyes got fearful, and she glanced at the ceiling light, the doorknob, anything to avoid looking directly at me.

"Tommy Callahan says he hired you to sleep with Lucho Braga the day he died. Grover says you do parties -- two, three men at a time. You did not like being around a cop that was at the party. Maybe it's none of my business, but I don't want to see Shorty going around misinformed."

"It's over," she said. "It was a lousy thing to do, and I felt terrible about it. I quit."

"When?"

"Jesus," she said, and slugged back some of the gin and tonic. "Did you ever have someone die on top of you in bed? I mean, here's this dead guy, and he's lying on top of me, and I can't breathe, and like he's still.... *inside* me. The old guy, Braga, he was the last. I had nightmares for weeks after that. I figured even starvation was better than screwing for a living..."

There was knock on the door. Before either of us could get up, it swung open.

Spanky Gallo had worked for Sylvester Reynard for years. He was a fair-to-middling light heavyweight boxer in his twenties, until he developed a glass jaw and a hundred dollar a day cocaine habit. He had been off the drugs for years, but he had slowed a bunch and had gone to suet working the bar.

Gallo did a little bit of everything for Reynard - running errands, bouncing, and occasionally squaring an overdue score. He was dangerous enough, I suppose, but he had never given me any real trouble. Now, standing in the doorway, he looked as if he wanted to make up for lost time.

"What in hell are you doing here, Gallegher?"

"Spanky, nice to see you again."

"Answer the question." His voice was dry and gravelly, and his teeth had this yellow junkie dinge on them.

"I'm having champagne with Lucy here. Would you like to join us? If you'd like, Lucy'll take off her clothes."

He ignored me.

"Mr. Reynard would like to see you."

Great.

"Tell him I'll see him when I'm finished with Lucy," I said.

Spanky was wearing a pair of designer jeans, and one of those godawful shirts without collars, just this band around his bull neck and the shirt buttoned all the way up. Over the shirt was a linen blazer. He pulled the blazer back to show me his automatic stowed low in a shoulder holster, with the intent of intimidating me.

"Mr. Reynard says now."

I didn't think through what happened next. It just happened. Maybe it was Gallo trying to muscle me, or maybe it was just the gun. I reached into the plastic champagne bucket, came up with a handful of ice and water, and I tossed it in his face. He reared back against the wall. Before he could get his bearings, I yanked his pistol from the shoulder holster.

Lucy jumped up and backed against the far wall, probably thinking that I was going to draw down on Spanky Gallo right there, and then maybe kill her to get rid of the witness.

Gallo mopped at his face, which was flushed bright red from ear to ear, and glared at me.

"I do not like guns," I said. Then I turned it sideways and showed Gallo the safety. "I do, however, know a thing or two about them."

I flicked the catch back and forth.

"Safety on, safety off. Safety on, safety off. Don't ever try to threaten someone with a locked gun, Spanky. It's embarrassing."

I turned to Lucy.

"I guess I have to go see Mr. Reynard, now. I'll take you at your word, Lucy. You say you're out of it, then you're out of it. I just wanted to protect Shorty."

I stuffed the automatic into my pants, and gestured for Gallo to lead the way. I followed him down the hallway, and then up a short flight of stairs to Reynard's office. He opened the door, and then held it while I walked in.

I'm a sizable fellow, standing about six and a half feet tall in the shower and running enough above two-seventy that I don't divulge it openly, but even so Reynard made me feel small. About twenty years earlier, Sylvester Reynard had been whacked across the throat with a beer bottle during a bar fight in Algiers. It did something to his thyroid, and he started gaining an alarming amount of weight. He had tried diets, surgery, pills -- nothing had worked, and he just kept gaining weight like those lab rats whose limbic systems had been ablated.

He sat on a loveseat set up on bricks behind his desk, because he could no longer find an office chair that could contain him. He wheezed all the time, as his overworked heart strained to catch up with his need for oxygen. His face was florid, and his nose was deeply crisscrossed with scarlet veins. His hands were like Italian sausages attached to birthday balloons.

As humans go, he was a real mess.

"Jesus, Sly," I said as I sat down. "No more Twinkies for you."

"Gallegher..." he said, as if he wasn't at all pleased to say it. The sound came from deep inside him, like an echo off the Grand Canyon, and it rumbled around the room. "I ought to kick your ass."

"I don't think you can kick that high," I said. I pulled the automatic from my waistband, and dropped the clip into my free hand. I laid the gun on Reynard's desk. "I took this from Spanky. I hope you'll understand if I leave the clip with the bartender downstairs."

"You got a smart mouth, dickwipe."

"It's an accessory. It came with the first class mind."

"You got a lot of balls coming in here like this."

"It wasn't something I preferred to do. What happened between us was a long time ago."

"I lost a lot of money on that deal."

"It wasn't your money."

"You stuck your nose in where it didn't belong. You screwed up a sweet situation for me."

"It's over and done. Think of all the sweet situations I haven't screwed up for you since then."

"What are you doing with one of my girls?"

"This doesn't have anything to do with you, Sly. It's personal."

He leaned forward. I could swear I could feel a shift in the tectonic plate underneath the city.

"Anything having to do with one of my girls concerns me," he rumbled. He had that tone of voice that made it clear that he'd just as soon have zagged me. Given our history, I figured it was time to make a little peace.

"She's been seeing the bartender over at my club. Several guys I know have told me she was hooking. I thought maybe I ought to check it out."

"My girls don't hook," he said. "I catch them screwing the customers, they're out on their ass. I don't need that kind of trouble with the cops."

"From what I hear, she might have been moonlighting. You might not have known about it."

He nodded, fold of flesh beneath his chin wobbling obscenely.

"You might be right. What'd she tell you?"

"She said she was, but it was a long time ago. She said she stopped maybe six months back."

"You believe her?"

I shrugged.

"I don't have any reason not to. She admitted everything I was told. She was straight with me on that. I figure she's telling the truth."

"Well, then..." Reynard said, drumming his hammy fingers on the scratched desktop. He was wearing about fifty pounds of rings on that one hand. I wondered where he had found a Big and Tall jeweler. "So you got no more business here, then?"

I shook my head.

"None that I can think of."

"Then you'll be going now?"

"Works for me," I said, standing. I walked to the door, where Spanky Gallo stood, still trying to kill me with his x-ray eyes. I turned back to Reynard.

"Hey, Sly, are we cool here?"

"What do you mean?"

"This thing between us. It's over and done with, right? You don't have any old contracts floating around on me out there, do you?"

He seemed to be laughing, but it was hard to tell under all that blubber.

"Man, I wouldn't even put a Haitian kid on you, if he offered to do it just for the action. You ain't that important anymore."

"Good," I said. "Just checking."

I turned to leave.

"Hey, Gallegher," Reynard called.

I looked back.

"You watch your ass. You could become important again, you know."

I nodded, and decided to let him have the last word. I lumbered down the stairs, and handed the clip to the wide-eyed bartender as I passed by.

As quickly as I could, I walked out the front door into the piercing sunlight of Bourbon Street. It was still early in the afternoon, before the gutters had started to fill with beer. A cold front had laundered the air, which smelled like new-mown wheat. It felt good to be out of the bar, good to be alive.

I should have bottled that moment. I wouldn't feel that good again for a long time.

TWO

Merlie was in my apartment, waiting for me to finish showering for dinner. We were going to Irene's for Italian. I was in the mood for shrimp parmegiana, which wasn't exactly on the menu, but they knew me well enough to make it for me anyway.

I stepped out of the bathroom in one towel, drying my hair with another. Merlie was standing next to my bookcase, which stretches the length and height of one full wall of the apartment.

"Looking for something to read?" I asked, as I turned to the mirror and tried to rake my hair into submission.

"If you take any longer, I'll have time for one of those Russian novels."

"There's a Penguin edition of *Anna Karenina* over on the right side."

"Pass. Here's something, though. Ernest Hemingway."

"Oh," I said, as I rummaged through my drawer for underwear, "I like him."

"You would. He writes the way you live."

"Do tell?"

"Quickly, succinctly, no wasted movement..."

"Poetry in motion."

"You flatter yourself."

"Which book is it?" I asked, crossing the room to her.

"*The Sun Also Rises.*"

"Cool. Borrow it if you want. I know where to find you if you don't bring it back."

I pulled on a pair of Dockers and a Duckhead pullover sportshirt Merlie had bought me before our last trip to Barbados.

"Who's Laurence Beaudry?" she asked.

"Hmmm?

"Here, in the front of the book, inside the cover. It says *Ex Libris, Laurence Beaudry.*"

"Oh, he's just this guy, the original owner. The book's a first edition. I bought it at an estate sale a year or so ago."

"You have a lot of first editions?"

"Baby, I *am* a first edition," I said, as I finished tying my shoes. "You ready to go?"

There was a knock at the door, and Merlie stashed the book in her oversized purse on the way to answering it. Shorty stood in the hallway.

"Hi, Merlie. Mind if I talk to Gallegher here for a minute?"

"Not at all," she said. "I'll just wait downstairs."

I could see by the pain in his eyes what had happened. I decided to deal straight with him.

"You spoke with Lucy?" I said.

"Uh huh," he said, closing the door behind him.

"And?"

"You want to explain why you went down to the club to hassle her today?"

"The story loses something in the translation," I said. "Though, looking back on it, she might have seen it that way."

"She says you took Spanky Gallo's gun away from him. Scared the shit out of her."

"What else did she say?"

Shorty doesn't get angry often, but when he does he wears it like a wetsuit. His fists clenched a couple of times, and you could have steamed cauliflower in his ears.

"Just what in fuck were you doing there, Gallegher? You want to explain that? You want to tell me what you were doing buying a bottle of champagne and taking her backstage, staring at her naked like that? Do you know how that makes me feel?"

I sat down on the couch, trying to keep my composure.

"*If* it had happened like that, I would presume you would feel betrayed, angry, maybe even a little violent. Would you like to hear it from my side?"

"You admit you were there?"

"Yes, Shorty, I do."

"And you bought that champagne and went backstage with her?"

"Does this mean you don't want to hear my side?"

"What else is there?"

"What did she tell you?"

"You tell me!"

He was fuming. Shorty's a squared off, runty kind of guy, who comes up maybe to my armpit. He's been rousting one way or another all his life, though, in traveling shows, strip joints, or bars, and he's all muscle. I figured, if he were to really blow, he could do some damage.

"Okay. Buying the champagne was the only way I could get to talk to her alone. It's her job to take off her clothes, Shorty. It's what she does. When she tried to in the back, I told her to put them back on. I wasn't there to ogle your girl, which I might add made me a minority of one."

"So why'd you want her alone?"

"Man, she ought to be the one telling you this."

"You tell me."

There was no getting around it. I could have told him to blow off, go call Lucy, ask her what the deal was. That would have been easy. Maybe he would have done it. Maybe he would have tried to dent my face first. Maybe I would have been forced to hurt him, and I didn't want to do that.

So I told him.

"... And that's how it is," I finished. "After what Tommy and Grover told me, I was concerned about whether you knew or not. I wanted to know if she was still punching. I couldn't just go to you and ask if you knew she was a hooker. I was hoping she had already done that herself."

Halfway through the story, he had sat heavily on the other end of the sofa. The color drained from his face like melting ice, and I could see the disillusion come across his eyes as they turned cold and dead.

"This is a hell of a thing," he said at last. "This is a hell of a thing."

"Yes it is," I agreed. "It's a hell of a thing. I really wish she'd told you first."

"She wouldn't do it that way," Shorty said. "That's why she called me. She knew that you'd tell me if I came after you with it. She's... she's not a strong person, Gallegher."

"Maybe she's stronger than you think. She says she hasn't turned a trick in over six months. She's trying to stretch her finances to get by without it."

"No, she's not that strong. I been helping to support her for a couple of months. She never told me about the other thing. You think maybe she knows I own most of the bar? You think she's just hanging on for the money?"

It's a tough deal being someone like Shorty. He's not tall or witty or urbane. He spent a lot of his life out in the air, working jobs nobody would ever choose given an alternative. The sun and the wind have etched his features until he looks like he washes his face with a weed eater. On the other hand, like every other human who draws breath, he has this innate need to be loved and accepted. That's been a rarity in his life, and when, once in a while, someone gives him more than a passing glance, a guy like Shorty can glom onto that and wring it to death.

I had a feeling that Lucy had really liked him for what he was. Despite his inconstant past and his rough exterior, Shorty can be a real sweetheart.

Once he knew the truth, though, I could tell that it was all ruined for him. The nagging doubt, born of the realization that Lucy had kept a dreadful secret from him for so long, would fester and grow suspicions like mushrooms in the dark. It didn't matter if her slate was clean and her heart was purified by his love, he would always look at her and wonder, and that was all it would take to poison their love.

It was a hell of a thing.

"I don't think that's it," I said, finally. "I think she likes you for you."

"So what am I gonna do, now?"

"Damned if I know. You have to decide whether you want her for what she is now, or drop her for what she used to be. Merlie's not interested in the seminary student I used to be, or the psychologist I was before I came here. I don't think she'd be interested in either of those guys. Those guys checked out for the coast years ago. Maybe that's the way you have to look at it with Lucy."

In the end, he sat there for five or ten minutes, and then he stood up, and he walked out of the apartment. He didn't say a word. He was alone with his own problems, and he would have to take his time to sort out all the briars I had tossed into his head.

I felt sorry for the little guy, but there was nothing else I could do.

I told Merlie about my conversation with Shorty over dinner that night. She listened attentively, but I could see her eyes cloud over when I told her about my visit with Reynard. She seemed especially perturbed when I described the disarming of Spanky Gallo.

"You shouldn't have gone," she said at last.

"Perhaps not," I agreed, taking another bite of the shrimp. It was butterflied and battered in seasoned bread crumbs, then fried golden brown, and then smothered with Irene's best meat sauce and four cheeses, and baked until just *so*. It was elegant and sublime, and I hated wasting it with self-reproach. I took another sip of the valpolicella I'd ordered to go with it.

"It wasn't your business," she continued.

"I seem to remember agreeing with you."

"It was dangerous," she said.

She seemed to be summarizing her points.

"I can handle dangerous. You're right about the other things, though. I poked my nose in where it didn't belong, and got it whacked. I promise never to do it again."

She rolled a fork full of spaghetti like a pro, using her spoon to shape it just to fit past her full, ripe lips.

"Liar," she said.

"Probably."

A stocky black man sitting behind her mumbled something, then nodded to himself. He was sitting alone, dressed in clean but apparently well-worn slacks and a plaid flannel shirt. His eyes looked worrisome.

You run into all types in the Quarter. The place is like some kind of geographic No-Pest strip for every loosely wrapped bozo who ever hit the road. Some of them are just kooky but harmless. Some you need to watch closely. Some defy all prediction.

"*Rule number one*," he mumbled, "*Never get high on your own supply.*" He sang it like a rap song, beating the table with his forefingers.

"On the other hand," I said, "What if Shorty and Lucy had gone on for years without him knowing?"

"You don't know all of my history," she said. "How do you know there's not something deep and dark back there?"

"*Rule number two*," the man behind Merlie chanted, beating out the rhythm on the table top. "*Never show your hand when you dealin' with the man.*"

"Are you trying to tell me something? Is your conscience getting the better of you, dear?"

"It's not that," she said. "I mean, *what if*? Would it matter to you if I did something a long time ago that I was ashamed to admit?"

"*Rule number three.*" Ratta, tatta, tatta. "*Never be unstrapped, even when you take a crap.*"

"Like what?" I asked, but my attention was drawn past her shoulder.

The rapper was packing.

I could see the outline of a revolver at the small of his back, and he was acting way too unstable for my comfort. His face was beginning to tense, there were beads of sweat on his brow, and I could make out a strange, other-worldly look in his eyes.

"It could be anything. Maybe I did juvenile time as a kid. Maybe I had an abortion when I was eighteen."

"Maybe you married a transvestite banker," I ventured.

"Rule number four." Thumpit, thumpit. *"Go ahead and shoot if some asshole takes your toot."*

"Well, I did, of course. But you already know about *that.*"

The man was scanning the room, his eyes darting about like ping-pong balls. I could see the yellowed sclera, and in an instant I could see his whole story, and a glimpse of the future. He was a hype, and he had just ordered a meal he couldn't afford. That didn't matter, though, because I could tell by the sweat on his face and the agitation that he was strung out about two stops to the right of reason, and he planned to use the revolver to make his world righteous.

He was planning to knock over the restaurant just as soon as Bourbon Street was blocked and the cop cars couldn't rush through the crowds.

"Rule number five," he mumbled absently. *"You gonna have the jerks, if you' caught without your works."*

"Can you do me a favor?" I asked Merlie. I pulled my car keys from my pocket and placed them on the table. The back of Irene's is a parking garage, which is also the location of the restrooms. As it happens, I keep my Pinto there. It's pricey, since parking space in the Quarter is hard to come by, but sometimes I need quick access to my wheels. "I left a couple of books in my car that I need to drop back by the library. Would you get them for me?"

She stared at me with this quizzical look on her face, then she caught my eyes looking past her, and for the first time she seemed to notice the chanter behind her. I could see her pupils dilate with the first adrenalin rush, and color started to rise in her cheeks.

"It's no big thing," I said, trying to make my voice calm and serene, hoping she wouldn't throw a rod. "I just haven't finished eating yet. While you're out there, you might want to visit the ladies'. Your nose is a little shiny."

Merlie and I hadn't been a couple for long, but she had already learned to recognize when I meant business.

"Rule number six. Every chump's a mark, and they're easy in the dark."

Merlie grabbed the keys from the table.

"No rush," I said, conversationally. I hoped she caught it as the warning I intended. If she were to grab the keys and run toward the back exit, it was a cinch she'd tip off the hype, and maybe he'd go off before I was ready for him.

She nodded, and picked up the keys.

"I was just thinking about paying a visit to the little girls' room anyway. I'll be right back."

"Take your time," I told her as she stood. The skin around her eyes was tight, and her forehead furrowed a bit.

She mouthed *Be careful* to me. Then she was gone.

I took a moment to fill my wine glass, and poured the rest of the bottle into Merlie's glass, before placing the empty on the floor next to my feet. The junkie was up to number nine, and he was doing the sitting jitterbug in his chair. As he finished the rap, I saw him reach back to grab the revolver, and start to stand. With my left hand, I speared a piece of shrimp with the fork, but my good hand was around the neck of the wine bottle as soon as the guy had his back to me. The revolver was out now, and he was facing the cash register at the front of the restaurant.

"Okay, motherfucker," he said. "Give me the *money*!"

I crossed the floor in about a second and a half, the heavy wine bottle already in a roundhouse swing that came from somewhere near Baton Rouge.

I think he knew, in that last tenth of a second, that I was coming for him, but it was too late to do anything about it. He seemed to turn, maybe an eighth of the way toward me, just before I connected with the bottle. It made a sick, empty, thudding sound as I brought it across the back of his head. He went down like laundry. The gun skittered across the floor and banged off the base of the front counter. The hype rolled on the floor, cradling his head, screaming like Tarzan. I looked around, and the other eight or ten diners were staring at me like a circus freak, this big, hulking old white fart who had just taken out a dangerous felon with a bottle of dago table red.

"Call the cops," I said to the cashier.

"What the hell'd you do that for?" the hype screamed between wails of pain. "What the fuck'd you do that for?"

I saw the back door open, and Merlie peeked in from the garage.

"Is it over?" she asked.

I grabbed a couple of napkins and tied them together in a neat sheepshank, and then wrapped them around the skell's wrists as a sort of makeshift pair of handcuffs.

Within minutes the police arrived, and the owner explained what had happened. The older cop looked at me like I had two heads. He told me what an idiot I was for stepping in, that I could have been killed. I didn't bother to tell him the odds that, strung out as he was, the robber might have just opened up with the gun at the first sign of resistance, because that would have been useless. Cops have a fairly narrow frame of reference, which comes from looking at too many dead tourists.

"The answer," I told Merlie as we sat back down to finish our wine, after the cops hauled the junkie off, "is that I would love you no matter what you did in the past. Shorty, though, is not me."

And that was pretty much the way dinner went.

"Okay, Rambo, you want to explain what went on back there?" Merlie asked as I closed the door to my apartment over Holliday's.

I pulled my ancient Conn band cornet from its case, and fingered the ivory inlaid keys, checking the action. A faint drift of oil caressed my nostrils. It smelled sweet, like frying onions.

"I could see the guy was going to try to knock over the restaurant. I figured I could do something about it."

"Not that," she said, dropping down on the couch and crossing her arms. "I'm talking about the Sir Galahad routine, making sure I was out of the picture before you got down and dirty."

"Oh," I said, lifting the mouthpiece and fitting it into the horn. "That."

I lifted the cornet and did a quick downward scale. I wondered, briefly, in the moment that Merlie gave me, whether I had any inkling when I joined the band in eighth grade that it would lead to such a life as the one I now led.

Probably not.

"Put the cornet down, Pat," she said. "I'm trying to get a hold on this. Are you going to go around thinking I need protection for the rest of my life -- our lives?"

"I don't know," I said, placing the horn on a stand next to my recliner near the window. "That's a long time. I have a hard time focusing that far ahead. Let it go, Merlie. It's no big deal."

"You're not telling me something."

Damn her intuition. Merlie runs a shelter for runaway and throwaway kids over in the Garden District. She's used to hearing all kinds of diversionary stories and outright stalls. It was stupid to try and blow her off. She deals with some of the world's most creative liars day in and day out.

"I didn't want you involved," I said.

"With the robbery? With busting that guy's skull?"

"With the whole thing. I explained this a long time ago, dear. I do not travel in the most savory circles. The guy I saw today at *Les Jolies Blondes*? Reynard? Three years ago he put a contract out on me. He says it's been canceled, and I suppose I believe him, but I still look over my shoulder from time to time. For better or worse, I've made this life of mine, and I have to manage it. I don't have to force it on you."

"I see," she said, shaking her head. "So the boundaries of our... relationship, whatever, are limited. You've staked out areas I'm not allowed to enter."

"Something like that," I said, sitting in the recliner. I grabbed the horn and did another scale.

"And suppose I can't deal with that?"

"That would be a shame," I said, sadly. "I would regret that a lot. It's for the better, though."

"Oh," Merlie said.

She gathered her sweater and her scarf.

"I suppose it's nice of you to make that decision for me. It could get real troublesome if you left something that important to li'l ol' me."

She walked toward the door.

"Call me when you evolve a little, Pat," she said as she reached for the knob.

"I don't want you to die," I said quietly. "Like the others."

She froze, her hand still on the knob. She didn't turn, or stiffen up, or even seem to flinch. She just froze, and she spoke without looking at me.

"Maybe you ought to explain that."

So I did.

I told her all the stories I had held back, the real horror tales about the women I had failed to keep alive. I told her about Claire Sturges, all cool strength wrapped in shimmering silk, the product of two centuries of careful New Orleans social breeding, the woman who took me into her life after I found the man who killed her former lover, Baxter Flatt. I had run to Claire when a deranged, dying man, Adam Kincaid, who hated me more than anything or anyone, called and told me he was coming to New Orleans to kill me as a last act of vengeance before his cancer took him out.

That story ended with Kincaid splattered on the concrete six floors below Claire's apartment, me sprawled against the wall sobbing, and Claire with a hole in her chest the size of a navel orange, her glazed unseeing eyes staring vacantly out the window, after Kincaid had shot her when I grabbed for his pistol.

"You blamed yourself," Merlie said.

"Blamed is not the word. I was immersed in guilt. I had a choice, after all. I didn't have to stay in New Orleans when Kincaid came hunting for me. He couldn't have found me if I had just gone on the road. He would have died by New Years, and that would have been all there was to it. Instead, I had to drag a woman I cared about into my own personal adventure, and it killed her. It took me a long time to get over it. I heard the rustle of the robes, Merlie. I felt the breeze as Death walked by me, when it was rightly my time, and took her instead. It wasn't right. "

"It was the way things happened," Merlie told me, taking my hand. "Believe it or not, darling, some things are out of your control."

"It wasn't right to pull her into it. That's what tonight was all about. I knew I was going to do the two-fisted rumba with that junkie, and that there was the possibility that either he or I would bite the big one. I didn't want you involved. I didn't want you to catch a piece of shrapnel off my brittle karma. This is the way it is, you see. I am what I am. Like it or not, I've become this occasionally violent creature and, also like it or not, I love you too much to let you get caught up in that violence. I won't let it happen to you."

I didn't know what else to say. There were a thousand unarticulated thoughts in my head, raw emotions mostly, but none of them seemed capable or willing to expose themselves openly. I could only hope that Merlie understood, if just a little, and that she wouldn't be scared off by my rampant paranoia.

She didn't leave. Neither did she come any closer.

It was a hell of a thing I'd done, laying heavies on her so early in the evening. I had just told her that there were secret, dangerous places in my life where she was not welcome, no matter how devoted we might be to each other. It wasn't the kind of thing women like to hear. She needed time to absorb it all.

"I have to go to work," I said, after a few minutes. "You don't have to go... wait. That came out wrong. I'd like it if you could stay, okay?"

She looked up at me, her thoughts far away.

"I need to think," she said at last. "I can't do that here, with you just twenty feet away, separated from me by nothing more than the floor. I think it's best if I go."

I nodded. Being a gambling addict, if nothing else, had taught me that the cards don't always fall your way.

"I understand," I said. "You'll call later?"

"I'll call," she said. "It may take a while, but I'll call."

She stood and kissed me on the cheek, and then she was gone.

It was a hell of a thing.

Some days, life really sucks.

THREE

Merlie didn't call the next day. That kind of hurt, since it was my birthday. I woke up on the day I turned fifty with a cool breeze blowing in through the open sash of my window over Toulouse Street, and a hangover the size of Biloxi. Outside, clouds were gathering in the noonday sky, and the air felt scummy and oppressive.

After dressing, I walked down Toulouse to the cafe from which Lucho Braga used to run the New Orleans mob before he died, and found it a changed place. Gone were the *soldatos* and made guys lining the bars and guarding the door. At the table where Braga had taken his breakfast for every day of the previous twenty years, there was a young couple sitting with two preschool kids, eating pancakes and eggs. The man wore a teal and purple nylon Charlotte Hornets jacket, and his redheaded wife had on a Carolina Panthers sweatshirt. The kids, a boy and a girl, picked at each other incessantly.

Tourists.

I stifled the impulse to sit next to them and regale them with stories of all the mob deals that had gone down at that table, the hit contracts and the money laundering, and instead I took a table near the door.

I sensed someone standing behind me. I took it to be the waiter, coming to take my order, and I turned just as Tommy Callahan slid into the seat next to me.

I was not amused.

"Whattsa matter, Gallegher?" he asked, feigning insult. "I'm not good enough to sit at your table?"

"You've been following me?"

He shrugged.

"Hell no, man. I still work here. They got me chained to a desk upstairs. I saw you on the TV."

He pointed over the bar, and I saw several cameras secreted among the liquor bottles.

"And I thought I was just paranoid," I said.

"It's a bitch. New management's scared to death Phang Loc's gonna try a hit now that Lucho's gone. Every made guy in this town, Vietnamese and Sicilian, knows this is the mob's counting house."

"Do tell."

"Oh, yeah, we do all our books here."

"I really don't think I wanted to know that."

"No big deal, Gallegher. It's all gonna be moved any day now. The new bosses, bunch of wingtip types from Houston, think it's bad for business to centralize the operations. So whatcha gonna have? Choose anything you like. It's on the house. Birthday special."

I was probably the only person in New Orleans who knew that Tommy Callahan was actually a federal agent working deep cover in the French Quarter gangland. I had discovered it by accident when he kept a teenaged Haitian killer from zipping me and a ten year old girl named Louise Onizuki on a lonely road out in the Atchafalaya Basin six months earlier. He knew his secret was safe, as long as nobody tried to torture it out of me.

I have a relatively low tolerance for torture.

"Eggs Benedict, then," I said. "and a split of Korbel."

"Alcohol so early in the day?"

"I have a *katzenjammer* from last night. Hair of the dog."

He surveyed me from head to toe. It took quite a while.

"Yeah, okay," he said. "You just see to it that dog don't bite back, you hear? I gotta take a whiz and get back to work. You enjoy your breakfast."

The food was good, and I spent the breakfast listening to the tourists at Braga's table debate where to go and what to do that afternoon, like it was the hardest decision they had made since their wedding invitations. The kids just kept bickering.

I was just three days back from the Caymans, but a vacation sounded pretty good. It had been a long time since I had spent a week in a strange, colorful city just exploring. About a year and a half earlier, I'd recovered about five million dollars for a new widow named Clancey Vincour, money her husband had skimmed from a ponzie deal he'd been running with Lucho Braga. I'd kept about a million of it as a finder's fee, and had squirreled it away in a Cayman bank. All my trips these days were to places like the Caribbean to visit my money. It was hard to believe that I could afford to just up and leave any time I felt like it.

Despite my relative comfort, I felt like this big lump of inertia.

I spent the afternoon at a movie, some action-adventure piece of fluff where the hero gets blown up every six minutes but never seems to die or even get his hair badly mussed. After it was over, I headed over to a sports bar I know and caught a Hawks game. They played Sacramento. The Kings took it by fifteen points. I lost ten imaginary bucks to the bartender, in addition to what I paid for my drinks.

As a gambling addict, I should have known better.

When I got back to Holliday's, I found Farley Nuckolls sitting at one of the tables, nursing a Pepsi. He was just sitting there, staring off into space, like he was running this endless loop of sixteen track audio tape in his head.

He picked up the narrative verbally as I walked through the door.

"...So I ask this cop, '*You say this was at Irene's*' and he says '*Yeah*', and I ask him what this citizen avenger looked like. '*He a big guy?*' I ask, and the cop, he says '*Yeah*', and I say '*Goes about six and half, maybe two-seventy, got a head of hair like he cuts it with a chainsaw?*' and he says '*Yeah*', and I say '*Goes by the name of Gallegher?*' and the cop, he looks at me like I'm David Copperfield or something and says '*Yeah, how'd you know that*', and I tell him that this guy Gallegher is the only person I know's got balls big enough to disarm two thugs in one day and still have time for a nice Italian dinner."

Farley is a better-than-decent cop. He's certainly one of the more honest detectives I've known in the time I've spent in the Quarter. He's gaunt, a damn near emaciated fellow who stands maybe six feet in his Rockports. It seems as if he has a closet full of white short-sleeved shirts and tan khakis, and about six seersucker sport coats of varying hues. The only other sartorial constant about him is his Panama hat, which he wears tilted back at improbable angles over a face that would have made Ichabod Crane's mother wince. His liquid blue eyes stand guard over a beaky nose and this incredible overbite that yields to a chinless turkey wattle that blends in almost without notice to his neck. I never see him without thinking of a turtle.

Damn fine cop, though, smart as a teenaged chess prodigy, and tenacious as hell. I had also discovered, somewhat by accident, that his dangerous past included a stint in at least one covert branch of government service. I had a feeling that my occasional adventures paled beside his own, before he became a resort city sleuth.

"Ah," I said, "At long last, fame."

"Oh, you have no idea how famous you are."

"Two thugs, you said. You spoke to Reynard. He told you about my meeting with Spanky Gallo."

He nodded, taking a long drag from the Pepsi.

"Great," I muttered, as I fished an Abita out of the ice tank behind the bar. "I can't imagine Gallo filing a complaint, though."

"He didn't."

"So you're just here to give me a hard time? Maybe razz me a little over what happened at Irene's? Somehow, I don't buy it."

"And why's that, my portly Irish nemesis?"

"Because you're on the clock. You only have soft drinks here when you're working. Otherwise, it's beer. What's going on?"

He snapped his Panama hat forward on his head, and stood as he started putting on his jacket.

"It's a hell of a thing," he said, not looking at me, "when I get to drop by and let you know you're in the clear."

I sucked down about a quarter of the beer, once again lamenting that Abita doesn't make them for people my size.

"What didn't I do this time?" I said.

"That business at Irene's last night? Really sweet. In front of about fifteen witnesses, too. Then there's the interview with the cops. All that gave you an incredible alibi, Gallegher."

I felt a tingle at the base of my spine that burned like a fuse as it worked its way toward the back of my neck.

"What's happened?"

Nuckolls made a show of pulling a notebook from the breast pocket of his seersucker jacket. He riffled the pages until he found the one he wanted.

"At around eight thirty last night, Ms. Lucy Nivens, an employee of Mr. Sylvester Reynard at *Les Jolie Blondes* on Bourbon Street, ordered a bottle of horse piss champagne to take back to a private room at the rear of the bar. She apparently intended to share this bottle of champagne with a gentleman."

"I know the routine."

"At eight this morning, a horse patrolman working the far end of Bourbon near Esplanade noticed a hand sticking out from behind a dumpster. That hand was attached to the rest of the late Lucy Nivens."

"Oh," I said, sitting heavily at the table. "Shit."

"It was really grisly. You want the details?"

I shook my head.

"Spare me."

"Suit yourself. Anyway, in the course of my typical thorough investigation, I questioned the other employees of *Les Jolie Blondes*, and they mentioned that her customer was a tall, heavyset fellow wearing a Saints cap. Meant nothing to me at the time, until I questioned Spanky Gallo, and your name entered the conversation."

"I'm sure you were thrilled."

"It was better than sex. I was beyond ecstatic. I thought I finally had you. Gallo described your waltz with him in the back room, and how you deprived him of his property, and I thought to myself, *Hey, Gallegher looks pretty good for this thing*. Then I talked with Reynard, and he told me about the conversation he had with you afterward. It was a setback. Then I get back to my office, and there's a copy of the police report from Irene's last night, and that was the end of my good day."

"Sorry to disappoint you," I said, trying to slow my thoughts just long enough to deal with him intelligently. "Remind me to send that hype I clobbered a thank-you note."

"So," Nuckolls said, watching himself straighten his tie in the mirror behind the bar. "You got any idea where I might find Shorty right about now? You see, I gotta arrest him for killing his girlfriend."

It was the first night in years that Holliday's went dark. Shorty had run the joint for so long that he had the money details all to himself. He would run to the bank in the afternoon to make the deposit from the night before, and pick up the till money for the evening. He would take care of the vendors over the course of the afternoon, sign for the beer kegs, clean the taps, ice down the bottles, and fill the pretzel bowls. The general cleaning he left to Brucie Epps, the retarded kid Merlie talked him into hiring about six months earlier, and who worked his tail off in the afternoons wiping down tables, mopping the floors, and sprucing the place up.

Of course, on this evening, my fiftieth birthday, Shorty was cooling his heels in the Rampart Street lockup. Brucie, who had a hard time dealing with changes in his routine, still showed up to do the cleaning, and Sockeye Sam, who hadn't been anywhere else at night for over a decade, arrived at his usual time to play the piano. I sat in a chair next to the bar, drinking a Jax from the ice cooler and trying to work it all out.

It had been a tough scene when Shorty showed up from the bank, about fifteen minutes after Farley told me about Lucy's murder. Shorty bounced in with his roustabout's quickstep, and found me and the detective staring him down.

"Nuckolls," he said, nodding at Farley as he crossed behind the bar.

"Come out from behind the bar, Shorty," Nuckolls said sternly. "Keep your hands where I can see them. I know you keep a .38 auto back there."

Shorty froze then, his eyes boring through Nuckolls like ruby lasers.

"What the fuck?"

"Just come on out," Nuckolls said, keeping his voice level. I could see his temples pounding, though, and I knew he was seconds away from doing it the hard way.

"Do what he says," I added, trying to make my voice urgent enough to make Shorty aware he was in real trouble.

"Keep out of this, Gallegher," Nuckolls ordered, never taking his eyes off Shorty.

Shorty stood there, his eyes flashing back and forth between Nuckolls and me. Then, as if nothing had happened, he shrugged and walked around the bar.

"Damned if I know what this is all about," he said, and if he had anything else to add it was squelched when Farley took him by the shoulders and turned him to face the bar for a quick pat-down before cuffing him. Seconds later, Shorty was sitting in a chair turned ass-backward, facing Farley, who was peppering him with questions.

"Where were you around eight-fifteen last night?"

"Here."

"Anyone else here at that time?"

"Naw. Brucie had left for the evening, Gallegher was out to dinner, and Sockeye didn't get here until around nine. Most of our regulars don't get here before then. Around eight-fifteen, I was icing down the bottle beer over there..." he nodded toward the bar. "What in hell is this?"

"Farley," I said, quietly. "Maybe you'd better let me tell him."

Nuckolls gazed at me for a moment, weighing the options. I guess he finally decided that Shorty already knew Lucy was dead, and would have formulated his own cover story over the past twenty-four hours, or he didn't have a clue, in which case telling him wouldn't hurt anything. It's the conclusion I'd have come to, and Farley is every bit as smart as I. He nodded, but he kept his attention on Shorty.

"It's like this," I told Shorty. "Something's happened to Lucy."

I could see Shorty's eyes glaze over, and something feral and self-protective flooded into them from an ancient and suppressed region of his head.

"She's dead, Shorty," I continued. "Someone killed her last night."

Some guys might have broken down into a blubbering heap at that point. Some may have gone all stony and catatonic from the shock. Shorty, who dragged around a long history of dashed hopes and broken promises, went ballistic.

"No," he half-moaned. "I don't believe you."

"It's the God's honest truth," Farley added.

"It's not true!" Shorty shouted, almost a wail, and he stood and kicked the chair on which he had been sitting. He hit it just right, and it sailed up toward the stage, ricocheting off Sockeye's piano. He started pulling against the cuffs that held his hands behind his back, all the time bellowing and kicking at the chairs and tables around him. "It's not true!"

Farley made a grab at him, trying to restrain him, but Shorty had built a head of steam and it was going to take an army to hold him back. He was bouncing against tables and chairs, sending the furniture skittering around the room. At one point I thought I had a handful of his shirt, but the fabric tore against my grasp.

The tantrum ended as quickly as it began, when Shorty attempted to upend a table with his hip, and instead slipped and fell to the floor, on his side. As if the fall and the shock sobered him, he curled into a fetal ball and sobbed, saying over and over again that it wasn't true. Farley knelt down beside him, and laid a hand on his tortured shoulder.

"I gotta take you in, Shorty," he said softly. "It's what I gotta do, you see. Sly Reynard says Lucy was hooking, and she told Gallegher about it, and Gallegher already told me he'd discussed it with you. Reynard says you probably killed her. It's the way things happen around here, crimes of passion, that sort of thing. So I gotta take you in. I don't think you ought to say anything else right now, understand?"

He read Shorty his rights, and helped him up from the floor. In the course of two minutes, Shorty had gone from rage to grief, and he sat in another chair, weeping, his chin flush against his chest, as his tears soaked his shirt, and Farley called for some uniform cops on his two-way.

He had a heart, though. He arranged for the squad car pull up in the alleyway behind the bar, so he could take Shorty out the back way, where he wouldn't be seen by every tourist on Toulouse Street being loaded into the back of the car with cuffs on.

Hours later, I sat sucking down a Jax while Sockeye rattled off some forgotten honky-tonk tune he had filed in the back of his head back when he worked the Storyville whorehouses. Brucie had picked up the scattered tables and chairs, and was wiping everything down for the fifth or sixth time, mostly because he couldn't think of anything else to do.

"It d..d..d..don't seem like Shorty to d..d..do that to Miss Lucy," Brucie said. He had a horrible stutter that likely had nothing to do with his retardation. It was just an additional impediment for him, and tonight he was stumbling over his 'D's.

"No, it doesn't," I said. "But you never know, Brucie. Sometimes, people do stuff that isn't in their character, that isn't like them."

I had backtracked, recalling with some embarrassment that Brucie probably didn't know what '*character*' meant.

"You think he d...d...did it?" Brucie asked.

"It doesn't sound right," I admitted.

"So, what you gonna do about it?" Sockeye called out, suddenly, and I realized he had stopped playing.

"What?" I asked.

"I said, what you gonna do about Mr. Shorty? How you gonna get him off?"

"I don't understand," I said. "What can *I* do?"

"Listen, Gallegher, I may be old, but I ain't deaf, and I ain't daft. You think I don' hear things up here playing this piece o' crap box night affer night? Well, I do. I do, shor' 'nuff."

I turned to face him.

"Go ahead and say what you're thinking, Sam."

He shook his bald wizened head and pointed a bony finger at me.

"You know what you gon' do, don' need some ol' nigger piano player to tell you. How many time have I sit here an' listen to you make a deal to do some po' asshole a favor? How many time that favor done work out to have somethin' to do wif somebody dyin'?"

I don't think I had heard Sam string so many words together at one time in all the seven years I had worked at the club.

"You want me to take a look at this Lucy Nivens killing?"

"Ain' what I want, boy, it be what you gon' do, whether I wan' it or not."

"How do you figure that?"

" 'Cause it in your blood. 'Cause it what you do. You ain' gon' stand by and let them sen' Shorty off to the prison wifout you take a look into it."

"The cops are already investigating," I said. "It's an open case. If I start looking at it, Farley will have me up on obstruction charges before the week's out."

Sockeye cleared his throat and spat into the cup he kept on the piano.

"Ain' never stop you befo'," he said. "Shouldn' stop you now. Tell you what, I got five large I'm gon' pay you to work for me."

Where Sockeye came across five hundred dollars was anyone's guess. He worked for tips at the bar.

"I don't want your money, Sam."

"Then use it fo' expenses. Ain' that what all the TV detectives say? Two hunnert a day an' expenses?"

"I'm not a detective," I argued.

Sam just laughed, and played some quick melodramatic *Dragnet* riff.

Dum de dum dum.

"Then you jus' this lucky son of a bitch who be good at findin' things. So you go out and you find who kill Miss Lucy."

I took a long pull from the Jax, and suddenly became aware of Brucie staring at me the way twelve year old kids admire Michael Jordan.

"What?" I said.

"Miss Merlie, she says you're the b...b...b...bravest man she ever m...m...met. You gonna find out who k...k...killed Miss Lucy?"

"Are you guys ganging up on me?" I asked.

Neither of them answered, but I saw Sockeye grin, and Brucie could have turned down the adulation a stop or two.

"Well, what happens if I find out Shorty really did kill her?"

Sockeye rocked back and forth on his piano stool, apparently having decided that we had a deal, and that I was going to investigate.

"Well, Gallegher," he said, "I guess we gon' just have to burn that bridge when we get to it."

FIVE

I started by calling Cully Tucker. Cully would be the living embodiment of the Peter Principal, in which genuine talent is rewarded by being promoted to just the right level of incompetence, if in fact he had ever shown the slightest aptitude for the law.

He was a lawyer, though, admitted to the Bar and everything, and just about the only one I knew that I could afford. Given his track record, it was a dead-bang even bet that he would have Shorty pled out to manslaughter before lunch the next day. It was a chance I had to take.

"Gallegher!" he greeted over the telephone when he finally returned my page. I could hear music blasting in the background, the kind Lucy Nivens might have done a lap dance to before her messy demise. It would be like Cully to be in some pussy bar at one end of Bourbon or the other. "How's the birthday boy?"

"I'm surprised you remembered."

"I remember everything, you big stupid mick. What's up?"

"I need your help."

"Wait a minute."

I heard a rustling, and suddenly the music became muted and distant. Cully's voice took on a reverberation that spoke of tiled walls and porcelain fixtures. He had moved to the men's room so he could hear me better.

"I recall a time," he began, "when you could sit all night at a hootchie-cootch and just nurse your beer. Nowadays some girl wants to sit on your face for pocket change every five minutes. No sense of propriety. I hadda scoot into the crapper just to get a little privacy. So what's the problem?"

"It's Shorty. He's been arrested. For murder." Somehow, the problem seemed too big to fit into one big sentence. I felt an imperative to break it down into digestible bits.

"Hold on a minute. Gotta dig out some earwax. I thought I heard you say Shorty was popped for murder."

"You heard right. Farley Nuckolls took him in couple of hours ago."

There was a moment of silence, save for the faint music and some ape-like hooting in the distance, and then Cully came back on.

"Sorry, man, I had to find a pen. So who'd he kill?"

"I'm asking for help here, man. I would feel better if you didn't go into this with the attitude that he's guilty."

"Okay, okay," Cully said in a conciliatory voice, with irritatingly patronizing overtones. "Who's he *accused* of killing?"

"Lucy Nivens."

"The chick he had at the party the other night? The blonde with the rock-hard store-bought gazongas?"

"She's all rock hard now. The police found her behind a dumpster at the Esplanade end of Bourbon this morning. Farley talked to Sly Reynard, who turned him onto Shorty."

"Reynard? What in hell does he have to do with this?"

"It's a long story, and I'd rather not go into it over the phone. Here's what I want you to do. First, come over so I can fill you in on the whole story. Second, I need you to negotiate with the DA tomorrow and get some kind of bond set."

"It's gonna be steep," he said. "Murder two -- that's what this sounds like to me -- it's gonna be a lot of bills."

"Don't worry. Shorty owns controlling interest in Holliday's. He can put up the bar for collateral. If he can't -- well, I'll take care of it. Just get yourself over here, though. I still have some visits to make tonight."

While Cully tended to Shorty, I decided that if Nuckolls was going to bust me for obstructing, then I might as well get popped doing something big. I went to *Les Jolie Blondes* to see Reynard.

I could hear the blaring music a block down the street. Reynard had hired a guy to wear a Charles Boyer tuxedo and stand out front of the club to herd in the tourists. As I reached the doorway, I hit a solid wall of stale beer stench, cigarette smoke, and raunch. I pushed by the barker and entered the club.

Spanky Gallo saw me the minute I walked in the door. He intercepted me halfway down the length of the bar. He was wearing yet another linen jacket over a white t-shirt and a pair of beltless trousers and some white bucks. I think it was his Fredo Corleone outfit.

"He don't want to see you," he said, as if they had expected me to show up.

"Tell him I just got in a new shipment of Ho-Hos. He won't be able to contain himself," I said as I ducked him.

"I think you better take a hike, Gallegher."

Gallo grabbed me by the sleeve of my nylon Saints jacket, and started to hustle me toward the door. I don't like being hustled, so I did the only thing that came to mind at that moment.

I pantsed him.

While he was tugging at my jacket, I reached down and popped open his Sans-a-Belts. Before he could stop me I had dragged them straight to the floor. Underneath, he was wearing these really ugly red paisley bikini shorts cut high on his prickly-pear thighs.

Gallo was mortified. His face turned pink, then ruddy, then carmine, and finally scarlet, as the girls around the bar laughed along with the regulars. The college kids never took their eyes off the twats thrusting back and forth onstage.

By then, of course, I had his gun again, which I stowed in my jacket pocket.

"You know where you can find this," I told him as he struggled to pull his pants back up. I left him to his task and lumbered up the stairs to Reynard's office.

When I opened the door, I found Reynard getting a hummer from a girl who looked like she had just flunked eighth grade. At least, I think it was a sexual act. With all the flab jiggling on Reynard's pelvis, she might have been bobbing for lost food.

"Jesus, I told you not to..." he roared, then saw it wasn't Gallo. "Shit, Gallegher. What in hell are you doing here? Where's Spanky?"

I crossed the office to his desk, while I ejected the clip from Spanky's gun, and placed the automatic on the blotter.

"I had to disarm your monkey again. I have a couple of questions." I gestured toward the child-woman who still rooted about his thighs like she was a truffling pig. "You might want us to be alone."

Before he could answer, I felt something hard and cold burrow into the base of my skull, and heard the metallic *sprong* sound as a pistol hammer was pulled back.

"Okay," I said. "Let me guess. Spanky was packing a spare."

"You know what they say," Gallo said, digging the barrel into the back of my head. "*Fool me once, shame on me -- fool me twice, shame on you.*"

I nodded, slowly and deliberately, so Gallo wouldn't think I was about to attack him with my skull.

"You know, Spanky, you got that almost precisely, but not entirely, wrong. How long did it take you to pull up your pants downstairs?"

"C'mon, Sly, lemme cap him," Gallo demanded.

"Why were your pants down?" Reynard asked.

"Asswipe pulled 'em down when I tried to bounce him. C'mon, Sly, gimme the word."

Reynard gazed at me, his eyes two little onyx beads buried behind folds of cheek fat.

"You yanked down Spanky's pants?"

I tried my infectious *aw-shucks* grin, the one I use when the tax man comes around.

"Yeah."

For a moment I couldn't tell whether he was appreciative or livid. With a guy like Reynard, all the more subtle emotions tend to get swallowed up and digested before they can escape his gargantuan face, the way a celestial black hole swallows up all the light that crosses its event horizon.

Then, he chortled, a slow rumbling sound like distant thunder, which grew into a sort of phlegmatic cough, and finally into raucous gales. He slapped one thigh, and for a moment I thought his chippy was going to be thrown across the carpet by the tidal motion.

"He yanked down your pants, Spanky. That's rich."

"Yeah," Spanky said, and I could hear the furor in his voice, "Well, let's see how rich it is when I spread his brains all over your desk, Sly."

Reynard stopped laughing.

"Oh, get real, Spank. Ain't gonna kill a guy here in my office. Besides, I have a feeling I got some business to do with Gallegher here."

"I'm gonna cap him right here!"

The pistol barrel dug deeper into my scalp, and I wondered which sense would go first when he pulled the trigger. Worse, I couldn't help wondering which would leave me last.

Reynard grabbed the twist's arm and lifted her up. She was wearing these threadbare jeans cut off near the crotch, with the outside seams split all the way to the waistband, and nothing else. As she faced me, I realized that she was every bit as young as I had imagined. Something in my stomach did flip-flops. I don't enjoy seeing kids exploited.

"Tell you what, Spanky," Reynard said. "I'll make you a deal. You don't zip Gallegher, and you can take Rosie here downstairs for an hour or two. Think you'd like that?"

I could almost hear Gallo salivating as he looked the girl over. He didn't say anything, but I could feel the pressure against my skull ease up.

Within a couple of minutes, Reynard and I were alone in his office, and I had discovered which of Gallo's heads made all the big decisions. Reynard had performed some kind of circus act pulling up his pants, and was seated on the elevated loveseat behind his desk. It had been a memorable sight. I was still trying to hold down my dinner.

"You got two questions," he said, gesturing for me to sit in a rickety wooden leather-covered chair across from him. After checking for trap doors, I slid into it.

"I said a couple of questions. It was intended to indicate an indeterminate number."

"You're not sure what you want, are you?"

"Sometimes one thing leads to another. Sometimes you wind up in a place totally different than you thought. Sometimes I just get curious."

"Yeah," Reynard said, "I remember. Okay, so ask your questions."

"You told Farley that Shorty killed Lucy Nivens?"

"No, I did not."

"Farley seems to think otherwise."

"Nuckolls tends to jump to conclusions. What I told him was that you came to see Lucy, and then we talked, and you told me that she was dating Shorty, and that she had been hooking. Shorty, he's got this cop brain thing going, he puts two and two together, and he figures Shorty put the zotz on her."

"You had to know he would reach that conclusion."

"No I didn't. I didn't hafta do nothin'. As it happens, though, I kinda hoped he'd think *you* did it. You know, just to give you a hard time."

I let that one slide. After all the grief I had given Reynard, he probably had one coming.

"Did anyone actually see Shorty here in the bar last night?"

"Naw, but that don't mean dick. There ain't no lock on the back door. The girls gotta have someplace to go smoke or toke up. I don't charge no cover here, neither. So anybody could come in the back and drag her out to the alley without being seen."

"So who was seen with her last?"

"I don't know who he was. Look, I didn't see anything anyway. I talked with my staff later, when I heard that Lucy got killed. Some of the girls said they saw her go backstage with some guy, big ugly white dude, but none of them saw her after that."

"Anyone see the big guy later?"

"No. He disappeared too. Don't mean nothing. Like I said, he coulda gone out the back before Lucy left."

I nodded, trying to collate all the data.

"So, nobody saw Shorty here, nobody saw Lucy leave, and nobody saw the big guy she took to the back leave. The only person they saw come and go was me, and that was earlier in the day. So the only factor connecting Shorty with the killing is me, and the fact that they were an item."

As I worked it all through, Reynard sat wheezing wetly, and nodding, as if he had already processed it himself, and was just waiting for me to catch up.

"You tell Shorty his girl was a punch?" he asked.

"Yeah, I did. Just before dinner last night."

"What time was that?"

"Around seven, seven-thirty."

He nodded again, as sagely as his bulk permitted.

"Plenty of time for him to get here. Plenty of time for him to do the job."

"I made it clear, though. I told him she was out of it."

Reynard laughed again, shaking like rippling pond water.

"Man, you wanna park that Boy Scout head of yours at the door for five minutes? I deal with this shit all the time. A girl starts takin' in dicks for a living, she don't get out of it. Maybe she takes vacations now and then, but this is a lifelong occupation, being a whore. Sooner or later, the rent's due, or the car payment's late, and here she is sittin' on this perfectly good pussy what ain't producin' no revenue. I asked a coupla the girls, and they told me Shorty had put Lucy up in an apartment somewhere."

"He was helping her, yeah," I said.

"He was helpin' her, all right. An' he was helpin' himself to that snapper of hers. It's all commerce, Gallegher. It's all just tit for tat. Like the truckers say, *gas, cash, or ass, nobody rides for free.*"

"You're saying Shorty probably became enraged, thinking Lucy might have been taking advantage of him, while she was still giving it up for money, and he lost control."

Well...." Reynard said, as if considering a chess move. "Maybe that was it, and maybe it wasn't, you know?"

"Give me an alternative."

"What do you know about how she was killed?"

I realized that I had cut Nuckolls off when he tried to give me details about the murder.

"Less than you, apparently."

He shifted in the loveseat, causing the earth's axis to move a couple of degrees, and placed his hands on the desk.

"Word gets around, you know? Three hours after they found Lucy, I get this telephone call from Lucien Fleck over at Twin Peeks. Lucien and I don't pass the time of day very often, you know, being pretty much in competition. He called me, though, wantin' to know if it was true one of my girls got zagged. I told him it looked that way, and he got real quiet for a minute or two, an' then he says to me, just like this, *Me too*."

"He told you one of his dancers was murdered?"

"Girl named Hayley something. Lucien, you know, he don't give a crap if his girls twist on the side. He says this Hayley took some big guy to the back to do the juicy watusi, and nobody saw her again until a dumpster crew emptied her into the back of a truck the next day."

From some blocked part of my brain, a voice I hadn't heard in ten years echoed.

Damn, we got another one, Pat.

I tried to shake it off. The implications were too dreadful to consider. I looked down and realized my hands were sweaty and tremulous.

"How was she killed?"

"I don't know. I don't know how Lucy Nivens died either."

"When was this?"

He took a sip from a beer bottle that had been sitting on his desk, and he waved a hammy hand in the air.

"Maybe two weeks ago. Now this is where it all gets really hinky. Maybe an hour later, I get this call from Huey Fontine over to Pink Snapperz, and he also wants to know if it's true Lucy got squibbed."

"There's a lot of interest in one dancer here," I noted.

"That's what I thought. So I tell Huey he heard it right, and he says he thought so because he had just got off the phone with Lucien, and then he tells me the strangest thing."

"One of his dancers was murdered, too," I said flatly, and the ancient voice with the flavorless boiled-dinner New England accent resonated in my head again.

Damn, we got another one, Pat.

"Within a month before Lucien's girl Hayley got it," I finished.

Reynard lit a cigarette with a Zippo, and flipped the lid shut before tossing it on the table.

"Damn if you ain't fast. I heard you was a smart guy. People talk about you, you know that? They say you stick your fingers in other people's business, get all sticky with it, but that you're smart, and you're a lucky son of a bitch."

"Everyone seems to think so."

"You sure as shit got in my business a coupla years ago."

I think I was listening to him with one ear, as my brain chugged up into fast-forward. Pieces of information started to fall into place, snippets of small talk, near-forgotten newspaper articles, all of it seemingly unconnected, started to coalesce in my head like gathering storm clouds.

Reynard was still droning on about how I screwed up his deal, when I interrupted him.

"Someone out there is killing dancers," I announced.

He blinked once or twice, and then nodded, his protruding, bloated neck wattle bellowing in and out from the compression by his chin.

"It looks that way, don't it?"

"Yeah, it does."

"Thing like that, Gallegher, it's bad for business."

"And it's hell on the dancers who get killed," I reminded him.

"Well, yeah, I s'pose..."

"How was Lucy killed?"

He shrugged, his face as blank as a new blackboard.

"Nuckolls didn't say."

"He tried to tell me. I cut him off."

"Seems to me," Reynard said, "like maybe you ought to go talk to him again."

SIX

It was too late in the evening to go to Farley, so I went home instead. Sockeye and Brucie were long-gone. The bar sat empty and silent and musty as a mausoleum, save for the insistent hum of the beer cooler. I grabbed a couple of Dixies and trudged up the stairs, where I eased down into my recliner and hung my feet out the window to pollute the atmosphere.

I was still sitting there hours later when the stars started to wink out and the sky to the east began to glow red and orange like the last five seconds of a campfire ember, and streaks of multihued illumination pinballed between the few pigiron clouds hanging on the horizon.

I suppose I should have been thinking about Lucy, or Shorty, or maybe the other two strippers who had been killed, but there was a futility to that. Perhaps I should have been formulating the questions I would ask Farley later in the day, but there was nothing there.

I hadn't been lucky or good or fast the previous evening. I had been slack and sloppy, and I had allowed Spanky Gallo to no-exit me to within a muscle spasm of worm food. The thought kept skittering away from me like a water balloon smeared with vaseline, but from time to time it would turn and stick a knife in my nuts and wink villainously as it whispered a raspy accusation

You almost met the Reaper tonight, shithead.

Spanky Gallo was nothing more than a mile-long laundry list of shattered dreams and botched opportunities, and maybe he was just waiting for the right asshole to come along and piss in his gumbo and grin about it before he decided to go out like a swinging dick.

I had nearly fulfilled his wish.

I wasn't still sucking oxygen because I had been cat-quick or steely or even terribly clever. There was no *fortuna* in my salvation. Like sinners throughout history, I owed my continued existence to the sacrifice of an innocent. The only thing, ultimately, that had kept Spanky from shagging my sorry ass was that Reynard had thrown him a piece of meat in the form of the piteous waif who had been servicing him when I walked in.

I owed for that one. I just couldn't figure out how to balance the books.

The first blinding yellow light of the sun pierced the horizon, turning the solitary clouds a translucent silvery gray with borders of gold, like God's own fine china, creating a dome of luminescence that spilled like milk over the umber sky, chasing away the demons of the night and bringing the reassurance of yet another day. The long vigil of darkness was over. The night was driven away, the day was begun, and there was no place in it for self-doubt.

Whether it was by luck, the fortuitous confluence of active and passive principles in the universe, or simply a karmic tradeoff in which my own life was traded for the degradation of a fourteen-year-old girl, I was alive. I would have to deal with all the other stuff later.

There was work to do.

I caught Nuckolls at his desk, where he was reading over arrest reports from the previous night, and sipping coffee from a mug that said, *Take my advice. I'm not using it.*

I leaned against the doorway to his cubicle, and stared at him.

"You look like shit," he said, as if that was a good thing.

"Yeah, it's the damnedest thing. This self-portrait I keep in my attic just gets prettier and prettier. I think I'm doing something wrong."

"I think you're doing your whole life wrong. What do you want?"

I pulled up a wooden chair and sat in it backward, leaning the back toward his desk.

"How did Lucy Nivens die?"

"Thought you weren't interested."

"You arrested my meal ticket. Now you have my attention."

"Your meal ticket got sprung about five minutes ago. That walking toilet of a lawyer you hang out with talked a bondsman into flushing twenty large on him. Next question."

"How did Lucy Nivens die, Farley?"

He put down the coffee mug and picked up a rubber band that he twirled between his two index fingers like a bad movie bureaucrat, as he drilled a few holes in my head with his carbide tool eyes.

"This bothers me," he said at last.

"My sudden interest?"

"Exactly. Why am I swept by this premonition that you are about to complicate my life?"

"Poetic. Maybe I am, but then you could also be wrong. I'll make you a deal. You tell me how Lucy Nivens died, and I'll do my dead level best to go easy on you."

He weighed the possibilities. It was difficult for him. I had tossed hand grenades into the middle of more than one of his cases. On the other hand, Farley had often made use of what he calls my Bourbon Street Irregulars, the slapped-together collection of bozos, yahoos, and loose change that had seemed to accumulate around me since I arrived in the Quarter over seven years earlier. Sometimes I was a benefit to him.

Often I was a pain in the ass.

He produced a wheezy, asthmatic sigh, and grabbed a thin manila folder from the center drawer of his desk.

"I just got the coroner's report this morning. I was saving it to read over lunch. I don't have to, though, to know how she died. She was ripped."

"Ripped?"

"Eviscerated. Someone took a blade and opened her from pubis to sternum."

I considered this as I helped myself to a doughnut from a box on his desk.

"It's not as easy as it sounds," I pronounced.

"How so?"

"Well, first, you have to be pretty strong. That blade had to pass through a lot of stuff -- muscle, mesentery, the diaphragm, the organs aren't as soft and yielding as you might think. Anyone who's tried to cut up chicken livers can tell you that. The abdomen is actually a pretty tough place, which is a good thing, because that's where we keep all our goodies. How do you get someone to stand still for all that, and how do you keep them quiet while you do it?"

"Maybe she was already unconscious. Maybe he did it while she was lying there."

"That could happen. It doesn't fit well, though. That makes it a coldly calculated act, requiring some forethought, a plan, and execution. Quicker to just slit her throat. It sure as hell doesn't sound like a crime of passion."

"You're just trying to get Shorty off."

"Of course I am, but not the way you think. I told Shorty about Lucy around seven-thirty. Lucy disappeared around eight-thirty, and presumably she died shortly thereafter. That's not a lot of time to put together a plan like this. What did the killer use to knock her out? Were there any head injuries, or did he use chemicals, choral hydrate, chloroform, ruffies? What does the tox report say?"

Farley slowly closed the folder and placed it back in the drawer. Then he leaned his own chair back to an improbable and well-practiced angle, placing his hands behind his head.

"You talk like you've done this before," he said.

"You know damn well I have."

"Crazy Ed Hix?"

I nodded, chewing on the doughnut. It was a Dunkin'. I like them, a lot.

"Among others. Just how thick a file do you have on me, anyway?"

"You're on your second volume. Get to the point, Gallegher. Why are you here?"

I polished off the doughnut, and went for another one. Farley grabbed the box and slid it out of my reach.

"Pretty cheap with the pastry, there, aren't you?"

He didn't say anything. He just tapped his fingers on the top of the box.

"Okay. Another doughnut, and I'll tell you what I know."

He slid the box back toward me.

"You read that report again," I said, as I lifted another doughnut from the box, "and you tell me what jumps out at you. There will be something you don't usually see. It will make the hair on the back of your neck stand up. I'll wait."

I chewed while he read. It didn't take long, so it's a good thing I'm hell on doughnuts.

"There's a word," he said at last, peering at me over the folder. "The killer, or someone, wrote a word on her left breast. *this*."

"*This*? That's it?"

"All lower case letters. *this*."

"Nothing missing? She was wearing all her underwear? Had both her shoes? No obvious jewelry taken?"

"She was wearing her panties. The autopsy said she wasn't raped. She wasn't wearing a brassiere."

"Maybe she wouldn't have been, given her business. Or, maybe the killer took it as a trophy."

"You want to make your point, Gallegher?"

I closed the doughnut box for him.

"I think you're already way ahead of me, Farley. I think you've already put it together, so I'm going to tell you where to go next. Somewhere around here, probably in that same drawer, is another murder case file, involving another dancer, named Hayley something-or-other, worked for Lucien Fleck over at Twin Peeks. She will have been similarly ripped, and there will be a word written on her body."

"*that*," Nuckolls said.

"Beg pardon?"

"The word, the one written on Hayley Stout's body. *that*."

"And on the body of the woman that worked for Huey Fontine over at the Pink Snapperz?"

"*oh*," he said.

"*this, that*, and *oh*," I mumbled. "Not much to go on. Not a terribly articulate killer, is he?"

"How'd you find out about all this?"

"Same place you did, I'll bet. I visited Reynard last night. He got calls from Lucien and Huey yesterday, after Lucy was found. There are jungle drums banging in pussy bars all over town. Everyone's getting the heebie-jeebies thinking there's one person behind all these stripper murders. I tend to agree, now, after what you told me."

"One might infer that you are suggesting a serial killer."

I pushed my Saints cap back on my head and scratched at my hairline.

"You're the cop. You tell me."

He had his seat teetering on the edge of balance, as he often did when I was pushing him on some matter. Finally, he let it settle back to the floor without a sound.

"I've considered the possibility."

"And?"

"There may be something there."

"I see," I said, tempted to reach for another doughnut. Damned things were addictive, but there were only a dozen to begin with, and they were almost half gone. I didn't want to wear out my welcome, at least not before I got some answers. "So you want to tell me why you rousted Shorty, if you suspected a serial?"

"It's my job. The guys upstairs want action on killings like this. You arrest someone, they get good ink in the papers, and they get off your back so you can get on with finding the real killers."

"Uh-huh," I said, nodding. "And how many guys did you arrest in Hayley Stout's murder?"

"It doesn't matter."

"So, for all practical purposes, Shorty's off the hook?"

Farley's chair went back again, and he put his hands behind his head, regarding my like some child for whom he had to spell things out.

"No, Gallegher, Shorty is not off the hook. In fact, the way I see it, the only person who's off the hook is *you*. I will, however, do two things today. First, I'll find out where Shorty was at the time the other two girls were killed. Second, I will call the Fibbies and find out if they're interested in this thing as a serial case. Would that provide you with some sense of closure?"

"It would be a start," I said, smiling as warmly as Farley was likely to buy. "I would appreciate it very much."

"Think nothing of it," he said, with just a faint sneer in his voice. "After all, we are here to protect and to serve."

It was still early, so I grabbed a quick breakfast of beignets and chicory coffee at Cafe du Monde, and then strolled across Canal Street in the general direction of the Garden District and *A Friend's Place*.

While I walked, I considered my reasons for going there. It was a Friday, which meant that Merlie, the shelter director, was going to be up to her armpits in requests for beds from Social Services. It happened every week. Desperate to get out of town for the weekend, social workers would descend on the shelter like acid rain, each trying to place his or her new crisis kid for seventy-two hours so the child wouldn't be brained by his hammerhead parents or left on the streets.

The calls usually began around nine, and didn't stop until after six, when most of the workers knew that the available beds would have been exhausted hours earlier. Still, they would call, because it was their job to use up all reasonable efforts for placement.

This meant, of course, that Merlie's attentions would be focused elsewhere than on working through our own problems. She wasn't likely to have time to sit and talk, and in a sense I was invading on her world anyway.

I didn't stop walking, though, and almost before I knew it I had rounded the corner and *A Friend's Place* was half a block ahead of me. There was the usual gaggle of adolescents lounging on the front gallery, listening to something vaguely musical under the rotating ceiling fans. I nodded to them as I reached for the handle of the screen door and walked into the living room.

One of the counselors recognized me from my many visits in the past. She smiled at me, and pointed toward Merlie's office. I took it as an invitation, because I wanted it to be one.

Merlie looked up when I tapped on her open door. Something like a cloud seemed to pass across her face, but she stood and crossed the room to me. She closed the door and put her arms around me as if she hadn't seen me in weeks, and rocked back and forth without saying a word, until I realized she was wetting the shoulder of my jacket with tears. I wanted to look in her eyes and ask what was wrong, but she clung to me like spider webs.

Finally, she pulled away, but only far enough to face me.

"Don't say anything," she said. "Let me talk first. I'm so sorry I didn't call on your birthday. I started to, but I didn't know what to say. Every time I picked up the telephone, I became confused and dumb. I even started to dial a couple of times, but I never made it through all seven numbers because I was afraid you might be there and I'd say something stupid and blow it. By the time I figured things out, it was too late."

"I had a feeling it was something like that," I lied. "I was busy anyway. I probably wouldn't have been around to answer the phone."

I told her about Lucy, and about Shorty being arrested.

"That's horrible," she said, suppressing a shudder. "You don't think Shorty would do something like that, do you?"

"It doesn't seem to matter much what I think right now. But, no, I don't. I talked with Detective Nuckolls this morning. He's working on another angle."

She took my hand and led me across the office to a sofa against the far wall, and we sat.

"I have something to ask you," she said. "You said you didn't want me to die *like the others,* but you only told me about Claire."

I told her about Meg Coley, and how she had conspired with Sammy Cain to seduce me and then frame me for killing Lester Vincouer. I told her how it all ended in a bloody mess on the *Mariposa,* Vincouer's cabin cruiser, out on Lake Pontchartrain. I told her how Meg had been laced up by one of Justin Leduc's bodyguard's machine pistols, and how I cradled her on the spattered deck of the boat as the lights faded from her eyes, and what her last words were.

You are one lucky son of a bitch.

"You tried to save both of them," Merlie said quietly.

"I failed to save both of them. I lived. They died. I've asked myself, hundreds of times, whether I was too absorbed in saving my own ass, whether I subconsciously weighed the odds, tapped the scales, and came to a split-second conclusion that it was me or them. I've nearly driven myself crazy wondering whether, without meaning to, I might have sacrificed them to give me an extra half second to salvage my own life."

"That doesn't sound like you," she said.

"Maybe you don't know enough about me, then."

She took my hand, and held the palm to her cheek.

"All I can tell you is this," I said. "This is what I know, what I've learned the hard way. When it comes down to just you and the other guy, and your whole life shifts up into slam-dancing mode, all you can think about is being faster, better, and cleaner. That's all that goes through your head until you're the last one standing in the blood and the smoke, and then all you feel is relief. It has nothing to do with good or evil or black or white. It's just instinctive, like the gazelle running from the cheetah. You kill the other guy because he needs killing, because it's better to kill him than it is to let him kill you. That's all there is. The rest you wrestle with later."

She rubbed her forehead with both hands, as if warding off a nascent headache.

"That's a frightening thing to know," she said.

"It's pretty scary to live it, too. This is the way it is, though. I can't protect you at the same time I'm protecting me. That could be fatal for both of us if you're in the line of fire when the black flag goes up. That's why I asked you to leave the other night. That's the way it has to be. I won't carry you around in my head like I do Claire and Meg. I just won't do it."

I could see the tears in her eyes, huge crystal droplets that danced about her lashes and refracted the sunlight streaming in through the windows until gravity pulled them down her cheeks.

"Let's leave," she said, snuffling back a sob. "Let's take off, go somewhere else. San Francisco, Seattle, Boston, anywhere. Let's leave all this behind, start fresh."

I felt sad, and a little empty.

She still didn't understand.

I shook my head.

"I can't. It wouldn't work, Merlie," I said quietly.

"Damn it, Gallegher, you're a fucking *expert* at starting over!" She was really revved, now, her eyes burning like finely polished amethysts. "You've spent your whole life leaving lives behind. Couldn't you do it one more time?"

"Maybe I could move. Maybe I could box up my books and my records and CD's, put all my clothes into a shopping bag, load up the Pinto, and drive off into the sunset. I probably wouldn't leave behind three people who would remember my name in five years. I'd just be one more guy who hit this town, stuck around for awhile, and then disappeared as quietly as he rode in. I could do that, maybe, but I couldn't leave my head behind. I couldn't just chuck my memories and fears and nightmares in the dumpster out back. I don't fantasize for a second that, by leaving New Orleans, I'd shuck Big Bad Pat the way you peel the shell off a boiled shrimp."

I crossed the room, and pulled her up from the sofa, and I drew her to me, her aroma surrounding me like smoke in a backroom poker game.

"This is what I am, Merlie. This is the man I've become, and everything I did or was before I came here is part of it. This is the man who loves you more than I can say, and if you ask again I'll leave with you, tonight, this afternoon. You have to know, though, you *must* realize, that the man you say you love is the same one I've described to you here. You want me, you take the failed priest, the psychologist, the knight errant, the killer. It's a total package, no substitutions, *prix fixe*. You can't have part of me and leave the rest behind."

"Oh, God, don't do this," she moaned.

"See me the way I am," I urged. "Stop looking at me with googly eyes and that trusting heart, and see the real person here. When we met six months ago, you told me you had given up idealistic infatuations, that you had become the ultimate realist. Get real, now, and take a hard keen look at me and not what you want me to be."

She pulled back, and cupped my size eight head in her meticulously manicured hands. One hand stroked my cheek, the other my hair. Then, seemingly without thought, she pulled me down to her and pressed her lips to mine, and they parted some, and her tongue danced across my lips and made them tingle. I responded to her urgently, the way she had always been able to make me do, and I picked her up in my arms, our lips never breaking contact, and her own arms wrapped around my neck and it seemed as if every molecule of air was squeezed from between us and time stopped for an entire lifetime and half of another.

"Don't you let me die," she said fervently. "Damn you, Gallegher, if you let me die in one of your crusades, there won't be room in your head for any other memories, and I'll haunt you as long as you live."

"I won't," I promised, and I kissed her again.

"Don't you dare let me die," she repeated.

SEVEN

I was on the stage at Holliday's, working on something melancholy and forlorn that sounded vaguely like *Ave Maria*. It had been a decent set, and for a change I was actually able to keep up with Sockeye Sam's frequent and maddening key changes. I suppose I was motivated by the constant awareness that, twenty feet over my head, Merlie was lounging on my couch reading Hemingway, waiting patiently for her soldier to come home from the wars.

Shorty was working the bar, slinging beers and shooting the shit with the usual crowd of ne'er-do-wells who show up night after night. He was working hard at it, like an actor who had been playing the same role for ten years and had a hard time juicing up for performances anymore.

It had been a rough day for him.

Lucy had not left any known relatives, so it was handed to Shorty to arrange for her funeral. He had elected cremation, partly because it was the least expensive option and Shorty wasn't a Kennedy, and partly (I think) because that way he didn't have to plant her somewhere in the city and have to drive by her week in and week out. Cremation was simple and decidedly final. Scatter the ashes into the Mississippi and let the current take them out to sea. Bury the memories instead.

I was seguing into Miles's *All Blues* when I noticed Shorty stiffen behind the bar and turn ruddy, his eyes squinting furiously.

"What in hell do you want now?" he said, pointing at Farley Nuckolls, who had sidled up to the bar.

Farley leaned across the bar and said something I couldn't hear, which didn't seem to mollify Shorty a bit. I decided it was time for a break, and I signaled to Sockeye to pick up the bridge.

After setting the Conn band cornet into its stand, I stepped down from the stage and wandered intently toward them.

"I thought you'd want to hear this," Farley said to Shorty.

"Put it in a fuckin' postcard, Nuckolls. I knew it all along. It doesn't mean you're welcome in here anymore. You got a lotta balls walking in here, after the way you treated me yesterday."

I sat next to Farley, and pointed to the beer cooler. Almost by instinct, Shorty reached behind and grabbed a Dixie, popped the cap, and handed it to me.

"I wanted an Abita," I said.

"Drink the Dixie," Shorty growled.

"So, um, Shorty," I said, "You want me to take this guy out in the back alley and kick the shit out of him, or what?"

Nuckolls gazed at me impassively, as if he wished I would try.

"This asswipe says I'm not a suspect no more," Shorty said. "Like he ever really thought I was."

"And this is bad news?" I asked.

"No more free beer," Shorty told Nuckolls, pointing a gnarled finger at him. "Go freeload somewheres else, you got that?"

Nuckolls held up his hands, palms out.

"Hey, no probs here, Shorty. I only come here for the cosmopolitan atmosphere anyway. I thought you'd just like to know you're cleared. Sorry if I dumped in your grits."

I put my hand on Nuckolls' shoulder and steered him toward an empty table.

"Some guys got no gratitude," he grumbled as we sat down.

"Well, you did put him jail and make him hock the bar for his bail, when he should have been out arranging funeral services for his dead girlfriend. Guys like Shorty take that personally. So tell me, Detective, how did you come to the conclusion that the boss wasn't the one that killed Lucy? I hope it was something I said."

"Actually, it was, sort of. The Fibbies like the serial killer angle. They're very excited about the prospect of some guy with a head full of razor wire stalking strippers in our fair city. They want to send a guy down here to consult on the case, do a little profiling."

"What does this have to do with Shorty?"

"The other murders took place while he was working here. I got that all confirmed. He got caught up in the circumstances the other night. The writing on the dead girls was all done with the same kind of marker. Shorty couldn't have done all three, so he didn't do Lucy Nivens."

"I take it the FBI guys have already run the M.O. through their computers for matches."

"Oh, yes. You have no idea how many blade-happy psychos there are out there."

"You might be surprised what I know. Who are the Feds sending to work with you?"

Nuckolls leaned back in his seat, but he didn't dare try to balance it in midair the way he did the one in his office. It wouldn't be seemly, I suppose, for one of New Orleans' Finest to flip over backward in a bar full of people.

"Galen Crosby. Heard of him?"

"Not in several years. Crosby was one of my trainers when I was doing forensic work in the Northeast. He's good."

"He worked on Crazy Ed Hix's case, didn't he?"

"That's the second time you've brought that case up, Farley. I think you're trying to stoke my nightmares."

"Anything for a friend."

"That case is closed, Detective. Understand?"

"Makes a hell of a story, though. Crosby was very impressed when I dropped your name. Told me shit that wasn't in the police files."

"You requisitioned the Hix case files?"

He nodded.

"Then you know everything there is to know. Forget what Crosby told you. He's a hell of a profiler, but he walks around with thumbtacks stuck in his scalp. He has a hard time letting go of the human algae he tracks. They all stay in his brain, taking turns at pouring lighter fluid on his soul and striking matches. The guy can stroll directly into the depths of a serial killer's consciousness, what there is of it, but he has a hard time finding his way out."

"Small world. He said something similar about you. Not in as colorful a vernacular, of course, but..."

"Drop it, Farley. I mean it. It was a long time ago. I got out of that business and Crosby didn't. He has ten years more road burn than I had when I punched out."

Nuckolls nodded, and turned to listen to Sockeye for a moment, tapping the fingers of his right hand against the table top in rhythm to some rag the ancient pianist had dragged from the musical encyclopedia of his brain. Then, as if he recalled some train of abandoned thought, Nuckolls turned back to me.

"It's a new guy," he said.

"Come again?"

"This ripper. He's new. You asked whether the Fibbies had run him through the computers. It's a new M.O.. We got us some fresh meat here, Gallegher. The guy's brand new."

"No," I said, trying not to get sucked in. "He isn't."

"Feds say he is."

"He isn't."

"You feel like elaborating?"

"Not really. He's not new. Start from there. And stop trying to bait me into coming in on this thing."

"Okay. If you say so," Nuckolls said, and turned back toward the bandstand. "Feds say he's new, though."

I felt the heat rising in my face. Farley was working a righteous shuck on me, and I didn't like it a bit. I had to get away for a minute, get Crazy Ed Hix and a half dozen other subhuman factory seconds out of my head long enough to think straight. I pushed back my chair and crossed the room to the bar, where I threw the empty Dixie bottle in the trash and fished a Heineken out of the cooler.

The hell with Shorty.

"They're wrong," I said, rising to the bait, as I sat back down at the table. "Even you can't be stupid enough to buy that crap. Look at the timeline. We have three murders in a little less than a month and a half. We have a well-developed M.O.. This UNSUB has refined his act, and he did it a long time ago…"

"UNSUB?"

"Unknown subject. Fibbie-speak for the ripper. This guy is exorcising some gruesome internal demon, using a ritual that is unvarying except for the word he writes on each victim. You got Lucien Fleck's girl murdered six weeks ago, Huey's girl four weeks later, and Lucy two weeks after that. The acceleration is almost geometric. It's like some kind of friggin' backwards inverse square law in action. You take the most recent victim, and start timing the difference between previous victims, and you get a compression of time with each successive killing leading up the most recent. With thrill killers, it's all about upping the ante, the way a junkie needs more dope more often the longer he uses. With guys who are working out some kind of intrapsychic garage sale, the voices in their heads are driven away for shorter and shorter periods, until they're killing every other day. So you've got four weeks between Huey's girl to Lucien's girl, and two weeks to Lucy Nivens. If this guy follows the pattern, he's going to do it again sometime the middle of next week, and then again during the weekend after that. He's been accelerating for a long time, Farley, and he's going critical. I suggest you tell the Feds to check the computers again."

"Jesus," he said, pulling off his Panama hat and running his fingers through what was left of his hair. "You really *do* know this stuff, don't you?"

"Quit buttering me up. What I know comes from another me that checked out before I turned forty, understand? You want answers? You go to Galen Crosby and ask him. You have one advantage on your side, though."

"That being?"

"These ripper types? As they go critical, get to one or two murders a week, they start getting sloppy. They make stupid mistakes. The New York police would have been another month catching Berkowitz if he hadn't gotten eager and pulled down a double-parking ticket during one of his murders. The drive to do the deed overwhelms everything, all caution, all method, even personal safety. It gets to the point with these mental cesspools that the only thing that matters is the stalk and the kill. You let this slimeball go long enough, and he's going to be chasing hookers though the Cabildo at high noon on Sundays."

"Uh huh," Nuckolls murmured, staring off into space. "You know, Gallegher, I'm gonna hate myself later for asking this, but how would you feel about throwing in on this thing a little? A part time gig?"

"How would you feel about biting me?"

"Just a thought," Farley said, before he turned back to listen to Sam. "Do what you want, though."

It was five in the morning. I was tossing and turning in bed trying to get to sleep. I was kept awake partly by the lingering aroma of lovemaking in the room, but mostly by the images and voices that kept flipping before my eyes like some kind of crazy nickelodeon.

Damn, we got another one, Pat.

He's gonna do it again, just you wait.

Watch out! He's behind you!

I shuddered once, and Merlie was awake beside me.

"What is it?" she asked.

"It's nothing," I said. "Go on back to sleep."

"You've been rolling like a typhoon sea for two hours, Pat. It has to be something."

I turned and sat up at the side of the bed, reaching for a glass of water I kept on the table there.

"It's Farley. He was shaking my branches tonight over a case that's been dead and buried for years. One of my serials. Now I can't get it off my mind."

She sat up, pulling the sheet up to cover her breasts. I could never understand why she did that, as many times as I had seen them, but I always found it endearing, even at the same time it was alluring.

"Why don't you tell me about it?"

"It's not exactly a bedtime story," I said.

"I have to get up soon anyway," she said.

I stood and walked over to the window. Outside, the street was littered with beer bottles and cigarette packs and takeout cartons, but no people. It looked as if someone had blown off an air raid siren in the middle of an orgy.

"I lied to you earlier, sort of," I said.

"Oh," she said, and pursed her lips. "I don't like this story already."

"It was a little lie, if that counts for anything. I didn't want to tell you about one of the men I killed. He was the first."

"The first time is always the hardest, I hear."

"Not in this case. The guy was named Ed Hix. He was diener."

"I don't know what that is."

"He worked in a morgue. He was the guy who pulled the bodies out of the drawers and transported them for viewing by the survivors. He signed the bodies in, and then he signed them out. These guys are always a little creepy, but you figure it goes with the job. Hix was a one-man horror show.

"There were some murders, isolated acts over a period of a couple of years, apparently unrelated. The only similarity between them, on the surface, was that all the bodies had been bitten."

"Bitten?"

"Gnawed, more like it. Nobody put them together, though, because the bites didn't match. Bite marks are like fingerprints. These were all different. Also, the victims didn't form a type. There were old ladies, young girls, a schoolteacher, a bar girl, a grocery store checkout lady, even a couple of homosexual men. We might never have found the connection, except for a couple of coincidences. There was this guy, another psycho, who was biting women on buses. He'd sit behind them and chomp just before he got off the bus. Some hotshot in the records department at the police station decided to collate all the records involving bites. We eliminated the murder victims immediately, since the guy on the buses wasn't killing anyone.

"This other detective, though, fellow named Skeezix - he looked a lot like that character Skeezix Wallet in the *Gasoline*

Alley comic strip - took a look at the bitten murder victims and noticed that they were becoming more frequent.

"At the time, I was consulting with the police department in Nashua as a forensic specialist, mostly doing competency evaluations for court hearings, but I had also done some training in serial profiling. So Skeezix called me up to his office and laid the records out on his desk.

"*When's the next one gonna be?* he asked me. How was I supposed to know? He told me he thought we had a serial killer, and I told him he needed to bring in the FBI, that this was out of my league. So he called the Fibbies, and they sent Galen Crosby, a hotshot psycho killer expert, to consult with us. He looked over the evidence, and told us to expect another killing about a week later. He said it would be on Friday."

"And it happened the way he predicted?" Merlie asked.

"Like he was psychic. I got a telephone call from Skeezix on Saturday morning. *Damn, we got another one, Pat,* he said. Some kids playing in a railway yard had found a body around two that morning. It was still warm when they found it, the blood still sticky on the ground. It was a woman who had sold tickets at the bus station. Whoever had killed her had bitten her on the upper arm and the left breast."

"And the bite marks didn't match any of the other cases?" she asked.

"Exactly. We were stymied. Skeezix figured it was some guy who worked in a dental laboratory, so he started screening those. He thought maybe some head case denture technician might be taking new sets of teeth out on test rides."

Merlie shuddered, and pulled the sheet tighter around her.

"Gives me the creeps," she said.

"It gets worse. This was about the time Wayne Williams was dumping young boys all over Atlanta, and Crosby was called away to work that case. He decided I was the closest thing Nashua had to a forensics expert. He gave me a crash course in advanced serial killer profiling. He headed off to Atlanta, and I was left to direct the forensic profiling component of the search for our murderer. Based on what Crosby had taught me, we decided that the murderer was a loner, a fellow who felt like he had been given the shaft by life, that he had never gotten any breaks. We figured he might have wanted to be a cop, or maybe he had been turned down for the Military Police. We decided he had to be a denture wearer, since he had to have some space to fit the choppers he used on his victims. He was strong, a lot of upper body strength. He probably lived alone, since he did most of his killing at night, when a family or spouse might have missed him. We knew his blood type from the saliva in the bite wounds, but this was long before accurate DNA testing, so that didn't help us much. I could go on and on. The description ran on to three or four pages. The worst part was that we had only about a week until he was likely to do it again.

"He's gonna do it again, just you wait, Skeezix told me. *Yeah*, I told him, *I know*.

"Meanwhile, Skeezix finished screening all the denture technicians in a three county area -- we had decided he was a local, since all the victims were from the same city -- but the last one he spoke with came up with an idea. He suggested that we look at the bite marks and try to match them up with denture owners through the laboratory and dental records.

"Skeezix could have kicked himself for not thinking about it first. He went back into the records and pulled all the bite photos, and we hired ourselves an expert in dental prosthetics, and he started visiting the labs and dentists' offices to compare the information from those photos with the records.

"We got matches on fourteen out of sixteen bites. Skeezix almost sprained his back trying to hug himself when the results came in. He saw himself making captain grade in six months. Then came the letdown.

"When he traced back the identities of the fourteen positives, he discovered that each and every one of them had died within a week of the murders -- not after, but *before*. Most of them had owned their dentures for more than a year. Skeezix couldn't figure it out. He had people being murdered by corpses.

"Oh, my," Merlie said. "I don't like the way this is going."

"I told you it wasn't pretty. Shall I stop?"

"No," she said. "If you stop, my imagination will drive me crazy all day. What happened?"

"It didn't take Skeezix long to work it out. If the dentures weren't being test-driven before they were delivered, then they had to be used after their owners died. Cutting to the chase -- and believe me, there were about a dozen angles to work out -- we discovered that the only constant in all fourteen cases was that the diener working the mortuary at the time of death was Ed Hix."

"I think I may be ill," Merlie said. "You're saying he was using the dead people's dentures to make the bite marks on his victims?"

"Precisely. We checked his medical records in the county personnel files, and found he had undergone extensive dental work, including the fitting of a complete set of store-bought choppers. Whenever a body came in with a full set of dentures, he would become obsessed with the urge to steal them and go hunting. Over time, the compulsion became so overwhelming that his frequency dropped to once every several days.

"Up to that point, though, we only had supposition. There were no facts to back it up. Skeezix set up a surveillance schedule. He had a hidden television camera installed in the mortuary, and he sat outside the place several nights running with a monitor, watching for Hix to grab off some spare teeth.

"I volunteered to keep him company on the third night. Hix worked the second shift, so he got off around midnight. At ten thirty, the camera caught him wheeling in a new body, which he placed in the cold storage. He took several minutes to look over the paperwork, and then he rolled the body back out. We watched as he pried open the corpse's mouth and..."

"Please," Merlie pleaded, "A little less detail?"

"Okay, so he stole the teeth and placed them in his pocket. Some of these bodies were there for three, maybe four, days. He had plenty of time to commit the murders and then get the dentures back into their rightful mouths. They were either buried with the bodies, or disposed of by the funeral homes. It was an almost perfect M.O..

"We followed him when he left the mortuary that night. First he went to a bar, and tossed back a couple of rock and ryes, I guess building up his courage. Then he drove to a rest stop on the interstate, where he went into the bathroom and stayed there for almost a half hour, until he finally walked out with a kid, maybe twenty-two years old, who had gone in moments earlier. They started hiking out toward the woods behind the rest stop, and Skeezix decided it was a murder going down. He radioed for assistance, but it would be five minutes or more before anyone would respond, so he opened the glove box and handed me a .32 Airweight he kept in there for emergencies.

"*You know how to use one of these?*" he asked. I told him I could manage, and we took off toward the woods. It was a bloody mess, thrashing through the trees and undergrowth, looking for them. After several minutes, Skeezix held up his hand, then pressed his finger to his lips, telling me to be quiet. It was a full moon. I could actually see shadows on the ground. Skeezix gestured for me to make a lateral move toward a broken-down wall, which I did. I was, maybe, twenty-five feet from him when I saw Hix dash out from behind a boulder with a huge knife, and make a run toward Skeezix.

"*Watch out!* I yelled. *He's behind you!* Skeezix dropped to the ground and rolled, at the same time I flipped off the safety, jacked a round into the chamber of the Airweight, and drew down on Hix. I was too slow, though. Skeezix got off one shot, which hit Hix in the shoulder, before the slimeball dove on top of him and drove the knife into his chest, right up to the handle. Hix was covered with blood, and his mouth was... I'm sorry, too much detail. Let's just say he had already killed the kid, and now he had Skeezix, too.

"It was like he was in a frenzy. He didn't care that I had him in the crosshairs. He was obsessed, and he had to carry out the act even at the peril of his own life. He bent over Skeezix with those stolen dentures, and started to take a chunk out of his neck...."

I stopped, as I realized there were tears on my cheeks. Decades later, and it still wrenched my heart.

Merlie wiped my tears with her meticulously manicured fingers.

"I splattered the top of his fucking head all over the woods," I said. "I emptied the clip of the Airweight into his face from five feet away. I was still trying to work the action on the pistol when the state cops caught up with us. One of them took the gun from my hand and my fingers kept jerking. I had never killed anyone before. I was in shock. I couldn't take my eyes off Skeezix, lying on the ground with that knife sticking out of his chest, and this *Oh Shit* look in his glazed eyes.

"A psychiatrist I worked with gave me tranks to keep me from climbing the walls. After a few weeks, I noticed that there was this numb place in my brain, where I was able to toss all the memories and lock them up. I was a little harder, a little less sensitive. I started volunteering for murder cases, the more bizarre the better. It was like when I was a kid, and I couldn't wait to go the *Oddities of Nature* show at the carnival.

"I know the rest," Merlie said, her arms wrapped around me from behind. Her face rested against my shoulder. Her lips brushed my ear, and I heard her whisper, "It's all right. You survived."

"Did I?" I asked softly. "You really think so? I think maybe I actually died in those woods, that maybe I lost everything important that I believed about myself, and then I had to manufacture something to take its place. Perhaps everything I am now is just defense, layer on layer of fortification to keep me from being devoured by the Crazy Ed Hixes of the world. Maybe I'm still an *Oddity of Nature*. It could be that the defenses are the only thing that keep me alive."

She turned me around and pulled me down to the sheets, and held me close against her cool perfect skin, and stroked my wiry graying mane.

"Maybe you're just lucky," she said.

I sighed, and silently gave thanks to whatever supreme deity had brought this tough old broad to me, and I nodded.

"Everyone seems to think so," I said.

And, finally, I slept.

EIGHT

Despite her plans to leave shortly after sunrise, Merlie slept in. It wasn't a big deal. When you're the director of a program like *A Friend's Place*, I suppose nobody makes you punch a timecard. On the other hand, judging by the way oversleeping rattled her, I figured it wouldn't be a good idea to encourage it as a regular indulgence.

I woke up at ten to find her dashing about the apartment gathering her things, trying to put on makeup, and brushing her hair, all at the same time.

"Oh, hell," she blurted, exasperated, "It's no use. I'll have to go by my house first. You are a terrible influence on me."

I settled back on my pillow and watched her wrestle with a vest she didn't know was twisted in the back.

"If you had any idea how many women have told me that..."

"Oh, that's fine. You can go back to sleep. You don't have to go to work until tonight. For all I know, though, my business burned down while I was dozing here."

"Don't be silly. If it had, they'd have paged you."

She stopped fumbling with the vest, and attacked it scientifically, which is to say she actually looked at it to figure out why it refused to be worn. She straightened it out, shooting me one of those *duh* looks. Then she padded across the room and sat at the side of the bed.

"Do you realize you were crying last night?" she asked.

"You must have been hallucinating."

"No, I mean it. Real tears and everything."

"Don't tell anyone. Everyone will want to see it."

"It's our secret. I have to tell you, though, it was kind of sexy."

"You're much more sadistic than I'd even imagined."

"Not the tears, actually. It's nice to see you have feelings that deep, though. Women like that kind of thing. Sensitive guys can be a turn-on."

I rolled over onto my back.

"I shall have to add that to my list of reasons to kill Alan Alda."

"Most guys, that would sound far-fetched. You know, we're reaching a critical moment in our relationship."

"Being?"

"The holidays, darling. Thanksgiving is only a few weeks away, and then there's Christmas. We have to decide what to do about that."

I propped myself up on one elbow and squinted at her. I could remember a time when my vision was crystal clear the instant I woke up. These days, I had to give it a few minutes.

"What's the problem?" I asked. "Neither of us has any family to visit. You know you're welcome to come to midnight mass with me at Dag's church on Christmas Eve."

"And that's it?"

"About covers it."

"I take back everything nice I just said about you," she said pouting. "You are not a sensitive man at all."

"Now you're just sucking up. What did you have in mind?"

"We usually have a big meal at the shelter for those kids who can't go home or don't have a home on Thanksgiving. The counselors and I put it all together. One of the local churches gives us a couple of turkeys, and we buy the rest. You could come over and have Thanksgiving there."

The idea of breaking bread with six counseling majors and nine runaway kids actually gave me the shakes, but it seemed like a good time to compromise.

"I'll think it over. How would you like to go somewhere for Christmas?"

"You mean, other than New Orleans?"

"Yeah, someplace white."

"What about Dag's midnight mass?"

"We'll take the redeye. If we go west, we could arrive almost before we leave, still get a good night's sleep, and wake up to a white Christmas."

She leaned over and hugged me.

"Ooooh, sounds delicious. It could be expensive, though."

"We've had that conversation, dear," I said, reminding her that I am, for all intents and purposes, independently wealthy.

"Let's talk about it over dinner tonight. My place?"

"Cool. Now get out of here and let me get some sleep."

I don't think I ever heard her leave, but when I woke up there was this big red set of lip marks plastered on my cheek.

I came downstairs sometime after noon to find Shorty sitting at the bar, sipping a soft drink through a straw. I hadn't expected to see him. I felt a little awkward.

He raised a hand and gestured for me to come over. I sat on a stool next to him.

"Gallegher, I... um, well... I never got a chance yesterday to thank you for getting that shyster friend of yours to bail me out. He called a little while ago. Since the police dropped the charges, the bondsman is clearing the books."

"That's good. I'd hate to see anything happen to the bar."

"I... ah, also understand, you see.... well, that you had something to do with getting Nuckolls to look in another direction. On Lucy, I mean."

"Did Cully Tucker tell you this?"

"No. Um.... Nuckolls called me this morning, see, and he told me."

"That was nice of him," I said.

"Yeah, it was. Look, this is hard for me, you know, since it's all happened so quickly. But, is it true that Sockeye and Brucie hired you to find out who really killed Lucy?"

I drew in a breath and tapped a little cadence on the bar top.

"Not exactly. Sockeye offered me some money to find a way to get you off, but I never intended to take it. I never said I'd find out who did the murders."

His eyes widened, accenting all the little scars left over from his days in the ring as a kid.

"There are more?"

"It looks that way. That's not official, though. You can't go around spreading that word, understand?"

"Oh, yeah, of course, I get it. But, look.... ah, how would you feel if I... I mean, would you consider taking a look at..."

I held up both hands.

"Wait a minute. This is still a police matter, Shorty. Nuckolls is handling this case."

"I know that, but I just figured you might be able to, you know, help out a little. You know, behind the scenes, like."

I rubbed my face a couple of times, buying time, trying to find a tactful way out of committing to him.

"I don't think so," I said, finally. "Nuckolls already asked me if I wanted to help. He's bringing in a whiz-bang expert on serial murders from the FBI. I know the guy, from back when I worked in New Hampshire. He's good, very good. He's going to be a lot better help for Farley than I could ever be. So it's covered, Shorty. You don't have to worry about it. Take it from me, ninety-nine percent of these pervs get caught sooner or later. They're going to catch him, man. I mean that. You just have to be patient."

His hands were trembling, something I had never seen. Lucy's murder had shaken something loose deep inside of him, and now it was rattling around in his soul like a can full of gravel. His eyes were all bloodshot. If I were still a betting man, I'd have wagered a week's pay he hadn't slept all night.

"Okay. Patient. That's a good idea. Yeah..." he turned and stared at his reflection in mirror behind the bar, the one which still had the bullet hole in it from the time Barry Saunders came back from the dead to try to kill me, so he could get away with murder and insurance fraud.

"Look," I said, "You have to get some rest. Take it from me. If you let this thing eat you up inside, it will. I know. Do yourself a favor. Go home and take a nap, at least. You'll feel better."

I stood and started to walk to the door. He kept staring at himself in the mirror. I had just reached the door when he spoke again.

"Twenty years," he said. "It's been twenty years since I let myself fall for a woman like I did her. And it's not like I've had a lot of chances at it, with a face like this, all bent up and punched in. She said she loved me, Gallegher. You think she meant it?"

What could I tell him? That the whore with a heart of gold dropped the fast life so she could give it up only for him? Reynard had left enough doubts about that for me to wonder if Lucy had told the truth about leaving the life. The fact that she might have been lured out of *Les Jolies Blondes* didn't help. What could she have been attracted by, if not the promise of easy cash? Maybe, I even mused, my visit had pushed her back over the edge. It was possible that, after confronting her the way I had, she had decided that she was condemned to prejudice no matter how hard she tried to change her life. If everyone was going to presume she was handing out ten-dollar hummers, then where was the motivation not to do it?

That was too much for my conscience to handle so early in the day, so I simply nodded.

"Yeah, Shorty," I said. "I think maybe she did."

"That's good. The funeral's tomorrow. It's not much, just a few minutes at the undertaker's. I'd consider it a favor if you'd...." He stopped there, as if he had lost the ability to speak. He turned to me, and there was this sad, distant, defeated look on his face. It was the look of a man who genuinely believed, in his heart of hearts, that his last chance at happiness had been wrenched from him and torn to shreds.

"It's okay, man," I said. "I'll make a point of being there. If you'd like, I'll even play something. What was her favorite song?"

He chuckled, a short, barking laugh that shook his body as his head rocked back and forth.

"Man, ain't that a shitter?" he said, his voice starting to break. "I don't even know..."

NINE

John Lennon once wrote *'Life is what happens while you're making plans for life'*. Considering the way things went down for him, I guess you'd have to say he had a handle on it.

Several things happened very quickly over the next several days.

On Saturday, Merlie and I were lying on a big blanket on a grassy hill near the Riverwalk, reading. I had a copy of *The Dancing Wu Li Masters,* a book linking quantum physics and Sufi mysticism. I couldn't make heads or tales out of the damn thing, but it was fun trying. Merlie was still working on the Hemingway she'd borrowed from me.

It was just warm enough to take the weak rays without a jacket. The sky was dotted with wisps of cumulus that the jet stream was batting around the way a kitten does with balls of yarn, and there was a steady stream of working ships making their way around the kink in the Big Muddy, headed out toward the lake and, eventually, the Gulf of Mexico. Somewhere far off, there was the faint rancid odor of decay, since fall comes even to the near tropics, and leaves drop from the trees here just as surely as they do in Vermont. I had brought a mini boom box from home, but the CD player had run out of tunes, and I had turned on a local jazz station on the FM.

Around the top of the hour, the news cut in, and after the usual string of stories about Washington scandals and various military uprisings in countries I hoped never to visit, a reporter cut in with the local stuff.

The lead story was about a murder in the Vieux Carre, involving a dancer from a dive called the Shag Palace, located on one of the less traveled streets near the old Storyville. She had been found early that morning, and all the reporter seemed to know was that she had been 'brutally mutilated', as if there was a civil way of doing the deed.

Merlie must have read my thoughts.

"Leave it alone, Gallegher," she said, pinching my thigh.

"Sure thing. None of my business," I said, as I turned off the radio.

I tried to concentrate on the book, but it was futile. Somehow, all the permutations of a serial killer operating just under my nose was just too much competition for the dancing *wu li* masters. I started thinking about dates and times, and despite my best efforts to block it out, a profile started to form in my head.

"Wednesday," I said, staring at a tanker with the name *Fairy Maiden* written on it, as a river pilot steered it by quietly.

"What?"

"Wednesday. That's when this guy's going to do it again."

She put down her book and punched me in the arm.

"Owww! Cut it out."

"No," she said, "*You* cut it out. Solve murders on your own time."

"Sorry. It's a reflex."

We both tried to resume reading, but after a couple of minutes she put the book down again and made an exasperated face.

"Okay, damn you, why Wednesday?"

"Couldn't get if off your mind, either?"

"No. Why Wednesday?"

"It's the way these guys operate. At first, at the time this freak began killing, it probably scared the crap out of him. Maybe not at the exact moment he killed the victim, but later, when he realized that he had these bloodstained clothes and shoes, and this contaminated knife to deal with. Maybe he got really frightened about being caught. Maybe he imagined that everyone who looked at him suspected that he was the killer, and they were just waiting for enough proof to pin him down. The adrenalin rush he got must have been better than sex, a real head buzz that lasted for days. You know the neurologists have discovered that adrenalin bonds to the same brain receptors as amphetamines? These serial murderers are just as hooked on the stuff as any crankhead you run into on Bourbon Street."

"And you're saying that, like the druggies, they need it more often?"

"Exactly. With each successive murder, the effect is decreased, so it doesn't last as long. They get desensitized to it. Lucy was murdered about a week ago, on Thursday, and today is Saturday, which means that this girl from the Shag Palace was killed on Friday, more or less. The girl before Lucy was killed three weeks ago. So figure this guy will do it again in three or four days. Wednesday, at the outside."

"Does it ever bother you that you know so much about these monsters?"

"*Oddities of nature*, dear. *Ego challenged. Socially alienated* and *isolated*. We must, after all, be sensitive and politically correct."

"Oh, the hell with that. Sometimes I think it would be horrible to live in your head."

"You should see it from my side. That's why I got out. The moment you start thinking about these moral primates in sympathetic terms, you lose something of your own humanity. You join the club, sort of. Read the transcripts of every serial killer trial on record and, somewhere, you'll run across the testimony of some hired gun shrink whose job it was to soften up the jury's images of the 'monster' they were judging. Take all those experts' testimonies, bind them together, and it will read like one long book with the same chapter written over and over and over. Physically and sexually abused kid raised by an emotional cripple of a mother, and no father. Every one of them has this bizarre history of fire setting, bedwetting, and animal cruelty by age ten. Most of them started out as peepers -- voyeurs, getting their kicks out of watching middle-aged women take off their clothes without knowing they were being seen. Some progressed to burglary, some to rape. All of them wound up in the same place though, when they killed their first victim. From there on, it's the same song, second verse."

She tossed her book on the blanket, and stared out over the water.

"I've had kids like that..." she said, sadly.

"They're the lunatic fringe of the testosterone set. Get one sitting in a chair across from you, though, and you realize you have more integrity and stability in one fingernail than he has in his whole body. These guys are held together with hormones and chutzpah, which is a good thing. No matter what the media likes to portray, mad killer genius and all, the real story is that eight out of ten of them have a hard time mustering up a triple digit IQ."

"What do you do with someone like that?"

"You bust 'em or smoke 'em," I said, trying not to sound overly cold. "You don't try to relate to them, rehabilitate them, nurture them, analyze them, or empathize with them. You chain them up and toss them behind a stout door with no keys, or you turn them into a rancid memory. I might add that I prefer the latter."

She turned to me with leaden, moistened eyes.

"It's cheaper," I added.

She nodded, and picked up her book.

"You know what I think?" she said.

"What?"

"I think you're still jerking that trigger on Crazy Ed Hix. I think you're still trying to save Skeezix."

"You don't like that."

"It's more complex than that."

"Bet your ass it is. I seem to recall a day last spring when you demanded that I rip Jimmy Binh's heart out and stomp on it for you."

"Twice."

"Twice?"

"I told you to rip out his heart and stomp on it *twice*."

"Ummm," I said, picking up my book. "So you did. Complex."

"It's different when you're personally involved, Gallegher."

"Damned right it is."

"He did horrible things to his stepdaughter."

"Yes, he did."

"He deserved anything that happened to him."

"Probably."

"So you're proving my point."

"Only the one where you said it was *complex*, dear. And, if you'll recall, I agreed with you on that one right off."

"So you're saying that, if you were to catch the creep that killed Lucy, that killed all those other strippers, that you could kill him the way you might squash a bug?"

"I wouldn't even give it the dignity of calling it a killing. I might zip him, squib him, smoke him, ice him, lace him, nail him, or smear him, but *killing* I reserve for people who haven't yet checked out on the human race."

"That's frightening."

"Of course, as you've also noted, I'm already involved. He did kill Shorty's girlfriend, after all."

"You're not feeling just a little guilty, are you?"

"Guilty?"

"About being one of the last people to talk with Lucy? Maybe you're sorry that you took up one of her last hours making her face herself so openly? Is it possible you want to make up for some of that?"

"Hell, I don't know," I said. "So much of my life is driven by guilt, it's hard to figure out where one transgression ends and another begins. What's the difference, though? I'm not actively involved in this one. This time I'm just one of the bit players. This one I can leave to Farley and Galen Crosby. They're welcome to it."

She seemed a little relieved then, as if tossing this miscreant back into Farley's lap lifted a great weight from her own shoulders. It probably did. I had managed to save Louise Onizuki, the little girl who brought Merlie and me together, from Jimmy Binh, her abusive pimp stepfather, without either sparking off a gang war or killing a single person. I didn't like to admit it, but that had scored a lot of points with this gorgeous auburn-haired love of mine. She didn't like to think about me returning to my wicked, wicked ways.

"So," she said, "Wednesday, huh?"

"At the latest."

"You're sure of that?"

"Pretty certain."

"Want to make it interesting?"

"Kind of ghoulish."

"Dinner at the Court of Two Sisters?"

"I don't bet anymore, you know. It got me into a lot of trouble."

"This isn't money, honey."

"Not for matchsticks, bottle caps, paper clips, or soda crackers. You don't offer an alky just one beer."

"Would it endanger your recovery if I congratulate you for being right?"

"Not at all," I said. "I can use all the self-esteem I can get."

Sunday was visiting day. Every other Sunday for about six months, Merlie and I had driven out to Bayou Teche to visit Louise Onizuki. After I nailed her stepfather, Jimmy Binh, for killing a couple of hookers in the process of taking over Phang Loc's Vietnamese gang in the Quarter, and for kidnapping Louise to make it look like she died a runaway's death on the streets, she had been sent to live with a foster family. Merlie and I, as something of surrogate parents while she lived at *A Friend's Place*, had promised to see her at least every couple of weeks.

I dropped Merlie off at her house in the Garden District before driving into the Quarter to park at Irene's. It was a short walk from there to Holliday's, off Toulouse Street. I considered stopping off at Kacoo's for a takeout of steamed crawfish, then thought better of it. It was off-season for mudbugs, and frozen just wasn't as good as fresh. I could grab an oyster po'-boy later.

Farley Nuckolls was sitting at a table in Holliday's when I walked in. Brucie Epps was mopping the floor on the far side of the bar, and Shorty was nowhere to be seen.

"You waiting for me?" I asked as I slipped behind the bar to grab a couple of Abitas.

"I don't know," he said. "I couldn't think of anywhere else to go."

I handed him one of the beers.

"If this is the only place you can think to go, seek professional help immediately. It signals a seriously stunted social life."

He twisted the cap off the Abita, and pulled a Licenciado Corona from the pocket of his seersucker jacket.

"Want one?" he asked.

"Don't mind if I do. You're off duty?"

"Yes, I am." He clipped the end off one of the cigars with the scissors of his penknife, and handed it to me before repeating the process with another.

"Want one, Brucie?" he called across the bar.

Brucie looked at the floor and shook his head shyly.

"N...n...no thanks, Mr. N...N...Nuckolls. I don't sm...sm...smoke."

"Then do me a favor, okay? Take a break. Go get a Coke or something."

"Y...y...yes sir."

Brucie leaned the mop against the wall and walked slowly to the back door of the bar.

Farley handed me a lighter, and I fired up the stogie.

"That was pretty rude," I said.

"I offered him a cigar."

"That's not what I meant. Brucie's retarded. He's not a piece of furniture. He has feelings, too, just like you and me."

"Speak for yourself."

"Oh," I said, drawing on the cigar, and savoring the sweet Cuban seed tobacco. "We're doing *honesty* tonight."

"Some guy at the Times-Picayune called me this morning. Says he's gonna dub this skell the Stripper Ripper. Get used to it. Name like that tends to stick around like an ugly girlfriend. So, when's he gonna do it again?"

"Your guess is as good as mine. Stripper Ripper's a cute name, though."

I took a long drag from the Abita, and followed it with some smoke.

"Aw, hell, gimme the beer," I said. "Cigar like this calls for something better."

He handed me the beer, and I took it behind the bar to toss it in the trash barrel. I grabbed a couple of snifters from the rack over the bar and poured some VSOP brandy into them.

He held his snifter up and swirled the liqueur around to watch it catch the light from the pots badly illuminating the stage.

"To what shall we drink?" he asked.

"Fermentation," I said, and I clinked glasses with him. "I'm way out of practice on this kind of thing, Farley, but if I had a vote, I'd say your dude's going to light up again sometime around midweek, probably Wednesday."

He dipped the wet end of his cigar into the snifter. Farley is all class.

"Yeah," he said. "That's what Galen Crosby told me."

"He's already on the case?"

"Nope, not anymore. That's sort of why I'm here. Crosby spoke with me yesterday, by telephone, after that twist from the Shag Palace got ripped. He told me to look for another murder around midweek."

"So, why's he off the case?"

"Because, about two hours after we hung up, he swallowed the loud end of his service automatic."

I set the snifter down.

"Run that by me again."

"He killed himself, Gallegher. He sat at his desk and stuffed his nine to the back of his throat and pulled the trigger. Would you like to know what the suicide note said?"

"Not particularly."

"It was very short. '*They won't go away*'."

"The faces."

"I kind of figured it was something like that."

"Crosby was a great profiler," I said, "but he had one major fault. He got too close. He identified too much with the assholes he was trying to catch. That scorches you after a while. He was four-fifths of the way to self-destruction when I last saw him. I figure he was living on borrowed time for years. It's a shame."

"Yeah. I know a couple of cops who bit the barrel. Mostly they did it shortly after retirement. Three or four months of downtime, a little too much alcohol, the realization that you're not part of the action anymore, that kind of thing can make you pretty desperate."

We sat there, smoking and drinking, for several silent minutes.

"Could you do it?" I asked, finally.

"Blow myself up? Hell, I don't know. I'm not tempted right now. What about you?"

"It's a mortal sin, Farley. I was almost a priest, you know."

"Horseshit. You're about as religious as the O'Hair family."

"In my own way."

"C'mon. Could you kill yourself?"

I took a sip of the brandy. It had been a good idea.

"Farley, I was a profiler, sort of, just like Crosby. I didn't do it for long. One thing I learned, though, is that one of the prerequisites for the job is an active, florid imagination. I can imagine a lot of things, man. I can imagine situations in which I might kill *you*. So, yeah, I can imagine doing myself in. I can think, right now, of about ten conditions under which I might do it. None of them, thankfully, exist. One of them got to Crosby, though. The faces he mentioned. *They won't go away*? They weren't the killers. He couldn't get the faces of the *victims* out of his mind. He put away over twenty serials in the time I knew him. Want to know how many actually rode the bolt?"

"None?"

"Not one. Every one of them is still alive, in prison. Crosby had the chance, at least twice that I know of, to do what I did to Crazy Ed Hix. He couldn't do it. I think that came back and took a big bite out of his ass."

Nuckolls nodded, and took another sip of the brandy.

"So," I asked, "Have the Fibbies put anyone else on the case?"

"No. Nobody's available. It seems that everyone's tied up with other situations around the country, at least for a couple of weeks. With Crosby dead, a lot of them are going to have to put in the overtime taking up his slack."

"That's a shame."

"They did have a suggestion, though. Seems there's a guy down here, a faculty member over at Loyola, who used to be a pretty hot profiler."

"Yeah? Maybe I know him. What's his name?"

"Clarence Evers."

I set the glass down again. I was lucky I didn't swallow the cigar.

"*Clever* Evers?"

"You know him?"

"Hell, yes. I didn't know he was down here. Man, Farley, this is not your day. You are truly shit out of luck."

"How do you figure?"

"Evers is a head case. He profiled the wrong guy in Tallahassee some years back. Cops arrested this garbage collector on a pile of circumstantial evidence. This was about the time they fried Ted Bundy at Raiford. The governor – can't recall his name -- got a little chair crazy and pushed through the execution. The perp went up like a dried Christmas tree. The only problem was, he wasn't the real killer. The real guy confessed about six months later."

"I remember that case."

"Clever lost it. Went all mental, had to be hospitalized. He tried to commit suicide two or three times. Finally, he chucked it all and retired from the Bureau. I lost track of him after that. So, Clever's here in town?"

"That's what they say. Look, Gallegher, I was hoping you knew this clown. Fact is, I tried calling him yesterday and today. He didn't return my call yesterday, but I caught him at home today. He told me to ram it, and he hung up on me."

"People who get out of this serial killer business aren't too keen to be dragged back in."

"So you say. What about this guy? Is he any good?"

"He *was*, a long time ago. Maybe he was the best. His grasp of theory was as good as any I've seen. Evers has this photographic memory thing going for him -- he remembers everything he reads. You ask him a question, and he can provide a dissertation, complete with bibliography."

"So they call him Clever."

"It was a convenient nickname. I wouldn't count on getting him to come in with you on this ripper case. He was seriously burned on the Florida serial. He hasn't worked a case since, that I know of."

Farley drained the rest of the brandy and blew a couple of smoke rings.

"You wanna talk to him for me?" he asked.

I stared at him, using the killer evil eye that I reserve for only the most malevolent of my enemies.

"Aw, c'mon, Gallegher," he protested. "You know I didn't show up here because I like looking at your ugly mick face."

"You said you were off duty."

"And so I am. This is an unofficial inquiry. This guy, Evers, he won't talk with me. You know him. All I want is for you to do is catch up on old times. Give him a call. Drop by his house. Hell, I don't have to tell you how to do these things."

"I do not like being shucked," I growled.

"And I don't like having some butcher roaming the streets of my city cutting up working girls. All I'm asking is that you talk with him. Feel him out. Let me know if I have a chance of pulling him in. This sack of shit killer is gonna do it again in maybe seventy-two hours, and I don't have clue how to stop him. Maybe Evers can help."

"He won't do it," I argued.

"Then we'll find another alternative. The Fibbies say he's my go-to guy, though, and I want to give it a shot."

I finished my brandy. The last shot went down like warm rain, and I could feel it singe my throat as it rolled through.

"You're going to owe me big for this," I said.

"We'll deal with that later. Will you do it?"

"You're asking me for a favor?"

He nodded.

"You know about the favors I do?"

"I've heard the rumors. I've also seen the bodies."

I rolled the cigar around in my mouth, and sucked in some smoke.

"I always liked Licenciados," I said. "Of course, I hear they're a pretty sorry substitute for some of Uncle Fidel's product."

"What the fuck...?"

"I bet Chester Boulware over at the Justice Department owes you a favor or two."

"You don't know what you're asking."

"All the gang busts he does out of Baton Rouge -- smugglers, racketeering, that sort of thing. Bet they confiscate all kinds of stuff. I'll even bet they've come across the occasional box of Cuban stogies."

"Jesus, Gallegher..."

"Hey, I'm not unreasonable. Tell you what -- I'll give Clever Evers a call. If he comes on board, I'll take a box of Cubans. If he doesn't, you don't owe me a thing. How's that for a deal?"

"Do I have a choice?"

Of course, he didn't. I knew very well that he was stuck. The haggling only took a couple of minutes, and when it was finished we had worked out the fine details.

Donald Trump would have been proud.

TEN

Clarence Evers lived on a cul-de-sac in a quiet residential section of New Orleans just to the west of the Garden District. The house was, like many in the town, designed to capture, however imperfectly, the ambience of the low country plantation cottage -- that is, if you could ignore the woefully inadequate front porch and the vinyl siding. Even the dormers on the ersatz second level were little more than vertical skylights, illuminating the vast empty space of the cathedral ceiling inside. Clever Evers' house was a masterpiece of deception.

As I touched the doorbell button, I could hear electronically reproduced Westminster chimes from inside the house. Within seconds a speaker attached to the doorbell crackled, and a tinny voice accosted me.

"What is it?"

"Fuller Brush man."

"Fuck off," the voice said, and the speaker chirped as it was switched off.

I pressed the button again.

This time it took almost a minute before the speaker came to life.

"I'm going to call the police," it said.

I gave him Farley's telephone number.

"Smartass," he said, and again the speaker chirped off.

I leaned on the doorbell button, and the Westminster chimes played over and over for almost a half minute.

That did it. I heard a succession of deadbolt locks being thrown, and finally the doorknob turned. As the door slid open, the double barrel of an over-and-under shotgun snaked out and was planted against my ample torso.

"Now you can get, or the law says I can blow you to kingdom come," he said.

"Actually, I think you have to lure me inside first," I told him.

"Like hell I do. I don't see you leaving."

"Clever, this is the third time in the last week that someone's held a gun on me. I'm beginning to feel a little unpopular."

I felt the tension in my belly relax a little, as the gun was pulled back.

"What in hell..." he said, the the door swung open a bit more. "I know you."

"Older, fatter, and wiser. I'll bet the same goes for you."

The door opened wide, and Evers leaned the shotgun against the jamb.

"It's Gallegher, right?"

"Roy Patrick Gallegher."

"From New Hampshire. You were loaned out to assist in that case in Boston -- what was it -- fourteen years ago?"

"Thereabouts. I just heard you were in town. Thought I'd drop by."

"Well, then come on in. Hot damn, but if it isn't good to see a face from the old days once in a while."

I followed him into the house. It was dark, compared to the steely sunlight cascading on the cul-de-sac outside. The rooms were furnished comfortably, but cheaply, which was befitting a fellow who lived on an FBI pension. There were art prints on the walls, but none of them were signed or numbered.

There was dust everywhere.

Clever stood about five inches shorter than my six and a half feet. He was walking around in terrycloth bathroom slippers. He was portly and black, his head shaved to the skin in the popular fashion that year. He wore beltless slacks and a pullover sport shirt, the kind of garb you see often in golf course clubhouses. His eyes, though, were quick and full of life, and they darted over my body as if cataloging my soul.

"Man, you weren't shitting me. You've put on a few pounds since Nashua."

"The years have been kind to me."

"Somehow, I don't think so, but have a seat anyway. How about a beer?"

He disappeared for a minute and came back with two bottles of Sam Adams. His Boston habits were dying hard.

"So," he said, after taking a sip, "What have you been up to? You live here?"

"In the French Quarter. I play a horn in a bar over there. You ought to drop by one night."

"You any good?"

"I'm the best horn player in my bar. Beyond that, I avoid comparisons."

"Got out of police work, eh?"

"It was a mutual decision. I tried teaching, but that didn't work out the way I planned. I've been here for about seven years."

He leaned forward. "Just between you and me, how do you like it?"

"It's hot as hell in summer, and there's no snow in the winter, and in between it just rains, except for during hurricanes, when it rains like hell. I like it fine."

He stared at me.

"It'll do," I corrected. "I haven't found any compelling reasons to leave. What in hell are you doing here, though?"

He took a sip of the beer, and placed it on a coaster on the occasional table beside his chair.

"Same as you. I didn't want to work in law enforcement anymore, so I took early retirement and accepted a teaching position at Loyola. Psych department. Two sections of Abnormal, and no research or irritating grad students to worry about."

"I hope you find it more satisfying than I did."

"It's fun, sometimes. I like watching the skin crawl on some of those pipsqueak undergrads when I really get into a story about some mouthbreeder like Ed Hix."

I hoped my eyes didn't narrow. It was strange of him to mention Hix right away, especially since he didn't work the case.

"Don't remind me," I said.

"So, what are you doing for the police?"

I suppressed a startle response, and decided not to let him get the upper hand in the conversation. It only took me a breath or two to remember that Clever had eidetic imagery -- photographic memory. Farley had called him only a day earlier. I had quoted Farley's number at the door. A guy like Evers wouldn't have had any trouble putting the pieces together.

"I'm supposed to be recruiting you for this Stripper Ripper case."

"Stripper Ripper?" he said, chuckling. "What smartass newspaper punk came up with that one?"

"Guy at the Times-Picayune."

"Figures. Forget it. I'm not interested."

"Did Detective Nuckolls tell you why he's asking?"

"Said the Bureau referred him."

"Galen Crosby was working the case."

"He's good. He can handle it."

"He's dead, Clever. He kacked himself a couple of days ago."

"No shit," Evers said, and drained the beer. "Well, that calls for a drink. Get you another one?"

I nodded and handed him my empty.

"Don't get the wrong idea," he said, as he walked into the open kitchen at the far end of the great room. "I had nothing against Galen. I just wonder who had that date in the office pool."

"You expected him to kill himself?"

"Everyone did," Evers said, handing me a fresh beer. "That boy was wound tighter than a cheater golf ball."

"Weren't we all?"

"Whoa," he said, holding the beer with all but his index finger, which was pointing at me. "What's this *we* shit, white boy? What makes you think your pitiful angst can hold a candle to what those of us in the Bureau went through? You weren't nothin' but a hired puke consultant for a podunk little police force. How many of these monsters did you actually cross swords with, besides Crazy Ed Hix? Two, three? Over how many years?"

"I'm not going to defend my life, Clever," I said, aware of my own growing irritation.

"Nobody's asking you to. Just consider what it would have been like to immerse yourself dick high in mental waste products like Hix, three or four at a time, for twenty years."

"It's hard to imagine."

"Try dragging a cheese grater across your soul for a couple of decades."

"I'm Catholic. It's not such a stretch."

"Try sending some innocent guy across, sometime."

I thought, painfully, of Claire Sturges for a second.

"*That* I can relate to."

"Even so, you ain't one of us, boy. Guys like Galen Crosby were *born* to bite the blue steel. We all saw it coming."

"So why didn't anyone do anything to stop it?"

"What were we going to do? Lock him in his room? Hell, every guy in the Behavioral Science Unit took turns urging Crosby to retire. I called him three or four times myself, tried to get him to take a few weeks off, come on down here and get a taste of it. He wouldn't listen. Always said he was too busy, too many bad guys to catch. The guy was a workaholic. It's like any addiction, man. Sooner or later it eats you up."

"Like it did with you and Larry Bondurant?"

He frowned as I invoked the name of the kid his investigation sent to the electric chair in Florida -- wrongly, as it turned out.

"Now who's goading who?" he said.

"I'm not interested in yanking your chain. I wasn't all that big on coming in the first place. Farley tried to bring me in on it, too. I told him I wasn't interested. I was kind of curious to see how you'd turned out. You look good, Clever. Retirement agrees with you."

"Thanks."

"It's a shame, though. This is the kind of case a guy like you could really latch onto. Lots of spooky ritualistic stuff."

"Oh?"

"Like the words on the body...." I stopped. "Jesus, I didn't even ask. Can I use your telephone?"

He pointed toward the bar separating the kitchen from the great room, where a wall phone had been installed. I picked up the receiver and dialed Farley's number. He answered on the third ring.

"Detective Nuckolls."

"Hey, Farley, this is Pat. I'm over at Evers' house killing a couple of brews, and I just realized that I forgot to ask what word was written on the latest victim."

"This is kind of confidential, Gallegher. I probably shouldn't have told you about the other three."

"Yeah, but you did. It might help."

"Does Evers look like he might come into this thing with us?"

"It's too early."

"Well.... okay. The word was '*too*'."

"Like the number two?"

"Like in '*also*'. T-O-O."

"'*This, that, oh*, and *too*,'" I said. "I don't see any pattern here."

"You're not alone. See what you can do about bringing Evers on board. Maybe he has some kind of insight that we're missing."

I hung up the telephone.

"So, your killer has literary aspirations," Evers said, as I walked back to the couch.

"Yeah. He's writing a novel, one body at a time. All the victims are strippers, so far. Each one has been eviscerated, pubis to sternum."

"That's not easy to do," he said.

"Exactly what I told Farley."

"You're yanking my chain, you know that?"

"Of course. Farley does it to me all the time."

"You said you wouldn't do that."

"No I didn't. Said I wasn't interested in it. Never implied I wouldn't."

Evers stared off into space for a moment, his face wrinkled, as if he were recalling a particularly tart dill pickle.

"And he's writing on them?"

"Not much, but each one has had a single word written on her, usually over one breast or another."

"*This, that, oh,* and *too,*" he said.

"So far."

"And you don't see the pattern?"

I took a sip of the beer, and scratched my head.

"No. Nothing comes to me."

"The letters. There are only six letters in all the words. *T, H, I, S, A* and *O.*"

"Okay."

"So, maybe this ripper of yours is anagramming something."

"I don't know..." I said.

"You have a better idea? Look, Gallegher, this is how we would have done it at the Bureau. You have to look at all the possibilities. These serial killers run around with all kinds of loose neurons rattling around in their heads. It's hard to say what might motivate one or another until you look at all the angles. You can't hit what you can't see."

I took a pen out of my jacket pocket, and one of my Holliday's cards from my wallet, and wrote the letters down in sequence.

"*T, H, I, S, A* and *O,*" I said. "Not much to go on."

"Rearrange them."

I tried several combinations.

" '*A IS HOT* ' " I read.

"So maybe the guy's name starts with A, and that letter is like a nickname."

" '*I SO HAT* '?"

"Beats me."

" '*HIS TAO* ' "

"There's a possibility. Some of these mass murderers are into Eastern religions."

" '*HOIST A* ' "

"Hoist a what?"

"Damned if I know. Maybe he hasn't used all his letters yet."

I rearranged the letters again.

" '*SAITH O*' "

"I like that one. Again, you might have a guy whose name starts with the letter *O*. The *saith* part sounds like religiosity."

"Maybe it's not an anagram."

"You're probably right, but you have to look at all the potentials. Anything you overlook could be the key."

"Yeah, I remember. Crosby taught me that, too."

"You don't need me," he said. "You may not have spent twenty years with the Bureau, but you can handle this."

"No deal, huh?" I said. "I can't talk you into helping out on this one?"

"No thanks. I take my life without sleazebags, now."

I set the bottle on a coaster on the coffee table.

"I'm sorry I wasted your time, then."

"It wasn't a total waste. We checked out one potential lead."

I stood, preparing to leave.

"That's it?" he asked.

"Yeah, pretty much," I said, putting on my Saints hat.

"So, what were you going to get out of this?"

"We made a deal," I said as I walked toward the door. "If I brought you into the investigation, Farley was going to get hold of a box of Cuban cigars."

"Hold on," he said.

I stopped and turned to him.

"Real Cubans?" he asked.

"Yeah. Look, I've taken up enough of your time, Clever. Why don't you drop by the bar sometime?"

I handed him the card for Holliday's.

"Wait up. Honest to Pete Cubans? Not that bullshit Cuban seed stuff."

"That was the deal."

"Genuine Havanas."

"Well, that's what I asked for. But it doesn't make any difference now. I mean, you decided not to help out."

"I'll be damned," he said, as I turned the doorknob. "You sold me out for a box of cigars."

"*Cuban* cigars," I corrected.

"I'm worth at least a case."

I slipped on a pair of sunglasses, and looked back at him, standing in the semi-gloom of his foyer.

"You're probably right," I said. "See you around."

ELEVEN

Tuesday night, I was jamming with Sockeye and some kid who had breezed in on the bus with a couple of saxophones and a face full of peach fuzz. I think he dropped into the first bar he came across, hit on Shorty for work, caught him in a weak moment, and drew down a one-night stand wailing for tips.

The kid was, maybe, twenty-two or twenty-three. He wasn't bad, but he hadn't grown enough of a life to make the music real. He just kept playing textbook improvs and variations on themes, which was fine with me. He was easy to keep up with, and he gave my mind some wandering room.

I knew the Ripper would strike again within twenty-four hours. Somehow, the nagging realization kept clattering around inside my skull, begging for attention. I found myself going through the same emotional phases I had back in New Hampshire and Boston -- the anxiety of waiting for the other shoe to drop; the dread of knowing that someone out there, someone who didn't deserve it, was going to be savaged soon for no other reason than some spiritual ashtray needed another adrenalin fix; and the disgust that I could do nothing to stop it.

It was a macabre frame of mind. I figured it would be much like this if you were the only person on the planet who knew about an impending asteroid strike, and all you could do was watch the heavens and wait for the damned thing to drop.

Farley came in around one in the morning, carrying a satchel, but he didn't take a seat. I saw him out of the corner of my eye standing at the foot of the stairs to my apartment and, when he saw me looking, he jerked his thumb toward my apartment door.

The gesture had all the warmth of a court summons. I stowed my cornet on its stand, and dropped out of the set. After picking up a couple of Dixies at the bar, I led the gentleman caller up to my pad to see what he had in mind.

The building that houses Holliday's used to be some kind of mill warehouse, before it was subdivided into sections and let out for rent. The second floor, as was typical of such buildings, boasted carefully hewn heart pine floors which had developed their own warped personalities after seventy or eighty years of wear. After the building was split up, somebody came through and sanded and polished the floors a beautiful deep natural hue, so beautiful that I would have considered it a sin to carpet it. So, I threw out a couple of small area rugs for accent, and left the rest of the floors bare.

Fully one wall of my apartment is made up of a bookcase, housing maybe a thousand volumes ranging from intro psychology texts I never got around to tossing out, to the complete works of Charles Dickens bound in leather. The bookcase runs from floor to twelve-foot ceiling, where I attached a used rolling library ladder I cadged at an auction.

The rest of the apartment is furnished in early functional. I had bought a new couch about three years before, with money left to me by Claire Sturges, but the rest was pieced together from consignment shops and second-hand stores. I had a king-sized Murphy bed, a sagging recliner, a couple of tables, some lamps, and that about did it.

I don't own a television. Reception is lousy in the Quarter, and I didn't feel like forking over to support the cable barons. I do have a state-of-the-art stereo, the components of which are updated every year or so, and an old RCA monaural record player I use for my collection of '78's from the Jazz Age.

Farley glanced around and clicked his tongue a couple of times before plopping down on the couch.

"I can never get over it," he said.

"What's that?"

"How you live like some kind of fuckin' monk librarian."

I held up one of the Dixies.

"You want this, or are you on duty?"

"Hell, yes, I'm on duty, and you're damn right I want it."

He didn't seem in a mood to argue, so I handed him the bottle. He twisted the cap and tossed it onto the coffee table.

"So, dear," I said, "How was your day?"

"Don't get cute," he said, and took a swig from the bottle. "You know this new Chief we got in the department?"

I did. Three years before, Farley may have been the only honest gold shield in New Orleans. At the same time the city was becoming the most crime-ridden in the country, the force at that time was also listed as the most corrupt. Besides the usual graft, there were reports of detectives selling crack and horse spirited out of evidence storage, ponied-up shootings of alleged informants, and at least one contract killing arranged by a beat cop.

The city finally decided to do something about it, and brought in a new chief from up north. The guy had almost immediately fired over two hundred cops, and put another third of the force on notice. It was time to clean up Artful Dodge City.

Since then, the murder rate had plummeted, though there were still far too many stabbings of tourists in the darker corners of the Quarter. You could still set your watch by the shootings over in the agonized streets of the projects. Yet, it did seem perceptibly safer in this town.

"You can tell me how many teeth he still has by counting the marks on my ass. He is not happy about this Stripper Ripper affair."

"I can understand that," I said. "Doesn't look good in the out-of-state papers. Makes his crusader's armor look a little tarnished."

"Just what in hell did you say to Evers, anyway?"

The sudden turnaround in the conversation took me by surprise.

"Mostly what I told you. He didn't seem very interested in working the case, but he couldn't resist making a couple of inferences. I'm not so sure they're helpful..."

"He's in."

"Come again?"

"Evers called me several hours ago. Said he's given it some thought, and he thinks he might be willing to help out -- indirectly, of course."

"Indirectly?"

"He wants to be anonymous."

"That shouldn't be so hard. Most of these cases have the Fibbie profilers working in the background. It's always the local cops who make the announcements, take the credit..."

"You don't understand, Gallegher. As far as this investigation goes, Evers' only condition for working with us is that *he does not exist.*"

"So you keep him under wraps."

"It's not that easy. He wants a diversion. He wants someone to play the beard for him. That way, even if the press gets suspicious, we have someone to trot out as our go-to guy."

I set the beer down on the coffee table.

"I don't like the direction this conversation is headed," I said.

"See," Farley continued, ignoring me, "the problem here is, if we parade some expert in front of the press, those guys aren't gonna take our word for it. They're gonna check things out, look into backgrounds. They're gonna want to *know things.* So we can't just hire some bozo to look professorial and learned. We gotta have someone who can really deliver the goods, someone with a past that makes him plausible to the reporters."

"Don't do this," I pleaded.

"It's not like you would actually have to do anything. Evers would do all the work. All you have to do is stand in front of the cameras, if it comes to that, and take the credit."

"Forget it."

"You're the natural choice, you know. You got that fuckin' psychology doctorate, you have all that forensic experience, and the icing on the cake is that you were trained to glom onto these psychopaths by the very guy who killed himself while working the case."

"No way."

"It's great human interest, Gallegher."

"I said *no.* I'm not interested."

"I thought you'd say that," he said, reaching into the satchel he had been carrying. He pulled out a package wrapped in brown paper, and sealed with cellophane tape. He held it out to me.

"What's that?"

"Just take it. It won't bite."

I hefted the package. It didn't weigh much at all.

"My birthday was over a week ago," I said.

"Hey, Christmas is only six weeks away."

I peeled away the tape and the wrapping, and found myself holding a bundle of cigars.

"Your payment," Farley said. "You got Evers to come on board, and I'm holding up my end of the deal."

The cigars were sealed inside freezer bags, which were wrapped loosely in rubber bands. I counted five bags.

"No shit Cubans?" I asked.

He nodded.

"If I'm lyin', I'm flyin'. Those are genuine Cohiba Havanas, hand rolled by three-dollar-a-day cheap labor out of primo Cuban leaf picked from the mountaintop fields of Guantanamo by naked-breasted voodoo girls, and cured in the bright Caribbean sun. You are holding, by my figures, about two grand worth of God's own stogies. Fidel himself smokes those. You can't do any better than that."

I walked over to the bookcase, where I kept a teakwood desk humidor, and I started to place the cigars into it. Thinking better of it, I unsealed a baggie, and drew one out to sniff.

"Jesus," I whispered. "Where in hell'd you get these?"

"Chester Boulware, up in Baton Rouge. Cuba, you know, is only a few hundred miles from the mouth of Lake Pontchartrain at the Gulf. You'd be amazed how many of these things sneak their way up the Mississippi on freighters."

I held up another cigar.

"You want one?"

"Don't bother," Farley said, reaching into the pocket of his seersucker jacket. "I took the liberty of holding back a couple for myself."

I pulled a cigar tool from its place next to the humidor, and gingerly clipped the cigar before rolling it around my mouth to wet the end. After lighting up, I tossed the tool to Farley. Within minutes, we were blowing Cuban smoke rings at the ceiling.

"I'm disillusioned," I said.

"Something wrong with the smokes?"

"No, they're everything I ever hoped. I'm just a little surprised at you. This is a blatant federal offense. I always took you for a real stand-up guy."

"You weren't wrong," he said. "I'm honest as the day is long. Matter of fact, I got special dispensation, in the interest of public safety, to provide you with this payment in order to assure that we have the very best chance of nabbing this pervert killer."

"Dispensation," I said, warily.

"From Boulware himself, who got it from the Department of Justice. Now, if you-all would be so kind as to retrieve my cigars from the humidor and hand them back over, I have to be going."

I had been raising the cigar to my mouth, but it stopped inches from my face. I peered at Farley through a haze of blue-gray smoke.

"What in hell?"

"Well, you haven't delivered, yet. I told you I'd get you these felonious stogies if you arranged for Evers to get in line with this investigation. He won't do it unless you stand in for him. You say you won't play the beard for him, so I guess we have to start looking for another qualified shrinkologist. Maybe some fellow over at Tulane..."

"You devious fuck."

"That's Detective Devious Fuck, *Sir*, to you," he growled, his voice suddenly colder. Then, he seemed to warm up again. "Now you either want to enjoy the fruits of the Cuban hand-rollers' art for months and years to come, or you don't. I wish you'd make up your mind, though. I still have another stop to make this evening, and it's unfashionably late for calling."

He patted the satchel by his side.

"What else do you have in there?" I asked. "Thumbscrews?"

"Not at all. In this satchel, I have another bundle of cigars, which I promised to give to Clever Evers if you agreed to stand in for him during this investigation. He's waiting for me at his house now. I'm in kind of a hurry, so I can only give you a couple of minutes to decide."

And that's how I went to work for the cops.

TWELVE

Around nine the next morning, there came an insistent banging on the door to my apartment. I was sprawled across my murphy bed, having dropped off to sleep only an hour or two earlier after winding down following my shift on stage.

My stomach was roiling with acid as I turned over, waking slowly.

"Go away!" I yelled.

The knocking continued.

"Damn it," I muttered, and got up. I belched twice, trying to calm the demons dancing in my gullet, and trudged across the heart pine to the door.

"I'm fifty goddamn years old," I said as I opened it, "I need my sleep!"

Clever Evers was standing on the other side. He was wearing a plaid flannel shirt, a pair of khaki slacks, and some shoes made for walking the Appalachian Trail. In his hand was a folder.

"C'mon, Gallegher. Time to get to work," he said.

"Like hell," I said, and turned my back on him. "This is your show. I'm going back to bed."

Evers followed me into the room and looked around.

"Jesus. You live here?"

"Mostly I sleep here," I said. "Go away and let me do it, okay?"

"Can't do that. Nice bookcase."

"The gaping hole next to it is the door. Don't slam it on the way out."

"There's too much to do. It's a beautiful day out there, Gallegher."

"On second thought, take the window."

I fell back into bed.

Seconds later, I was sopping wet.

It took me a moment to realize that Evers had emptied the glass of water from my bedside table more or less into my right ear. I flew out of the bed, and took a clumsy swing at him.

"Damn it, you Fibbie asshole! I worked until four this morning and I didn't get to bed until six! If you're looking for a week in traction, you're on the right track."

"Go to the bathroom and dry off," Evers said. "And while you're at it, I'll tell you what I've figured out so far."

One of the most important steps in the recovery process from any addiction is recognizing the necessity of finding peace and happiness in the cards you've been dealt. This is referred to as *accepting the things we can't change*. Therein may be found the path to serenity. I figured Evers wasn't going anywhere unless I chucked him out the window, and even then it was a fairly decent bet that I wouldn't get any sleep because of the cops. I resigned myself to the situation. For some reason, I didn't feel a damn bit more serene.

"This is the way I see it," he started, as I toweled my hair. "What we have here is one of those moralist killers. This is the kind of guy who looks in a magazine and sees an ad for underwear, and he decides that the models are automatically whores because they let everyone see them in their scanties. The killer sees a polarized world -- black and white, good and bad, sweet and sour. You find where he lives, and it will be like walking into an operating room. I see practically bare walls, probably white. I see furniture of a single color, either black or dark brown. No magazines on a glass coffee table, or if there are magazines, they're all one title, and arranged *just so*. Not a speck of dust."

"The guy's a clean freak," I said, as I walked out of the bathroom and rummaged through my dresser for a shirt.

"He's compulsive. This is a crime of obsession and compulsion. The crime is just another extension of the killer's mental process. You look in his closet, and the shoes will all be arranged in neat rows, or even on some kind of rack, probably metal because wooden racks might carry germs. In his bathroom, every drawer is perfectly neat, and the mirror gleams. Everything in this miscreant's life gleams. Oh, and he shaves his body."

"Come again?"

"The coroner's reports indicate no evidence of any kind of hair on the victims' bodies that didn't originate there. The killer doesn't leave any hair because there isn't any to leave."

"His whole body?"

"Yeah. Everything's shaved: head, eyebrows, chest, back, underarms, pubes, maybe he even yanks out the hair on his ass."

I grimaced.

"Maybe he uses a depilatory. It would burn like hell, but the result would last longer."

"Or perhaps he doesn't have any hair for another reason," I suggested.

"Like what?"

"I don't know. Genetic alopecia, problems with his endocrine system, chemotherapy, radiation. Maybe the guy's a burn victim."

"That could work. If this guy has undergone medical treatment that caused total hair loss, he might be paranoid about germs and dirt. That would fit with the rest of the profile."

I pulled on a pair of jeans and sat on the couch to do the socks. Clever seemed almost hyperactive, pacing the floor and scratching his head.

"So you think," I said, "that this guy sees these girls he's killing as somehow -- what? -- *infesting* the population? Because they do the bare-assed hootchy-kootchy in the clubs, and some of them hook on the side, they're *bad*, and need to be eradicated?"

"It makes sense."

"So you have to wonder how he got that way."

"I've been working on that. We had a similar case in Kansas City a few years back. The perp in that case came from a deeply religious background, real holy roller stuff. He was very respected in the community, worked as a loan administrator in a local bank. Kiwanis type, real button down, double-breasted sort of guy. The only problem was, whenever he went out of town on business he had some difficulty keeping his dick in his pants. He said later he wasn't getting any at home from his similarly straight-laced wife, and when he did get it she would just lie there and stare at the ceiling.

"So, whenever he hit a new town, he'd grab the phone book and turn right to the escort services. He was a long way from home, after all, and who was he likely to run into? So, he'd squire around some dynamite-looking piece of fluff, take her to dinner, liquor her up, and then spend the night annoying the tourists in the next hotel room.

"Then, one day, he comes home from work, and his wife is sitting in the living room with his baggage packed and a letter from her attorney. It seems she was having some kind of nasty infection, you know, *down there*, and she went to see her doctor, who told her she had contracted herpes. Thank goodness for her, this was in the days before AIDS. Wife leaves the poor fuck, and over the months to come she makes good on a threat she had made on their wedding night, when she told him that if he ever cheated on her she would steal his dreams.

"Shortly after the divorce is final, hookers start turning up dead all over the metroplex. There was nothing elegant about the killer. He'd just locate a streetwalker, waltz her down an alley, and tell her to get on her knees while he reached for his belt. Before you could say Free Willie, he would shoot her in the top of the head and walk away. Always the same caliber weapon, always in the top of the head. It was like he wanted to get caught. He even used a registered weapon, stupid fuck. We caught him when the frequency got to about once a week, and he confessed right away. He said he had to kill the bad girls, so that they wouldn't tempt good men to go astray."

"What happened to him?"

"He's still in the can. His lawyer pleaded him out on second-degree, claimed dim cap, and he got seven consecutive twenty-year terms. With good behavior, I figure he may get out about six days after the Apocalypse."

I shook my head, smiling grimly.

"Diminished capacity," I said.

"More like mentally handicapped. You know how they say all roads lead to Rome? Well, that's the way it was with every scrap of evidence in his case. I'm hoping that's the way it will be with the guy we're looking for. Come on, now, we have to visit a few places before lunch."

Clever drove while I rested my head on the back of the front seat. I was hoping he had planned a long trip, but the ride only took a few minutes.

He pulled into a sand and shell parking lot next to the most rundown bar I had ever seen, near the intersection of Esplanade and Bourbon.

At one time, before the Great Fire, it might have been a stable or some kind of barn. The dive was only a single story, made of stucco with huge chunks broken out of the walls, exposing wire and lath underneath. The roof was clay shingles, most of them cracked or broken in at least one place. The front door was as wide as it was high. I could tell that, at whatever times the place closed to customers, the door simply slid into place on a makeshift runner built into the header, and was secured by two heavy-duty hasps on each side. It was a major firetrap waiting for some kind of spark, the kind of place where drinking was just a means to an end, the kind of joint where men gathered to toss back shots of rye and complain about all the assholes who were getting rich on their backs, while they themselves had to scratch and bust hump for a lousy forty dollars a day, and someday, by Gawd, they were going to get even.

From somewhere inside the bar, nerve-jangling zydeco poured out at roughly the volume of a Boeing 747. It was a wonder that the structure could handle the constant pounding of noise and remain standing.

Clever got out of the car, and led me around to the back of the bar, where some container company had placed a battered steel dumpster. Huge flakes of dull green paint were flecking off of it into the sand.

"He dumped one of them here?" I asked.

"Mmm," Clever said, nodding as he stared at the ground. "Lucy Nivens."

I shook my head, as much to loosen the cobwebs as in pity.

"Jesus, what a lousy place to bite it."

"Tell me what happened, Gallegher."

I looked up at him.

"Too early. My head doesn't start crank over until at least noon. You do the honors."

He straightened up, his hands at the small of his back, as if the effort of bending over to survey the darkened spot in the sand had left an immense ache, and he sniffed the air as he looked all around. He walked to the other side of the dumpster, and he kicked at the shells and the sand a little, raising a failure of a cloud which settled back to the lot as quickly as gravity allowed.

"He came from the south," Clever said at last. "By the time he grabbed Lucy from the bar, Bourbon Street had been closed for over an hour except to cross traffic. So let's say he parked along Decatur. He lured her out of the bar, or forced her somehow, and he took her to his car. He drove east on Decatur, and turned onto Esplanade, heading north. He pulled off Esplanade and drove behind the bar. He parked the car right here, with the headlights pointing at the back wall, and the trunk near the dumpster. He told Lucy to get out. The way the car was parked, it made a little shelter, with the car on one side, the dumpster on the other, and the wall making up the third side of the triangle.

"Lucy got out of the car, probably expecting that the guy would have her give him a hummer here in the closed-off area. He backed her up against the wall, though, and he opened a jacket or a coat, and he showed her the knife.

"It was sharp, but sturdy. Not a kitchen knife, like for slicing, but something beefy, like a hunting knife. A Bowie, maybe, or some kind of military piece. He showed it to her, because he wanted her to see it, to know what she was in for, and he wanted to see the look on her face.

"Maybe she started to run, or maybe she fought him. Maybe she knew what was coming, that there was no way for her to stop it, and she just stood there, pissing her britches and waiting for the pain.

"She didn't have to wait long. He stuck it in, quickly, about seven inches below the sternum, and slightly to the left, taking great care not to sever the abdominal aorta, because then she would have died instantly, and that wouldn't have done at all. He wanted to see her face, watch the realization come over it, savor the terror and the resignation and the ultimate submission.

"In her last moments, as the knife was eating away at her, she thought of her mother, of her first lover, of every lousy decision she had made since the moment she left home, of all the mistreatment and all the shitty jobs. She thought about stupid stuff, like maybe that the rent was due and there was no way she could actually be dying because if she didn't get the rent paid she'd get evicted. They say your whole life passes before your eyes in that moment, and in Lucy's case it was one long sorry list of missed opportunities, broken promises, and disappointment heaped on disappointment. Maybe she had always believed that there was a reason for it all, that maybe it's true that you can't have all this shit without a pony being around somewhere. Maybe she thought all along that there would be a reward for all her suffering. Now, with the killer's blade buried deep in her body, she realized that it was all shit, that there was no payoff, that she was just one more nobody who was born to die badly.

"That was what the killer wanted to see. He wanted that flash of realization, the ultimate loss of self-respect and dignity. He wanted to see in her eyes the moment she understood that there was no point.

"Then he ripped her. He twisted the blade, and he pulled it upward, slicing everything in its path, sawed right through the liver and the intestines and the stomach, and he could see in her eyes that it hurt like hell's own fire. Finally, he burst through the pericardium and bisected the heart the way you'd filet a bass, and she died right at that moment, staring through his eyes into his black soul and the last thing she ever knew was his hot acid breath on her face."

He stood there, staring at the place in the dirt behind the dumpster where Lucy died, and he shook his head.

I found myself shaking my own head along with him. I pulled off my Saints cap and ran my fingers through my thick, close-cropped, wiry hair. I could taste salt at the corners of my mouth.

"If I start walking now," I said. "I can be at Lucho's old restaurant for breakfast in about fifteen minutes."

He looked up at me. His sad eyes were suddenly full of question marks.

"I'm hungry," I said. "I worked until four this morning, and you yanked me out of bed after five hours sleep. I haven't had breakfast yet. I'm in no mood for this horseshit so early in the morning on an empty stomach."

"You don't understand..." he started.

"No," I interrupted. "*You* don't understand. This has nothing to do with me. If you want to put on some kind of show, go grab some rookie cop who gives a damn. I don't need to hear all this to know what happened. Write it down. Put it in a report, and spare me and yourself all the high school dramatics. Send it by courier. If the reporters want to know anything, I can fill in the blank spots. But I won't be your Watson on this thing. I don't have the time or the inclination."

I turned and started walking away, toward the heart of the Vieux Carre. I thought for a moment, a hopeful moment, that he was going to let me go. It was wishful thinking.

"Wait a minute," he said, and sprinted up to walk alongside me. "Don't you want to know what happened?"

"Pancakes," I said.

"What?"

"I want pancakes. A big stack. With melted butter running down the sides, none of that no-cholesterol margarine shit. And real maple syrup, the kind you can't get down here. I'm going to settle for whatever I can get."

"Jesus, you *are* nuts."

I stopped.

"Who said I was nuts?"

"Just about everyone. Not in so many words, but the meaning was there."

I grunted, and started walking again. Clever kept pace with me. It was difficult for him, being all torso with short legs. He was taking a step and a half for each of my strides.

"I don't have to hear what happened," I said. "You don't have to tell me what went on in their minds. You don't have to do the Ted Mack Amateur Hour routine. I know what happened. I can tell you exactly what her eyes looked like, right up to the moment they glossed over and fixed on infinity. I know what she thought. I've been there too many times. Go sell it to the tourists."

I picked up the speed, hoping he would give up and let me go. Instead, he stopped and stood on the sidewalk watching me. Finally, he spoke.

"Will you, for the love of Christ, please *stop*?" he demanded. "Just wait a minute!"

I did stop, and I turned back to him. I tried to look menacing, but I think I just came off as irritated.

"We'll take the car," he said.

THIRTEEN

"Pass the syrup," Clever said.

We were sitting in Lucho Braga's old restaurant. For the first time in more than a year, I had actually entered the place, taken a seat, and ordered breakfast without being harassed, stiff-armed, patted down, or simply given the evil eye by some gun monkey. I guessed that Tommy Callahan had told me the truth when he said they were moving the center of mob operations to another location. It felt weird. I kind of missed being bullyragged. I made a mental note to take that up at my next GA meeting.

"I came back because I was born here," Clever said.

"Apropos of what, in particular?" I said.

"When you came by my house the other day, you asked me how I wound up here in New Orleans. I was born here."

"And you came back?"

"Strange as it seems. I grew up just on the other side of Rampart, in the projects."

I took a bite of pancakes, and chewed for a moment.

"You don't strike me as a projects sort of guy," I observed, after swallowing.

"The projects weren't the same back then. It was the fifties, Gallegher. It was a different world. There wasn't any civil rights movement. We were *Negroes*, and we knew our place, if you listen to the white folks. Worst thing went on most Saturday nights over in the Desire was some dockworker would get all liquored up and beat his wife or get cut in a knife fight. My father didn't even drink. He also didn't work, but that was another story. Got his left leg blown off in the Second War, and we lived on disability. While he was recuperating in an Army hospital in England, some nurse gave him a copy of <u>*Great Expectations*</u>, and he read it cover to cover in a couple of days, so she brought him more books. Pap read like it was free for the taking, and he taught me and my brother and sister to read as soon as we could hold a book with both hands. He insisted that we get a good education, because it wasn't our fault we were poor, and he didn't want his own misfortune to make us feel like we *belonged* in the Desire. I bulled through Spellman on a full scholarship, and then took my doctorate for free at Vandy. I have a lot to thank Dr. King for, I suppose. By the time I got to grad school, colleges were pissing on themselves to recruit qualified blacks to give degrees to, just so they wouldn't look like they were standing in the way of progress. My brother's an MD, never paid a cent of tuition. Cammy, my sister, teaches Romance Languages at UT-Arlington. I got a lot of good memories of New Orleans, Gallegher. It just seemed natural to come back."

"You said it, though. It's not the same city."

"It's always the same," he said. "You always see it the way you remember it. If I walk down in the Desire today, it will be the same as when I lived there."

"If you don't get shanked by some Vietnamese kid who wants those fancy hiking boots, maybe. Look, I didn't mean to be nasty out there, but I really don't want to be part of this investigation. I had enough of that back in New England. If Farley wants me to front for you, that's one thing. But it's as active a role as I have any desire to play, understand?"

He gnawed on a thick slice of bacon, and nodded his head a couple of times.

"I feel very disappointed," he said. "I had hoped you wouldn't lie to me."

"About what?"

"Detective Nuckolls told me a lot about you, Gallegher. I already knew about Ed Hix, how you killed him point blank when he came at you with a knife after killing your detective friend up north. I had no idea, though, that you had been so... *busy* down here."

"Busy how?"

"You've killed three men that are documented..."

"All self defense..."

"And Detective Nuckolls suspects you've killed at least three others."

"He's entitled to his opinions."

"And you've been on the scene when at least five other people have died, including a local gangster earlier this year, and a Haitian punk out in a voodoo house in the Atchafalaya basin?"

"Just bad luck and ill timing, all of it."

"And on just how many of Nuckolls' cases have you provided critical evidence?"

"I don't keep count. Are you headed somewhere with this?"

"I don't know. It just seems to me that you never quit working with the police. You just went freelance."

I set down my silverware, lest I lose my temper and add to my body count.

"I'm going to say this once," I said, slowly. "Farley thinks he can read my soul in the dark, but he's wrong. Some of the things you've said are true. Some are nothing but speculation. It's like this, though. Life takes its twists and turns, and sometimes you drive it, and sometimes you're just along for the ride. I'm a gambling addict, Clever. I got in terribly deep with some loansharks when I hit town. I had a blackjack jones and an incredibly long string of bad decisions with thirteen on the table. One of the loansharks, guy named Leduc, made me an offer -- he would cover my debt if I would work for him shaking down other gamblers for overdue payments. I did this for almost four years. It was never full time, and I hated myself every time I came home.

"Once in a while, someone would come into the bar, and say they heard about me on the street, and they'd ask if I could maybe help them out with a little problem. If they came from someone I knew, maybe I'd help them. Sometimes, their problems involved dangerous people with malicious intent. Sometimes, in the course of helping out, I pissed off those dangerous people. Sometimes they tried to do something about that. At that point, Clever, you are just strapped in for the whole ride, and that's all there is to it. If some fellow comes at you with a gun and a plan, it just makes sense to have your own plan. If that means he takes it up the chute, well, maybe he should have had a better plan. I discovered over the years that, for better or worse, I don't kill easily. Some people regretted trying.

"I never asked for it, though. It's not like I blew into town, hung out a shingle, and started selling my services. Most of it is something that just happened, like ear wax."

"So," he said. "All this badness just blew around you."

"Sometimes it has seemed that way."

"And you're just this lucky son of a bitch."

"Everyone seems to think so. Let's drop it, okay? I haven't killed anyone in a long time, and I don't plan to anytime soon. As for investigating murders, I like to leave that to the pros. What I'm saying is this -- I'm glad you're working this case with Farley Nuckolls, but I really don't want to be part of it. You keep me posted. I'll understand what's happening. When the time comes, I'll stand on the steps of City Hall and play my part and smile for the cameras. I just don't want to be part of the process."

I stood and dropped a ten on the table.

"I'm full. It's been fun, Clever, but I'm really tired, and I'd like to go back home and sleep for a while. I'm having dinner with my sweetie later tonight. Maybe I'll get lucky, and I'd like to be awake for that."

"Hold on," he said, and fished in his shirt pocket, bringing out a card. "Take this. It's my phone number. If something helpful comes to mind, give me a call. Just because you aren't active in this investigation doesn't mean your brain is going to shut down. Anything at all, understand?"

I took the card and slipped it into my wallet.

It was not a day destined for sleep.

I got back to Holliday's, and undressed. My clothes felt tight and musty from the long walk across the Quarter, and my skin tingled when the rushing air from the ceiling fan washed across it and dried the film of sweat that covered me from head to toe. I tossed back the covers and dropped onto the sheets, aiming for at least five hours of dreams.

That was when the telephone rang.

I thought about ignoring it, but then I considered that it might be Merlie, so I picked up the receiver.

"We got another one," Farley said.

"Call Clever," I said. "He's your expert. Let me know what he says..."

"It's different this time, Gallegher. This asshole from the Times-Picayune, what's-his-name, he's on top of it already. He's already sniffing around the squad, looking for some shit to recycle into newsprint. Someone told him we have a profiler on the case, and he wants to meet you."

"I just got back to bed, Farley. Can't he wait?"

"Now, how in hell's that gonna look? We got this fresh body, and our expert profiler is catching forty over a bar on Toulouse? Come on, now, Gallegher, it's time to earn those Cohibas."

Outside the window, the breeze had built to blustering gusts, and the light on Toulouse Street had taken on a brassy, transcendental quality, and there was the smell of ozone in the air. Far off, I could hear the first tremulous rumbles of Wagnerian thunder, a portent of what was to come of my life until someone collared the ripper and I could return to my own dilapidated course. It was no use fighting the current, and I imagined as the wind built and whistled down the lanes and alleys of the Quarter that I could detect the faint roar of the whirlpool.

It was a shitty way to start the day.

"Give me an hour," I said.

"Yeah, whatever. And do me a favor, Gallegher. Try to wear something that doesn't make you look like you've been punching the monkey for the last ten years, okay?"

I was halfway dressed when the telephone rang again. Hoping it was a reprieve from Farley, I grabbed the receiver. It was Merlie. She sounded midway between worried and alarmed.

"I just had a telephone call from Louise," she said, referring to Louise Onizuki, the girl I'd saved from Jimmy Binh six months earlier.

"What's the matter?" I asked.

"She was scared. She said she was coming home from school the other day and saw a car parked at the far end of her block with a man sitting in it, watching her."

"An Asian man?" I guessed.

"She couldn't see that day, but she did later on, when she was waiting for the bus the next morning. She said he looked Vietnamese, and she thought she recognized him. What do you think?"

"It could be one of a number of things. Binh's filed the automatic appeal to his death sentence, but Louise shouldn't have to testify on that one. Maybe he just wants to even the score a little. He may have arranged for one of the few loyal men he has left to keep an eye on her."

"Oh, Pat. I don't like this at all. Should we call the police?"

"I don't know. It's also possible that Phang Loc has thrown up a screen around her, just in case one of Binh's flunkies might try to take her out. The guy she's seen may be protecting her. If that's the case, I don't want to foul up the works by tossing the cops into the mix." I paused, trying to figure all the angles. "You say she sounded really scared?"

"Yes."

I thought for a moment.

"Phang Loc owes me a favor," I said. "If I hadn't stomped around in Binh's kimchee last year, Binh might have had an opportunity to zag him and take over the Vietnamese gang. Maybe I can pay him a visit, maybe find out if he's posted one of his soldiers to look after Louise. If not, maybe I can convince him to look into the matter for me."

"When can you see him?"

It hit me right then that I hadn't told Merlie about my arrangement with Farley Nuckolls.

I had a lot of explaining to do.

When I was finished, the line went silent for several seconds, and then I thought I heard a whooshing sound on the other end, like wind coursing through a culvert drain. Then Merlie spoke, and I heard the sad tinge in her voice.

"I swear, Patrick, you make loving you a hard thing."

She used my Christian name. She meant business.

"You don't like what I'm doing?"

"You do what you do, is all. You don't ask ahead of time if it's okay. You don't *include* me in your decisions. Sometimes I wonder if you include me in your life, or if I'm just something you hang on the edge of it like a Christmas tree ball. Does it matter if I *like* it?"

Outside, the rain that had ridden in on the back of rumbling black clouds danced off the terracotta roof of the voodoo shop across the street, producing a constant low roar. There were no words for what I wanted to say. The telephone was a poor substitute for staring into her lavender eyes and hoping that our souls would do the talking for us. I kept the receiver to my ear and with my free hand rubbed the day's growth on my cheek and chin, waiting for inspiration.

"Don't answer that," she said, finally and flatly. "I just asked you to consort with gangsters, and then I jumped all over you for working with the police. You have proven to be a bad influence on me. My thinking's all haywire. Could I ask you a favor, though?"

I didn't say anything. She wasn't really asking permission. She already knew what I would do for her.

Damn near anything.

"Please keep me in the loop? Just talk to me once in a while and let me know what side of the street you're playing this week? That way, at least, I'll know what color to wear."

"How about this?" I said. "I have to run down to the Rampart Station to meet with Farley and some reporter from the Times-Picayune. There's been another murder, and Farley wants to parade his profiler so it will look like the NOPD is on top of things. After I get finished, I'll go find Phang Loc and see if he'll talk to me, and I'll try to find out who's watching Louise. If nothing else, we'll have a lot to talk about over dinner tonight."

"I suppose we will. Do you still love me?"

"Yes, I do," I said.

"Do I still love you?" she asked, more quietly.

"Oh, yes," I said. "You do indeed."

FOURTEEN

The rain was still driving down in torrents when I hopped out of the taxi and dashed up the steps of the Rampart Station. Drops the size of doubloons bounced off my Saints umbrella, and I flapped it a couple of times to shake off the soak before stepping through the double doors in front of the station, right into the brightest light I had seen in years.

Someone grabbed my arm and pulled me off to one side.

"Are you Dr. Gallegher?" he asked.

I squinted and blinked a couple of times, trying to place a face on that voice, through all the yellow and bluish spots dancing in front of my eyes. Eventually, I made out a thatch of frizzy red hair, a gaunt sallow face, and about a zillion freckles. Or maybe those were just more spots.

"Brian Templeton," he said, grasping my hand. "Times-Picayune. I'm working the Stripper Ripper case."

"You gave it that godawful name?" I said.

"Yeah, but it's selling papers like nobody's business. Can we talk a minute?"

Before I could answer, we were surrounded by more lights. It seemed that every television station in the lower half of the state had sent a camera and a talking head to cover the latest butchery.

"No," I muttered. "I need to talk with Detective Nuckolls first."

His grasp on my arm seemed to tighten.

That was the wrong thing for it to do.

"I'd really like to ask a few questions," he said, leaning in so close I could tell he had andouille with his eggs that morning.

As my eyes cleared, I could finally see that he was just a youngster, no more than twenty-five. He was probably on his first job out of school. He needed to learn respect for his elders. I reached down and surreptitiously grabbed the thumb of his hand latched onto my arm. In a second, I had it bent back as far as it was going to go, at least willingly. Templeton's eyes grew big, and his mouth made this funny zero shape.

"Listen sonny," I whispered. "You don't let go of my arm, I'm gonna walk into Farley's office and lay your thumb on his desk blotter. You may get your interview later, but it's going to be awful damned hard to type the spaces, know what I mean?"

As if my body had been charged with electricity, he jumped back, loosening his hold on me. By that time, several other muckrakers had figured out who I was, and all the cameras were turned in my direction. I figured it was a lot like dying, walking into that light. As I progressed, however, they parted, and before I knew it they were shooting my back as I walked down the hall toward Farley's cubicle.

"You said one reporter," I growled as I walked in and sat down in the heavy wooden chair across from his desk.

"What can I say?" he said, shrugging his shoulders. "This is a hot story."

Outside the cubicle, which was surrounded by glass and Venetian blinds, the lights seemed to congregate and turn our way. I don't know what they thought they were filming. I felt like one third of the Yalta Conference.

I sat in the chair across from him and silently repeated my Serenity Prayer.

"You're enjoying this, aren't you," I said.

"Oh, hell yes," he said. "This is just like a party. Nothing I like more than to be dragged out of bed at five in the morning so I can hang out in some back alley watching flies feast on the entrails of some ripped twist. This is better than Mardi Gras."

I waved him off.

"Okay, okay, I get it. What's happened?"

He pulled a file from his desk drawer. I almost felt the air pressure increase as the crowd of reporters outside the cubicle pressed against the office glass.

"Girl's name was Sherry Francine Gordon, but she went by the professional name of Molly Mounds. Beat cop ran across her behind a motel over near the Superdome."

"That's a long way from the Quarter."

"About six minutes by car, if the traffic's good."

"Where'd she work?"

"*Bottoms Up*. It's the same story as before. A couple of other girls remember her giving a lap dance to some big white guy, in a dark corner over to the side of the main stage. The next thing they knew, she was gone."

"Their descriptions match the ones from Lucy Nivens' killing?"

He shrugged again.

"Big. White. Guy. That's all there is. Sounds the same, but how many of them are there in this city? Hell, for all I know, I ought to be scoping out the entire front line of the Saints."

"I don't think they're vicious enough," I said, grinning. "So what was the word this time? What did he write on Molly Mounds?"

"This is a strange one. It's a repeat. *Too*."

"He wrote *too* again?"

Farley nodded.

"Damned strange," I said, scratching at a badly shaved spot just under my chin. "Think maybe he just lost his place?"

"Doesn't seem likely, does it?"

"No, I guess not. *This*, *that*, *oh*, *too*, and now *too* again."

"So, what does Evers think about this?"

I pulled off my wet jacket and rolled up my sleeves.

"He's got this image of the killer as being some kind of obsessive-compulsive neat freak. Says he thinks the guy is operating under this idea that he's somehow cleansing an infestation in the city. Clever drove me out to where Lucy bought it this morning, and did this song and dance about the killer's motivation. According to him, the fellow likes to watch the lights go out behind their eyes when he rips them, so he would have to be facing them and very close at the moment of death."

"Not real tidy."

"No. If the guy is all that compulsive, he sure wouldn't want to get himself all messed up with blood and gore and stuff. I asked Clever about that on the way to breakfast. He suspects that the killer has a murder kit he carries around, with a fresh set of clothes, maybe lines the back seat of his car with plastic bags or something, and that he ditches the soiled clothes right after the murder."

"Does it play?"

"It's been done before. A lot of these serial killers have a set of tools at hand all the time, just in case they get the urge for an impulse whack. Hell, if he changed clothes right away, bagged the bloody duds, and then dropped them in a dumpster two or three miles away, he probably wouldn't leave any evidence around at all. What with all the dumpsters in this city, it would take a hundred years to find anything."

"Maybe not," Farley said, his eyes closed. He leaned his chair way back, to the limits of gravitation and balance. I could never figure out how he did that. "If we could get a body fast enough, and alert the beat cops immediately, they could probably scout out the surrounding radius of four or five miles, each cop searching just his own beat. We might be able to find the bloody clothes before they're carted off."

"Worth a try."

"Five girls, five clubs," he mused.

"What's that?"

"Each of the five girls has come from a different pussy bar. What's that about?"

"It makes sense, if the killer is trying not to get caught. Let's say it is this big white guy. A fellow like that draws attention when he walks into the room. If he were to hit the same bar twice, he might set off a memory in one of the girls who saw him the first time."

"It's a good way to get nabbed."

"Which, of course, defeats the idea of being a career serial killer."

We both sat there for several seconds, me reflecting on what I was going to say to the dogs of the fourth estate, and Farley just balancing his chair with his eyes closed. Finally, he spoke again.

"Guy's gonna run out of clubs sooner or later," he said.

"In this town, he might run out of women first."

"Very unkind, Mr. Gallegher."

"That's *Dr.* Gallegher, Farley."

"So it is," he said, righting his chair. "Which reminds me of why I invited you down here in the first place. Shall we meet the press, Doctor?"

I walked down the front steps of the Rampart Station an hour later, trying very hard to wipe the scowl off my face. The remnants of the news crews were packing up the last of their equipment and getting ready to haul ass to some other breaking story of the day. Overhead, the clouds had begun to break up, and there were patches of translucent electric blue peeking through the heavy dishwater sky. The air was damp and close, but the Quarter smelled like a new dollar bill, all the ferment and garbage washed away into the ancient storm sewers criss-crossing the firmament beneath the cobbled streets.

It had been as bad as I expected. Maybe even a little worse. It had been a long time since I had faced reporters, and they seemed to have gotten even more ravenous and predatory than I recalled. This was an old trip to a familiar town for me, though, and I knew enough to say nothing in as many words as possible.

I was about a block away, my fists clenched deep inside my jacket pockets, as I walked along staring at the sidewalk, when Clever Evers fell into step beside me.

"Damn fine job back there," he said. "You really shined them on but good."

"Fuck off," I said, and stepped faster.

"Why're you mad at me?"

I stopped, glared at him for a moment, and then decided that I was on treacherous ground. Digging a hole in the pavement with Clever was clearly not on the program for New Orleans' newest media darling. I stuffed my hands back into my pockets and started walking again.

"I have something I have to do," I said. "You can't come along."

Maybe he was deaf. Maybe he didn't give a rip what I wanted. He just kept pace with me and talked.

"I particularly liked the way you handled that television geek," he said. "You know, the one that kept asking about your qualifications..."

I stopped again. I was rapidly becoming sick of him.

"I was there, Clever. I remember everything. This is just beginning, you know. I bet there will be twenty phone messages for me when I get home. These newsie assholes are going to dog me day in and day out. What happens when one of the smarter ones finds out what I've been doing for the last decade?"

"What happens? Shit fire, man, it's gonna be the biggest story this town has seen in ages. This is pure human interest. We're talking about redemption, here. Former hotshot forensic psychologist falls on hard times and is brought back to life by a series of murders committed by some crankshaft spinning his bearings. He's reaching down the toilet and pulling you back up from the sewer. Lemme tell you, my friend, that's the stuff that *People* magazine articles are made of..."

"Precisely my point, Clever. Nobody's pulling me up from any sewer. Believe it or not, I actually like my job. In the peace and contentment department, it is by far the best gig I've run across in fifty years. I do not want to be redeemed. Look, I mean it, I really have to go."

"I can keep up."

"You don't understand. Where I'm going, I can't take you."

He stared at me for a second, and then some idea took root and his eyes cleared up.

"Oh, I see. Why didn't you say so? Look, you wanna get your wick dipped, you go right ahead..."

"It's not like that," I said. "There's this thing I have to do for Merlie."

"If it's not all *that* personal, I'd really like to tag along. I have some ideas for your next press conference I'd like to run by you. Hey, did Farley tell you about the word written on the Mounds girl? Freaky, huh...."

It was useless trying to shake Evers. I had become his alter ego, and he was about as likely to let me go as he was to divest himself of his shadow.

Screw him, I thought. *He wants to ride along, I'll let him.*

Phang Loc was a Vietnamese refugee who had fled from Saigon about fifteen seconds ahead of the Viet Cong. He might have made it out earlier, but he was dragged down by all the bags of money he brought out with him.

Twenty years later, he was the head of all the Vietnamese gangs in New Orleans. Like the Italians, the Vietnamese were a tough, razor-sharp lot, but unlike the made guys they didn't give two hoots for honor or *omerta*.

Phang Loc, on the other hand, owed me something of a favor. A half-year earlier, one of his most ambitious lieutenants, a subhuman spit cup named Jimmy Binh, had tried to stage a coup and take over the entire Vietnamese operation. Binh was a degenerate child abuser, and what he did to his stepdaughter, Louise Onizuki, would haunt her for the rest of her life. That's where I came into the picture, as her protector and guardian angel. I had stopped Binh in his tracks, and managed to hang a murder conviction on him in the process. Phang Loc had made it clear that he was grateful, and had urged me to contact him if I was ever in need.

This seemed like a good time.

Phang, like most gangsters, had to have a legitimate front for his business activities. His was a second mortgage loan office operating about a block from the courthouse.

I walked into the office with Clever closely in tow, and the secretary, a drop-dead gorgeous Eurasian with almond eyes and yardstick straight ebon hair, gave me the head-to-toe look as I stood at her desk.

I asked for Phang Loc. The girl behind the desk shook her head.

"Mr. Phang not seeing people today," she said.

"Tell him it's Gallegher."

"Mr. Phang not seeing people today," she insisted, her headshake becoming more pronounced. "You come back tomorrow."

I heard Clever suppress a snicker behind me. He was enjoying watching me get hung out to dry. That irritated me. I turned to him.

"Let's try to act a little more dignified, or Madame Butterfly here is likely to cut you in half with the sawed-off shotgun she's holding under the desk, okay?"

Clever's smile disappeared, and his eyes grew large.

I looked back at the girl. Her eyes were pretty big, too. Her hand stayed under the desk.

I hoped she wasn't the impulsive type.

"Let's try this again, Madame," I said. "You get on the phone and tell Mr. Phang that Mr. Gallegher is here to see him, and tell him that I was sent by Lucho Braga."

"Mr. Phang not seeing..." she started, before she processed everything I had to say. By the time she got to the part where I invoked the name of the late boss of all the Sicilian mob in New Orleans, she figured out that she was running with the big dogs. Six months dead, and his name still opened doors. That's real juice.

She picked up the telephone and said some words I didn't understand, and then I heard my name and Braga's, and then some more gibberish. Then she nodded and hung up the phone.

"You wait," she said, pointing toward some leather-upholstered office chairs lining the far wall. "Mr. Phang be out in a moment..."

She stopped for a second, and then added, "... *sir*."

I put on my best smile, the one I use to bring out the sun on a cloudy day, and nodded.

"Thank you."

We weren't sitting for two minutes before the inner office door opened and Phang Loc stepped out. He was about a foot shorter than my rough two meters, and wide in the muscular way that Asian gymnasts get when they quit working out and start going to a lard-based metabolism. His hair, obviously colored, was stylishly cut and combed to within an inch of its life. I could have eaten for a year on what his suit cost. He crossed the waiting room floor in about three steps, his hand already extended in greeting.

"Mr. Gallegher, so good to see you again. How long has it been?"

"Six months, sir," I said, taking his hand. "This is Mr. Evers. He's insisted on staying with me for the time being. I hope you will accept my word that he won't repeat any of our conversation."

Phang Loc took Clever's hand, but he kept his eyes on mine.

"I have come to depend on your word, Mr. Gallegher."

"Even so, sir, I'll make every effort not to use names."

"That would be... appreciated."

He led us into his office. It was spartan by most American corporate standards, with just a standard-sized wooden desk, several office chairs, and a cloth-covered sofa against one wall. Phang gestured for us to sit in a couple of office chairs facing the sofa. He sat on the sofa.

"I'll be brief, sir," I said. "I would like to remind you of a man, a child molester who was, until recently, associated with you."

"I remember this man."

"He had a stepdaughter."

"Yes," Phang said, nodding. "Very sad. I believe she lives in Bayou Teche now."

"That's correct. The child called her court-appointed guardian today. She was afraid. She said she's seen a man watching her at school and near her home. A Vietnamese man."

Phang Loc didn't say anything. He just nodded.

"I was wondering," I continued, "whether this man is protecting her, or whether he means her harm. I will not ask you whether he is working for you. I just felt that you should know that he's there, and that he's been seen. If he does work for you, you would want to know. If he doesn't work for you, then it could be assumed that he's working for your former associate. In that case, the child could be in danger."

Phang didn't say anything for a minute. He stared at the ceiling for a moment, then at his nails. The room was silent, except for the gentle whoosh of air sailing through the clogged air filter in the wall next to his sofa.

Finally, he nodded, and stood, extending his hand.

"Thank you for bringing this to my attention, Mr. Gallegher," he said. "Please feel free to tell the child, and her guardian, that she will not see this man again. You have done me a favor."

"No more than you've done for me, sir," I said, clasping his hand. "I appreciate you seeing us on such short notice. I hope I won't need to disturb you again."

"Do not concern yourself. I am in your debt."

He ushered Clever and me to the lobby, where the receptionist still looked a little shell-shocked. I thanked him again, and then we were out on the street.

We had walked almost a half-block before Clever said anything.

"Jesus," he wheezed.

"Excuse me?"

"You know what you just did back there?"

"I have an idea."

"That guy stinks to high hell of mob."

"Uh-huh," I said.

"You're pretty cool, considering that you may have just had some guy squibbed."

"I try not to think of it that way."

"Damn, you are such a block of ice. What in hell happened to you?"

I didn't bother answering. It was too long a story.

"I'm going home now," I said. "Between you, Merlie, and the dogs of the fourth estate, I haven't slept in almost twenty-eight hours. Please do me a favor and see to it that no strippers are killed for a day or two, okay?"

FIFTEEN

I was too tired to dream much. Lulled by the drone of the fan next to my window, I fell asleep in five minutes, and the rest of the day was lost.

I was vaguely aware, in that five percent of my consciousness that remained active while I was asleep, of the door to my apartment opening. Shortly after, there was a rustle of my sheets, and I could feel cool bare skin against by back and legs. I wasn't alarmed. I had caught the fragrance of Merlie's perfume, the one she always wore, the second the door opened. In more vigorous times, I might have roused myself to greet her. On the other hand, I was still wiped out, and she knew her way around the place.

She nuzzled my neck. I could feel her breath wind around my scalp like island zephyrs. It was almost too much for one human to bear.

"Do you know why I'm here?" she whispered.

I cleared my throat.

"I can only hope it's because your soul felt my soul crying out for it, and you were drawn to me by some feral, ancient yearning."

"Nice try. You didn't show up for dinner."

I raised my head and glanced at my clock. The digital readout glowed in the inky light of my room.

Nine o'clock.

"Oh, shit, I'm sorry," I said, turning to her. "I didn't get to bed until almost two."

She stopped me with a kiss.

"I know. I saw you on the tube. You clean up nicely."

"I can be dressed in fifteen minutes," I volunteered. "As nights go, this one is still pretty young."

I started to roll out of bed, but she stopped me again, this time by grabbing the nearest available appendage.

"Why bother?" she said. "I'm already undressed..."

Some time later, I heard her murmur softly. She kissed my chest, and then raised her head to nuzzle my neck.

"You have to go to work," she said.

"It's not like I have a long commute."

"Would you like me to go down the street and get a takeout?"

"Sure," I said. "But let me pay. I owe you for not showing up tonight."

"O-kay," she said, wistfully, like a contented sigh. "Here I go. I'm getting up."

But she didn't. She just lay there, breathing deeply and stroking my chest. I liked it.

"I, uh, visited Phang Loc today," I said.

"Umm hmmm" she murmured.

"He assured me that Louise wouldn't be seeing that man anymore."

She shuddered slightly, as if she had a chill.

"I'm not going to ask what that means," she said.

"Neither did I. I just told him the situation. He told me he'd take care of it. I don't want to know the details."

She rolled off me and sat up against the bars at the head of my Murphy bed. She pulled the sheets up to cover herself.

"It's kind of creepy, you know," Merlie said, "It's very strange to know someone who has this kind of power."

"I call it *juice*," I said. "And, besides, for all I know I was just informing him that one of his employees was being sloppy. It's like being a Secret Shopper for the mob."

"Or maybe you set up this guy watching Louise to be killed."

"That was Clever's interpretation, too."

"This isn't troubling to you?"

"Not as much as the thought that some goon might be trailing Louise."

She chewed on her thumbnail a little, staring down at me. It was kind of cute.

"You have some interesting values," she said.

"Probably nothing more than a keenly crafted set of rationalizations. You think I should hustle down to the parish church, maybe confess to Dag?"

"Do you feel guilty?"

"All the time. I am Catholic, you know. And I kind of left Jesus standing at the altar when I dropped out of seminary. I figure I have a lot to atone for, but that doesn't include what I did today."

She didn't say anything about that, so I figured it was time to change the subject.

"I really looked good on TV?"

"Well, you know, the camera puts on ten pounds..."

"Oh, great. So, instead of looking like a whale in a suit, I looked like a whale in a suit, with a glandular condition."

"I wouldn't say that. You looked big. Impressive. You looked like you knew what you were doing."

"Proving, once again, that Lincoln was right."

"Mmm?"

"You can fool all the people some of the time."

I decided it was my turn to take the initiative, so I tossed off the covers and walked into the bathroom to start the shower.

I had just lathered up when the door opened, and Merlie stepped in. She squeezed between me and the tiles, and stepped under the water. She ran her hands through her auburn hair, which turned a coffee shade as the water soaked it. I took the opportunity to wash her back.

"Are you close to catching him?" she asked, her eyes shut tightly against the spray.

"The Ripper?"

"Umm hmmm," she sort of said, mixing the affirmative with her apparent approval of my scrubbing.

"Not even in the same zip code. You know what we have so far?"

"What?"

"*Big white guy*. That's it."

"Should I be nervous?"

"I have an alibi, remember?"

"That's all there is? Big white guy?"

"That and a lot of theoretical mumbo jumbo. Clever thinks he might be bald as a cue ball from head to toe. He's probably obsessed with order and cleanliness, and he thinks he's sanitizing the city by eviscerating these dancers."

"Your turn," she said, gesturing for me to turn around. I complied, as she began to rub the soap between my shoulder blades.

"Doesn't sound like you have much to go on," she said.

"You never do, at this stage. Things will start to fall together, though. Little pieces will emerge, constants in each murder will be recognized, and sooner or later the guy will get sloppy and tip his hand. It's really not my problem. I'm just the acting mouthpiece for the department."

I turned and put my arms around her chest, pulling her toward me. Her naked, wet, substantial breasts formed to my ribcage. It felt like heaven. I kissed her under the showerhead. For a moment we were both in danger of drowning.

She pulled away at last, acutely aware of my growing excitement.

"Oh, no, not again," she said, teasing me. "I may put out once, but for sloppy seconds you have to buy me dinner."

I reached over and turned off the water.

"Let's eat," I said.

Brian Templeton showed up at the club around midnight. I had just finished my first set, and I was sitting with Merlie at the bar, chowing down on some jambalaya from the Gumbo Shop down the street. My obligatory bottle of Dixie was almost down to the foam, and I asked Shorty for another as I saw the reporter come in the door.

"Aw, hell," I said.

"What is it?" Merlie asked.

"This kid from the Times-Picayune just strolled in. I think I'm busted."

His eyes adjusted to the dark, and Templeton finally saw me. His expression seemed to change to something like victorious, and he quickly crossed the bar to where I was sitting.

"I didn't believe it when I heard it," he said, ignoring Merlie and focusing on my eyes. "This guy tells me that the cops' chief profiler is actually a horn player in some dive bar over near Decatur, and I said, '*No shit, really?*', and he dared me to come over and find you."

"Your lucky night," I said. "Merlie Comineau, this is Brian Templeton. You may have seen him hanging with Lois Lane and summoning Superman with his signal watch."

It took Templeton a moment to register the reference. I wondered for a second whether Jimmy Olsen still used a signal watch in the comic books, but that's just the way my mind works.

"Comineau?" he said, as if accessing some kind of file. "Wait, I know you. We met at the Charities Ball during last year's Mardi Gras. You run some kind of halfway house, don't you?"

"It's a runaway shelter," she said, graciously.

I made a mental note, while they talked, that Templeton might look like a smart-aleck kid, but he apparently had a good head for names and faces.

"I work here," I said. "I'm on a break. You have some questions about this serial killer?"

"The Stripper Ripper?" he asked.

I winced.

He turned to Merlie.

"I made that up, you know."

"You must be very proud," she purred.

"Actually," he said, turning back to me, "I'm here to do some background stuff on *you*. When Detective Nuckolls told me you were doing the forensic work on this case, I drew a complete blank. I thought I knew everyone over at the Rampart PD. I ran your name through the computer, though, and it tossed back some very interesting facts."

"Do tell," I said, before taking a long swig of the Dixie.

"Well, it's nothing definitive. It just seems like, a number of times over the last several years, you've been on the scene when someone died."

"Happens to doctors every day," I said.

"Not doctors of psychology."

The kid was quick. I had to give him that.

"Your point being, I presume, that it looks awful damned suspicious that I have the awesome bad luck to stumble onto these murder scenes year in and year out."

"Well....," he said, surprised that I would admit it, "Okay, yeah."

"You are absolutely right to think so."

"I am?"

"Oh, yes. It *is* awful damned suspicious. I'm surprised some intrepid investigative reporter hasn't run across this incredible string of coincidences before now. As a matter of fact, I think it reflects admirably on the quality of journalistic talent being churned out by our better state universities these days that you were able to figure this whole thing out. Congratulations."

"I, uh.... well, thank you. You want to talk about it?"

I slammed down the rest of the Dixie, and settled back against the bar.

"About what?"

"This string of... well, amazing coincidences."

I leaned forward. I knew I had him when he leaned toward me. I winked at him in my most conspiratorial way.

"I don't think that would be a good idea," I said. "You could get into a lot of trouble."

"I don't understand."

"You know what this is all about, don't you? Bright young guy like you, you must have figured it all out already."

For a moment, I had him on the ropes. Then he seemed to recover.

"I have my suspicions, Mr. Gallegher..."

"*Doctor*," I corrected.

"...Doctor Gallegher. I can't print suspicions, though"

"Of course you can. Papers do it all the time. Some political scandal breaks out, and reporters fall all over themselves to put it to ink. Most times, it isn't as important to be first with the right story as it is to be first, period. I suggest you go with your suspicions."

"I can't do that," he protested. "I'd really appreciate it if you could give me a little something to go on."

I made a couple of desultory glances around the room, as if checking for spies, and then I lowered my voice.

"Deep background?"

"I don't know..." he started.

"It's that or suspicions. Deep background, and no citations. I don't want to see in print that this came from me, or you won't even get past the front door here from now on. My buddy Shorty will see to that..."

I poked a thumb at Shorty, who was now in on the game. He snarled appropriately, and went back to pouring a beer.

Templeton thought about it for a minute. Finally, he nodded.

"Okay, deep background is better than nothing."

"Good. Now, you know what this is all about already."

"Sure..." he said, "At least... well, I think."

I leaned forward again, and this time I took my voice all the way down to a *sotto voce* whisper.

"Intelligence."

He watched me for a moment, waiting for more.

"Intelligence?" he said, finally.

"Intelligence. Let's say, just speculating here, that you were Detective Nuckolls. Now you know Farley. He practically reeks of cop. There are places he can't go, and things he can't do. So, still speculating, let's say you need someone with contacts on the street, someone who doesn't smell like a tin badge. There are people like that, all around, but how many have some experience working with the police? Do you have any idea what kind of network you could put together just by knowing most of the pimps, loansharks, gangsters, whores, three-card-monte dealers, street musicians, murphy artists, and bartenders in town? We're talking about tapping into the fountainhead of information, here, kid."

"That's you," he said, pointing toward my barrel chest.

"I'm not going to confirm or deny that. But *you* put it together. You already know that I keep showing up at the scene of the crime, right? Let's say that Farley does have this insider doing all the slimeball networking out in the Quarter. How do you suppose he would network if he didn't know all about the crime being investigated? You see where I'm going here?"

He nodded.

"I think I do."

"Good for you. Now, let's take this hypothetical situation just a little farther down the road, shall we? Would you be willing to admit that the process of putting together our little band of Bourbon Street Irregulars might involve a substantial amount of time and effort?"

"I can see that," he was nodding involuntarily, by that time, and I knew he was mine.

"I knew you were sharp. What do you suppose Farley might do to some young, intrepid muckraker who exposed not only the existence of such a network, but also its organizer and coordinator?"

Some kind of light seemed to brighten behind his eyes.

"How many people know about this... arrangement?"

"Including you?"

"Including me."

I leaned back against the bar.

"There's Farley, of course. Merlie's in on it. I imagine Farley's boss, the police chief, has been informed. Shorty knows, because sometimes I have to skip out on work to go to a crime scene and... ah, gather information. And then there's you. You wouldn't want to screw up something this delicately protected, would you? It sure might make it hard to get the hot poop and straight skinny from the NOPD from now on…"

He stroked his bare chin, and put away his pen.

"I see what you mean. Can I ask a favor for keeping this thing under wraps, though?"

"You can ask."

"Would it be too much to ask that you give me the first take when you do get this Ripper guy?"

I reached out and patted him on the shoulder, the way my father did when he wanted me to go away.

"You'll be the first person I think of, when that happens. Now, if you'll excuse me, I have to finish my dinner."

He thanked me again, and then left the bar. I turned back to my jambalaya, which was beginning to get cold. It took a couple of bites for me to realize that Merlie was staring at me.

"What?" I asked.

"You are one devious bastard."

It sounded like admiration.

"Thank you. All I did, though, was tell him a lie in the form of the truth."

"Did you ever do that with me, when we were first dating?"

I polished off the jambalaya and washed it down with the rest of the Dixie.

"Only when it was absolutely necessary. Want to hang around for the next set?"

She nodded.

"I don't think I should let you out of my sight."

SIXTEEN

I didn't sleep very well that night. Maybe it was because I had spent most of the previous afternoon and part of the evening in bed. Perhaps it was what Merlie had said, that despite my apparent lack of concern over what I had done with Phang Loc, I was feeling a little guilty over the possible results. Maybe it was the other stuff that was going on, all the Stripper Ripper stuff that kept roiling around in my head like superheated quicksilver.

When I did drop off, I kept having this dream I couldn't shake. In the dream, I was replaying the scenario that Clever had described in the dusty shell parking lot at the far end of Bourbon. The Ripper was dusky and indistinct, but I had looked into Lucy Nivens' eyes, and I knew what was there, and it was as if, at one point, I melded with the killer, and was looking into Lucy's eyes at the moment the knife pierced her skin.

It was all about eyes, I realized. The Ripper wanted to see the lights go out. That was the moment of ecstasy for him, the moment that filled him with power.

No matter what Farley said, this couldn't be a new perp. This guy had been working on his sick rigmarole for years, either secretly or far, far away.

I was becoming wrapped up in the case, in a way I really didn't want. While the largest part of me wanted to shut out the horror, to separate from the din and hubbub of the hunt, there was a cruel, cold, analytical part that was fascinated with the puzzle, and wanted to work at it incessantly, the way a child turns and turns a

Rubik's cube. It was happening again, the unbidden, involuntary attempt to solve the riddle of the Stripper Ripper. I couldn't stop it, no matter how I tried, because that was the way I was.

This sick miscreant was sucking me in, just as surely as if he had planned it from the start.

Since I couldn't sleep, I got up around eight, dressed, and took a walk over to the Rampart Station to see Farley. There was a mist in the air that seemed to form at the level of the rooftops, and obscured the sky above it, save for the occasional mere silvery glimpse beyond, as if it were a keyhole on heaven. By noon it would burn off and leave one of those rare tack-sharp brilliant fall days in the Quarter that eliminate any argument about the existence of a Supreme Being.

Farley was in his office when I arrived. I could not remember a time I had arrived before him in all our encounters. I think he slept in his office chair, and maybe had his food trucked in.

I sat across from him, in one of the rickety wooden chairs that furnished his spartan office.

"I'm not happy with the facts of this case," I said.

"Is that so?"

"Have you heard any more from the FBI or NCIC on this guy's record?"

"No."

"It just doesn't fit, Farley. This guy is working out of a scenario so well defined, he has to have honed it somewhere else along the line. Is it possible that he's from another country?"

Farley leaned forward, allowing the front legs of his chair to return to the earth which they met so infrequently.

"It's *possible* that he's from Mars," Farley said. "And I might have just as much success getting a rap sheet from the Justice League of the Universe as I might of getting it from Europe or some other place. NCIC is rickety enough, pal, but you ought to see how hard it is to coordinate information between the States and other countries, unless you're with the White House or the CIA. Even then..." he shrugged his shoulders.

"So this may not be a new killer. He could have been doing this for several years outside the country."

"Sure. Why not?"

"It occurs to me that, while coordinating information like this between international police agencies might be difficult, a nutcase like this should have made waves wherever he was operating."

"Okay..."

"And, if he did, maybe it made the newspapers there."

Farley nodded, but his eyes were focused somewhere in Baton Rouge.

"Your point being?"

"Just this. If there are news accounts of killings like those of our guy, we might be able to find them on the Internet. If we can pin down the country where he's been operating, presuming he's not new and that he's been killing women somewhere else, we could then look for foreign nationals entering the country from there for a month or two back from the first killing here. That would at least be a place to start."

Farley stroked his chin, then took off his Panama hat and ran his fingers through what was left of his hair.

"You know, Gallegher," he said, "I don't know why everyone says you're so stupid. That's not a bad plan at all."

He jotted some notes down on a pad he kept next to his telephone. As he did, he spoke again.

"So, tell me, Mr. Wizard, when's our bad boy going hunting again?"

I shrugged.

"What's Clever say?" I asked.

"He's predicting another murder by the end of the weekend."

"In that case," I said, "I figure this Ripper dude's going to strike again by Saturday. Sunday at the latest."

"You aren't going out on a limb or anything there?"

"And argue with the experts? If it were left up to me, he'd never come out to play again. It wouldn't hurt my feelings a bit if this guy were lying on his bathroom floor right this moment, jerking around with a burst artery in his brain. Too many variables,

Farley. We still don't know what's driving this guy. Clever says by Sunday? Sounds good to me."

"Uh huh," Farley said, his chair delicately pushed back to the vanishing point between balance and disaster. "But between us swinging dicks, when do you really think it's gonna be?"

I scratched my wiry scalp and thought for a moment.

"If he were playing by the rules, I'd say Clever is right on the money. This killer is different, though. It's like he *understands* what he's doing."

"You might want to put that in smaller words."

"People see too many movies. They expect the bad guy to be some kind of evil genius. You and I, though, we know better. Most of the bad guys we run across have all the brains of wallpaper paste. The blinder the violence, the more likely it's some kind of stimulus-response event that, given the opportunity, the perp would refer to down the line as *just one of those things*. You take some of the most prolific killers of the last twenty years, and toss them in a room, and it would look like just a bunch of dumb losers in a room.

"Once in a while, though, some guy comes along, and he's really thought this whole thing through. Guys like this have a soul of pure liquid nitrogen, and they've made it, like, their *mission* to jam up every poor sucker who gets in their way. These are the guys who aren't just knee-jerking their way through life. For them, there's this grand design of death, and they're checking off the punch list as they work their way through it. I think maybe this Ripper guy is one of those.

"Let's say he really is brand new at this killing business. That would mean he's done his homework. He's read up on the serial killers of the past, and he knows the M.O.'s. He's skipped right over the preliminaries and gone straight to the main event. That's why we started off getting the killings so regularly. He knows how the progression is supposed to look. Maybe he wants to jerk us around a little, think we can predict him. Maybe he plans to go underground for a while, make us think he's quit, or dead. Worse, maybe he's planning to change his methods the next time he hits. Maybe, instead of killing dancers, he plans to start taking out priests, and maybe his signature will be the knots he uses to hang them from the bell pulls. Maybe that's been his way of working all along. Maybe every time the cops start getting close to him, he turns into a different kind of killer."

Farley closed his eyes, as if he were trying to mentally visualize the type of skell I was describing. Finally, he nodded, and opened his eyes, and he settled the front legs of the chair to the floor.

"I don't know how to catch that kind of guy," he said at last.

"You remember the name of the guy who nabbed Jack the Ripper?"

His gaze was stony and he drummed his fingers on the dented and scratched desktop, as he realized where I was going.

"Nobody ever caught Black Jack," he said.

"Yeah."

I got back to Holliday's around ten. Spanky Gallo was waiting for me outside the door. He was wearing a Houston Rockets sweatshirt over a short sleeved green sport shirt, judging by the way the collar stood straight up on his neck. He was in designer jeans that accentuated his muscled thighs, and a pair of snakeskin Tony Lama boots.

"Damn," I said, "Now those pants are gonna be tough to yank down."

I stuck a finger down and hooked it under the right side of his sweatshirt. When I pulled up the edge, I saw the bottom of his hip holster poking out.

"You here to muscle me, Spank?"

"Hell, no, Gallegher. I'm here to thank you. That little girl Sly gave me to keep me from shaggin' your sorry ass was the tightest little twist I'd had in months."

"Probably the smartest, too," I said, trying hard not to switch his ears around for him. I made a mental note to clean his clock someday when he wasn't packing, and to make sure he knew why.

"What do you really want?" I asked.

"Mr. Reynard wants to talk to you."

"What if I don't want to talk to him?"

"He could care less what you want."

"It's '*couldn't care less*'."

"What?"

"The saying. If he could care less whether I want to see him, then he would really *want* me to want to see him. Understand?"

Of course, he didn't. He just gawped at me for a moment, the way a golden retriever stares at a ceiling fan.

"Look, all I know is that Mr. Reynard tol' me to bring you around this morning so he can talk to you."

What the hell, I figured.

I didn't have anything else interesting to do.

Reynard was in his usual place when we got to the club, sitting behind his elevated desk on his elevated love seat, chowing down on a plate of *boudin* and eggs. He had slopped a ton of catsup all over the eggs, and there were flecks of the catsup on his shirt. I wondered what food must look like from his perspective. I took a seat in one of the ancient wooden dining chairs sitting in his office, and crossed my legs.

"Don't let me interrupt your meal," I said. "I can read a Russian novel or something while you finish."

God love him, he actually continued eating. I sat there, checking my nails, examining the crease in my trousers, counting the stains on the ceiling, anything to avoid watching the feeding frenzy across the room. Finally, he had consumed everything on his plate. Rather than start in on the desk itself, he turned his attention to me.

"Saw you on TV," he said, in what sounded like half a burp. He wiped his chin, badly, with a cloth he grabbed from his lap.

"How'd I look?"

"When'd you start working with the cops?"

"It was very sudden. They were all over me before I knew what was happening. Kind of like the Moonies."

He didn't have a clue what I was talking about, so he went on.

"I had a meet last night with Lucien Fleck and Huey Fontine and some of the other club owners. This Ripper thing is hurting business. Not just here, but all over the Quarter. It's like that AIDS thing. When it came out that it wasn't just the fags that was carrying it, that you could get it from plain ol' pussy, the hot pillow joints all over town took a big hit. Nobody wanted to pay fifty bucks to catch something what would put him under."

"I thought there was no such thing as bad publicity in your business."

"Yeah, well, that's why you're a shithole horn player in a stinkin' little hole in the wall dive."

I sat back and crossed my arms.

"Charm me some more."

"I ain't doing this right," he said.

"Alienating me? Oh, I think your approach is right on, Sly."

He blinked twice, looking vaguely reptilian.

"Naw, that's not… I mean… Look, I called you here for a reason. We was talking last night, the other owners and me, and we thought maybe we could, like, help you out some."

"Me, personally?"

"The cops. Nobody knows how the clubs operate the way we do, and we keep a pretty tight watch on things. We thought, maybe, we could like work together and share information, keep in touch each night. Maybe this guy, he's scouting out several bars a night before he takes some punch out. If we could get enough information together, you know, what he looks like and stuff, we could keep an eye out and identify him for you."

While syntactically disastrous, it actually wasn't an off-the-wall idea.

"You may have something there, Sly," I said. "How many of the other club owners are willing to pitch in?"

"Hell," he rumbled, with something that might have been a chuckle, but ended up just jiggling everything from the waist up, "All of 'em!"

"You want me to take this up with Farley?"

"You don't got the authority to okay it yourself?"

"This police thing is a part-time gig for me, Sly. Believe it or not, I'm not even drawing a paycheck. The FBI guy originally assigned to the case snacked on his service nine, and the Bureau didn't have anyone else to handle the profiling. I have some experience in the area, so I was called in. I don't have the authority to lift a box of paper clips from the supply closet. Everything has to go through Farley. You want me to talk with him?"

He seemed to mull the idea over for a moment, or maybe it just took that long for the decision to work its way around his skull.

"Yeah, you talk to Farley. I think we can help you guys out for a change. We'd all like to see this Ripper dude squibbed, so we can get back to business."

"Okay," I said. "You get with Lucien and Huey and the boys, and start putting together your net. I'll talk with Farley and get back to you."

"Have you guys worked up an Identikit picture of the Ripper yet?" I asked as I sat across from Farley.

"Didn't you just leave a few minutes ago?"

"I'm back. I just left *Les Jolies Blondes*, where I made a command appearance before Sly Reynard.."

"My, you do get around, Doctor."

"Reynard and some of the other club owners have offered to set up a network, to let each other and the cops know when someone meeting the description of the Ripper walks into one of their clubs. It occurred to me that if we had a picture of the guy for them to refer to, it could be of some help."

He opened a drawer on the right side of his desk and reached in, and pulled out a sheet of paper. He handed it across the desk..

"What in hell is this?" I asked, as I looked over the paper. "This could be a friggin' happy face."

The picture was about as nondescript and innocuous as a drawing could get. *White bread and mayonnaise*, was my first impression.

"This could be anybody," I said.

"It's the best we can do, so far. You gotta remember, Gallegher, these girls in the clubs see about three hundred faces a night. You get right down to it, the only faces they give a damn about were on Washington, Lincoln, and Jackson. I told you a couple of days ago – the only real description we have is this: *big white guy, wearing a baseball cap.*"

The picture was - well, it was bland. That was the only real word I could find. Oval face, straight nose, no marks, normal mouth, no hair because it was all shoved under a baseball cap with no logo. His eyes were empty and useless, probably because they were created from reports from ten or twenty sources, and the more people you interview, the more the description begins to gravitate toward nothing special. This could be any guy, anywhere, wearing a baseball cap.

"I have to take this back to Reynard and tell him this is the guy he's looking for?" I asked. "Do you have any idea how many false positives we're going to get on this thing?"

"It's a good idea," Farley said. "The more people we have looking out for us, the better. Tell Reynard to look for someone at least six and a half feet tall, and built like a fullback. Tell him to disregard the face. There can't be that many hulks around."

"What about the cap?"

"Clever thinks that whatever hair he has under there is a wig, and he needs the cap to keep it in place until he's ready to kill his victim."

The telephone on Farley's desk rang. He picked up the receiver.

"Yeah," he said.

The color started to drain from his lips.

"Where?"

He scribbled something on a notepad, and thanked the caller.

"Let's ride, Gallegher," he said. "Our boy got impatient. He hit a couple of days early."

SEVENTEEN

It's amazing, how quickly a body can begin to bloat. Even on a cool day in November in the French Quarter, even when it's been lying in the shadows of a quiet alley cul-de-sac, and even when it has been slit open like a hot boiled smoked sausage, the gases of putrefaction seem to find little hidey-holes to accumulate and blow up the body like a hideous birthday balloon.

The girl was lying on her back, her loosely curled blonde hair billowing out from her dumbfounded features. Her silk shirt was slit, away from the buttons, revealing the clumsy evisceration underneath. Some cop had brought in a fan to keep the flies down, and there was a cloying antiseptic smell of phenol in the air, to keep the investigators from ralphing all over the crime scene.

On her left breast, which seemed curiously flattened and deflated against her bony chest, the Ripper had left us another piece of his puzzle message.

solid.

"What in hell does that mean?" Farley asked.

I didn't hear him the first time he asked. I couldn't hear much of anything over the roar in my ears, and the distant rumbles of Adam Kincaid's .45 automatic, and the half-heard truncated scream from Claire Sturges as his misdirected bullet slammed into her chest, cleaving it open the way a fist would open a ripe watermelon. The blonde's empty, flabbergasted eyes, already clouded over with the cast of death, bore into me in the same accusatory way that Claire's had as the light faded from behind them and I spiraled down into the blackest void of my life.

"Hey, Gallegher!" Farley interrupted my flashback. I became aware of the satiny sheen of sweat on my face, and a trickle that ran down the small of my back.

"You got any idea what that means? *Solid?*"

"Why in hell am I here, Farley?"

"The press is gonna be swarming like these damned flies in a half hour. I can't have Evers hanging around. You're our expert of record. Now what in hell does this asshole mean by *solid?*"

"I don't know," I said, trying to keep my head from floating back to Claire's apartment. "Some musicians use that term to mean righteous, or right on, or, well, you know. *Good.*"

"You think he took particular pleasure in ripping this one? So he, like, commented on the kill?"

"I don't know. Nothing is falling together on this case. For all I know, he's picking out words at random."

Farley turned to one of the uniformed cops standing around looking green.

"Anybody found out who this is?" he asked.

One of the uniforms stepped forward.

"There was a wallet lying against the wall over there," he said, pointing toward an ancient brick exterior wall lining one side of the alley. "I gloved up and took a look. The license looks kind of like this girl. Her name was June Gable." He pulled a small notebook from his pocket. "Uh, thirty-four, lived over on Beaufair Terrace. Apartment nine. We have the wallet in a baggie in the squad over there." He pointed toward a patrol car at the entrance to the alley.

"What's your name?" Farley asked him.

"Lawrence, sir. Ashley Lawrence."

"You thinking about making Lieutenant, Lawrence?"

"That would be great, sir."

"Think you might want a gold shield someday?"

"Even better, sir."

"Then let me give you a hot tip, kid. Gloved or not, baggie or not, don't you ever again move a piece of evidence before the investigating detective gets on the scene. You understand?"

Lawrence seemed to shrink, probably so that he could make up for the strip of meat Farley had just carved out of his backside, and he nodded his reddened face.

"Uh, yes sir. I understand. It won't happen again. Uh, sir, would you like for me to replace the wallet in its original position?"

Farley pushed his panama hat back on his head. I could see the squiggly veins in his temples begin to pulsate.

"Yeah, Lawrence, why don't you do that. And after you reconstruct the crime scene and put it back roughly into the shape it was in before you fucked it all up, why don't you also do CPR on Miss Gable there and maybe she'll come back to life long enough to tell us where to find the asshole that tore her apart."

Lawrence held it together long enough to nod and say , "Sir."

He turned and walked unsteadily away. Somewhere, later that evening, he would sit in a bar and pour down bottle after bottle of beer, and with each beer he would find even more colorful words to describe the gold shield who stuffed a two-by-four up his ass until he tasted splinters.

"This is all wrong," I said.

"The killing?"

"The schedule is too tight. This guy is going critical way too early. This is two killings in two nights. That doesn't make sense."

"You applying logic to the criminal mind now?"

"This kind of criminal mind, yeah. The Ripper is breaking rules like he meant to do it from the beginning."

"What do you make of that?"

"Hell, I just said it doesn't make sense. It's like he's in a hurry or something, like he's fighting against some sort of deadline. I was with Clever on this thing. I didn't expect him to hit again for two, three days."

"Speculate on that," he said.

"What?"

"Carry that on out for me. You're my fuckin' profiler, here. Do some of that psycho mumbo-jumbo, put yourself in the head of the killer. Tell me what kind of schedule he's buckin'."

"That's Clever's job…"

"Yeah, well, Clever's not here right now. I need something to work with. You've done this before. I just promoted you to the first string."

I looked back at the body, and for a second my head tried to do another flashback to Claire Sturges' apartment. I shook it off and tried to focus. At the mouth of the alley, I could hear people gathering, and there were bright lights beginning to cast long scarecrow shadows into the lane. The reporters were pulling together, and they were going to want something to spew back to their waiting public.

"Not here," I said.

"What in hell…"

"I can't do it here, not with… her, the body, lying there. I need quiet."

"Go sit in the car. I'll hold off the press."

He knelt back over the coarsened body of June Gable, and I turned my back to him.

The car was in the midst of four or five cruisers, all with their red and blue lights flashing like the inside of a gambling riverboat. That didn't help, the association with my primary weakness. It was times like this that my mouth went dry, and I contemplated running to the nearest casino to bury my angst in the green velvet of the twenty-one table. I hadn't done a meeting in two weeks, and I realized now how bad a mistake that had been. However it fell today, I was going to have to make a meeting before dark, or Merlie would have to chain me to one of the pillars in Holliday's to keep me from making the long short drive to Biloxi.

Farley opened the driver's side door, and slid in beside me.

"What'cha got?" he asked.

"There are all kinds of deadlines," I said. "This has only been going on for a few weeks. Maybe the killer, like I said earlier, is from somewhere else. He's been in the city on business, or a vacation, for a few weeks, you know, kicking back, taking in the sights, eating a little Cajun food, knocking off a few strippers, but now it's time for him to go back home, wherever that is, and he's getting a real jolt out of all the attention in the press. So he's jacking up the frequency, compressing the timeline, so he can get the maximum bang for the buck before he climbs onto a plane and jets off forever."

"He knows the city," Farley argued. "He has a feeling for where to park without getting a ticket. He knows where the lonely places are, to kill the girls and dump the bodies, so he can get far away before they're found. He knows the clubs, how to get in and out, where the back doors are. I don't see this guy for an outsider."

"So maybe he's sick," I said. "Like Kincaid was when he came for me."

I fought back the images that intruded my head, of Adam Kincaid, all the emaciated hundred pounds and change of him, lying broken on the sidewalk six floors below Claire's balcony, while the wind of her last breath whistled out of the gaping hole in her chest. At the same time, I could almost feel the waxed, satiny crispness of a fresh pack of Hoyle playing cards as I tapped the six, telling the dealer to hit me so I could make it and the seven next to it truly righteous.

"Sick…" Farley urged.

"Bad sick. Like he thinks he's going to check out any time now, and he wants to finish it."

"Finish, like how?"

"Like getting caught. Or maybe he wants to make a big exit, suicide by cop, before whatever is eating him up does the job for him."

"He might want to be found, so he can go out like a swinging dick?"

"That's a possibility."

"He'd have to be really sick to move this quickly."

"Yeah. I know where you're going. Big white guy, strong enough to overpower these women, to rip them open like a boil-in bag. That doesn't match up with being that sick. I'm just throwing out the directions this hurry-up is taking me."

"What else?"

I looked down at my shaking hand. In my fantasy, the dealer dropped the prettiest little eight I had ever seen, and I scooped up the chips like a greedy kid with chocolate coins.

"He's anxious," I said. "He's got it bad, this killing jones. I was right earlier. He's been at it a long time, here and there. Maybe he's a drifter, never in one place long enough to set up a pattern. A girl here, a girl there, then back on the long lonesome road. So he set up shop here, and he tried to control it for as long as he could, but he needs the killings to stave off the anxiety and all the secret fears that eat him up at night. He didn't want to do it again, and he tried to stop it for a while, but there was no chance. Once you take that big step, you can't go home again. So he's fought it, losing all the way, and now he lies in bed at night, fighting off the shakes, maybe hearing his mother tell him over and over again in his head that he's an exasperating little shit and born to lose, and finally he can't hold back anymore, and he gets up, gets dressed, and goes out hunting. The killings don't stop the voices in his head anymore, so needs a daily fix to calm things down."

"I like that one better."

"Except that the information we have from Washington doesn't support it. This is a new M.O.. There're not only no matching patterns for this killing, there are no matching killings."

"So, like you were guessing earlier, in my office, maybe this guy is from outside the country."

"It's possible," I said. "It's possible."

"What's left?"

"You won't like it."

"At this point I'd listen to anything."

"He's playing with us."

"I don't like that one."

"I knew you wouldn't."

"Playing with us."

He shook his head.

"He knows the drill. He knows what we're expecting, so he violates those expectations. He's having a great time, watching us dance while he calls the tune. It's the ultimate power and control trip, and he has the stones to pull it off. The killings aren't driving him, he's driving them. Somehow, he can tell what we're thinking, and he stays one step ahead of us."

"This is crazy," Farley said, slapping the dashboard. "I can't take that to the press. Can you see the headlines? "*Stripper Ripper Goads Police*". How's that gonna look, him dicking us around like that?"

"Just the way he wants it to look, Farley. That's where he gets his laughs. He isn't getting the charge from killing these dancers. The real jolt comes from watching you squirm."

He pushed the panama hat far back on his forehead, and stared out the window at the throng of rubberneckers who had congregated on the sidewalks beyond the yellow police barriers, straining to see what little there was to see in the darkening alley.

"Let's play him," Farley said.

"What?"

"He's getting his rocks off making us jump back and forth, playing his game. Let's turn the tables on him."

"You'd better be a little more specific."

"Come on, Gallegher, you play chess. How many games have you won playing pure defense?"

"None, but…"

"So, we've been five steps behind this skell for days now, because we assumed he was playing by the rules. He knows the serial killer routine, so he can predict how we're going to react to each killing. He thinks we're going to go ballistic now, because he's chucked the playbook. So, we write a new playbook, and get a few steps ahead of him."

"How?"

"We might be able to draw him out tonight. I can place plainclothes cops in each of the pussy bars in the Quarter, and maybe some of the others in the outlying neighborhoods. You contact Reynard, and tell him and the other owners to contact me the moment any of the girls gets suspicious."

"How are you going to draw him out?" I said. I didn't like the way the conversation was going.

"We go on the record. We give the press something so friggin' outrageous, so inflammatory, that he will go through the roof. We

need to find something absolutely insulting, something he won't
be able to resist. He'll go on the hunt tonight, bent on showing us
we don't know shit. When he does, we'll be waiting for him."

"I won't do it," I said.

The conspiratorial smirk faded from his face, and he shook his
head.

"What now, Gallegher?"

"It's too dangerous. I know what you're saying. If he's so
stable that he can run the show, we can destabilize him and try to
take the upper hand. But what if we can't? Maybe we can enrage
him, make him want to strike out and show us how wrong we are,
but what if we can't stop him then? Wouldn't that make us, at
least, partly responsible for what happens? I don't know about
you, Farley, but I don't know if I can handle walking around
knowing that I was complicit in the death of a woman who didn't
necessarily have to die."

"Damn it, man, this freak is already killing. He's done two
women in two nights. For all we know, he's already scoped out
tonight's victim."

"Then we do exactly what you said. We set up the net in the
bars, and we wait to be alerted. We don't have to push this guy. If
you're right, he's coming out whether we inflame him or not."

Farley stared out the window, toward the gaggle of reporters
huddling behind the police line. Officer Lawrence was standing in
front of them, trying to keep them from stampeding the crime
scene. Maybe it was because he had been verbally stripped down
by Farley, but he seemed particularly enthusiastic about his job.

"Okay," Farley said, the word coming out as a resigned,
whistling sigh. "We won't try to inflame him. I need to do
something, though, to send him a message. Disinformation. That's
the way we used to do it in…" he stopped.

"What?"

"Never mind."

Farley had come very close to divulging what I already knew. I
had discovered, half a year earlier, that he had been wrapped up in
the Phoenix Project in Viet Nam, as a part of a strike team
designated to take out key military leaders. That made him a

spook, or at least a former spook, since Phoenix was all bundled up with CIA. If it had anything to do with disinformation, Farley probably knew how to do it.

"You're sure," he said, "that this clown is playing us like a two dollar violin?"

"No. It just makes as much sense as anything else."

"All right. Let's adopt that as our working hypothesis. If that's the case, how does he see himself?"

I thought about it for a minute.

"Adept, wily, smarter than the average bear. The more he gets away with, the more superior he feels to us common mortals. Each time he pulls off a murder and doesn't get caught, his self-esteem jumps up a dozen percentage points."

"And if he thinks he's got us stymied, headed in the entirely wrong direction?"

"It'll be like hitting the chocolate mother lode. He'll be so full of himself that he won't be able to stand it."

"Yeah," Farley said, tapping his protruding incisors with his index fingernail. "Yeah."

"What are you thinking?"

"Those stories you were telling a few moments ago. I liked the one about relieving anxiety."

"Okay."

"I especially liked that bit about hearing his bitch mother's voice ragging him in his head."

"It might be true."

"Would it be consistent with this idea of yours that he's jerking us off?"

"Possibly. Not necessarily."

"Would it hurt to put that information out if it is true?"

"I don't know. If it's true, he might think we're getting too close, and he'll back off for awhile, or move on."

"And, either way, our problem is at least temporarily solved."

"Yeah…"

"And if it's not true?"

"Then he'll figure that he's got us running. He'll think he's on the right track, that we don't have a clue about him, and he can strike with impunity. It would be like being the invisible man."

"Which, for all we know, is what he plans anyway."

"For all we know…"

"So, cutting loose with that anxiety relieving story probably wouldn't hurt, and it might help?"

"Maybe."

Farley nodded, and let his head fall backward until it reached the vinyl-covered headrest. He was figuring all the possible angles, all the eventualities, trying to find the weak point in his plan. It couldn't have been that difficult. I could think of dozens right off, including the nagging reminder that, no matter how much we thought we knew, we were basically pissing up a rope and hoping not to get splashed in the process.

Finally, he opened his eyes and raised his head.

"Right. Let's go with that. Once they cart the body away, I'll call the press over to the car, and we'll do this impromptu briefing. I want you to lay it on thick, like we got this guy in the crosshairs. We know everything but his birthday and where all his moles are. Push the bitch mother thing. Make that his motivating factor. Maybe make it like when he's killing these dancers he's actually ripping into mamma. The press loves all that Oedipal bullshit. It makes good copy."

I pulled off my hat and ran my hands through my coarse, prickly hair.

"Is that all?"

"Why am I telling you all this? I've seen you in action. You know how to lay it on."

Without waiting for me to argue, he tossed open the car door and headed back down the alley. Before the door closed, I could hear the reporters calling after him, like a poorly coordinated Greek chorus.

Only one in the afternoon, and already the day had turned to pure shit.

EIGHTEEN

After shining on the press, giving them the song and dance that Farley and I had settled on, I had to make a trip over to *Les Jolie Blondes*, to meet with Reynard. The place had already cranked up for the evening, but there weren't many people inside. Two lonely looking women gyrated on the stage, looking uncomfortable and bored, knowing there wasn't much money to be had from the ten or fifteen men scattered about the main room.

I made a gun with my thumb and index finger, and fired it at Spanky Gallo as I walked by him, going directly to the stairway leading up to Reynard's office. He didn't try to stop me this time, That was the right decision. I wasn't in the mood, whether he had the automatic stowed in his belt or not. Maybe he saw it in my eyes, the wish that he would make any kind of move in my direction. Maybe he just figured I wasn't of enough interest to him.

Reynard was at his desk, reading the Times-Picayune. His lips were moving. As was his tragedy, when any part of his body moved, it had a ripple effect that spread out over his appreciable bulk and, I supposed, eventually affected even the orbits of nearby planets.

"We're on," I said, taking a seat.

"On what?" he said, looking up.

"The network deal. Farley Nuckolls is going to call in about a half hour and tell you he's placing a plainclothes guy in your bar tonight. Before he settles in, he'll let you or Spanky know who he is. You can pass the word on to your dancers. If they get suspicious of any of the slimebags who actually spend money here, they are to go to this plainclothes guy and offer him a lap dance or something. They'll also indicate who they want him to watch closely."

"What about the other clubs?"

"I want you to get on the horn and tell Fontine and Lucien Fleck what's going down. They can each call two other owners. I figure, by six or so, everyone ought to be in on the deal. Anyone who hasn't heard from Farley by seven should call him at the Rampart Station to arrange for coverage."

Reynard nodded.

"That's it?" he said.

"That's all I have."

"Okay," he said, and turned back to the paper. I figured I had been dismissed, and I supposed it was asking a lot to expect gratitude from a hairball like Reynard. I got up and started out the door.

"Hey, Gallegher," Reynard said.

I turned around.

"You wanna hang out here tonight? You can keep an eye out for this Ripper asshole. Maybe you'll get the chance to zip him yourself, know what I mean?"

"No," I said. "I *don't* know, Sly."

"Hey, it's all right, man. We're all in the club here. Everyone knows all about you."

I nodded, and tried to quell the red tinge closing in from the edges of my vision.

"Yeah, I'm famous, I guess," I said. "But forget it. Believe it or not, I really don't want to be involved in this whole mess."

"Yeah, right," he said, and started chuckling.

Rather than watch that spectacle, I let myself out.

It was four o'clock before I got back home. I was contemplating a quick nap and maybe a trip over to the Garden District to visit Merlie before going to work that evening. I was feeling sticky and my clothes smelled of cigarette smoke and ozone.

When I walked into the bar, Clever was sitting on a stool, chatting with Shorty. Clever was the last person I wanted to see at that moment. I waved at him and continued toward the stairs to my apartment.

He didn't get the message.

"Hey, Gallegher, wait up," he called.

I ignored him, and started up the stairs. He followed me. I stopped about halfway up, and glared back at him.

"Walk down or fly down," I said. "It makes no difference to me."

"I gotta talk to you," he insisted.

"I'm all out of talk for today. Take a hike."

"You have some explaining to do," he said. He sounded angry.

I continued up the stairs to my apartment. Before I could close the door in his face, he managed to squirt by me, and stood in the middle of my apartment defiantly.

"Well?" he said.

"What?"

"You want to tell me what all that shuck and jive was you did on the television this afternoon?"

"Talk to Farley. It was his idea."

"You had no business…"

It had been a long day, full of compromises I really didn't want to make, and I was already convinced that I was going to pay the freight in burn time. Clever was just handy, and had managed to push the liftoff button on my Big Bad Pat persona.

I reached out, grabbed the lapels of his shirt, and walked him backward into the wall. I could see the fear in his eyes, and for just a second it tweaked my conscience. It was too late, though. For better or worse, Clever was about to take the heat for all the shit I had endured over the last two weeks.

"Get… this…straight," I growled, almost a hoarse whisper.. "I am tired of being manipulated. I am sick to death of being pushed and pulled. I have had about all I can stand of reliving my own horror show every time some twist takes it in the ribs from this walking trash heap. I need a shower. I need a nap. I need about a week on some pink sand beach somewhere, and I just got back from one two weeks ago. What I don't need is some washed up hack profiler telling me what my business is. I've had it with armchair quarterbacks who don't have the balls to get into the game for real. You want to call the shots, then you come out of the shadows and take the grief for it. You have a problem with the way I handled that interview today? Fine. I have the telephone number for a certain ambitious cub reporter in my pocket that I'll happily give you. I'll even take you to him. Until you are ready to step up to the plate and take one for the team, though, I would suggest that you quit walking in my head with your dirty feet."

To accentuate the point, I pulled him toward me, and then tossed him back into the wall – not hard, but with just enough emphasis to assure him that I was serious.

He blinked a couple of times, as if waiting for me to finish him off with a nice roundhouse right. Droplets of sweat had popped out on his brow, and if he hadn't been so black I was sure his face would have turned a lovely scarlet.

I turned and walked away, toward my sofa.

"Go downstairs. Tell Shorty I said to give you a beer on me," I said.

"You made a big mistake today," he said. He hadn't moved an inch.

"You're making a bigger one."

"This Ripper dude knows you're not dumb enough to miss him this wide."

"What are you saying?" I asked, not really wanting an answer.

"You want him to think you're on the wrong track. You want him to believe he's invisible, that he can go on hacking up these chicks safely, because you're off chasing head cases who are working out their sexual attractions to their mommies."

"This is Farley's play," I said. "I already told you what I want."

"Maybe Farley's calling the shots, but you're the talking head on the tube. This guy we're hunting is no slouch, man. He's going to know you're spreading bullshit. You may have just sent him to ground, playing games with his head like that."

"Go away, Clever. Go talk to Farley. Tell him he made a bonehead decision. I'm too tired to discuss it."

For a moment, I actually thought he was going to leave. He turned toward the door, but then he hesitated.

"I almost forgot the other reason I came here," he said. "Have you read the Times Picayune today?"

He pulled a folded section of the paper from his back pocket, and held it out to me. I didn't reach for it, so he took a couple of steps toward the sofa.

"Take it," he urged. "You'll be interested in this."

I finally reached out and took the paper. It was the local section, a report with no byline. It was just a blurb along the leftmost column of page two, where they put the notices of no particular general interest.

Body Found, it read. At first I thought it would be about Molly Mounds, but that was splashed all over page one already.

Police in Bayou Teche discovered a body lying in a tidal pool late Thursday night, it began. *According to Parish Sheriff's Detective Sam Raborne, the individual had been shot twice in the head at close range. The victim, identified as Thuy Ninh Duc, a Vietnamese immigrant, was taken to New Orleans for autopsy by the Medical Examiner there. The investigation is continuing.*

Clever waited for me to finish reading.

"The Vietnamese gangs have been immersed in an internecine squabble with the other gangs for months," I said. "You want to know how many Asian immigrants have wound up in bayous all over the area?"

"In Bayou Teche? Wasn't that the place you mentioned yesterday? Seems to me you might owe that slant we visited a thank-you."

There was a hollow feeling in my chest, but it was filling up with bile and acid.

"You don't know the whole story," I said.

"And I don't want to," he said. "Just do me a favor. Before you go off again and bitch and moan about being manipulated, maybe you ought to reflect on the way you push and pull people around yourself. You seem to have a particular knack for it."

He left then, perhaps before I could try to get in a last word.

As if I had any.

I was going to have to do without the nap. It was going to take a really long shower before I would feel clean again.

The Ripper didn't strike that night.

I took Merlie out to the Court of Two Sisters, where I had my favorite house specialty, the *pompano en papillote*. We had gone there on our first real date. We sat near the fountain this time. I was distracted several times when I realized that people were looking at me. It wasn't my guilty conscience or anything, but rather my newfound fame. With my picture plastered all over the front section of the Times-Picayune, and flashing on the television screen every thirty minutes in news teasers, I was losing my low profile but fast. I tried to return some of the stares. Most of the people would carefully glance away when I made eye contact, as if they did not want to be tainted by my association with this vile murderer. Nobody came up to ask for an autograph.

After dinner, we went back to my place. I didn't tell Merlie about Sly Reynard's invitation to hang out at *Les Jolie Blondes*. I tried not to talk about the Ripper situation at all. I didn't feel like making love. Actually, I didn't feel like anything. I wondered whether Merlie had seen the article in the paper about the late Thuy Ninh Duc. She didn't mention it, and I didn't bring it up. We sat for a while, and finally went downstairs to catch a game on the television. We sat at the bar, me with an Abita and Merlie with her white zinfandel.. Some of the regulars dropped by to pass the time, but they didn't hang around.

About halfway through the game, the local station cut to a teaser for the eleven o'clock newscast. There I was again, looking rather lame and scurrilous, talking about how the Stripper Ripper was consumed by his obsession over his bitch goddess mother. I tried to shut it out.

I didn't have to work that night, so Merlie and I took a walk in the Quarter. Out among the thousands of tourists crammed into the eight square blocks, I felt a little more anonymous. It became tiresome after awhile, though, threading our way through the drunks and the panhandlers and pussy club barkers, so we decided to call it a night. Merlie wanted to stay with me that night. We went back to my apartment and went straight to bed.

I think she felt my lack of desire, and she went right to sleep. After a couple of hours, I got up and padded over to my easy chair near the window, where I sat until the blue-black hours of the morning, long after the tourists had retired to their hotels and boarding houses. I waited for the telephone to ring.

It never did.

The Ripper didn't come out to play the next night either, or the night after that. I visited Farley on the third day following the murder of June Gable. He was strung out. The pressure of maintaining the deathwatch in the bars was beginning to tell on him. His face, never a robust countenance, had grown even more lean and wan. There were dark circles under his eyes, and his wattle seemed to sag even more precipitously than normal.

He smelled.

"Did we scare him off?" he asked.

As if I knew.

"What does Clever say?"

"He came in here two days ago and tossed a real hissy. Said if we didn't want him around to just say so. He claimed we were blowing the case, playing fast and loose with the psychoanalytic routine, that this clown was too smart to fall for that horseshit."

"Maybe he's right."

Farley stood and sniffed at himself. His face made it clear he didn't like what he found.

"I gotta go home and shower," he said. "Just so you know, I got authorization to maintain the plainclothes guys in the strip bars for three more days. After that…". He shrugged his shoulders.

"That's a mistake," I said.

"That's exactly what I told my commander. You wanna see the new asshole he chewed for me?"

"The minute you pull those plainclothes cops, this headcase is going to crank back up."

"You're so sure of that?"

"Yeah, I'm sure. He knew the minute we posted them. That's why he dropped off the gameboard. Somehow, he has some kind of connection with the bars – maybe his girlfriend's a stripper, or he's next to some bartender. Whatever the reason, he's still a step ahead of us."

"Maybe we were righter than we thought about the mother fixation," Farley said. "Maybe we scared him into pulling up stakes."

"I don't think so. You pull that coverage in the bars, and you'll find out I'm right."

Deep down, he knew it too. I could see it on his face, this hangdog defeated expression that said he had used all his best tricks and was left with nothing but instinct and adrenalin. He pulled on his seersucker jacket as he nodded. He started to walk out of his office, but stopped and looked back at me.

"You really beat the crap out of Evers?"

"No. I just bounced him off the wall of my apartment to get his attention."

"Uh huh," he said, tapping on the jamb of his office door with his index finger. "Well, next time you feel like getting his attention, make sure we've caught the Ripper first. We almost lost him over that little incident. Be a shame to lose Clever. Then I'd be stuck with you."

"You could do worse."

He stared me down on that one.

"Are you coming, or staying behind to clean my office?" he said.

· The Ripper didn't strike again that night. For that matter, everything was quiet for almost a week. We were in the midst of the Thanksgiving season. I, for one, was thankful for the lack of activity, and I was hopeful that the Ripper had pulled up stakes and gone somewhere far away.

I'm lucky, but I'm apparently not that lucky.

As a sort of olive branch to Merlie, I agreed to break bread with her and all the little urchins at *A Friend's Place* on Thanksgiving. As I may have mentioned at some other point, I don't know which end of an oven you blow into. I can cook a mean Pop Tart, but that's about the limits of my culinary expertise. I do, however, have a more than nodding acquaintance with most of the best chefs in town. Being a silver-tongued devil, I had managed to talk several of them into preparing the pieces of a genuine holiday feast, complete with Cajun seasoned roast turkey, oyster dressing, a delightful cranberry compote, several varieties of veggies, and a caramel spice cake, all of which I delivered to the shelter just at dusk.

There were, maybe, eight kids in the house that night. Some had come from as far away as North Carolina. None of them felt particularly nostalgic for their hammerhead families, but they were all, seemingly, possessed of ravenous appetites. They ate as if they hadn't seen food since Reconstruction.

I sliced the turkey, which required almost no kitchen skills whatsoever, and was serving onto the donated plates used at the shelter, doling out the largest portions I could in all good conscience manage. I looked up, and Merlie was gazing in my direction from the head of the table. She had been offered that place of honor by the kids themselves, who regarded her as some sort of beneficent goddess. They were, obviously, bright and astute children.

She didn't turn away when I caught her eye, but rather winked at me, and her face conveyed something beyond the usual drowsy lust, something that approached admiration and tenderness. Something I was doing was making me seem paternal and charitable. I determined right then to figure out what it was and not do it again. Any act I perform which leads Merlie to even look at me with that syrupy Daddy Potential leer is, by definition, a bad thing, and should never be repeated.

Merlie said grace. She was barely past the second syllable of the "amen" before all her charges dove in like gravediggers, and for several minutes the only sounds in the room were the clink of flatware against china, and the occasional slurp as one or another gulped down tea.

Despite myself, I did enjoy the evening, though I was separated from Merlie by this gulf of dinner table. The kids seemed really satisfied, and within a half hour they had cleaned their plates down to the etching, and vanished, almost as a group, to the front porch. The steady *whump whump* of hip-hop shook the front of the house, which, I suppose, signaled the end of a wonderful evening.

So I thought.

I tried to help Merlie gather the dishes for washing, but she stopped me. As I had, after a fashion, "cooked" dinner, I was banished from the cleanup. She summoned one of the children from the porch to help her, and sent me to the living room to relax.

I turned on the television, just in time to catch the second half of the Minnesota-Dallas football game. The turkey was beginning to work its tryptophan magic on me when the telephone rang. Merlie had sent the staff home for the evening, and she was occupied, so I answered.

It was Farley Nuckolls.

"Shorty told me you were at the shelter," he said.

"What's up?"

"Do you have access to a computer?"

"There's one in Merlie's office."

"Is it hooked up to the internet?"

"I don't know."

"Write this down."

"Wait," I said, and grabbed a pen and scrap of paper. "Okay."

"Write this down. *Alt.binaries.pictures.erotica.tasteless.*"

"What in hell…"

"Its a Usenet newsgroup. It's kind of a bulletin board where people post messages."

"I understand newsgroups, Farley. What's this have to do with me?"

"Access the newsgroup I just gave you. Scroll down to a series of postings labeled *French Quarter Rips.*"

"Oh, hell…"

"Just do it, and then call me back at this number and tell me what you think." He gave me his telephone number, and hung up.

I called Merlie into the living room, and asked her about access. As it happened, her computer was hooked in with one of the major Internet service providers. She gave me her password as soon as I told her what was happening.

It took me a minute to log on. I ignored the cheerful voice that told me I had mail, and clicked immediately on the Internet icon, and then on the Newsgroups icon. Since the specific board Farley had directed me to was not on Merlie's list, I had to expert add it quickly. It took me another couple of minutes to scroll down to the specific messages *French Quarter Rips*. I double clicked on the first heading, and ordered the computer to save the download into Merlie's briefcase. It automatically opened the file as it downloaded it.

I almost lost my meticulously prepared dinner.

The first picture was of Lucy Nivens, splayed on the ground and opened like a biology lab frog. It was apparently shot at night, with a bounce flash, judging by the lack of red in her eyes. On the other hand, I had never heard whether dead eyes shot red, and Lucy was undoubtedly dead when the picture was taken.

I killed the picture and pulled up the next JPEG file. This one I didn't recognize, but there was a word on her left breast.

that.

Hayley Stout, the second victim. The pose was similar, along with the sad, surprised look on her face.

I ran through each of the pictures, until I got to a picture of June Gable. She was lying much as she was when Farley and I examined her, but the background again indicated that the photo had been taken at night, with a flash.

There was a crash behind me. I jumped, startled, and whirled around to find Merlie and one of the kids from the shelter standing in the doorway to her office. The kid had dropped a plate with a piece of cake on it, and it had shattered on the floor. Her mouth was open, and there were tears in her eyes. She turned to Merlie, panicked, and buried her face in Merlie's chest.

"Pat," Merlie said, nodding toward the screen.

"Oh," I said, and turned back to kill the image.

The girl was crying by then. I hoped it was because she was worried about breaking the plate, but I knew better. Merlie walked her back into the living room, away from the office, and spoke to her quietly as she stroked the tormented youngster's hair.

I sat in the office and felt low and dirty. It hadn't occurred to me to close the door.

I signed off the computer, and picked up the telephone to call Farley.

"You look at them?" he asked.

"Yeah. I'm guessing those aren't purloined copies of the investigation photos?"

"First thing I checked. I have all the pictures we took on my desk. They don't match."

"How'd you find out about this?"

"Anonymous tip. You check out the other files on that newsgroup?"

"No."

"Really raunchy stuff. Lots of piss drinking, a couple of bestiality shots. Some guy who subscribes to the newsgroup apparently ran across these pictures, realized that they weren't some kind of stunt, and he called the Rampart Station watch captain to report it. Cap took one look and called me in. Hell of a way to spend Thanksgiving."

"It does answer one question, though."

"The trophy angle?"

"Gad, you're fast, Watson," I said.

"Way I figure it, the Ripper takes pictures of his victims as his trophy, rather than taking panties or something."

"*Take a picture, it'll last longer.*"

"That's sick."

"Of course it is. We are not dealing with a mental health poster child here, Farley. This guy has a box of pictures in his house that he uses when he masturbates. He thinks about the feeling of power and control he achieved while committing the murders, and he really gets off on it. He's stretching out the thrill."

"So why's he posting them on the internet?"

"I can think of several reasons," I said. "One, he's sending us a message. He wants us to know he's not gone, that we didn't scare him off. He wants us to think about him, a lot. Maybe he wants us all bollixed up with worry about when he's going to strike again. Two, he's challenging us to find him. By posting the pictures, he's raising the stakes. This isn't our little party anymore. One guy saw these pictures and called. Want to guess how many others saw them and didn't report it? Maybe because they were getting off on them as much as the Ripper."

"Jesus," Farley wheezed. "This asshole's building a fan club."

"And, in the process, he's pissing in the well. I noticed that, on every picture he posted, the word written on the victim was prominently visible. He just gave away his trademark. From now on, we're never going to know if a murder was committed by him, or by some copycat."

"You think there's another trash head out there hinky enough to do this kind of thing?"

"I think this Ripper dude could fill a platoon, just in the metro area. He's just the only one who's currently shown the balls to act on his impulses. If word gets out that the cops can't touch him, it's likely to set off a flurry of imitation killings."

"He's looking for safety in numbers."

"Let me guess. You traced back the history on the posts and ran up against a brick wall somewhere in Northern Europe."

"The Netherlands. This guy sent his postings through a re-router that we can't touch. By the time we work through all the international law tangles to get a subpoena the re-router's records, you, me, and the Ripper will be long dead."

"It wouldn't be any good anyway. These re-routers have figured out that game. They purge their files several times a day. You won't catch this Ripper that way."

"So he's done exactly what he wanted. He has us over a barrel. He's telling us he's won this round."

"It sure looks that way. Did you notice, though, that the pictures were all in color?"

"So?"

"So, black and white is pretty easy to develop. Any guy with the chemicals and a good dark bathroom can do it. Color is something else. Most color film is developed by something called the C-41 process. On the way to New Orleans a few years ago, I stopped off in a couple of towns and worked odd jobs to pay my way. One of them was with film developing company. This C-41 process is kind of tricky, and it requires a lot of special chemicals. Since it's really cheap to do at the local drug store now, most people don't bother developing their own film. Maybe if you scour the local photography stores, you'll find a record of a big white guy who likes to process his own color photos."

"That's a lead?"

"Best one we've had yet. Of course, there's always the possibility that he used a digital camera."

"And if he did?"

"Then you're screwed."

"Serial killers using digital cameras and posting their work on the Internet," he mused sullenly. "Whatever happened to plain old cops and robbers?"

"It's a new world, Sparky. I'm not so sure we were invited. I told you this guy's smart. What's Clever say about all this?"

"Nothing. I can't raise him. Got his answering machine and left a message. He's probably out for the holidays."

"He didn't mention anything about going away."

"Yeah, well, maybe he just stepped out to the market. I expect he'll call back soon."

"You don't sound like you'd care much one way or the other."

There was a short, deliberative silence on the other end of the line.

"What are you saying?"

"Just that it seems you're leaning on me more than Clever the deeper we get into this Ripper business."

"Maybe. You're a known commodity. I can usually figure out which direction you're going to bounce. This Evers fellow, he's different. Spooky."

"Flaky?"

"Quirky."

"I suppose he is," I said. "But I warned you about him before you brought him on board. He hasn't been the same since he tagged Larry Bondurant to get the fire knocked out his ass at Raiford."

I caught a reflection in the window next to Merlie's desk. She was standing in the doorway of her office. She didn't look happy.

"Look, Farley, I gotta boogie here. Merlie needs me to help her with something. Do me a favor and keep me posted on what Clever says, okay?"

"If I ever hear from him again…"

I hung up, and swiveled around in Merlie's chair.

"I'm sorry," I offered.

"You damn well ought to be. What do you mean, bringing this perverse investigation into this house?"

"I didn't know what it was going to be. Farley didn't tell me beforehand. When I found out, I just forgot to close the door."

"Well, you just gave Shelley out there a Thanksgiving for the scrapbooks. I probably won't be able to get her to sleep tonight. I can't go into details with you, but she isn't really in shape for the kind of trauma she just had."

"I said I was sorry," I said, beginning to feel a little irritated, and even more guilty for feeling that way. "Would you like me to talk with her?"

She shifted from one foot to the other, her arms crossed protectively in front of her generous bosom.

"What would you say?

Excellent question.

"I don't know. You and I both know, though, that this can't be left hanging."

She glanced off, as if deliberating.

"What are you getting into, Pat?" she said, at last. "You're just supposed to be covering for Evers. Now I see you on television, and the cops are calling you their expert. This is all damned difficult."

"That was the plan before. As far as I'm concerned, it still is. Do you want me to talk to the girl?"

"Shelley," she said.

"Do you want me to talk to Shelley?"

It took her a long time, but she finally nodded.

"She's in the parlor."

I went to the kitchen, and cut another piece of cake for Shelley, and one for myself. I put them on a tray with a couple of glasses of milk, and carried them into a room off the main living room, which had been dubbed the "parlor". It was really just an eight by eight room with a couple of small loveseats, which was used for family visits and counseling.

It would get a workout tonight.

Shelley was sitting on one of the loveseats, her legs drawn up underneath her. She was staring at a picture on the wall, a print of a painting of two kids, viewed from behind, as they walked down a leafy forest trail surrounded by mist and bowered trees. It reminded me of Hansel and Gretel, but that's just the way my mind works.

"I brought you some cake," I said.

"Already had some."

"Go ahead, have some more. It's free."

I placed the plate and the glass of milk on the table in front of her. I sat down in the other loveseat, and tried to make myself comfortable.

"First things first," I said, "I didn't mean for you to see that picture on the computer. It was an accident."

She didn't say anything. She had pulled the sleeves of her sweater up, though, and I could see the old healed railroad ties of self-inflicted mutilative knife cuts. Whoever had undertaken to screw up this kid's life had done a banner job. I hadn't made things any better. On the other hand, it gave me an idea.

I held up an index finger, right in front of my nose.

"Look at me," I said, gently but with a tone that said I meant it.

She stared at the floor.

"Look at me," I said again, more sternly.

She looked up, with this surprised expression. She hadn't expected me to take the offensive.

"There are bad people in this world," I said.

She nodded.

I softened my voice.

"You've known a few of them, I'll bet."

She nodded again.

Good. We were communicating, sort of.

"I've known a few of them, too."

She nodded one more time, but then she said something, just over a whisper.

"Do they scare you?"

"All the time," I said. "I have been so scared, once or twice, I had no idea where to turn. You go through that a few times, and you begin to think about ways to take care of the bad people. Right?"

As I expected, she agreed.

"Right," she said, tentatively.

"The guy who took that picture you saw is a very, very bad person," I told her. "He hurts people because he *likes* to hurt people. Do you want to know what I'm going to do about that?"

She didn't say anything, but her eyes remained stuck on mine.

"I'm going to take him out of the picture. When I'm finished with him, he isn't going to hurt anyone ever again. I was looking at that picture because I'm working with the police. The police want this bad person locked away. Now, look at me."

I waited, as she surveyed my impressive bulk.

"Do I look like the kind of fellow who is going to let this bad person go on hurting people?"

She shook her head.

"When you're done," she said, "Would you do something about my uncle?"

I suppressed a sigh.

I had suspected that an uncle, a stepfather, or maybe even the kid's father, had abused Shelley until she couldn't take another moment.

I hated Shelley's uncle already, and all I had seen was his handiwork..

"Have you told Ms. Comineau about your uncle?" I asked.

She shook her head, her eyes remaining locked on the weave of the carpet.

"I… couldn't," she said.

"He told you not to tell."

She nodded.

"He told you that if you let anyone know what he did, he would do something to you?"

She shook her head.

"Your sister?"

A single tear flowed from the corner of her eye, and coursed slowly across her plump cheek. I hadn't known for certain that she had a sister, but I did know how these slimeballs worked.

She nodded, slowly.

"What's your sister's name?"

"Lindy."

"How old is Lindy?"

"Nine."

"How old were you when your uncle started hurting you?"

She snuffled a little, and I handed her a tissue from the ubiquitous box on the arm of the couch. She rubbed her nose with it, but she never stopped examining the floor.

"I was nine…"

"I'm going to ask you a very hard question," I said. "Do you really think your uncle is going to leave Lindy alone just because you keep quiet?"

More tears. More snuffling. A forlorn shake of her head.

"You know what we need to do?"

She nodded.

"I'm going to take care of the monster who made that picture you saw on the computer," I told her. "What are you going to do to your monster?"

She sat quietly for a long time, occasionally wiping her nose or eyes. The pile of spent tissues grew beside her on the couch, like empty promises. I hadn't been out of the therapy business long enough to forget that sometimes the most important gains came in silence.

"I wanna talk to Merlie," she whispered finally.

"I'm right here," Merlie said, standing in the doorway. I had been so focused on Shelley that I had no idea how long she had been there.

"I'll take it from here," Merlie told me, and the way she squeezed my shoulder as she said it made it clear that everything was going to be all right.

I excused myself and walked out onto the front porch. The kids had decided to take a walk, and I was out there all alone. I fired up one of the Cubans and sat in a rocker, watching the leaves still hanging stubbornly on the trees of the front yard tremble in a gentle breeze from the Gulf. I practiced blowing smoke rings for a half hour or so, and between puffs I thought about all the people I had hurt over the years, doing a meditative Eighth Step of my recovery program in my head. For each one, living or dead, I imagined how I could make it up to them, provide some kind of feeble restitution for the havoc I had wrought in their lives. I tried to make it as little like a litany as I could.

Merlie stepped out on the porch and sat in the rocker next to mine. She reached over, took the cigar from my hand and, in some kind of show of butch camaraderie, she took a drag from it and let the smoke waft about her perfect features.

"Shelley gave me permission to call Social Services," she said. "I knew someone had misused her, but I didn't know who. I made the report."

"It's going to be a long road," I said.

"Damned rocky, too. Roads go places, though. That's more than she had when she came here."

I took the cigar back from her, and puffed on it.

"So that's a Cuban," she noted.

"Yep."

"Can't see what all the fuss is about."

"Forbidden fruit."

"So why in hell did you get out of the therapy business, Pat? What you did in there was as good as I've seen lately."

"We've had this conversation, dear. *Oddity of Nature*, remember?"

"Maybe you were working on the wrong people," she observed.

"Maybe."

"Ever think of working with kids?"

I shifted in my chair. The wooden slats were carving ravines in my fat fanny.

"Sure. Dismissed the notion every time. Too much heartache. Too much responsibility."

She stood and leaned over the rail of the front porch, and looked both ways down the sidewalk. At the end of the block, the kids from the shelter rounded the corner and headed for home.

"Reconsider it," she said, before she walked back into the house.

NINETEEN

I hung around the shelter until midnight, when the overnight staff waddled in, stuffed with their own Thanksgiving dinners. Once Merlie had done the turnover staffing, updating the overnighters on all the news, she and I drove over to her home and turned in for the night. It had become an interesting arrangement, as most nights it seemed that we stayed together either at her place or mine, but there was never any discussion of picking one or the other. It was just something that happened naturally, the way birds pick up in autumn and flock to the south without meeting about it first.

On some nights we just decided to sleep separately.

A friend had given me tickets to the Saints game the next day, so we rose early, for me, and had a light breakfast before walking toward the Superdome, which was about a mile from Merlie's house. The Aints struggled in futility against the Packers, in a year when neither team was much to write home about, and in the end Green Bay took it by about six. I didn't really mind. I was there mostly for the hotdogs and the beer.

After the game, we walked to Merlie's and grabbed my car to go back to the Quarter. I had to work that evening, and Merlie and I had decided to drop by The Gumbo Shop first for a bite.

The bar was empty when we walked in, which was to be expected at five in the afternoon. Brucie had come and gone, and Shorty was probably out at the bank getting the till money. We stepped up the back stairs toward my apartment, where I almost tripped over the thick manila envelope lying on my doorstep.

Nothing was written on it, which first raised my suspicions. I asked Merlie to stay on the landing. I unlocked my door and stepped over the envelope to check all my telltales, just to make certain that nobody had invaded my home while I was gone. Everything seemed in place, so I called her in. She stooped to pick up the envelope.

"Don't," I cautioned, maybe a little louder than was necessary. She froze.

"What?" she asked.

"Don't touch it yet. Just come on in."

She stepped inside and stared at me.

"I'm not expecting any packages," I said. "Why don't you go into the bathroom while I check this out?"

That troubled look I hate crossed her face quickly, but she didn't argue. After she closed the bathroom door, I knealt in the doorway to examine the envelope. There were no strings attached, but that didn't mean anything, necessarily. I recalled stories Scat Boudreaux, a former Viet Nam sniper I know, had told me about booby trapped mines. For all I knew, there was a hole carved in the floor underneath the envelope, just big enough for a Bouncing Betty claymore mine, waiting to give the big stupid Irish cornet player a nasty surprise.

I sat there in the doorway for almost five minutes, debating my options. It was that old quantum physics problem I had read about in _The Dancing Wu Li Masters_ a week or two earlier – the Schrodinger's Cat mystery. In an airtight, lightproof box is a cat and a vial of cyanide, which is triggered to go off when some random unpredictable event takes place. Is the cat dead or alive? According to Schrodinger, it is both dead and alive, until you check, when it becomes one or the other.

The envelope was either dangerous or it wasn't, but I wouldn't know until I checked. I had the familiar buzzing sensation in the back of my neck, the old feeling I recalled whenever I stared at thirteen on the green felt and contemplated the universe of possibilities which might be unleashed by telling the dealer to hit me.

Finally, I took a deep breath and picked up the envelope.

Nothing exploded. There was no sudden invasion by black-robed ninjas. The Spanish Inquisition did not break down the doors.

The envelope was light, much lighter than I would have expected from its overstuffed appearance. I prodded the manila delicately, searching tentatively for some solidity, any discordant shape which might be explosives, but there was nothing but the yielding softness of paper. That was also meaningless. I had heard, again from Scat Boudreaux, about a new explosive that would be shaped as flat and thin as a piece of sixty pound bond.

My damnable curiosity got the better of me, and I pulled open the seal. Inside I saw wadded tissue paper, which had given the envelope it's bulk. There were several sheets of paper inside. I pulled them out.

All the air seemed to be sucked out of the room in an instant. I leaned back against the door jamb and tried to catch my breath as I examined the photos in my hand.

Schrodinger had been wrong. Even after examination, the contents of the envelope were both harmless and dangerous at the same time.

The bathroom door opened, and Merlie peered out.

"What is it?" she asked.

"Pictures," I said. "Of you and me."

"Let me see."

She crossed the living room to where I sat in the doorway, and looked over my shoulder.

There were six of them, all eight by ten glossies, mostly in black and white. They had a glow about them, especially the ones taken at night, which led me to believe that they were video captures from a low-light camcorder of some sort. One showed us walking along Toulouse. Another was of us sitting on the front porch at *A Friend's Place*. There was one that showed us in my bed, apparently taken through the window of my apartment from the roof of the voodoo shop across the street.

Someone had taken a marker, and had drawn a circle with crosshairs over our chests in each of the pictures.

Merlie turned and walked to the sofa. She sat heavily on one end.

"Is it him?" she asked quietly.

"Probably. These are a message."

"Oh, I figured that one out already."

There was a cold edge to her voice, as keen as the bite of a scalpel. I didn't like it.

"This guy's turned things around," I said. "I'm not hunting him anymore. He's hunting me."

"Bullshit."

I turned to her.

"He's *found* you," she said. "What now?"

I pulled myself to my feet and joined her on the sofa.

"I need to show these to Farley."

She stiffened.

"All of them?"

I pulled out the photo of us in bed, and laid it on the coffee table. She seemed to relax.

"All but that one."

She didn't speak for a long time. I knew what was going on in her head, though. We had not been involved with each other for even a year, but she had learned, the hard way, how I operate.

"This is personal now, isn't it?" she asked.

I nodded.

"About as personal as things get."

"And, after you speak with Farley? What then?"

"Then," I said, "I'm going to find this bastard, and I'm going to yank his heart out through his asshole."

If the pictures had been only of me, I could have handled that. One way or the other, I've been in a lot of crosshairs over the years, and nobody's pulled the trigger yet. With Merlie involved, though, things were different. Even before I spoke with Farley, there were arrangements to be made.

At the far end of Bourbon Street, long after you blow by the pussy clubs and Hurricane stands, even past the courtyards and fancy wrought-iron balconies, past the antebellum home of Colonel Beauregard, there is a seedy section filled with small businesses that somehow managed to escape the restoration afforded the touristy venues. Most of these buildings feature wormy, dry-rotted doorways and painted glass storefronts. If you have the time when you visit, you may drop by some of them and find the true treasures of New Orleans - rare book stores, architectural salvage companies, antique havens, and the occasional off-beat voodoo shop. If you stroll long enough, you'll come across a nondescript, olive drab shop with a simple wooden sign bolted to the door, which reads *Semper Fi*.

Walk inside.

At first it looks like any other military surplus, with racks of ugly green jackets, bulky sweaters, boots, camping paraphernalia, and the odd piece of hardware. Behind the counter is a fellow named Sonny, who wears an eyepatch with a Jolly Roger on it. I have never entered *Semper Fi* without finding him wearing the same fatigue pants and camo tee shirt. I guess he dresses off the rack in the store.

What isn't apparent, at first glance, is that *Semper Fi* is a clearinghouse for extremely deadly weaponry, dealt from a storeroom in the back of the shop by Scat Boudreaux, the Cannibal Commando.

Merlie is extremely uncomfortable around Boudreaux. She has her reasons. A lot are good ones.

Scat grew up in a two-room shack way back in the Atchafalaya swamps, where a couple of nutria rats can make a damned nice stew. His father, who couldn't read or write his own name, did pass along to his son the talents of hunting and tracking. Word on the bayous was that the Boudreauxs, *pere et fils,* could follow the day-old trail of a duck in flight. I had personally seen Scat's abilities with a rifle demonstrated, when he passed a Winchester .308 handload round under my nose at slightly more than the speed of sound, in the process of killing one of Justin Leduc's bodyguards, who was trying to kill me at the time out on Lake Pontchartrain.

Scat Boudreaux's main claim to fame, however, was a legendary trek across North Vietnam in the late '60's. Through a series of tragicomic circumstances, Scat was drafted into the army at the height of Johnson's war. He was ultimately pegged as a sniper, and scored over thirty one-shot kills before his luck ran sour. Some second lieutenant was busy in the bathroom with a Playboy and his good hand when he should have been directing a Huey to the recovery zone to pick up Scat after a mission. As a result, Scat was captured and spent the next year in a tiger cage courtesy of Uncle Ho's finest.

Captivity did things to his head, dark crawly things that changed his already limited perspective on qualities like morals and humanity. He fashioned finger knives from the bamboo of his cage, and used them to kill one of the guards when he was served his rice one day. After using the guard's knife to open the cage, he killed the rest of the Viet Cong in the camp.

Scat knew he had a long way to go to reach friendly territory, so he stoked up on protein before starting his journey. As it happened, the only real protein-rich biomass available to him at that moment resided in the bodies of the Cong, and that explains how Scat became the Cannibal Commando.

When he finally reached ARVN lines, the story of his improbable trek made front-page headlines in *Stars and Stripes*. As the gory details were revealed, his story moved progressively further back in the paper, until it disappeared altogether when he was quietly discharged to spare the military any unnecessary embarrassment.

I have had occasion over the last several years to take advantage of Scat Boudreaux's considerable skills, usually when I felt the vague burning in the back of my neck that indicated I was being watched, and I needed someone to watch the watcher.

Among Scat's other gifts is the apparent ability to become invisible at will. Six months earlier, I had hired him to watch Merlie when Haitian gang members employed by Jimmy Binh vandalized her house, and she never knew she was being protected.

Now, it seemed, I needed his help again.

Merlie and I walked into *Semper Fi*. Sonny was lounging in a new recliner behind the counter. At his feet was a German Shepherd who sprang to its feet and growled at us. Merlie instinctively drew back to hide behind me.

Sonny opened his one good eye, and said something in a foreign language to the dog, who immediately sat and panted as Sonny scratched him behind the ear. Sonny knows I have no business with him, not being into the whole military scene, so he just smiled and jerked his thumb back toward the store room.

Merlie and I passed through a couple of doors into a warehouse with shelves that stretched twenty feet to the ceiling. Scat was sitting behind a desk, reading a copy of *Mercenary Times*. Like Sonny, he wore camo fatigue pants, properly bloused where they were tucked into his spit-shined boots. His tee shirt, though, was strictly non-issue. It was black, and across the front was an advertisement for a new video game, with a picture of three heavily armed commandos, and the legend *You Can Run, But You'll Just Die Tired*.

The last time I had seen Scat, he had shaved his head. Now, he sported an austere buzz cut flattop, with the front waxed to a rigid wall of hair. He looked up as we entered the room.

"Well, if it ain't that media darlin', come to visit," he said, as he snapped to attention behind the desk. "Kinda wondered when you were gonna show up."

He gestured toward the couch positioned in front of his desk, and we sat.

"How's it hanging, Scat?" I asked, almost afraid of the answer.

"Well, you know how it goes, Doc. You cain't drink the water 'cause of the fluoridation and the chlorine, you cain't breath the air on account of the PCB's, and then there's those guys on the television who keep tellin' me to do stuff I just don't wanna do."

I felt Merlie's arm snake around my own, and she applied pressure. Scat scares her.

Scat scares a lot of people.

Hell, sometimes Scat scares *me*.

"I been readin' about you in the papers, ol' son," he continued. "Seems you been comin' up in the world. Looks like you finally took ol' Scat's advice and quit hangin' around the guinea gangs. This Stripper Ripper, though, I don' know about that boy. Reminds me of that guy over in Yorkshire a few years back. Of course, we both know what that was all about. Friggin' Labor government was in bed with the Commies, tryin' to put together their One World Disorder over there, put a buncha people on the breadlines. Didn't help that Georgie Bush Senior was in the White House. You know he was CIA director, don'cha? You know what that means. Ain't been a CIA director since Wild Bill Donovan what wasn't in the pocket of the Masons and the Illuminati. Have you looked at the back of your dollar bill lately, Doc? You look there, and you're gonna find what -- a pyramid with an eye on it, Masonic symbols both of 'em, and right underneath what's it say? Don't bother checkin' your pocket, Slick, 'cause I got it memorized. It says *Novus Ordo Seclorum*. That's Latin, and they say it's a dead language, but we all know it's the language of the Illuminati, and it means *New... World... Order*. Look it up, and you'll see that I'm right. So who uses Latin anymore? I don't have to tell you, sittin' over there with your P.H. friggin' D. The only folks usin' Latin anymore are lawyers! So who makes up half the Congress and Senate, the guys makin' the laws and approvin' of CIA directors? Lawyers, the only guys still using the language of the Illuminati, and they got Masonic symbols on the back of our foldin' money."

He stopped there, and thrust his chin forward, but somewhere in his eyes I thought I saw a moment's confusion, as if even he had gotten lost in his own rant.

I took advantage of the moment to drop the envelope with the pictures in it on his desktop.

"What'cha got here, Slick?" he said, as he picked up the envelope. It took him a moment to flip through the photos, then he tossed them down on the table.

"Okay, I get the picture," he said, grinning at his pun. "This guy you been huntin' has figured out where you live, and he's tryin' to scare you off the case. Cain't say for sure, but these look like video captures – the image is grainy and not as well defined as you'd expect from a good SLR camera with a long lens. That means he prob'ly has a bunch more footage what's not represented here."

"Anything else?" I asked.

"Yeah, the guy don't know shit about guns. He ain't a shooter. Got the crosshairs all wrong in the drawing. If I read the papers right, though, and you know you cain't trust them worth a damn, but what I've read makes it clear he's a blade man. Likes to work in close."

"Can you keep him from getting in close?" I asked.

He gave me a look that translated roughly to something like *Is it possible that you really are that fucking stupid?*. He was kind enough, though, not to say the words. I guess he didn't want to make me look dumb in front of my main squeeze.

"You want coverage for both you and the missus?" he asked.

Merlie stiffened a bit at that. I let it go.

"Yes. I'm worried this Ripper character might try to get to me through her."

"So, why don'cha just send her off?"

"Come again?"

"Find some place far away, safe, until this thing blows over."

I could feel the vibes pinging off of Merlie like sonar. She didn't like the way this conversation was going.

"Merlie has a life, Scat. She's responsible for an entire program for needy kids. She can't just take off indefinitely."

He waved his hand in the air, as if to dismiss the idea.

"Okay, I gotcha. We need to watch over the both of you. No big deal. Twenty thousand."

"That's all?" I asked.

"A week."

"For twenty thousand, I need assurances."

"What?" he asked. "Assurances that you ain't gonna get filleted on Toulouse Street? That's easy."

"No. I need assurances that this guy keeps breathing if he shows up. I don't want him splattered."

He sat in the leather chair behind his desk and surveyed me with flat eyes that would have made a shark look almost compassionate.

"Rules of engagement?" he said. "We drawing the lines here, Slick? Gonna dictate a hard deck ol' Scat can't cross?"

"He's committed at least six murders," I said. "He has to answer for that. I'm not calling the shots here. I'm just the hired help. The cops are making the rules."

He thought about it for a minute.

At least, I *think* he was still thinking about the case. With Scat, it's sometimes hard to tell.

"Twenty thousand a week. We'll keep you alive, both of you, and this Ripper dude don't get to watch his intestines unravel before he dies. We catch him, you'll get him with his eyes open and his mouth working. Cain't promise he won't be bruised a little."

"Works for me," I said. "I'll arrange for the money to be transferred to you in the form of a cashier's check on a weekly basis."

"That's cool," he said. "Before you go, though, I wanna lay something on you. I know you don't like carrying ordnance, even if I never could cipher why. I got this piece in my desk here I want you to have, though."

He reached into the desk drawer, and pulled out a pistol.

"Smith and Wesson Model 1076. Ten millimeter automatic. A silly millimeter stronger. This hog'll stop any bad guy dead in his tracks. You get a good body shot anywhere, and the hydrostatic pressure will do the rest. It's a beast, nowhere near as user-friendly as that Browning I gave you last year, but I don't got that gun no more. I'll give you a pancake holster, too, so's you wont have to go stuffing this nut buster in your pants."

"I'd rather not, Scat…"

"Listen to me, Slick," he said, cutting me off. "Crazy knows crazy. This Ripper wouldn't know reality if it buttfucked him and called him Nancy. You confront him, and he's just as likely to run right through you like a Greyhound bus through a Toyota as he is to turn tail and run. He's already got a sweet tooth for you, judging by these pictures. Take the gun. Call it overkill if you want, but take it anyway. I'll sleep better at night."

I had a feeling that Scat wouldn't be sleeping at all, since he would likely be perched on the roof of the voodoo shop across the street from my apartment, or tailing me at a respectable distance that still fell within his considerable kill zone. I wasn't really worried about his sleep. I *was* worried about what Farley might do if he caught me strapped without a license to carry concealed.

I pushed the gun back across the desk toward Scat.

"Not this time, I'm afraid," I told him. I felt Merlie relax against my arm. She doesn't like it when I play with firearms. "I'm working with the Department on this one. They don't like their consultants walking around with undocumented hardware."

"Suit yourself," Scat said, as he stowed the pistol back in his desk drawer. "Just tryin' to do you a favor."

"You already are," I told him.

The Rampart Station was overflowing with angst as we walked in. People filing complaints lined one entire wall, and the desk bull with the bulging proboscis veins was playing ringmaster, trying to coordinate the flow into something resembling order. I bypassed it and led Merlie back to Farley's glassed-in cube.

He was sitting at his desk. It had been a busy day for him, too. He had apparently just come back into the station, hadn't even bothered to remove his Panama. He was hunched over his desk, speaking furtively into the telephone receiver, and waved us in when he glanced up and saw us in his door.

"Thanks," he said into the phone, "I'll get right on it."

He replaced the receiver. Merlie and I had already taken our seats across from him.

"That was the Fibbies' computer science unit in DC. We may have a lead on this asshole. He seems to have made a big slipup."

"Tell me," I said.

"Well, I don't completely understand it, but it concerns those pictures he uploaded to the Internet."

"The ones he routed through the data laundry in the Netherlands?"

"The very ones. This is all very sophisticated, but apparently every file uploaded to an Internet site is tagged in some way. The language used for these things, this hypertext language, includes some tricky subroutines that not everyone understands. Apparently, every computer has a code implanted in the primary microprocessor chip, a bunch of numbers and letters or something, and it's like a fingerprint. No two computers have the same code.

"Anyway, the Fibbie computer geeks tell me that they can open the file uploaded to the internet, and take it apart line by line. Somewhere in all the dits and dahs is this code. You have to be a really spectacular nerd to keep it from being implanted in your uploaded message, and our boy doesn't qualify."

"They found his code?" I asked.

"Exactly. So far, all they know is that he used an Intel Pentium 2 processor, but they're contacting the manufacturers to see just where this processor chip went after it was manufactured, and where the computer it went into was sold."

"And from there," I surmised, "they can find out who bought the computer. Damn, that's fine work."

"Give the credit to Evers. He came up with the idea."

"Clever's surfaced again?"

"He was never gone. Seems he gets melancholy over the holidays. Says he was holed up in his house, drinking Michelob and watching football games. Says he ignored the telephone when it rang."

I pulled the envelope with the pictures in it from my jacket pocket, and tossed it on his desk.

"Couldn't ask for better timing," I said. "These showed up on my doorstep this morning."

He opened the envelope and riffled through the photos.

"Shit," he said, as he laid them on the desk. "I'm sure sorry, man. I never intended for you to be targeted by this spitwad. Do you need protection?"

"It's already arranged."

He stared at me from across the desk. I could see what was going on in his head. He knew that I had been involved, however tangentially, with the New Orleans gang scene over the previous years. He probably figured I had worked out some kind of deal with the bent-nosed types to cover my six. I could also tell he didn't like it much, but I wasn't about to blow Scat Boudreaux's operation. Farley knew Scat, and he didn't like him. Scat was probably the most dangerous man in Louisiana, but to Farley he was just mayhem-in-waiting.

"Yeah," he said finally, "Whatever."

"I thought you'd want to know about these," I said, "It tells us something about our guy."

"Like what?"

"Like we were right about him. He's outside the mold for serial killers. He's smart, and he's playing us for fools. This is all wrong. He accelerates, then he pulls back, stop and go. That just doesn't fit the profile. This is the screwiest method I've ever seen. Now, he's turned the tables, and he's hunting us."

"Uh-uh," Farley said, shaking his head.

I waited for him.

"He's hunting *you*. You've done something to him, struck a nerve. Maybe it was when you went on TV and made him out to be some kind of Freudian poster boy. This Ripper wants to take it out of *your* hide."

"I'd thought about that."

"Kind of makes it personal, doesn't it?" he said.

I glanced at Merlie. She nodded.

"You're not the first person to point that out to me," I said.

He nodded, and finally pulled the panama hat off his head. He set it on the desk, on top of the offending pictures.

"Now I'm getting nervous," he said.

"You think I might get personal right back at him?"

"It seems to be your style."

"It's different this time."

"How so?"

"I'm on the inside looking out for a change. I'm working with the guys in the white hats. There's no mobster pushing my buttons. Shall I go on?"

"I get the picture. You're gonna color inside the lines."

I nodded.

"Well," he said, "I gotta tell you, that would take a huge load off my shoulders, if I thought for a second I could believe you."

TWENTY

Merlie and I got back to Holliday's around nine. I figured it would take Scat a few hours to put together our coverage, so I wanted to keep her close by until I could be certain of her safety.

When we walked into the bar, I saw Brian Templeton sitting on a stool, chatting up Clever Evers. It made my heart skip a beat. I led Merlie over to the bar, and asked Shorty for a couple of Dixies.

"I've been waiting for you," Templeton said. "Thought you'd never show up."

I nodded at Clever, and said to Templeton, "So you're harassing my regulars?"

"Oh, you mean Dr. Evers here? Hell, Dr. Gallegher, we go way back. I interviewed him when he first arrived in New Orleans, just after he retired from the FBI. You, umm, *did* know he was with the FBI, didn't you?"

I glanced past him at Evers, who shrugged his shoulders. I was, apparently, on my own.

"Of course I did. Dr. Evers and I collaborated on a case in Boston, about ten years ago."

"The Chuckie Hamrigt case?"

"Yeah, that one," I said, distracted.

"I knew that, of course. Just testing you. Imagine my surprise when I walked in and saw Dr. Evers sitting in your bar. Made me wonder whether he might be involved in this Stripper Ripper case."

"He isn't," I said.

"I'm not," Clever said, almost at the same second.

"Dr. Evers is retired," I said.

"So were you," Templeton observed.

"Let's just say that Dr. Evers isn't as big a sucker as I am," I said.

Clever hoisted his glass of beer and took a long draught.

"I just come here for the music," he said. "The FBI was a long time ago. I'm just a simple college professor now. The police wouldn't be much interested in my opinion."

"I would, though," Templeton said, and turned to me. "I was just talking with Dr. Evers about this Ripper case. I was wondering whether he had any ideas."

"Did you tell him who you were?"

"Of course."

"Did he have any ideas?"

"We were just getting to that when you and Ms. Comineau came in."

He turned back to Clever, who was munching on a pretzel. He washed it down with some beer, and cleared his throat.

"Well, as a matter of fact," Clever started, "I think I do have an idea or two about this monster who has been preying on our city's loveliest, and most available, young ladies."

Templeton pulled a hand-held memo recorder from his pocket, and placed it on the bar.

"Mind if I record this?" he asked.

"Not at all. Like I was saying, it occurs to me that you have to look at motive, means, and opportunity. The basics, you know. We know the means, and we all know there's plenty of opportunity. Right, guys?"

He playfully jabbed Templeton in the ribs. Templeton flinched slightly.

"So, that leaves motive. I learned a long time ago that there are only a few motivations strong enough to convince someone to kill another. There's money, of course. There's jealousy. Greed, need for power, need for attention. Revenge is a biggie. Some people kill just because they can, because they are incredibly sick fucks who just want to see what it feels like to blow someone away. Fortunately, there aren't many of those around.

"This Ripper guy, though, he's really interesting. Given what little I know about the case - from the newspapers and all, you understand - I'd say we're looking for a young fellow, maybe in his twenties. He's single, which gives him lots of freedom to hang out in the stripper bars. He craves attention, maybe he's in some kind of job that brings him to the attention of a lot of people, puts him in the public eye. Maybe a politician, or a movie star, but I don't think so. He also has to have something to gain from the killings. Validation, maybe, or perhaps some kind of material profit."

He took another draw from the schooner of brew, and continued.

"Now that I think of it, it appears that the folks who have gotten the most out of this case have been those in the media. They're selling papers hand over fist, selling advertising time on the TV and radio at premium prices. This has been awful good for the news folk. Now, when I was investigating murders, I'd immediately look to those folk who had gained the most from them. Right now, that looks like the media.

"What is it they call this piece of shit committing all these murders? The Stripper Ripper? I bet – and you make sure you quote me on this, young buck – I'll bet if you find whatever muckraker coined that dumbass name, you'll find the person who has gained the most from the murders. That's your man, I'll wager."

He gestured to Shorty to bring him another beer, while I watched Templeton blanch and slowly turn off the recorder.

"You were just jerking me off, weren't you?" he asked Clever.

Clever just stared at him. The stare went on for almost fifteen seconds. I waited for him to blink.

He never did.

Shorty delivered the beer Clever had ordered, and glanced back and forth at the two, staring each other down.

Finally, Templeton broke the spell. He turned back to me.

"Actually, I came here tonight to talk with you. It's been almost a week since the last killing. My editor's getting jumpy."

"In that case," I said, "I'd imagine you'd better get on the stick. There's a couple of joints over Esplanade that haven't had dancers killed yet. Want me to drive you over? You can make an early night of it."

"Knock it off," he said, but I could see him getting edgy. "I wanted to ask you if there were any new developments."

"Don't you want to turn on that little tape recorder first?" I asked.

"Do I need to?"

This kid was beginning to get on my nerves.

"No," I said. "As far as I know, there are no new developments. No deaths, no hot leads, no confessions. Nothing to report. Your editor is just going to have to suck it up."

I followed it up with my really mean look, the one that turns weak men into stone.

"Well…" he said, "just thought I'd check."

He slipped off the bar stool and straightened his jacket.

"You'll call me if anything turns up?"

"That was our agreement, Brian," I said.

"Okay, then. Well… I guess I'll go work on another story."

"You do that," Clever and I said at the same instant.

Templeton nodded at me, then at Clever, and he walked out of the bar.

I introduced Merlie to Clever, and asked Shorty for another beer. Merlie had drunk only about a quarter of hers. Despite her ravenous appetite for food, she tended to nurse her alcohol.

Merlie could tell that Clever and I wanted to talk business, and she didn't seem to have the stomach for it. She excused herself and went up to my apartment to read.

I took Clever by the arm and led him over to a table near the bandstand.

"Asshole's been taking pictures of Merlie and me," I told him. "All over the place. Even took some through my window. What do you make of that?"

"Same as you, I'd imagine. He's trying to intimidate you, scare you off the case."

"Or maybe he's playing games."

"Could be. You've noticed, I suppose, that this guy is breaking all the rules."

"And how. It's almost like he knows what we're going to do before *we* know it. You think it might be a cop?"

"Wouldn't be the first time," he replied. "You know the profiles as well as I do. Lots of these guys wanted to be cops, but washed out. Maybe this one slipped under the radar screen, made the cut. Want to guess how many bad cops there still are in this city? How many of them resent the changes made by the new chief? It works for me."

"There's a lead," I said.

He leaned forward as I told him about the computer fingerprint code.

"Shit hot," he said. "It's just a matter of time, then. Soon as they place that machine, the cops can just pick up the dude and take him in. Possession of that computer will constitute probable cause, just like owning a gun that matches a murder weapon. I checked out that Internet site after Nuckolls finally caught up with me. Pretty raunchy stuff."

"You should catch the live show. Do me a favor, okay? Don't fuck around with the press. Templeton's a kid, but he's also bright. You can dick him once or twice, but if he starts digging he's likely to figure out what's going on."

"Yeah," he said. "You're probably right. If we're lucky, though, we won't have to worry about him for long. That computer thing pans out, we could have this guy in custody by the end of the weekend."

He took another drag from the bottle of Amstel, and placed it back on the table.

"Those pictures have you rattled?" he asked.

"A little. It's covered, though. I hired someone to watch Merlie and me. Things are pretty safe now, as long as it doesn't take much time to catch this killer."

He reached across the table and chucked my arm.

"Betcha can't wait to get back to real life, huh?"

"Don't you know it. You plan to hang around for a while? I go on in an hour or so."

He sat back in his chair and grinned.

"Think Shorty has enough beer?"

I never went on stage that night.

I had been in my apartment for about a half hour, smoking one of the Cubans while Merlie was curled up on my couch. I was fingering some tricky combinations on the cornet, but didn't want to waste my smoke on blowing.

The telephone rang.

I picked it up.

"Gallegher, this is Nuckolls."

"Did you run down the computer code?"

"They're still working on that. We've got another one."

It took me a moment to register what he was saying.

"Another killing?"

"Just got the call about ten minutes ago. Looks like this dude wrapped up his Thanksgiving holiday by carving another bird."

"Where?"

"The body was found behind a dumpster at the Superdome. After the game on Friday, there was plenty of trash to cover her with. I'm going to need you on the site. Fifteen minutes. The press is going to be crawling all over the place. I need my profiler there."

"Clever is here in the bar," I said. "You want I should bring him along?"

"Too risky. He might decide to bolt, what with all the pressure. Go ahead and tell him about the murder, let him know we'll be consulting with him later on tonight. Okay?"

"Superdome," I said. "Fifteen minutes."

I hung up the phone, and started to plan what I had to do. Then I caught Merlie's eyes locked on mine.

"Another killing," I said. "Body's at the Superdome."

"Do you have to go?" she asked.

"Seems I'm locked in. I wish it had come tomorrow. By then Scat will have us covered. Tell you what, why don't I get Clever to come up here and keep you company? Soon as I hear that Scat has his troops in place, you can go home."

She wasn't in a mood to argue this time.

"You be careful," she said. "I love you."

"Love you back," I said, then I bent down to kiss her before dashing out the door.

I caught Clever sitting at the bar, shooting the shit with Shorty. The television was on, showing a Hawks game. I didn't have time to check the score as I sidled up to Clever.

"He's done it again," I said. "I have to go meet Farley at the Superdome. I have a huge favor to ask. Merlie is up in my apartment. I don't think our protection is in place yet. Would you mind going up and keeping her company until I get back?"

He nodded solemnly.

"You'll call me with the details when you have them, right?" he asked.

"The minute I know what's going on, you'll hear about it. Thanks for helping out with Merlie. I'll call later."

It was already party time on Bourbon Street so, rather than retrieve my car from Irene's and fight the cross street traffic, I dashed down to Decatur and grabbed a taxi.

It took ten minutes to cross Canal and shoot through the Garden District to the Superdome. I directed the cabbie toward the flashing blue and red lights across the parking lot.

Farley was at the scene already, along with ten or fifteen uniforms, and a suit I hadn't seen before. They were clustered around a heap on the concrete, their faces half-inked in shadows from the spill of the halogen lamps set up to illuminate the scene. Small billows of steam rose from the lamps as they turned the water vapor around them into plasma.

Farley was talking to the suit as I walked up. He kept talking, giving details on the discovery. Only when he finished did he turn to me.

"Gallegher, we got some new talent on this case. This is Truman Selden. He's with the Bureau."

"A Fed?"

Selden extended his hand.

"Dr. Gallegher. I can't tell you how grateful the Bureau is that you've agreed to work on this case. I'm just sorry Dr. Evers couldn't make it out tonight. I've been a fan of his work for a long time."

I shook his hand, and nodded in the direction of the heap.

"What do we have?" I asked.

"Same as the others," Farley answered. "A security guy in a bubbletop was cruising the lot, and saw a bunch of cats around this dumpster. Wouldn't be so unusual, but it turns out this guy's a cat freak, and he saw a coupla breeds he likes. Drew his attention. Then he saw the body lying just behind the dumpster. He had heard all about the Ripper, so he called the cops right away."

"Has the medical examiner arrived yet?"

"Get real. I only got here ten minutes ago. Let me do his work for him, though. She's dead. She was ripped. And, she was written on."

I walked over and looked down on the body. The wound was identical to the others. There was no steam rising from the entrails, so she had been there for awhile. She had probably been killed the night before. The cats had been there long before us, and it showed.

For some reason, I didn't fuzz out this time. There were no intrusive visions of Claire lying on her living room floor, or Meg on the deck of the *Mariposa*. I figured I was becoming inured to the gore.

I didn't consider this a good thing.

As with the others, there was a word written on the body of the victim.

flesh

As before, it was all in lower case letters. The word was written over her left breast, what was left of it. She had apparently had implants put in at some point. The killer had excised them. He hadn't been very careful about it.

"What's he mean, *flesh*?" Selden asked. I hadn't heard him walk up behind me. Probably used that super-secret stealth walk they teach all the grunts up at Quantico.

"It's the only thing yet that's made any sense," I said. "That's all these twists are to him. Flesh. Meat. They're his instruments."

"Come again?"

"He's using them to get to us. We keep thinking the killings are the object. They're not. The killings are the method. The object is to play us for chumps."

"That's what Dr. Evers says?"

"The hell with what Evers says. *I'm* saying it. He's giving it to us, right up the chute, just to let us know he's the dude."

Farley walked up and stood with us over the body.

"It's not a cop," I said.

"What?" Farley asked.

"Clever and I were talking about a half hour ago. He wondered whether this Ripper guy might be a cop. It isn't a cop."

"You're sure?" Farley asked.

"Empirically? No. But the feel is wrong. This guy enjoys serving it up to the cops. He's digging the feeling that he has the cops chasing their own asses."

"What about an ex-cop?" Selden asked.

"What in hell are you doing here?" I asked him.

He blinked a couple of times.

"Gallegher..." Farley said.

"No, Farley," I interrupted. "Where have the Fibbies been all this time? Now, all of a sudden, they're interested?"

"It's okay," Selden said to Farley. "He's right. It looks weird. Gallegher, it's the computer thing that brought me in. Up until now, the Bureau figured things were covered down here. The Behavioral Science Unit is stretched to the seams with Crosby gone, and they decided that Dr. Evers could handle the case for the time being. When the computer stuff broke, that made it interstate, and I was assigned. I'm on purely to help out until we catch this guy. If we can't hang the murders on him, we'll get him on pandering obscenity interstate over the Internet. You know, wire fraud. The Communications Decency Act."

"What do you mean, if you can't hang the murders on him?"

"They're covering their asses," Farley said. "like the only thing they ever got on Capone was tax evasion. It's a backup. The murders still belong to the NOPD."

"So, what about an ex-cop?" Selden repeated. "Someone who was fired, or had to take early retirement? Some guy with a beef against the department. The way this new chief's been cleaning house, there ought to be a lot of candidates."

Farley scratched at the wattle connecting his lower lip with his Adam's apple, and thought about it.

"Screw around with the department long enough, until the parish council gets sick of it and decides to can the new chief? Seems like a pretty poor motive for serial murder, doesn't it?"

"How else do you explain the way this creep stays two steps ahead of us?" Selden argued. "It's like he's getting inside information. Sounds like you have a leak somewhere, Detective."

Farley started to do the long slow burn. An outsider might not have noticed, but I had hung around him long enough to know the signs. I had also seen the fallout from one or two of his tantrums. At this point I didn't think he wanted to fight a beef for assaulting a federal employee. I took him by the arm.

"I need to discuss something with you, Farley," I said, and led him around to the other side of the dumpster.

He glared at me, strange shadows playing about his scrunched face from the halogen lights.

"One of you needed a time out," I said quietly. "I don't know Selden well enough to drag him behind a dumpster."

"Goddamned Fed jerkoff…" he started.

"It's still your case, Farley. He's just here on the computer angle. Keep telling yourself that."

He stuck his hands in his jacket pockets and bent over, taking a deep breath. It seemed to clean his head out a little. When he straightened back up he seemed better controlled.

"Okay, so it's not a cop," he said. "What else are you getting from this one?"

"Something strange. I can't put it together. You know how it is when you're right on the edge of recalling some guy's name, and it keeps flitting in and out of your head, too fast to catch?"

"Yeah," he said, nodding. "More and more, lately."

"Time and tide, man. Well, it's like that. There's something in my head that's pulled itself together, but I can't force it to the surface. The word on her. *flesh*. Soon as I saw it, I got this shiver, like it completed the puzzle."

He started counting on his fingers as he recited the words.

" '*this*; *that*; *oh*; *too*; *too* again; *solid*; and *flesh*'," he recited. "Ain't doing a thing for me, Gallegher."

"It's something I should recall," I said. "This guy's telling us something. I can feel it."

"He's telling us we're a bunch of morons running around with our thumbs up our asses, that's what he's saying."

"It's more than that. I just can't seem to dredge it up."

"So, what's that tell you about this creep? Any forensic insights?"

"Maybe if I can knock heads with Clever for an hour or two. Perhaps, between us, we can come up with something. He's at Holliday's. He was there when Merlie and I got back from your office this evening. That reporter, too. Templeton. They were sitting at the bar, talking like old friends."

Farley turned and surveyed the crime scene again. The corpse lay under the arc lights, looking smaller and lonelier by the moment. A police photographer finished shooting snapshots, and started to make videos with a portable camcorder.

Farley turned back to me.

"I don't like that," he said.

"Clever and Templeton?"

"What's goin' on there? First Selden suggests a leak in the department, and then I hear our secret profiler is chummy with a reporter."

"Clever seemed to be stringing him along. Even suggested that the police might do well to look for the guy who came up with that

Stripper Ripper name. Templeton went five shades paler. You should have seen it."

"Yeah. Maybe I should've."

"He was joking, Farley. It's not Templeton."

"Who says? This kid shows up in my office, the first scandalmonger to run down the story on these murders, and he's talking like he knows what's going on. I'm so used to these reporters hanging around the station, all of them with some kind of inside dope, I don't recognize when it doesn't fall together right."

"What do you mean?"

"Templeton. I never saw him before. I checked him out, of course, after he paid me a visit. He's been with the Times-Picayune for a coupla years. But he's been doing some kind of social beat. He's not a crime reporter, up until now. Maybe I ought to check him out again."

I let him think that one over, while I glanced back at the body again. Someone had dragged a black body bag over to the area, and had spread it out next to the dead girl. It was a perfunctory act. It would be a good hour before they'd need the bag. Suddenly, I didn't feel like hanging around.

"I'm going back to the bar," I said. "Let me talk with Clever for a while, and I'll get back with you. We'll see if, between the two of us, we can come up with something you can use."

My taxi was long gone. Farley called one of the uniformed cops over and directed him to drive me home.

It was the first time in years I had ridden in the *front* seat of a bubbletop.

TWENTY-ONE

We were almost back to the corner of Toulouse and Decatur when the radio crackled, and a dispatcher's voice came of the speaker, telling the uniform driving me that he should change to another channel to speak with Farley.

Farley's voice had that tube-like sound the cop radios impart, full of over-modulated static.

"Give me Gallegher," he said.

The uniform handed me the microphone.

"Gallegher," I said.

"Tell that guy driving you to hit the lights and make straight for *Les Jolies Blondes*," he said. "Spanky Gallo just called in. Told us Reynard spotted the guy who was in the club the night Lucy Nivens was killed. I'll meet you there…"

"We're on the way," I said, and handed the microphone back to the officer driving the car. He switched back to the original channel and barked some instructions to the dispatcher, telling the mounted cops in the Quarter to clear a path using the barricades, so we could get through to the club.

By the time we arrived in front of *Les Jolies Blondes*, two other bubbletops were already there. Another light was coming up the cross street. I figured it was Farley.

Before the cruiser was fully stopped I popped the door and hopped out, on a dead run for the entrance to the club. One of the cops at the door tried to stop me.

"I'm Gallegher," I said, "Farley told me to come."

By then, Farley's unmarked Crown Vic had stopped in front of the club.

"Let him in!" he shouted as he jumped from the car, flashing his badge. "He's with me."

Together, we entered the bar. The music was playing, but there were no strippers on the stage. Two girls in thongs and nothing else were standing with a uniform cop over Spanky Gallo, who was sitting on the floor, his back against the mahogany of the bar, holding his head between his hands.

He saw Farley and me and shook his head.

"He tried to leave," Spanky said. "I figured I could stop him."

"He hit you?" Farley asked.

"Guy's like a fuckin' Bigfoot," Spanky replied. "I grabbed his arm, and he came after me with both fists. Damn near took my head off. Guy shows up again, you'd better have a platoon or a SWAT team to take him out."

"Did you get a good look at him?" I asked.

"Big guy, about your size," he told me. "But he's blond. Not like he was born that way though. Peroxide, like Dixie here."

He pointed to one of the topless girls, whose hair had been bleached so white it was almost translucent.

"It couldn't be a wig?" I asked.

"Sure it could. It could be a fuckin' mop, for all I know. I was a little busy at the time getting the shit kicked out of me. I'd love to get that asshole in a ring with some ten-ounce gloves…"

I turned to Farley.

"You called me about three minutes ago, no more than four. How far could this guy have gone?"

Farley didn't bother answering. He belted out instructions for the uniforms in the room to fan out across Bourbon Street and the three parallel and cross streets to look for a blond me.

I bolted up the stairs to Reynard's office. He was standing, rather uncomfortably, at the one-way mirror overlooking the bar. I wondered just how often he actually left this office. It was a cinch he would take an hour getting up and down the creaky stairs.

"How long was he here, Sly?" I asked.

"Don't know," he wheezed. "One'a the girls, Keely, she came up and said she thought the guy that was here the night Lucy got squibbed was back. I came over to the window here to look. He was sitting about two rows back from the stage, watchin' the dancers, drinkin' a beer. I told her to go down and offer him a lap dance, try to keep him around long enough to call the cops. Told her to send Spanky up so I could fill him in. I guess the creep got suspicious, tried to bolt. Spanky grabbed him and the guy stomped all over him.

"Did you get a good look?"

"Only at the top of his head. You don't get much of a perspective up here. He's big, though. Real big. Bet he'd be a match for you."

"I hope it won't come to that. It was good of you to call, Sly."

He waddled over to his desk and slowly lowered himself to his loveseat.

"Gotta catch my breath," he gasped. "Damn fat. You wanna know how many diets I been on in the last thirty years, Gallegher? Even had my jaws wired back in the seventies. Think it did any good? This bar, these girls, they're all I got. Any chance I had at a real life, a home, kids, that shit, well it went out the window the day that punk slapped me in the throat wit'a beer bottle. I'd do anything to protect this place. It's the closest thing I got to security. What I did, I did to protect this place. *Good* don't got nothin' to do with it. You wanna do me a favor?"

I nodded.

"Sure, Sly."

"Go find that asshole and tie a coupla knots in his intestines for me. I'd do it myself, but I can't even get outa my own fuckin' way."

I left him to the only real home he had every known, and returned to Farley in the bar. He had made the bartender turn off the music, and had his radio on the bar. The chatter was running non-stop, with each of the beat cops combing the Quarter reporting in. The voices were different, but the word were all the same. There was no sign of the Ripper on any of the side streets.

"Maybe he holed up in a building nearby," I said.

"I thought of that," Farley said. "I called my chief to ask for clearance to do a building-to-building search. He doesn't want to concentrate that much manpower in the Quarter yet. Figures if the guy has gone to ground, he's gotta come up for air sometime. The cops in the area will keep a wide eye out for him through the night. We'll add to the daytime coverage in the morning. If he's still here, we'll get him. Why don't you go home, Gallegher? This could take a while."

"You'll call me if something turns up?"

"Yeah. I know where to find you. Get out of here. I need to monitor this chatter."

I left *Les Jolies Blondes,* walked the three blocks to Toulouse Street, hung a left, and was at Holliday's about three minutes later. Sockeye was at the spinet, mostly noodling some Tin Pan Alley stuff. The bar was about half full. I didn't bother to speak with Shorty, but rather ran up the stairs to my apartment.

It was empty.

I picked up the telephone and dialed Merlie's number. It had only been a couple of hours since I had left, but it was possible Scat had called to give her the all clear, and she had returned to her home.

The phone rang until the machine picked up.

"It's Pat," I said. "Give me a call when you get in."

I tapped the button to break the connection, and called Clever. Bunches of rings. No machine.

When I dropped the receiver back on the phone, I was acutely aware of the sensation of a boring bar pressed against the back of my neck.. Something was amiss in this situation, and I was beginning to worry. Was it possible the Ripper had left *Les Jolies Blondes* and come to my home to confront me, only to find Merlie and Clever?

I ran back down the stairs, found Shorty at the bar pulling a draft Miller into a pitcher for a gang of college kids at a nearby table.

"Where did Merlie and Clever go?" I asked.

He looked at me strangely.

"Didn't see them leave," he said. "Aren't they still upstairs?"

"Did you see anyone unusual come in over the last half hour? A big guy, maybe my size, bleached hair?"

He shook his head.

"Doesn't mean he hasn't been here. I had to take some trash out to the dumpster a while back. I was out of the bar for a few minutes. What's up?"

"The guy who killed Lucy did it again last night after the Saints game, dumped the body at the 'Dome. He showed up at Reynard's place tonight and beat up Spanky Gallo before running out. I thought he might have shown up here."

"Haven't seen anyone like that. You bet I'll keep an eye out, though. I'd love to get a piece of that son of a bitch…"

I didn't hear the rest of it, because I was busy dashing out the door.

It took me five minutes to make my way through the revelers on Toulouse Street to Irene's, where I retrieved my Pinto. I drove straight up Toulouse to Rampart, threaded the narrow boundary between the Quarter and the projects to Canal, crossed it and Poydras, and drove straight to Merlie's home.

Her house was dark when I pulled into the drive.

As soon as I stepped out of the car, a shadowy figure floated out from behind some hedges. It wasn't a man, really, but rather the suggestion of one, all dressed in flat black from head to toe, including a black ski mask. I instinctively reached back into the car for my billy, two feet of ebony dowel I had gun-drilled and filled with lead. I keep it around in case of trouble, and this guy looked like a bunch of it.

The figure saw me pull out the sap and stopped, his hands held up to show he had no visible weapon.

"It's me, Gallegher," Scat Boudreaux said. "Put that damn thing down."

He pulled the mask off. I dropped the billy back into the Pinto.

"Where's Merlie?" I asked.

"She's not with you?"

Something like a bolt of lightning flashed across my chest. If a spook like Boudreaux had missed her, she must not have come home.

"How long have you been here?" I asked.

"Not more'n ten minutes. I couldn't scare up any help for tonight, so I decided to cover her myself. Don't you know where she is?"

"I left her at my place, with…" I stopped, realizing Scat had no idea who Clever was. "With a friend. He was supposed to stay with her until I got back. When I returned, they were gone. I figured you had called to tell her it was all right to come home."

He shook his head.

"What about that place she runs?" he said.

I thought that one over.

"Come on inside," I said.

I used the key Merlie had given me to open the front door. The house felt empty, that kind of still sensation that settles over a room when nobody has been there to stir up the air molecules. The lights were off.

"Girl place," Scat said, as I reached for the telephone.

"What's that?" I said, dialing.

"This house says girl all over it. A woman lives here, all right. Can even smell her, like flowerdy stuff, lilacs and jasmine, that kind of thing. Hint of perfume. She cleans a lot."

As the phone on the other end of the line rang, I stared at him. Scat spent the first eighteen years of his life in a stilt house out in the bayous of south Louisiana. He could probably shoot before he had a good word for what he was doing, and his father had trained him in tracking and hunting fieldcraft. It was the kind of training that had served him well in Vietnam, the kind of sensory awareness that stems from the most primitive regions of our brain, the one we used to keep ourselves from becoming a meal for something bigger, toothier, and better clawed than ourselves about a hundred thousand years ago. Scat was permanently tapped into that feral sixth sense, whether he was aware of it or not. It had probably kept him – and me – alive more times than I cared to ponder.

The phone on the other end, Merlie's private line at *A Friend's Place*, was finally answered. I heard a youthful voice I didn't recognize.

"This is Pat Gallegher," I said. "Have you seen Merlie around there this evening?"

As I said it, Scat started walking around the house, probably feeling the aura coming off the furniture. I hear crazy people can do that.

"No, Mr. Gallegher. We haven't seen her. Would you like me to take a message?"

I thought about it for a moment. Unlike most people in this modern world, I didn't carry a pager or a cell phone. There were times I liked being disconnected from my fellow man, secluded and unreachable. This wasn't one of them.

"If you would, have her call me at my apartment."

I gave her the number. Even if she missed me, the machine would kick in.

As I hung up the phone, Scat echoed my next thought.

"Who's this guy you left her with?" he asked. "Might be she's with him."

I dialed Clever's telephone number again. This time it was busy.

"Do me a favor," I told Scat. "Stay here, in case she comes home. I'm going over to Clever's house. If she shows up here, let her know I'm looking for her, and she can reach me through the bar. And, if she comes home, don't walk up to her wearing that damn mask. It'll scare the crap out of her."

Scat walked out with me, and stood on the steps as I locked Merlie's door behind me. I turned left at the bottom of the steps. I don't have a clue where he went. One moment he was next to me, and the next he had vanished.

Scat does stuff like that. Spooky as hell.

It took me another fifteen minutes to negotiate the web of side and back streets to get to Clever's house without hitting the major thoroughfares. I wasn't encouraged when I drove up. His house was dark, too.

I banged on the front door and rang the doorbell a few times, without any response.

I was closer at that moment to a sense of terror than I had been in years. This Ripper asshole had been drawing a bead on Merlie and me for days, if not weeks, and how she had disappeared on the very night he was almost caught.

I lunged back into the Pinto, banging my head on the doorjamb, and burned rubber as I backed out of Clever's drive. I chirped the tires through three of the first four gears on the way back up his street.

Ten minutes later, I arrived at the Superdome. As I drove into the parking lot, I could see the brilliant white glow of the halogen lights surrounding the scene where the Ripper's latest victim was found. While I had left Farley at *Les Jolies Blondes*, it had been over an hour, and I figured he would return to the 'Dome.

As I hit the first layer of uniformed cops set up to keep out the gawkers, I rolled down the window. I was lucky. The first officer I met recognized me and waved me through. He must have radioed ahead, because I wasn't stopped again until I drove up to the crime scene.

As I had hoped, Farley's car was there, the portable bubble light mounted on the dash, sweeping the area in front of the grille with an eerie intermittent blue flash. He was sitting in the car.

Next to him in the front seat was Clever Evers.

I pulled the Pinto up next to his car and jumped from it. Clever turned to face me just as I yanked open his door. I must have looked ferocious, because he recoiled as I leaned over toward him.

"Where's Merlie?" I demanded.

"What?"

"I left you at the bar to take care of her! Where is she?"

He seemed puzzled. He looked over at Farley and then back at me.

"What in hell are you talking about, Gallegher? She's at home, where *you* told her to go."

TWENTY-TWO

I couldn't speak for a moment, because all the air had been sucked off the planet. Finally, I was able to draw a decent breath.

"Where *I* told her to go?"

"Well, yeah. We were up in your apartment, like you told us to do, and about twenty minutes after you left the telephone rang. She picked it up, said a few words, and then hung up. She told me you had called to let her know this bodyguard you hired to watch over her was at her house, and she should go there."

Things were getting all crinkly at the outer edges of my vision, as the adrenaline surged through my bloodstream. This was what real terror felt like. I couldn't pull my thoughts together.

"And you *let* her *go*?" I finally asked.

"No," he replied.

"What bodyguard?" Farley asked.

"What in hell kind of person do you think I am?" Clever asked. "I drove her home myself."

"When?"

"Who's this bodyguard?" Farley demanded.

"We got there maybe forty-five minutes after you left." He recited her address. "When we got there, the house was dark, but she said that didn't mean anything, because the guy who was looking after her wouldn't be visible."

"Who are we talking about?" Farley nearly shouted.

"Scat Boudreaux," I said.

"Boudreaux?" he said incredulously. "You mean that head case who took you and Boulware out into the bayous after Louise last spring? Do you know anyone who *isn't* certifiably insane?"

I ignored him, and turned back to Clever.

"I just spoke with him about thirty minutes ago. He had only been at Merlie's house for ten minutes or so then. I never called Merlie. Whoever she spoke with must have imitated me."

I leaned into the car.

"Merlie's gone missing, Farley. I've been to her place and Clever's. I called *A Friend's Place*. She hasn't been there all night."

"You went to my place? When?" Clever asked.

"About fifteen minutes ago. I must have just missed you. I called from Merlie's, and got a busy signal. Couldn't have been more than a half hour. Did you go into the house with her?"

"Only for a minute or two, just to make sure it was safe. I never saw anyone else there. After she was secure, I left and went home."

"How'd you wind up here?" I asked.

"Well, that's the damnedest thing," Clever said. "I was sitting at home, and someone called. Said he was a cop, working with Nuckolls here. Said it was an emergency, and I should meet him out here at the Superdome. So I drove on out. I was just telling Detective Nuckolls about it when you drove up."

"This stinks," Farley said. "Someone calls your apartment and tells Merlie to go home, says he's you, makes her *think* he's you, and she does it. Someone called Evers at his house, tells him to come out here, and identifies himself as a cop. I didn't tell anyone to call him."

I stood upright, and tried to make sense of it all. In frustration, I banged a fist on the roof of Farley's car, then leaned back down.

"Bastard's playing with us again."

He stared out the window of the car, drumming his fingers on the steering wheel. Finally, he grabbed a pen and his pad from the inside of his seersucker jacket.

"Give me all her particulars, Gallegher. I'll have dispatch put them out on the computers in the cruisers around town. At least they can keep an eye out for her."

I told him everything I could.

"Where's your Fibbie guy?" I asked.

"Went back to his office to oversee the search for the Ripper's computer. He's on the job. It's a matter of time."

That was my biggest fear.

Did Merlie have enough time?

Farley sent me back home, told me to get some sleep.

I disobeyed him.

Instead, I spent the next four hours visiting every strip bar in town, meeting with the owners. I gave them descriptions of the Ripper, asked them to pass the word to their dancers and bartenders. I gave them the telephone number in my apartment, told them to call me right after calling the police if this monster showed up.

At every stop, I also called Merlie's number. She never answered.

By five in the morning, I was wiped out. I made my way back to Holliday's, and fell into bed without undressing. The dreams that came were tightly wound and screechy. Like an endless strip of recording tape, I heard myself promising Merlie over and over that I wouldn't let her die. I saw her face, the way she would look at me when I was contemplating doing something black and bloody. Somehow, I had the feeling she would condone me disassembling this Ripper character, but I had no idea where I might find him.

I finally awoke around ten, still exhausted but no longer drowsy. I showered, shaved, and dressed in fresh clothes, before heading straight to the Rampart Station.

Farley looked like he hadn't gotten any sleep, which was probably the case. He was sitting at his desk, drinking a cup of coffee and staring off into space.

"Any word?" I asked.

"Yeah, we caught him. I just forgot to call you," he said, his voice strained and biting. I forgave him the sarcasm.

"Still no word from Merlie," I said. "I have to presume he has her."

"This is a hard question," Farley asked. "But, as a profiler, do you think he'd kill her?"

"What do you mean?"

"She doesn't exactly fit the pattern. She isn't his type of victim."

I hadn't allowed myself to think of her as dead. Somehow, in my florid imagination, she was being held somewhere by the Ripper as a sort of *Get Out of Jail Free* card.

"I don't know," I said. "I still haven't figured out what's driving this bastard. I don't know what trips his trigger. I want to believe that she's all right. Beyond that, I'm too close to speculate."

"You made the rounds of the clubs last night."

I nodded. I didn't bother asking how he knew. A cop like Farley tends to cover all the bases. He was probably right behind me all the way.

"That was good. With both of us visiting, maybe the club owners will make it a priority."

He followed this statement with a giant yawn. We sat there for several minutes, nothing left to say. The Ripper had made his play. We'd responded.

Now it was his turn again.

The telephone rang. Farley picked it up. The conversation was very short, with Farley making a lot of disapproving grunts, and then hanging up.

"Bad news," he said.

"Not another murder," I said, apprehensively, hoping it wasn't Merlie.

"No. That was Selden. He's been pulled off the case."

I sat upright, my feet stomping on the floor.

"What?"

"It's just temporary. There's this computer virus, they call it the Boogie Man. It surfaced in Kuala Lumpur about ten hours ago, and it's been spreading like wildfire through email systems worldwide. It shut down most of the computers in Washington this morning around nine. All the FBI units specializing in data analysis have been rerouted to work on it. They're trying to track down the guy who set it off. Sorry, man."

"How long does he think he's going to be on this thing?"

"No more than a day, probably. They've gotten pretty good at tracking these things down. It takes time though, and until then we're back to doing street work."

I settled back, feeling the resignation and disappointment taking over. This investigation was falling apart at the seams. I looked back at Farley, and realized he must be mirroring my own haggard self.

"You look like shit, man," I said. "This Ripper mess is going to eat you up if you don't get some rest. Go home. Sleep a few hours."

He nodded, his head lolling like a tempest-tossed ship.

"You're right. If I don't get some down time, when we do catch this asshole I won't be able to stay awake long enough to cuff him."

He stood, grabbed his seersucker and his panama hat from the stand next to his desk, and started putting them on.

"Five hours," he said. "I'll be back around four this afternoon."

He pulled a card from his jacket pocket and tossed it to me.

"My pager number. You find anything out, you call. I know you're in tight with the strip club owners. They might call you before they call me. You'll do that?"

I nodded, and stuck the card in the inside pocket of my Saints jacket.

Without a word, he walked out.

I sat there for another ten minutes, trying to decide what I should do next. Nothing came to me. I had run out of options. I had never felt so helpless in my life, and it wasn't even lunchtime.

TWENTY-THREE

I ate something for lunch somewhere in the Quarter. To this day, I can't recall what or where. It was an automatic thing, a felt need to stoke the engine. It could have been rocks and bark, for all I know.

When I got back to my apartment, around one, the light on my answering machine was flashing. My heart stopped for a second when I saw it. Perhaps it was Merlie trying to get in touch.

I hit the button.

When the cheery voice hawking timeshares in Biloxi asked me to call back to set up my free vacation, I almost ripped the machine out of the wall and tossed it out the window.

I was about ten seconds away from imploding. All my gears and shafts were grinding away at each other, and I felt like I had just had the shit kicked out of me by longshoremen with pituitary conditions. My hands shook with this barely perceptible tremor that I knew was adrenaline, too much caffeine, and the scarcely contained fury I directed toward the Ripper who was trying to destroy everything I held dear.

It was the longest afternoon of my life. I started to smoke one of the Cubans Farley had given me, but they were suddenly distasteful. I pulled one out of the humidor on my bookcase, and had actually snipped the end when I stopped and looked at it.

What had I called it at *A Friend's Place*? Forbidden fruit?

I sat in my recliner, contemplating the cigar for a long time, using it to focus my meditation on my seemingly futile life. I had been so smart and clever, forcing Farley into a corner, making him do something tacitly illegal in order to secure my services. I thought it would be cool to surprise visitors to my humble quarters over Holliday's with a whiff of the illicit stogies. I hadn't considered what I was trading my anonymity and dignity for at the time. It was my own arrogance and self-absorption that had brought me to this precipice, and once more I feared that someone else, some innocent, was going to pay the freight with her life.

I thought of all the innocents over the years, the folks who were caught up in the wake of my fatal aura, whose luck was no match for my own. Like Galen Crosby, I saw their accusatory faces in the night, coming to me in my tortured dreams, wondering why I was walking about hale and hearty, while they lay in corruption.

I had promised Merlie that she would not join them. I had sworn to her, on my love and faith, that she would be protected. If I hadn't fallen victim to my own pride and conceit, had told Farley to find himself another patsy to front for Clever Evers, she would be here with me in my three rooms, or at work at the shelter, or maybe we'd be back in the Caribbean, enjoying a little pre-Christmas vacation. She'd be just about anywhere except wherever she was, facing whatever she was facing, outside my ability to protect her.

I sat there, staring at the unlit cigar in my hands, pondering my own futility, and waiting for the telephone to ring, until the shadows crept across my meager balcony and the first neon glow from the voodoo shop across the street permeated the dusk. Then it was dark and the revelers began to parade up Toulouse Street, with me sitting in my chair, the telephone silent, and I was so consumed by despair that every breath was an effort.

It was the shittiest afternoon of my life.

The telephone rang at a quarter after seven.

"Gallegher," Farley said. He sounded out of breath. "I'll be outside Holliday's in about five minutes. Be there."

"What's happened?" I asked, almost afraid to hear the answer.

"We've got him. Selden finally identified the computer the Internet images came from. We're going over to collar him now."

I was downstairs two minutes later. Farley drove up a minute after that, the light on his dash flashing bluer than the neon of the voodoo shop sign. I clambered in alongside him in the front seat.

A thick, greasy fog had descended on the city. It didn't slow things up a bit on Bourbon Street, where you were never more than twenty feet from a bright light, but after we left the Quarter the mist closed in on us, and Farley's headlights became solid cones of wet yellow steel extending twenty yards in front of the car.

"I've already sent a cruiser to get Evers," he said. "The guy's name is Arlen Grosbard. Get this; he's a student at the university, on an educational visa from Germany. Twenty-five years old, big, blond, all the stuff we're looking for. He has an apartment on the other side of Canal Street. Want to know what happens if you draw a line from his place to each of the dump sites?"

"They're equidistant," I said. "The guy's a creature of order."

"Too bad you didn't think about that a week ago. We could have drawn lines from each site to every other site, and the point in the middle would have been ground zero."

"There are a lot of things I should have thought about a week ago. Tell me more about this son of a bitch."

"You're gonna love this. His father was some kind of neo-Nazi agitator, but they got caught on the poor side of the Berlin wall when it went up in '62. Guy like Grosbard Senior, he's only gonna stay off the Commies' radar screen for so long. Only thing the Russkies hated worse than Wall Street tycoons was Nazis. They rooted out Grosbard's dad about fifteen years ago and put him in prison. He died there, maybe five years later. Nobody knows for certain, because it wasn't official."

"One night, someone just walked up behind him and put a round in the base of his skull, that sort of thing?"

"Probably. All the family ever found out was that he was dead. So Grosbard is brought up by this real Teutonic bitch of a mother, according to reports we've gotten so far. She was abusive, neglectful, all your classic stuff. Kid had a problem with … whatcha call it when they shit their pants all the time?"

"Encopresis."

"Yeah. Well, he had a real hard time with that. So he craps in his lederhosen one night and mom goes ballistic. She grabs a pot of boiling water off the stove and tosses it at the kid. He turns, but it still hits him in the top of the head…"

"Scalding his head and killing the hair follicles," I finished.

"You got it. This blond hair we been looking for? It's a wig. Probably some kind of tribute to Dad's Aryan perfection. Anyway, we have no way of knowing what all the kid did in East Germany, but after the wall came down he was pretty busy. Nothing really horrible, no prison time, but a number of assaults, mostly beating up girlfriends, that sort of thing."

"How in hell did someone like that get a visa to study over here?"

"Slipped in under the net. Lots of accusations, like I said, but no convictions, and no prison time. His grades in school over there were almost perfect. He looked good on paper, I guess."

"You've put a lot of data together pretty quickly on this one."

"Thank Selden when you see him. I guess I underestimated how quickly a motivated Fibbie could get cooperation from foreign agencies. It's just around the corner."

We turned right, and double-parked the car in front of a string of three-story apartment buildings tossed up during the Works Progress Administration under Roosevelt. I had been inside one of them before – real plaster walls, ten foot ceilings, heavy wooden moldings. The WPA had provided needed work for thousands of carpenters, craftsmen, and masons, and these buildings were built to last.

There were several police cars parked in the area, and a group of officers and suits were milling about in front of the building. I could see Evers huddled with Selden in one small group. None of the bubbletops had their lights flashing, and everyone seemed to be speaking in low whispers inside cones of crackling, living light projected by the mercury street lamps overhead.

Farley and I walked up to Selden and Evers.

"He's not here," Selden said. "I checked with a neighbor, who told me that he heard Grosbard leave about a half hour ago. I took the liberty of securing a federal warrant to search the place on the porno beef. If you want to tag along…."

He shrugged, in a distinctly conspiratorial manner. He was telling Farley that whatever they found while working on the federal warrant would probably be admissible in the Ripper case.

Another police car turned the corner and double-parked in front of the row house. Without turning off the ignition, an officer hopped out and sprinted over to Farley, an envelope in his hand. He handed it over.

"*My* warrant," Farley told Selden, holding up the envelope. "No use taking chances, right?"

"They trained you right in the…" Selden started, but was interrupted when Farley coughed loudly. I was probably the only one present who understood. Few people besides me knew that Farley had been heavily involved in the covert services before becoming a cop. He wanted to keep it that way.

Selden caught it, too, and clammed up.

"Well," Farley said, "no time like the present. Let's do it."

He signaled the uniforms to secure the area, and the four of us trotted up the stone steps to the entryway of the apartment building. Selden banged on the manager's door. It opened almost immediately. He was expecting us.

"Special Agent Truman Selden, FBI," he announced. "This is Detective Nuckolls of the New Orleans Police Department. We both have warrants authorizing entry and search of the apartment of Mr. Arlen Grosbard. Please hand over the keys."

The manager was a scrawny, nearsighted guy wearing a Hawaiian flowered shirt and a pair of worn khakis. He probably hadn't had this much excitement since puberty, and he couldn't cooperate fast enough.

"I'll take you up there," he said.

He led us up one flight of stairs to Grosbard's apartment. As he unlocked the door, Selden reached down and grasped the key.

"That will be all, sir. We can take it from here. We'll return the key when we're finished."

The manager stood there, blinking, trying to get a glance inside the apartment. Selden blocked his view.

"Thank you," he said, more sternly this time. "I suggest you go back to your apartment now."

The manager got the message, finally, nodded a couple of times, and slowly walked back down the stairs.

Selden, Nuckolls, Evers, and I stepped out of the hallway into Grosbard's apartment.

I stopped at the doorway, taking in the view, while the other three continued across the living room.

It was amazing. Clever couldn't have described it better if he'd had a photograph. The floors, made of tongue-in-groove oak, had been refinished and waxed to a fine gloss. The furniture was all chrome and black leather, with a chrome-framed thick glass coffee table in front of the sofa. There were several art prints on the walls, all by a single neo-modern artist, and all in severe chrome frames, with white matting. The walls had been painted with a high-gloss enamel, in an ecru shade, with the trim in a high gloss white. The place was as clean as an operating room. No magazines on the coffee table. No bookcases. No etageres full of bric-a-brac. It was sterile, yet designed for living, in a way.

I opened the door to my right, which led into a bedroom. The bed was made of brass, painted white to go with the wood trim in the room, and the comforter was black, made of some shiny material. There was a closet to the left of the bed, and I opened it. Inside were two horizontal hanging poles, on two different levels. The top level was all shirts. The bottom was all pants. Ten pairs of shoes, ranging from bedroom slippers to sandals to a pair of hiking boots, were arranged by weight on a wooden rack on the floor.

"Here it is!" Selden called from the other side of the apartment.

I followed his voice, and found the other three crowded around a computer sitting on a glass topped table, in front of a chrome and black leather desk chair. Selden sat in the chair, and was booting up the computer. He took a disk from his jacket pocket and slipped it into the floppy drive.

"Decrypting program, for bypassing passwords," he explained. "If it can't do the trick, it will automatically contact the mainframe in Baton Rouge using the computer modem, and that computer will do it remotely. We should be inside his puppy in a minute or two."

Surprisingly, Grosbard had not secured his desktop on the computer, so no password was necessary. Within a minute, Selden had accessed the MY COMPUTER menu, had hit C:, then WINDOWS, and then TEMPORARY INTERNET FILES.

A screen of files flashed across the monitor, and Selden scrolled down, until he saw one he liked. He clicked on it, and the computer announced on the margin that it was generating a preview.

A second later, we stared at a thumbnail picture of Lucy Nivens, sprawled on the shell and gravel of a parking lot at the far end of Bourbon Street, and split apart from pubis to sternum.

Selden closed the file, and went back to the C: menu screen. After a minute of searching, he clicked on a file, and the computer opened a photo program. It took a minute to run, but when it grabbed the file he had clicked, we saw the same picture again.

"This is the original," he said. "It's in a format used by digital cameras. He captured it using this program, and saved it as a JPEG file, then distributed it to the internet."

He pulled a radio from his jacket pocket, and keyed the microphone.

"This is Selden. It's the right guy. I want this apartment sealed off, and a crew up here to confiscate the computer and any other evidence we run across. I want a forensics crew up here to comb the place down for any indication of blood or other physical evidence."

"Roger," said a tinny electronic voice from the radio.

"Okay, let's go find that digital camera," Selden said.

It took them fifteen minutes to find the camera. In the mean time, I sat at the computer, checking out every image file I could find. Each time I hit a key, there was a catch in my throat as I waited to see if the next dead woman had auburn hair, and wide-open, accusing violet eyes.

There were all the shots I had discovered in the envelope left on my doorstep, and a couple more of me and Merlie in bed together, shot through the window of my apartment, apparently from the roof of the building across the street, but in all of them she was alive, breathing, vibrant.

As the last image file coalesced on the screen, I remembered to breathe again. Merlie wasn't dead anywhere on the computer. It was at that moment that Farley called from the second bedroom, where they had found a Sony digital camera stowed in the bottom of the closet.

Selden walked into the living room, carrying the camera.

"No new images," he said. "Whatever is in the computer should be all the victims."

There was a knock at the door, and three burly men in jumpsuits with FBI printed in huge letters across the back trudged in with handtrucks and boxes.

"It's time to go," Selden said. "These fellows will secure the apartment and take whatever we need to a storage facility in Baton Rouge. It's just a matter of time, folks. We know who this buttwipe is now. All we have to do is wait for him to come home."

Farley's radio crackled, and a distorted voice filled the room.

"… *at the corner!*"

Suddenly, there was the chatter of a dozen voices on the radio.

"…*around the back!*"

"*Get someone in the back of the building….*"

"….*didn't we post someone there?…*"

"…*damn fog is too thick….*"

"…*deploy the cars. Cover all the surrounding streets…*"

Farley had his radio in hand by then.

"This is Detective Nuckolls. I want Sargent Mays to switch to tac six."

He jiggled a button on the radio, and the chatter disappeared. A second later, a single voice came over the handheld.

"*He almost walked into us, Detective,*" Mays said.

As they talked, I ran to the back of the apartment, where a window opened onto a fire escape at the back of the building. Half a block down, I saw a large figure walk quickly through the spill of the street light.

"I've got him," I shouted backward, and then opened the window. "I'm going down there."

"Wait, Gallegher!" Farley shouted back, but it was too late. I was already out the window and stumbling down the steel stairway to the street.

The fire escape ended at the top of the first story. There was no time to extend the ladder. I leaned over, grabbed the bottom of the first landing, and swung myself around until I was hanging from the rail. I still had to drop five feet to the sidewalk.

As soon as my feet hit the concrete, I took off in the direction I had seen Grosbard walking. The sidewalk between the overhead lamps almost disappeared in the syrupy fog. There were side streets every hundred feet. It was stupid to take off after him this way, without a clue where he was headed, but I ran on regardless. Somewhere out in the muck was the guy who knew what had happened to Merlie, and I wasn't going to depend on the police to find him.

At a cross street, I jerked my head back and forth, looking down both directions. For an instant, I made out a figure rushing under another streetlight. It was the only human I had seen in three blocks, so I took off after him.

He must have heard my running shoes padding on the concrete, because the next time I caught sight of him he was at a dead bolt.

I was a fifty year old fat man who hadn't run as much as a hundred yard dash in twenty years. It wasn't long before my chest burned and my lungs ached. If I kept this up, I'd be dead long before I caught Grosbard.

The element of chance never let it come to that. A siren shrieked in my ears, and the fog turned alternating hues of blue and red behind me, casting multiple shadows of me against the ancient brick walls of the building I was passing.

"Put your hands on your head and lie on the ground!" said an amplified voice coming from the cop car behind me.

I turned to the car and pointed at the retreating figure I imagined to be less than a block ahead of me.

"He's headed toward Canal!" I shouted. "I'm working with the police!"

"Get down now!" the voice shouted again.

I was about three seconds away from getting unjustly plugged by a very nervous patrolman who saw a shot at glory. I turned one more time and tried to divine Grosbard through the viscous mist.

I couldn't see a thing other than the long row of illuminated cones cutting through the fog.

"NOW!" the patrolman shouted.

I felt the tears of rage and frustration coursing down my cheeks, as I slowly raised my hands and clasped them into the all too familiar position on top of my head. All I could think of as I dropped to my knees was how close I had come, and how I might have blown my last chance to save Merlie.

TWENTY-FOUR

"What in hell were you thinking, taking off like that?" Farley said, as we both sat in the back seat of the cruiser which had picked me up. "We got some goddamn ripper out there, probably killed this girl not forty-eight hours ago, and all the cops know is he's some big white guy. Not only did you confuse officer Beeker here, but you damn near got yourself killed."

"I had to do something," I said.

I didn't elaborate.

Didn't need to.

"You did something, all right, you fat mick. While Beeker was busy cuffing you, Grosbard disappeared."

"He'll resurface," I said. "He has nowhere to go. You have the bus terminals, the train station, and the airport covered. His car is impounded. Unless he takes a cab or hitchhikes, he's stuck in the city. He'll turn up sooner or later."

"Yeah, well what if he decided to go out like a swinging dick, kill a few girls a day until we catch him? Didja think about that?"

"Put the officers back in the clubs. That's where he'll go, one way or another. That's where he finds his flesh."

Farley was fuming. He crossed his arms and stared out the front window of the cruiser for a moment. I could almost sense what he was thinking. I was right, and he knew it. Whether we caught Grosbard that night, or the next, was simply a matter of the luck of the draw. He was going to be caught one way or the other.

"I'm going to talk with Selden," he said finally. "You stay here. Beeker, you keep an eye on Gallegher. If he even touches the door handle, do us all a favor and shoot him."

He didn't smile when he said it. He jerked the handle on his door, and crawled out of the car. Within moments, he had disappeared into the fog.

Beeker cleared his throat, and turned to face me through the thick steel mesh separating the front and back seats.

"I'm sorry about what happened back there," he said. "The detective was right, though. I saw you running along, and I had been told to look for a big white guy..."

"A big white guy with bleached blond hair," I said.

"You were wearing a baseball cap. I didn't have time to check your hair color. You fit the description, so I stopped you. I already said I was sorry. I was just doing my job."

"Yeah, I know. Want to do me a favor?"

"What?"

"I'm really wiped out here. Why don't you check with Farley, see if it's okay for you to take me back to my apartment? I can't think of any more good I can do here."

He keyed the radio microphone, and within seconds Farley instructed him to drive me back to Holliday's. He sounded relieved to give the order.

Ten minutes later, I sat at the bar, nursing the Dixie I had fished from the ice tank.

"We had him, Shorty," I said. "I was in the fucker's apartment. I looked at his computer, rifled his closet. I was in his goddamned world, man."

He nodded. He was wearing the sad face that night. In the midst of all my own problems, not knowing whether Merlie was alive or dead, I had almost forgotten that the woman he had loved had been a victim also.

"What happens when you nab him?" he asked.

"You don't want to talk about this, Shorty."

"I want to know. They gonna fry him up at Angola?"

"I don't know. He's not a citizen. I don't know how the law treats aliens who are convicted of murder. Best guess, though?

They catch him, he gets several consecutive life sentences and rots in prison."

"They don't zag you for doing something like this?"

"Not usually. It's all hinky in that system. If you kill one guy down in the Desire, and it's premeditated, yeah, you might get to suck the green gas. You kill a hundred or so, like that guy did in Oklahoma, using a bomb, you get burned. Draw it out, though, make it look like a ritual kind of thing, and the lawyers crawl all over it, dig up a bunch of traumatic shit from your past, and the next thing you know the jury is up to their balls in mitigating factors. Most serial killers don't get the death penalty."

"Some do?"

I nodded, and took a long swig from the beer.

"Yeah, some do. Not many, though."

He shook his head, wiped the counter, and turned to look at the television screen for a moment. It was still fairly early in the evening, but it was an off night for sports. There was an old movie on the screen, something with Humphrey Bogart, but I couldn't identify it. The sound was down low, and I didn't recognize some of the other actors.

"Don't seem right," Shorty said.

Sleep was a long time coming, and when it overtook me it was a guilty slumber. I had no right to be dreaming in my own bed, when Merlie was out there, somewhere, facing god knows what. I finally settled for a nap, just enough to keep my substantial body from breaking down entirely, then rose and dressed.

My first stop was *Les Jolies Blondes*. Like most joints on Boubon Street, it was closed this early in the morning. With the tourists and revelers cozy in their plush rooms in the hotels and bed and breakfasts, it was time for the Quarter to begin its daily regeneration. Two trucks had pulled up in front of *Les Jolies Blondes*, a beer distributor and a grocery truck. The purpose of the first was obvious. I figured the second was there to deliver Reynard's breakfast.

For once, I walked into the club without being accosted by Spanky Gallo or diving into a sea of cigarette smoke and beer fumes. The overhead lights had been turned on, for the cleaning crew which would arrive shortly, and in the glare of illumination the club took on a particularly depressing shabbiness. It was like Reynard, who claimed to care about the bar the way most men do their families, to leave it to crumble in disrepair.

I found him in his office. He was sitting in his elevated loveseat, behind his desk. His head rested on the pushed up fat of his chest the way most people use a pillow, and the force of compression had multiplied his chins to an almost exponential number.

I let the door to his office slam after entering the office.

He snorted, and his head flew upright, his eyes wide open suddenly.

"Gallegher," he said.

"The downstairs could stand a coat of paint," I told him.

He stared at me.

"I didn't have anywhere else to go," I said.

He looked around.

"Me neither."

"Pretty miserable, huh?"

I pulled up a chair, and sat facing the human train wreck.

"You want something?" he asked.

"Yeah. I want that slimeball who's been running around this town slicing and dicing dancers. He's out there, waiting, looking for an opportunity. We hurt him last night, Sly. We took away his base of operations. He's running in the cold now. He won't quit just because we took over his digs."

"What makes you think he'll come back here? He was just here two nights ago."

"I don't think he'll come here. I also think the police can't find him without a lot of help. I think, if he does materialize somewhere tonight, somebody's going to have to hurt him, maybe pretty badly, to keep him in place."

"And you're here for..." he waved an inquiring hand in the air.

"I want you to get on the horn. Call Lucien Fleck, and Huey Fontine. Call them all. We're going to reassemble the network here, today. I want to know the minute anyone in any of the pussy bars even thinks the Ripper is there. I want to get there before the cops. All I need is a five minute lead."

"I thought you was working with the cops," he said.

"This is personal. He has my girl, Sly."

"The Ripper?"

"Yeah. She's disappeared. I think he's using her as some kind of shield, an insurance policy. That's why I have to get to him first."

Reynard stared at me for almost a minute, sizing up his options. Maybe he was weighing his end on the deal. For certain, if he set up the net, and it worked for me, I'd owe him.

Reynard likes to be owed.

It wouldn't hurt his prestige, either, if he was influential in bringing Grosbard down. It might help his image over at the Rampart Street Station, maybe make it easier for the cops to turn a blind eye in his direction once in awhile, when it was crucial that he not be noticed. The police in New Orleans hadn't reformed so much, that a little corruption was out of the question. There was nothing but ups for him on this one.

He finally reached for the telephone, and started dialing.

"This is going to take a while," he said.

"That's okay," I said, reaching for the doorknob. "I have some more errands to run."

I stopped next at Merlie's house. Before opening the door, I looked around, and spoke, as loudly as I dared without alerting the neighbors.

"I need you inside."

I opened the front door and stepped into the living room. I sat on the couch for a few minutes, and then walked into the kitchen to get a soda.

When I walked back into the living room, Scat Boudreaux was sitting in the easy chair next to the fireplace. He was wearing jungle fatigues, and his face was smeared with multicolored greasepaint.

"Someday," I said, "you are going to have to show me how you do that."

I thought I made out a smile from behind the camouflage paint.

"Whatcha got, Slick?" he asked.

"I don't think it's necessary for you to hang out here anymore. It looks like Merlie's been nabbed by the Ripper."

"I regret that deeply, son. I feel kinda responsible."

"You aren't. The guy's cagey, Scat. He figured out how to imitate my voice, he ran everyone around like puppets, and in the middle of the confusion he made off with my girl."

"You have a plan?"

I took a sip of the soda. It was cloyingly sweet, after so many months without drinking it, but it gave me time to think.

"Nope. Not a plan, actually. I'm just changing the strategy. It's possible I'll run across this shitheel sometime tonight. He turned Spanky Gallo into a portable speed bag the other night. That would take some doing. I might not be enough of a challenge to keep him in one place without a little help."

"You want someone to watch your six, maybe provide a little support?"

"It would help. I think you'd clean up pretty good. Why don't you go home, change clothes into something civvie, wipe that warpaint off your face, and meet me at *Les Jolies Blondes* just before nightfall?"

He was motionless for a moment, staring at me. It seemed that I had a lot of people staring lately. I wondered whether I was beginning to look a little wild-eyed and vindictive. I was actually hoping I was. It might help when I had to face down the monster.

"Thought you didn't have a plan," he said, finally.

"Not a good one."

"Not a bad one."

I nodded.

He rose to his feet, looking damned malevolent in his battle gear.

"I'll be at the club around six. This one's a freebie, Gallegher. I don't like blowing a job the way I did the other night. Just one thing I ask."

"Yeah?"

"Don't start the party without me, you hear?"

Twenty minutes later, I walked into the Rampart Street Station. Brian Templeton was lounging on a bench outside the Homicide Division cubes. He jumped up when I sauntered in through the double doors.

I was in no mood to deal with him this morning.

"Dr. Gallegher, you have a minute?" he asked.

"No," I said, as I started to walk by without even looking in his direction.

"Have you heard anything..." he started, as if he hadn't even heard me. I was in no mood to be ignored.

"Sit down, sonny," I said, as I reached out and shoved his chest. He fell back hard, settled solidly on the oak bench, and expelled this sudden, violent *oomph* sound. If I had bothered to look back, I would bet his eyes were as big and round and wide open as his mouth.

Maybe next time he'd listen to me.

I didn't look back, though. I wasn't at the station to banter with the hounds of the fourth estate.

Farley was sitting at his desk reading the paper when I walked in.

"Gallegher," he said, putting down the paper. "I'm sorry. No word yet."

"I figured," I told him. I unzipped my jacket and pulled a bundle from underneath it. I dropped it on his desk.

"What's this?"

"Open it."

He took the bundle, wrapped in two thicknesses of plastic grocery bags, and hefted it in his hands. He knew what it was without examining it.

"My thirty pieces of silver," I said, as I sat in the chair across from him.

He thought about it for a second, then shoved the bundle of cigars across the desk toward me.

"Keep 'em. You've earned them."

"It's not about that," I said. "It was a bad idea, tossing in with the cops. It was a bad idea, pretending to be someone else, just to get one over on you. The whole thing has been one big bad idea. I'm out of it."

"What do you mean?"

"Out. No longer in. Not included. When you stuffed me in a bubbletop with Beeker last night, and told him to blast away if I tried to run – like he would – you drew the lines very clearly. You don't need me anymore. You have your killer. You won't need Clever, so I'm superfluous."

"So you finished your job. Keep the stogies."

I sighed, and settled back in the chair. Farley still didn't get it.

"On Thanksgiving night, I was sitting on the front porch of *A Friend's Place*, smoking one of those. Merlie tried it, didn't think much of it. I remarked that they were forbidden fruit, and that was the allure. Nothing in my life has fit together flush since I took those cigars from you, Farley. Accepting your bribe was the catalyst that set this whole tragedy into action. If I'd done like Clever, told you to ram it, I'd still be on the sidelines. Maybe I'd have done better than you catching Grosbard. Did I tell you that Sockeye and Brucie hired me to find him? I was already on the case before you ever recruited me."

"So, what's your beef? You got to play for the *A* team."

"This is *me*, remember? I don't like to play by the rules. I've lived to see a lot of guys get dirt shoveled in their faces by keeping my own regs. When I threw in with you, I had to do things your way. It hasn't turned out well so far."

He didn't say anything. I think he was beginning to see my position, and he didn't like it much. I had been inside, knew too much, had far too many pieces of information to make him comfortable. He could see Big Bad Pat peeking out from behind the curtains.

He didn't like that much, either.

"What do you think you're going to do now?" he asked.

"What I always do. I'm going back to my playbook, working off intuition and my vast backlog of accumulated trivial knowledge. I need to get close to this Ripper asshole. I need to smell him, get his scent in my head…"

I stopped. Somewhere in the back of my mind, a little red flag popped up. As if it had been working on a problem for a long time, deep in the background of my consciousness, I had come across something critical, something that mattered, something which might save Merlie.

It was still hidden, though. My head was telling me the secret was there, but it refused to bring it out in the open. I would have to dive back there, toss a few things around, and look for it.

"And then…" Farley said.

"What?"

"You need to get the scent of him in your head, you said. Then what?"

I tried to stifle a grin. Like in the kids' game, I was warm, and getting hotter. I could feel it. Somewhere, just beyond my grasp, the Ripper stood, waiting for me to discover his secret.

"Then I'm going to run him into the ground, and I dare him to try to get back up."

TWENTY-FIVE

I should have brought earplugs.

After sitting in the upper room at *Les Jolies Blondes* for three hours, the constant tom-tom beat of the music downstairs was beginning to give me a headache. It resonated through the floor, and began to be a physical thing.

Reynard seemed immune to it. I supposed his inner ears had been burned out long ago, along with his thyroid. He sat at the window, peering down at the stage, the way a proud papa hangs about the maternity ward window. It was creepy.

I had brought along a book, Maugham's *The Razor's Edge*, and was trying to concentrate on the exploits of Larry Darrell, but every time he got around to saying something profound, it just fell into this driving rap beat that made it all seem shallow and frivolous. Finally, I tossed the book aside, too frustrated to deal with it, and let my head fall backward to rest on the back of the sofa.

This was the hard part, waiting for something to happen. I slipped my hand inside my jacket pocket and hefted the ten millimeter Smith and Wesson Scat had given me. It felt foreign and intrusive. I don't like guns. They turn the brains of even the brightest and most rational of men to pure mush just by being around. Having a gun on hand made it too easy to resort to blowing away an adversary, and right now I needed mine alive and talking. On the other hand, I had seen Grosbard's handiwork on Spanky Gallo, and the way he had sprinted effortlessly away from my decrepit carcass in the fog the night before. The German was no lightweight. If push came to shove, I wanted something substantial to shove with.

Scat had chosen to take the watch down on the bar floor, after I gave him a description of Grosbard. I tried to imagine the variety of hardware he must be carrying, but my brain fatigued at the effort. He also understood the necessity of allowing Grosbard to continue breathing, but with Scat you never know how the cards are going to be dealt. His uncle had fought and died at the Remagen Bridge and, being of French descent, he had about as much regard for Germans as he had for the VC. Scat was a double-plus soldier, even if the year in a tiger cage had done strange, frightening things to his mind, and you never knew when he might revert to the military default in which the prime directive is to kill people and break things.

The telephone rang around nine-thirty. I had drifted off on a brief cat-nap, and the jangling of the bell woke me with a start.

Reynard had returned to his desk, and picked up the receiver. He mumbled a couple of words, and then looked over at me.

"For you," he said.

I crossed the room to his desk, and took the phone from his hand.

"Gallegher?" called Grover from the other end.

"Yeah, Grover, what do you want?"

"Man, I do not be believin' this. You and Sly Reynard cooped up in that tiny office. You know, I was talkin' with Huey Fontine, and he tol' me that you was holed up over at the *Blondes*, hangin' out with Jabba da Hulk, and I tol' him, ain' no way that shit goin' down, 'cause Reynard would jus' as soon carve your fat ass into strip bacon as look at ya. But then I call up, and by god there you are."

"Yeah." I tried not to sound irritated, since Grover had helped me in the past. On the other hand, I was hoping for a call from one of the clubs, and he was keeping the line busy.

"So, accordin' to Huey, you be lookin' for this big white dude with hair like it come out of a bleach bottle, right?"

I perked up immediately.

"Right. You know anything about him, Grover?"

"This dude talk funny? Like English ain' exactly his original language?"

"Probably. He's from Germany."

"Well, I think I know this guy. He a regular wit' one of my girls."

Now he had my full attention. I could feel the pressure start to build between my ears, and I wondered if this was the way stone age men felt when they caught their first whiff of an approaching mastodon.

"You have any idea where I might find him?"

"I don' know, man. Are we talkin' about a *bidness* arrangement?"

"Grover, this guy has killed seven working girls."

"Ain' none of them mine, Doc. Now I ain' sayin' he hadn't been into a little of the rough trade, if you know what I mean, but if he out there thinnin' the herd, that just mean my stock gettin' more valuable. What he worth to you?"

"Five large," I said without even thinking.

"Ten."

"Seven, Grover. This is important."

"Then you don' mind eight. Eight, an' you can lay eyes on this superhonky tonight."

"Eight. Where can I find him?"

"Well, lessee. Right about now, I would imagine he be … oh, maybe twenty-five feet away from me."

"What!?" I almost shouted into the phone. "Where are you?"

"Damn, man, you jus' about blew out my eardrum. Take it easy. I'm over to Rusty Flank's place, *El Tequila*. You know where it be?"

I knew.

"What's he doing?"

"Well, I know what he ain't doin' and that be travelin'. He jus' lay a twenty on the bar for a four dollar beer about ten minutes ago, and he ain' pick up his change yet. Look like he kinda thinkin' about movin' in. You comin' over?"

"In about fifteen minutes. Do me a favor. If he leaves, follow him. If he goes to the can, go with him. I don't care if you have to shake it for him, you stay nearby. Promise him a frequent flyer freebee with one of your girls, if you have to. I want him there when I arrive. After I get there, you wait five minutes, and then you call Farley Nuckolls…"

"Whoa, man, the cops?"

"We want this guy alive and kicking, Grover. I just need a few minutes with him myself, before they take him in. You'll do this for me?"

There was a long pause.

"Eight large?"

"And another hundred for keeping an eye on him."

"You bring it with you?"

I was about to blow a gasket with this redbone entrepreneur.

"Grover, I do not have time to stop by a bank on the way over. I've never stiffed you before. You know I'm good for it."

"Yeah, well…. I reckon. Okay, but I wan' the money by tomorrow. Might wanta take a trip somewheres."

"Yeah, fine. We're on our way."

I zipped up the jacket, and started for the door.

"We've got him, Sly," I called back. "I'll check back in with you in a few hours, let you know when he's locked up."

"Right," Reynard said. I started out the door, but he stopped me.

"Hey, Gallegher," he said.

"What?"

"Once you know what you gotta find out from this rimjob, you do me a favor and kick the shit out of him for me, okay?"

I didn't answer, but I had a feeling I would get the opportunity to accommodate him.

I found Scat lounging in a booth near the bar, facing the front door. By arrangement earlier in the evening, he had been unmolested by the wait staff and the ever more aggressive dancers.

"He's at *El Tequila*," I said. "Guy just called, says he looks like he going to be there for a while."

"Finest kind," Scat said, a weird cast coming over his eyes. "Lock and load, podjo."

It took us a little less than fifteen minutes to wend our way through the Bourbon Street crowds to *El Tequila*, a bar near the intersection with Canal.

"You take the back door," I told Scat. "There's no way I'm going to let him make it out the front."

Without a word, he disappeared around the corner.

I walked into *El Tequila*. The last time I had been in there, it had been a raw bar called *Shucksters*. Businesses come and go quickly in the Quarter, and as soon as one goes belly up there's another waiting in the wings to take its space. The sheer foot traffic on Bourbon Street makes it one of the highest dollar per square foot pieces of real estate in the country.

Rusty Frank was the owner of a couple of bars at either end of the most popular segments of Bourbon. He also ran a lucrative side operation as a coke dealer, but those customers were all over in the projects, and he had so many layers of dealers underneath him that the organization chart made him look like the King of Amway. This bar, not surprisingly given its name, had a Mexican theme, complete with sombreros and marimbas hanging on the walls, and festively colored pinatas suspended from the ceiling. Some kind of canned fiesta music played quietly in the background, so that it wouldn't interfere with the patrons' attempts to follow the ball games on the various television screens set up in the corners.

I blinked a couple of times to adjust my eyes, and finally found Grover sitting at a table to the right of the front door. He saw me first, and by the time I recognized him he was gesturing frantically toward me.

"He still here?" I asked as I sat at the table.

"Over at the bar, man."

He pointed toward the wall opposite the front door. Near the middle of the bar, I immediately identified Grosbard, sitting hunched over, munching on some pretzels and chasing them down with the last half of what I figured was not his first tankard of beer.

"He's just been sitting there?" I asked.

"Ain't moved once. Just jerks his hand toward the bartender whenever he get near the bottom of his mug. Big, ain't he?"

He sure was. I go six and a half feet in worn socks, and I tip the scales at between 270 and 280. If it was possible, Grosbard was bigger. He had shoulders like a fullback or a tackle, and his neck just sort of disappeared between them and his head. I recalled how I had intimidated the folks I collected from when I was working for Leduc, and I understood how Grosbard got his twists to stand still while he fileted them.

"What you gonna do?" Grover asked.

I stared at Grosbard, and considered my options. Scat had the back covered, but I didn't have anyone blocking the front door. It was a sure thing that Grover wasn't going to stop Grosbard from leaving. At his heaviest, Grover couldn't have gone more than one-fifty.

It was time to find out just how badly fifty years had eroded my strength and vigor.

"Call Farley," I said.

"Now?"

"Yeah, you want his number?"

"That okay. Got it on speed dial."

I didn't bother wasting the gray matter figuring out why a redbone pimp like Grover might have a police detective's number preset on his cell phone. I just chalked it up to the fact that this was, after all, New Orleans.

As he dialed, I got up and made my way to the bar. My mouth was dry, and I could feel my heart hammering away inside my chest. With each step, I imagined myself a yard closer to Merlie.

There was an empty stool next to Grosbard. I took it. I motioned for the bartender to bring me a beer. Grosbard was watching the television screen, which was on his other side away from me, so he didn't pay any attention when I joined him.

As he watched the screen, I studied his face. I could just make out the scald burns which flowed like congealing wax underneath the back of his wig. His right ear was partly gone too, and I wondered whether he might have hearing loss from the abuse by his mother.

I tapped him on the shoulder. He turned three quarters of the way around toward me.

"Pass the pretzels?" I said.

Without looking closely at me, he grunted, and slid the bowl down the bar in my direction. The television was showing a basketball game. I didn't bother to figure out who was playing.

I was sitting to his right. I unzipped my jacket, put my hand in the left pocket, and brought it up to the small of his back, so the jacket shielded my other hand, the one holding the Smith and Wesson, from the view of the rest of the bar. I stuck the barrel of the pistol in his kidney, and cleared my throat. He had been reaching for his beer. His hand froze halfway to the bar.

"Both hands on the bar," I said, just loudly enough for him to hear.

Slowly, he raised his other hand, and laid both on the walnut molding.

"So," I said, "Before we do anything else, I want to know one thing. What have you done with her?"

He stared straight ahead, at the mirror behind the bar, and I think he saw me, really recognized me, for the first time. He was cool. I kept my eyes on his face, and I never saw panic.

"You have mistaken me with someone else," he said. It was a deep voice, but not guttural, as I had expected. It was smooth, with a cultured European accent, almost foggy, like Clint Eastwood if he had been raised in Stuttgart.

"I don't think so, Arlen."

He did start then, just a little, when I called him by his given name.

"Who are you?" he asked.

"Nice try, asshole. This is a ten millimeter cannon I have in your back. If I pull the trigger, they'll be picking pieces of your spleen out of the alley behind this place for weeks. You have about three minutes before the cops storm the place, and I want to put them to the best possible use. Now, what have you done with Merlie Comineau?"

A lot of bad things happened in the next several seconds. Some of them still keep me awake at night.

Some guy who was headed for the bathroom after too many beers stumbled as he passed our stools. He reached out and grabbed the first thing that he could to steady himself, which happened to be the jacket I was using to hide the gun. He fell, and jerked my hand from the small of Grosbard's back.

A waitress saw him fall, and started to chuckle, but then her face went flat when she saw the gun I had jammed into Grosbard's midsection.

"Oh, my God!" she said, then screamed, pointing toward the pistol.

While I tried to figure out what to do, Grosbard whipped his right hand down from the bar and grasped my wrist. It felt like the steel jaws of a bench vise closing on my arm, and he pushed the barrel of the gun down toward the floor. I reflexively pulled the trigger, and the explosion got a lot of people's attention, right away.

In a second, customers were yelling and diving under tables. Some stampeded the front door. Others just sat petrified, the color draining from their faces as quickly they were voiding their bladders.

I yanked my free hand out of the pocket of my jacket, and punched Grosbard twice, very quickly, in the face. It was like pummeling someone in a football helmet, for all the effect it had on him.

I was either going to have to shoot him, or go at it with fists and teeth. Shooting him was a bad idea, under the circumstances, so instead of hitting him in the face I concentrated on his knuckles holding my gun hand down. The first hit hurt him, I could tell. It must have, because it stung my hand like hell. The second paralyzed his fingers for a second, during which I was able to lurch my hand free.

I tossed the pistol behind the bar, and Grosbard and I both watched it skitter down to the far end when it hit the wet floor. Grosbard backed away for a second, then charged at me again.

I had both hands free this time, and I assumed the closest thing I could manage to a street fighting stance. I snapped off a quick right and caught him bringing his own hands up. It jerked his head back.

His idea of fighting was to grab me around the chest – no mean feat, considering my coat size is a fifty – and tried to bend me backwards over the bar.

"Why are you doing this?" he shouted at me.

I didn't bother answering. Instead, I kneed him in the balls, and felt his arms slacken. I kneed him again, and he let me go.

He wasn't crippled, though, as I expected him to be. He stepped back for a moment, grimacing, and I took the opportunity to drive my left fist up into his midsection, trying to give it enough follow-through to make it hurt. He gasped as all his air rushed out, and I swung down across his temple with my right fist.

Amazingly, he was only dazed. He shook his head for a second, which was about the time I heard Grover shout from the front of the bar.

"Freeze yo' kraut ass, dickweed!"

From somewhere, Grover had produced a long-barrelled Ruger revolver, with a pearl grip, and had it trained on Grosbard.

A second later, two cops rushed in the front door of the bar, saw Grover drawing down on us, and drew down on him.

"Drop the gun!" one of them yelled.

Grover, conditioned by years of rousting by the police, immediately obeyed, and threw both hands up in the air.

"It's the Ripper!" he yelled, pointing toward us.

There was a single moment of confusion, just enough for Grosbard to take advantage, and he turned and dashed for the back door.

"Wait!" I shouted.

It was too late. He was out the door before I could warn him. Seconds later, I heard two quick, barking whipcracks, and I knew immediately what had happened.

Before the cops could decide to make me a target, I followed Grosbard out the back door. Scat was standing to the right in a shooter's crouch, the barrel of his Browning nine smoking just a bit.

I turned to the left. Grosbard was on the ground, on his knees, bent over with his palms flat on the pavement. Blood streamed from his mouth and nose, pooled under his face, and reflected the lights from the overhead streetlamps.

"I aimed low, Slick," Scat said. "Got him in the ass with the first one, but he twirled while the second was in the air. I think I lunged 'im."

I could hear the cops running toward the back door, their heavy rubber soles clomping on the linoleum of the bar floor.

"Run," I told Scat. "Just go. Get the hell out of here."

I turned back to Grosbard for a second, then toward Scat.

He had disappeared again, the way he does. There was nothing left of him but a faint, small cloud of smoke from his pistol.

I started jogging toward Grosbard just as the cops jumped out the back door.

"Call an ambulance!" I shouted, even as I saw one of them finger the radio microphone on his shoulder. I pointed at Grosbard. "That's the Stripper Ripper!"

One of the cops, the one not calling for help, tried to stop me, but I jerked free and ran to Grosbard, who still knelt in the alley, as if praying.

I dropped to my knees in front of him, and grabbed his face, pulling it up to face mine.

"Where is she?" I pleaded.

He didn't say anything. His eyes focused on a point at infinity, and began to glaze over. I had seen the look before.

"For the love of God!" I cried. "Tell me where she is!"

His eyes rolled upward, and he coughed just once, spraying my jacket with blood, before he collapsed in a heap, finally stopping as he rolled over on his side.

There was blood everywhere, on my hands, on my jacket, even on the knees of my trousers. The only chance I had to find Merlie was flooding out of him in cascades, and I could do nothing to stop it.

"Where's that goddamn ambulance?" I screamed at the cops.

TWENTY-SIX

Farley Nuckolls stared at me.

He didn't say a word. He didn't glare. He didn't scowl. He just stared, as if he couldn't believe what he saw.

We were sitting in a private waiting room just outside the operating room where Grosbard was in surgery. I must have looked grotesque. I had dried blood on my jacket and shirt, smears of it on my pants leg. I thought I could feel some congealed spots in my wiry, graying hair, but that might have been guilty conscience, and I didn't have the strength or the motivation to remedy it.

Grosbard had been in surgery for two hours. Scat had been right. The second bullet apparently entered about three inches below his right armpit, and had made two efficient holes in Grosbard's right lung before blowing out two of his left ribs on its way to Canal Street. It had missed his heart by about the thickness of a fingernail. As it was, it did crease the pericardium, the sac around the heart, which had begun to fill with blood.

The biggest worry, though, was the amount of time it took the ambulance to get to the rear of *El Tequila* to pick Grosbard up. In that time, he had lost a lot of blood, and may have experienced some brain damage. It would be fitting, considering the way I had gone cowboy with the Ripper, if he lost the brain cells that knew where he had stashed Merlie.

Fitting, and tragic.

I had a hard time meeting Farley's staring eyes. I had a very good idea what he was thinking.

He had a real problem on his hands. His very public profiler had confronted the Stripper Ripper in a bar on Bourbon Street, and had been seen poking a big bad automatic in Grosbard's kidney by only fifty people, more or less. Seconds later, Grosbard was lying in an alley behind that same bar, perhaps dying of a sucking chest wound.

I should mention here, just in passing, that the gun I had stuck in Grosbard's side had not been found. Apparently, after I told Scat to beat it, he had doubled back, knowing the bar would be empty, and had retrieved the Smith and Wesson.

Farley had a major league public relations dilemma. The easiest solution would be to tell the press that I had quit working with the police and had struck out on my own to find Grosbard. Under the circumstances, however, he knew I would be the benefactor of public sympathy, when it became known that Grosbard had stolen away with my sweetie. He could decide to continue the cover story, that I was working with the police. Then he had to explain how, not being a real cop, I had come to be in a public place sticking a roscoe into the Stripper Ripper's shortribs.

As if he had been reading my mind, Farley let out a long sigh, and shook his head.

"You son of a bitch," he said.

There was nothing I could say to that. I just nodded.

"Give me one good reason," he said. "Just one reason why I shouldn't raid *Semper Fi*, find the firearm your nutcase soldier boy used on Grosbard."

I didn't bother telling him what he already knew, that by now Scat's gun was lying on the bottom of the Mississippi, already covered with two or three inches of silt, along with the Smith and Wesson. I hadn't told him who shot Grosbard, but I suppose it wasn't hard to figure it out.

He got up, walked over to me, and sat close. His voice dropped to a whisper, but there was malice in it I had never heard from him.

"Now listen to me, asshole. I'm going to say this to you once. Against my better judgment, I'm going to pull your dick out of the fire. The thing saving you at this point is that the slug the doctor pulled out of Grosbard's pelvis is a nine millimeter, and the cops who walked into that bar were carrying nines. Right now, the Chief is drawing straws to decide which one of them is going to go on administrative leave and become a citywide hero for nailing the Stripper Ripper. The cover story is going to be that the gun you held on Grosbard was his own. You took it from him while he wasn't looking. You were using it to hold him until the police could contain the situation. Say it back to me."

"The gun was Grosbard's. I took it away from him, and I was holding him in place until the police arrived," I repeated, a little annoyed, but more relieved that I wasn't going to hang on this deal.

"Your pimp pal walks on this one too. He comes off as just a concerned citizen who stepped in until the police could take over.

"You and I both know that nobody will ever find the gun Boudreaux used to shoot Grosbard, and nobody saw him anywhere near that bar tonight. I want you to understand all of this for a reason. For the first time since I became a cop, I am doing something sneaky, underhanded, illegal, and corrupt. I want you to empathize a little bit with my situation. I have to live with this. I have to toss and turn in my bed for the next month rationalizing this decision. I don't like losing sleep, Gallegher. I *really* don't like it. Somehow, I am going to find a way to take that out of your hide."

Again, there was nothing I could say. I nodded again. In another time, I might have said something witty or caustic. Right at that moment, though, I was still unable to think clearly.

He got up and walked back to his own chair.

I sat through another half hour of staring.

Around two in the morning, a bleary-eyed surgeon wearing surgical greens stepped into the waiting room. He sat in one of the chairs, and ran a neatly manicured hand through his wavy salt and pepper hair.

"Okay, we repaired the lung after doing a lobectomy. That bullet did a ton of vascular damage, and it was better in the long run to cut out the damaged tissue rather than chance emboli later on. We had to remove one of the ribs, because it was shattered beyond repair. The pericardium is okay. He's going to need a hip replacement, but that can wait."

"What about brain damage?" I asked.

"He lost a lot of blood," the surgeon continued. "We put two units in before he even got on the table, and he was still almost a quart low. He was unconscious when he came in, and never woke up before we put him under for the surgery."

He looked up, into my pleading eyes.

"Your guess is as good as mine at this point," he said, finally. "The anesthetic should wear off in the next half hour. We'll see then if he wakes up. If not, we'll try an EEG, maybe do a CAT scan, see if there is any necrosis – tissue death – inside his head."

Farley spoke up.

"If he wakes up, and he's not gorped, how soon could we talk with him?"

"Well, he's going to be pretty groggy, and he's going to hurt like hell. Between the injuries and the drugs we're going to be giving him to cut the pain, I don't know how conversant he's going to be."

"He's going to live," I said.

He nodded.

"Yeah, he's out of danger for now. There's nothing going on at this time that's likely to kill him." He paused. "This guy really was this Stripper Ripper that's been all over the papers?"

I started to answer, but Farley cut me off.

"That's why we want to talk with him, Doctor. Will you do me a favor and let me know when he wakes up?"

The surgeon glanced back and forth at us for a moment. Maybe he could feel the electricity coursing between Farley and me, perceive the tautness of the atmosphere, stretched as tensely as the high 'E' string on a blues player's archtop. There was something in the room that bothered him deeply. He got up and headed for the door.

"You're welcome to stay here and wait for him to wake up," he said, just before leaving. "Someone will come and get you if Mr. Grosbard regains consciousness."

We waited all night. Around daybreak, I told Farley I was going down to the cafeteria for some coffee and maybe a little food. I asked him if he wanted anything. He just shook his head.

When I returned, about fifteen minutes later, Farley was gone.

I dashed out to the nurse's station.

"The police detective," I asked the man behind the desk. "Where did he go?"

The nurse looked up at me for just a second, then back down at the chart he was writing.

"Doctor took him down to Recovery Four," he said, pointing down the hall with his pen.

I jogged in the direction he had pointed until I saw a set of double doors labeled *Surgical Recovery*. I pushed through them, and found myself in a round room, dominated by a circular desk in its center, staffed with intense-looking medical folk.

"Number Four?" I asked one of them.

"You shouldn't be in here," she said, stiffening as she saw the dried blood on my clothes.

"I'm with Detective Nuckolls," I said.

She gave me a skeptical once-over, then pointed behind her.

"If the detective tells me you need to go, I'm calling security," she said.

I was already walking away before she finished the sentence.

Each of the recovery rooms was a self-contained intensive care unit, maybe ten feet square, with glass doors. By the time I joined Grosbard and Farley in Recovery Four, it was pretty crowded. The surgeon who had visited us in the wee hours of the morning was there, monitoring the lights and gauges on a machine trailing dozens of wires under the sheet covering Grosbard on the bed. I could see the top two inches of the gauze pad that covered the incision in his chest. It was already discolored by drainage.

As I walked in, Grosbard was talking, weakly, in a lightly accented but otherwise fluent English.

"...sorry, but I don't recall anything after that."

"Nothing from last night," Farley said.

"Like I said, the last thing I remember is walking up on the police cars in front of my building. I knew why they were there. I knew what would happen if they found me. So, I turned and walked away."

He seemed to notice me for the first time.

"I know you," he said, but I could tell he had a hard time fixing my face.

Farley turned to me.

"Dr. Gallegher is working with the police. You might have seen him on television."

Grosbard nodded.

"Ah, yes. The profiler."

"If you don't mind," Farley said, "I'd like to go over this once more. You know, to get the details straight."

"You wish to find out if I change my story, yes? To try to -- what is it?-- trip me up?"

Farley looked back at me.

"*NYPD Blue*," Grosbard said. "Great show. I watch it every week."

"Well, okay," Farley said. "So we're trying to trip you up. Start with the night a week ago when you made your discovery."

He stared up at the ceiling, and licked his lips. He began to recite the tale again, the one I had missed while eating.

"I was installing a new program on my computer, behavioral statistics. The machine told me it did not have enough memory to complete the installation. So, I started cleaning out the hard drive. It's nothing. It happens all the time. I found a folder, though, which had been hidden inside another folder. When I opened it, there were photographs – awful, horrible photographs...."

He stopped, looked at me again.

"You were in some of them, profiler."

Farley looked back at me.

"You and a woman. She is very beautiful, for an older lady."

He shook his head.

"The other pictures, though, I knew immediately what they were. I could not imagine how they had gotten on my computer. I checked the properties, and discovered they were all made with a digital camera, then downloaded onto my computer."

"What did you do then?" Farley asked.

"I stopped deleting files. I knew someone had tampered with my machine. I went to a friend in the computer department at the university. I told him what had happened, and he came over to my apartment. He found the other files, the ones in the Temporary Internet folder."

"You have an internet account?" Farley asked.

"*Ja*...yes," he said. "My friend, the one I asked to help, he used my account to find the newsgroup where the pictures were located. When he tried to download one of them, he was informed by the computer that he had already downloaded it. He told me that this meant whoever had placed these pictures on the computer had done it using my own account."

"Meaning," Farley interjected, "that someone broke into your apartment while you weren't there, installed pictures from a digital camera onto your computer, accessed your internet account using your secret password, went to this newsgroup, and uploaded the pictures. Then he downloaded them again, so that they would be placed in your Temporary folder?"

"That is what my friend said."

Farley turned to me.

"I have the friend's name. I radioed Selden. He's already checking it out."

He turned back to Grosbard.

"So, what did you think was happening?"

Grosbard rolled his head to the side. A tear seemed to form at the corner of his eye.

"I have done bad things, Detective," he said. "I have had bad things done to me. My head..." he reached up and ran a hand across the rubbery scar tissue. "I have had a problem with anger, with rage. I have hurt people. I know this. I knew it was wrong when I was doing it. I have been in therapy. I have taken medication. I have worked *hard*. Someone knew. Someone, whoever is actually killing these girls, found out about me, and decided to use me to cover up his crimes.

"As soon as I figured this out, I started trying to find out who could have done this. I spent the last several days talking with everyone I know, everyone who might have been able to get into my apartment. I was no closer to an answer on the night I saw the police outside my building than I had been when I started. The rest, after that, I cannot remember."

"One more question," I said.

Both Farley and Grosbard looked up at me.

"You go to strip clubs?"

Grosbard nodded.

"You like the girls?"

Grosbard nodded again.

"They are easy," he said. "I am…disfigured. Most women do not want to be around me. They are…disgusted by my appearance without my wig. The girls in the strip clubs, they don't mind. As long as I have money, they ignore everything else. I know they aren't sincere. I don't care. For a moment, I can pretend they like me, just as they do."

"Where were you between November twenty-third and November twenty-ninth?" I asked.

"That was Thanksgiving Break, from college," he said. "I took my car, and drove to Florida. I stayed at a hotel in Daytona Beach. I can prove that."

"I know you can," I said. "That's the period during which the Ripper didn't kill anyone."

Grosbard became tired soon afterward, and the doctor made Farley and me leave the recovery room.

Farley's anger at me had subsided. He was on the trail, now, and nothing mattered other than the hunt.

"What do you make of it?" he asked, as we walked out of the hospital.

"This guy's been playing us for idiots the whole way. He's been two steps ahead since the day you brought me on the case. Who's to say he didn't expect to get caught at some point? Maybe he built in this little setup to make us think he had been framed. I don't doubt for a second that Selden will confirm the story about the friend in the computer department. It won't take ten minutes to confirm the story about the hotel in Daytona beach. I'll even bet that when you check Grosbard's apartment, you'll find evidence that the lock was jimmied."

"Your point?"

"Grosbard's not off the hook yet. As smart as this Ripper guy has been so far, this could be just another way of twisting us around, make us feel sympathetic for our prime suspect."

"Give me an alternative."

I thought for a moment.

"He's telling the truth. Everything he said was absolutely righteous."

"That would mean the real guy is still out there somewhere."

We walked toward the parking lot. I didn't have a way home. Farley offered me a ride. He didn't talk a lot on the way back to Holliday's. Rather than park in the front, on Toulouse, he took Decatur to the alley, and parked behind the bar. As I started to leave the car, he reached over and grabbed my arm. His gnarled fingers felt like rake tines digging into my bicep.

"I don't like the idea that this guy might still be running loose," he said. "What's worse, I don't like the idea that the wrong guy might be lying in a hospital bed with three quarters of the lungs he had yesterday, because the Ripper made us jump through hoops again. I gotta know something, Gallegher. Can I trust you?"

"What do you mean?"

"You're either in or out on this thing. If you're in, I want you playing on my team, by my rules. If you're out, I want you *really* out."

"How can I be out?" I asked. "How in hell do you expect me to sit on the sidelines while Merlie is missing? For all I know, Grosbard is lying in that hospital bed, his head just overflowing with knowledge about where she is."

"Then you're in."

"What do you think?"

He nodded, and let go of my arm.

"You're in," he said, "then I expect you to let me know what you're doing. You think you know something, you make sure I know it too, before you start tearing bars apart. I gotta be in the loop from here on in. I'll keep you informed, but it's gotta go both ways. Understand?"

"Sure, Farley. I understand."

"No, I don't think you do. I mean this, Gallegher. If you do anything that fucks this case up any worse than it already is, I'll have your ass in the lockup so fast you won't have time to draw your balls up."

His eyes burned into mine. This was his last warning, and he wanted to make it stick.

"Okay," I said. "All right. Both ways. You tell me, and I'll tell you."

"All right then," he said. He put both hands on the wheel, and stared out the front window. "We understand each other. Go on upstairs and get cleaned up."

TWENTY-SEVEN

I showered for half an hour, and still didn't feel clean.

When I got out, I tossed the clothes I had worn the night before in the trash. Maybe I could have gotten the bloodstains out, but their ghosts would always be there.

I couldn't get rid of the persistent feeling of guilt that fell over me. Part of me wanted Grosbard to be the Ripper. That would make it all so easy. Everything would fall into place.

The guy we were looking for, though, had proven he was smart enough to make New Orleans' Finest chase their asses for over a month. That being the case, he was also probably smart enough to lead us down yet one more intricately constructed blind alley.

What really frightened me, when I considered the possibility that Grosbard had been framed, was what might have happened if Scat hadn't pulled his shots in the alley behind *El Tequila*. Scat was trained to kill, and he's very, very good at it. It took a lot of discipline for him to aim low. If his conditioning had kicked in, I might be sitting in my apartment with a dead suspect on my hands, and no way whatsoever of finding Merlie.

I slept until noon, just a nap really, but the dreams that intruded kept me from resting comfortably.

They come to you in your dreams, all the people you've sent across. Some I dispatched myself, others were mere passengers on my tragic trolley who got caught up in the heat of the moment and lost everything. They didn't go away, though. They still lived in the world of my dreams, and every once in a while they liked to come out and deliver one righteous ass-kicking.

Sleep being impossible, I got up, and tried to read. That was a bust also. I would scan the page, but the words wouldn't stick to my eyes. I found myself just turning pages, while my mind was stuck rolling the problem of Grosbard and the Ripper over and over, looking for a flaw in the crystalline structure of his story.

Around three, I went downstairs. The bar was empty. Shorty wouldn't come in for hours. I grabbed a Dixie from the cooler, and switched on the television over the bar. I wasn't really interested in watching, but I sure didn't want to sit drinking in the silence of Holliday's. I used the remote to casually flip from channel to channel, watching only as long as my mind didn't wander, which for the most part took only a minute or so.

I landed on a classic movie channel. They were showing one of the film versions of *Hamlet*, the one with Olivier. I recalled, from my reading, that Olivier had made this one just after his version of *Henry V*, as part of the war effort during The Big One, to help keep the British public enthusiastic, and maybe help them ignore the insistent whine of the buzz bombs which strafed London daily.

I settled back and watched the guards run scared from the Ghost of Hamlet's Father, just before Olivier made his appearance.

Five minutes later, I had dashed back up to my apartment, and was frantically dialing the telephone.

Farley answered at the other end.

"This is Gallegher," I said.

"Yeah?"

"I need you to do something for me."

"You're running a little shy on favors right now."

"This is important. The girls that were murdered. When we first discussed them, you didn't give them to me in order. I need to know which of them was killed first."

"Oh, that's easy. I have them memorized. The first one was the girl from *Pink Snapperz*, Cathy Heidenreich."

"And the word written on her?"

"*oh*."

"That's what I thought. I've figured it out, Farley."

"What?"

"I know what the Ripper is trying to say."

"Lay it on me."

I did.

Farley listened, then was quiet for several moments.

"I don't know what to do with that," he said. "That's out of my league."

"Would you mind if I took it to Clever? Try it out on him?"

"You tossing in on this again, Gallegher?"

"Let's say I'm following your directions. Let's say I've found out something, and I'm sharing it with the police."

"You wanta take this to Evers?"

"I can run it by him, and get back with you in a couple of hours."

"Maybe I oughta go with you."

"You want to pick me up? I can be ready in five minutes."

He seemed to bounce the idea around in his head for a minute.

"No, that's okay. You get back with me as soon as you finish with Evers, understand?"

I assured him that I would.

I retrieved my Pinto from the lot in back of Irene's, and drove over to Evers' house. It took two rings for him to come to the door. He squinted as he opened it up, and the daylight poured in from his western exposure.

"What do you want, Gallegher?"

"You heard about Grosbard?" I asked.

"Yeah, Nuckolls called me this morning."

"Well, I have some new information. I want to run it by you, see what you think."

"Okay, come on in."

He opened the door wider, and I followed him into the room. It was dark and dingy, and it looked like an untended man's home, with magazines scattered around on the tables, all of which sported several circular water marks from wet glasses left to stand too long.

There was something else, though. I couldn't define it right away, but I felt the all-too-familiar tension building between my temples. Something was out of kilter.

"Want a beer?" he asked.

"Not right this moment. Farley and I interviewed Grosbard this morning."

Clever disappeared into the kitchen, leaving me standing in the living room. I looked around while he rummaged through the refrigerator for a brew, and my eyes fell on his ornate, nineteenth century rolltop desk, piled high with papers, bills, and a single book.

Suddenly, I couldn't breathe.

"Yeah," Clever said, returning with an open bottle of Michelob. "He told me. Says that Grosbard is claiming he was set up. What do you think?"

"I tend to agree with him," I said.

"Grosbard?"

"Yeah. He seemed pretty sincere." I could hear the distance in my own voice, the detachment that I needed to pull all the snippets of information together and make a complete picture.

Evers surveyed me, waiting for more. I wasn't going to deliver. Not yet.

"Well, then, that must make you feel pretty bad, shooting him all up like that."

"I didn't shoot him, Clever."

"Yeah, I think Nuckolls did mention you had some help. That guy who was supposed to look after Ms. Comineau."

I couldn't sit down. Instead, I leaned against the wall next to the rolltop.

"There's more," I said.

"New information?"

"Yeah. I've figured out what the Ripper is writing on the victims."

"Do tell."

"Oh yes. I was confused by the word order. When Farley first presented it to me, he got the first three girls backward. Maybe it was my fault, working backward the way I was, trying to establish the decreasing frequency of the murders. When I got them in the right order, it went like this. *Oh – that – this – too – too – solid – flesh.*"

"Sounds familiar," Clever said.

"It's Shakespeare. *Hamlet*, Act 1, Scene 2. I looked it up in my library. The entire quote goes like this: *Oh, that this too too solid flesh would melt. Thaw and resolve itself into a dew...*

"Yes, I know it," Evers said. "*...or that the Everlasting had not fixed his canon against self-slaughter. O God, O God. How weary, stale, flat, and unprofitable, seem to me all the uses of this world.* I'd hoped they'd catch on earlier, make a big deal in the press about the Bard Butcher or something, but no such luck. I know *Stripper Ripper* is lurid and sells a lot of papers, but it's just not *me*, you know? It's terribly poignant, don't you think?"

"It is. Where's Merlie, Clever? Where have you taken her?"

He crossed his arms and stared at me. I waited for him to respond. It was a long wait.

"What gave me away?" he said, finally.

"Lots of things. On the first day I came here, I called Farley, who told me that the most recent victim had the word *too* written on her. I thought he meant the number, and I said so, but he corrected me. You couldn't know that, but you immediately started making anagrams with six letters -- not including *W*. I was suspicious when I realized it later, but I decided you were just lucky. It never occurred to me that you knew the word was *too,* because *you wrote it on her.*"

"Yeah," he said, "I thought of the same thing later. I figured you just missed it. My bad."

"Grosberg looked really good. I mean, he looked so sweet for this thing, but under interrogation our case started to break up. There was something else, something Scat Boudreaux noticed, but I had started to take for granted. When we went to Merlie's house, he noticed the smells, her perfume. I just realized that I didn't smell her at Grosbard's place. I did smell her here, though, when I walked in. It just took me a few minutes to figure it out. What finally sewed it up for me, though, was this..."

I picked up a book from the desk.

"*The Sun Also Rises*," I said. "Want to bet I can tell you what's written on the inside cover? How about *Ex Libris, Laurence Beaudry?*"

I opened the book and checked.

"Sure enough. You couldn't know it, Clever, but this book belongs to me. I bought it as a first edition at an estate sale over in the Garden District. I lent it to Merlie several weeks ago. You told me that you took Merlie home from the bar after she got a telephone call, without coming here. Yet, my book, which was in her possession, winds up on your desk. You killed those girls, didn't you?"

He sat in an overstuffed wing chair and gave me this conspiratorial smile.

"Of course I did. What are you going to do about it?"

"How did you set up Grosbard?"

He shrugged his shoulders, smirking just a little.

"That was easy. The college knew all about his problems in Germany. They were worried he might come over and start bouncing American coeds around the way he did in Berlin. They asked me to check him out – all my FBI credentials and contacts and all that. He was perfect. I assured them that he would be all right, that he had benefited from treatment over there. You know the funny thing? I was right. He's been very well behaved since getting off the plane. He had this one weakness, though."

"Strippers."

"Precisely. He couldn't stay away from the coozies. He had to get his fix, take a nightly lap dance. Guy his size stands out in a crowd. Old black fart like me, hell, I might as well be invisible. So I'd follow him at night, watch which girl he chose to do him up nice, and then I'd take her for a round myself. I flashed money, lots of it. It's the world's most perfect aphrodisiac, you know. They took the bait every time. All I had to do was pull them into the boat, and gut 'em."

"You took the pictures, put them on the Internet?"

"Nice touch, wasn't it? You learn a lot in the Bureau, my friend, including how to pick a lock. Yeah, I took those pictures. About three days before Thanksgiving, I waited until Grosbard was in class, and I broke into his apartment. That agent, Selden, had a disk with him to override passwords, remember?"

"You have one, too."

"Well, of course I do. It took me about a half hour to install the pictures from the digital camera onto the hard drive of Grosbard's computer and upload them to the newsgroups. Then I downloaded them again, just to make certain they were in the Temporary file. I hid the camera, just well enough so he wouldn't be likely to find it before the police figured out about the hidden codes, and then I… well, I went to lunch."

He chuckled at the nonchalance of chowing down so soon after setting up an innocent man to take the rap for a string of murders.

"Where's Merlie? What have you done with her?"

"You think I killed her, too."

"Don't play games with me," I said, feeling the color rise in my face.

"But that's the point, isn't it?" he said. "I've been playing games with all of you, and it's not over yet."

"Is she alive?"

He made a show of checking his nails, then shoved his hands into his jacket pocket.

"Yes," he said at last. "She wouldn't be worth much to me dead."

"Where is she?"

"She's safe," he said. "In fact, she's extremely comfortable. I sent her away, Gallegher. Remember when I told you that she had received a call asking me to take her to her home, that the person who was supposed to watch her was in place? I used the telephone in the bar, and paged myself. When the pager went off, I called my house, and pretended to be speaking with you. I told Merlie that her protector had been discovered and killed by the Ripper, and that you had instructed me to get her out of town. I brought her here.

"You'd have loved the act I put on, pretending to call in favors from various government agencies, working the telephone like a siding salesman. I made arrangements for her to go somewhere safe. I told her that you had said she shouldn't try to contact you, that the Ripper might be monitoring telephone calls. She bought all of it, every word. That is one trusting woman you have there."

I reached down and grabbed him by the lapels and pulled him up to within inches of my face.

"You think hiding her away is going to keep me from tearing you apart?"

Again, he put on this sublime grin.

"I was kind of hoping it would provoke you."

The room started to spin. Nothing was making sense. I let him loose and staggered back. I pulled the chair away from the desk, and sat down, trying to make it all work.

"The quote. It's about wanting to die. You weren't making a statement about the girls. It's you. *You* want to die."

"Do you know how many times I tried to commit suicide?" he asked.

"Only that you did."

"Six times," he said. "I slit my wrists, took pills, even tried to hang myself once. Galen Crosby had it easy. He had the guts to pull the trigger and the good luck to make it work the first time. I never could get it to go. I chickened out each time. Pretty stupid, huh?"

"I'm willing to give you another chance."

"It's no use. I just can't do it. I considered suicide by cop -- you know, take some people hostage, wait until the SWAT team shows up, then come out blasting, like Butch and Sundance, but that just wasn't my *style*, man."

"You wanted to make the police work for it."

"What did I do for twenty years? I chased monsters. Nobody knew more about them than I did. Hell, who gives two damn cents about someone like Dahmer or Gacy or... Crazy Ed Hix, for example. You can relate to that one. Scoot 'em off the planet and plant a tree where they last stood, s'far as I'm concerned. You ever heard the saying, '*play golf for a thousand years, and nobody calls you a golfer, but suck one cock, and you're a cocksucker forever*'."

"When you did the profile that helped send Larry Bondurant to the electric chair in Florida, you lost the magic. You thought everyone would see you as fallible, and nothing about that was going to change. So you decided to switch teams, and take the playbook with you. You engineered this whole string of murders just to taunt the police?"

"Something like that."

"Because you want them to kill you?"

"Well, at first. Now, though, I think it would be more fun if *you* did it. You have the motivation, after all. Your girlfriend. She's my insurance, you see. She's my guarantee that you will kill me."

He settled back into the chair. It took a second for his words to settle in, through my scarlet rage, but then it all fell together.

"No," I said, shaking my head.

"Oh, come on, Gallegher. You've killed lots of men. I wanted to give Galen Crosby the honor. He always craved a shot at zagging a real serial killer, but he never had the balls for it. It's a shame he blew his head off. He'll never know how close he came. I think you'll do much better, though. I got confidence in you, boy. Ain't nothing more reassuring than experience."

"I won't do it," I said.

"Not even to save her life?"

I turned toward him. His face had taken on this almost beatific peacefulness. He knew he had won, but I waited for him to lay it all out for me.

"Your woman is safe," he told me. "For now, at least, nobody will harm her. There are several people out there with instructions. Should I die, then one of them sends a sealed letter to a third party, whom I will obviously not identify, giving that third party instructions to call you and tell you where she can be found. On the other hand, if I am arrested for these murders... well, that would set off an entirely different set of consequences."

"You would have her killed," I said.

He nodded.

"This is really quite a dilemma for you. I want to die, you see, but I also want to *win*. I knew I could pull off the perfect serial killing, but what fun would that be? Killing these whores was easy, after all. The real fun was manipulating you and the police into all these spooky dark dead end alleys, and watching you squirm. You're a smart guy, though. I knew all along that you'd figure me out, sooner or later. On the other hand, spending the rest of my life in jail has no appeal for me at all. So, I'm at the end of the game. It's time to die, and you're going to kill me."

"I won't do it," I said again.

"Oh, you will," Evers argued. "And you'll do it sometime in the next forty-eight hours. If you don't, I'll be forced to turn myself in. I would, of course, be arrested. That would be horribly unfortunate for Ms. Comineau."

There was nothing left to say or do. Clever was way beyond reason, and I didn't have a good argument for him.

I suppose I could have done him right then and there. It wouldn't have been hard. I was furious at him, and not only for placing Merlie in danger. I knew the minute Farley approached me that Clever was nuts. I even told him so. Still, I had allowed Evers to pull my strings like a cheap dime store marionette.

Clever didn't know me as well as he thought. It was true that I had killed before, but never the way he wanted me to, never in anger or out of a desire for revenge, and never in cold blood. Every time I had yanked the chain on some subhuman toilet floater, it had been him or me. A second later, a single instant of indecision, and Pat Gallegher might never have met Merlie Comineau.

What Clever wanted was beyond me. Even if I could have convinced myself to wrap my paws around his neck to squeeze the breath out of him, I never would have been able to finish the deed. Something in my head, some sort of moral/ethical circuit breaker, would have made me break my grip before his eyes glazed over.

I thought about this all the way over to the Rampart Station.

Farley was sitting in his cube, digging in his ear with a paper match, when I filled the doorway. He must have seen the panic in my face.

"What in hell?"

"Grosbard didn't do it," I said.

He tossed the match into the trash, and straightened up his chair.

I pulled the door shut, and sat across from him.

"What did Clever say?" he asked.

I silenced him, by holding my hand up, palm out. I needed time to pull it all together.

"It was Clever," I told him. "*He* killed those girls. He told me so. He's been running us all like lab rats since the very beginning."

Farley looked at me the same way all those nursing students had years before. *Oddity of Nature.*

"I think you just jumped to the end of the story," he said, finally.

I told him everything, about finding the book at Evers' house, about Evers' confession to me. I also told him what Evers wanted, and what would happen to Merlie if I didn't somehow manage to smoke him in within two days.

"Look," I said, "I know Grosberg didn't kill those girls. You know Grosberg didn't kill them. We both know that Clever did it. If you arrest him, though, he's going to have Merlie killed..."

"We don't know that for sure," Farley argued. "You said it yourself. Evers is a devious bastard, a games-player. Maybe he did arrange for Merlie to go somewhere, but that doesn't mean the rest of his story holds water. For all you know, he just has her tucked away in a nice hotel somewhere only he knows about, and there are no letters, and he just told you he had arranged to have her killed if he was arrested to make you do something to him. The guy's a head case, Gallegher. He's Section Eight material. You're too close to the situation to think clearly. He's counting on that."

"And if you're wrong? What are you going to do then? Shake your head and mumble some kind of lame-assed, ponied-up apology? Tell me you were just playing the odds and it went sour this time? That's not good enough for me."

"Yeah? Well how do you feel about a stretch in Angola? Because, whether this sick son of a bitch killed those girls or not, and whether he kidnapped Merlie or not, you kill him and then I'm gonna have to come after you. It's the law, Gallegher. It's what I do. I've already compromised myself once on your behalf. Don't count on me doing it again."

"It doesn't matter. I don't have any intention of killing Clever, no matter what he says. He gave me forty-eight hours to get the

job done. That gives me the same time to find out where he has
Merlie hidden, but I'm going to need your help."

"You aren't really thinking about going along with this guy, are
you? You're gonna play it by his rules?"

The telephone rang on Farley's desk. He glared at me as he
picked it up. A second later, his mouth dropped open.

"Lemme put you on speaker," he said.

He pushed a button on the telephone and dropped the receiver
into the cradle. There was suddenly a mild buzzing noise in the
room from the cheap speaker in the phone.

"*Figured I'd find you there,*" Clever said. "*I just knew that was
the first place you'd go. It's what I would have done, in your
place, back when I was playing it straight. Did Gallegher tell you
everything, Detective?*"

"Enough," Farley said.

"*Well, that's all right. Makes it more fun for me. You coming
over any time soon? Plan on arresting the bad guy?*"

"Maybe…"

"*That would be dumb, Nuckolls. What's more, you know it
would be dumb. I checked you out too, you know. Want me to tell
Gallegher all about your sordid past?*"

"I already know it," I said. At least, I had made some educated
guesses.

"*Not all of it, I'm afraid. When it comes to killing, Gallegher,
you're a fucking amateur compared to Nuckolls. Did he ever tell
you why he became a cop?*"

"To protect and to serve?" I asked.

Evers laughed. It was a raspy, unpleasant, malevolent chuckle.

"*Yeah, right. I have a copy of the letter he wrote when he quit
working for the Feds. Man, was he pissed. Here's a tip, Detective.
Never write something down you might want to take back later.
Now, you gotta realize, Gallegher, that some of this stuff is still
classified. I could read it to you, but then Nuckolls'd have to kill
you, and I can't have that.*"

"Let it be, Evers," Farley growled.

"*Okay, okay. Listen, the real reason I called… See, I know what
you're thinking about doing, here. I gave you forty-eight hours, so*

you and Fearless Limpdick there are considering your options. You think you might be able to use the time to scour the area, check out all the possible places I might have Ms. Comineau stashed, maybe make a covert grab for her so you can arrest me without being afraid for her safety."

Neither Farley nor I said a word.

"Hey! You still there? I just want to give you a tip. Don't waste your time. I spent a little time doing the covert services thing too, Nuckolls. I know how to cover a trail pretty well. Believe me, wherever she is, she's not there under her name or mine. She's hiding, you see? She's playing the game too. She doesn't want the mean ol' Stripper Ripper to come after her, so she's following my directions to stay low, keep out of sight."

"And we take your word for that?" Nuckolls said.

"Yeah. You take that word to the fuckin' bank, Ursus."

Farley sat upright when Clever said *Ursus*, and grabbed at the receiver.

"Listen to me, you fat fuck," he snarled into the receiver. "That was another time, another place, and for goddamn sure another person. You want to meet face to face and talk about old times, that's fine with me, but you keep droppin' code around like bread crumbs, and maybe I'll pay you a visit myself. I won't kill you, but I'll see to it that you feel like absolute shit as long as you live. You got that?"

Whatever Evers said on the other end seemed to do the trick. Farley put the phone back down and stared at it for almost a minute.

"Okay," he said. "What's Plan B?"

There was no Plan B.

Farley rolled the situation over four or five times, and each time we came up with only one solution. He wanted to arrest Evers and take the chance that he was lying about making arrangements to kill Merlie.

In the end, I begged him for some time. We both figured Evers wasn't going anywhere. Farley would stonewall his chief, claim

Grosbard was still being questioned. He wasn't going anywhere either, and that gave us some wiggle room.

I left the station and drove straight over to the restaurant at the corner of Charles and Decatur, from which Lucho Braga had run the New Orleans mob for over twenty years.

"I need to talk with Tommy Callahan," I told the bartender, slightly out of breath.

"Who?"

"You know who. You've worked this bar for as long as I can remember. You contact Callahan, and you tell him Gallegher is in a jam. He'll know what to do."

"Look, buddy," he said, "You want a drink or sumpin'? 'Cause I'm too busy here to play cops and robbers."

"You get him that message," I said, "or Lucho is going to reach from his grave and tie your dick in a knot."

I didn't bother hanging around to discuss the matter with him. There were too many other people to contact. It was time to put the Bourbon Street Irregulars into action.

I started with Petey, the street saxophonist who had given me so many hot tips over the years. I caught him in front of a Greek restaurant over in Storyville, wailing away at something that sounded like Thelonious Monk. I dropped a hundred in his case.

"Take a break," I said.

He put the axe away and sat with his back against the ancient bricks of a former Storyville whorehouse, while I told him what I needed to know.

"Ain' gonna be easy," he said. "There's a lotta guys, you know, but I can ask around. Thing like this, though, I don' know if you talkin' about you' regula' muscle. Mebbe this fella, he bring in talent from outa town…"

"Yeah, I'm covering that one," I said. "I just need to know if anyone has heard about any talent suddenly spending like it's going out of style."

"I'll ask," he promised.

An idea hit me, and I thanked him. The hundred would keep him off the streets long enough to hit some dives and make his inquiries.

I stepped into the Greek restaurant and called Farley.

"I need a favor," I told him.

"What are you up to?"

"I have forty hours. I plan to do whatever I can to get Merlie back without squishing Evers. You're going to help."

"What can I do?"

He actually sounded sympathetic, like he wanted to help. I wasn't used to that from Farley.

"Don't contradict me, okay? I know you have a past. I know you were a hotshot in Phoenix, whether you admit it or not. You were probably connected in organizations the CIA doesn't know the initials of, before you became a cop."

"Gallegher…"

"I said, don't contradict me! This is important. We're going to assume that everything I just said is true. I also know that being covert is just like being a made guy – you never really cut loose. Somewhere in your head is a telephone number. I want you to call that number, and pull in a couple of markers. I want you to find out if anyone has been contacted by Evers over the last week or so about a job. Understand?"

"You're dreaming, man," he said. "You're making up fairy tales. Evers has gotten in your head and he's scrambling your brains with eggs."

I didn't say anything. I just breathed into the phone. I could hear my exhalations echoed back to me in the earpiece.

"I'll call you tonight," he said after several seconds. "You're fantasizing, but maybe I know a guy who knows a guy, you see?"

I saw.

I thanked him, and hung up the telephone.

It took thirty minutes to get back over to Holliday's. As I had expected, Tommy Callahan was sitting in the bar, reading a copy of the *Times-Picayune*.

"I don't have time to explain," I told him. "You have to trust me on this one."

Maybe he could see the desperation in my eyes. He just nodded.

"Somewhere out there is a guy. He's got a contract, and it's conditional. He might not be one of yours. He might be from Houston, or Miami, or Detroit, or Las Vegas, hell, anywhere. His assignment is simple. He gets a call, and he goes and kills Merlie Comineau."

Callahan seemed to jump.

"Your girlfriend…"

"It's complicated. There's this other guy, and he's made the arrangements. If something doesn't happen in the next…" I checked my watch, "…thirty-nine hours, or if he's arrested, then the order goes out."

"Tell me what you want," Callahan said.

"Find him. If he's on your team, maybe we can interdict him."

"If he's not made…"

"Then you'll just hit a dead end. I want the word to go out, though. This is not a mob thing. This guy who put out the contract is a sick fuck, and he's using old connections to kill an innocent woman. This isn't *omerta*, understand?"

He nodded earnestly.

"Look, Gallegher, I can make some calls. There are guys out there, though, guys we… *they* don't control. They're just hired guns, you know? They work for anyone who'll pay the freight."

"Do what you can, okay?"

He stared off into space for a moment.

"You owe me," I reminded him. "I could have blown your cover wide open months ago, but I've kept quiet. A year ago I'd have gone to Hotshot Spano or Lucho Braga, but they're both dead, and all I have now is you, understand?"

Callahan nodded, but his face made it clear he didn't like being backed into this particular corner.

"I like you Gallegher, even though you're way out of line. I'll do this for you, but after that we're jake. Do *you* understand?"

I nodded. I had pulled in a lot of final debts in the last two hours.

"I should know something by this time tomorrow," he said. "I don't think this is gonna pan out for you, but I'll give it a try. After that, though, you got no credit with me."

He stood and left without saying goodbye.

I made several telephone calls over the next hour, pulling in old markers, asking for new favors, hitting on any of my long laundry list of dark characters who might know who might have been hired to kill Merlie.

Then, despite what Clever had said, I pulled down the Greater New Orleans telephone book and started calling hotels, motels, boarding houses, bed and breakfasts – any place that might have a bed for rent. I gave Merlie's name, her maiden name, Clever's name. I even went with descriptions on the off chance that some desk clerk would remember a voluptuous auburn-haired lady with amethyst eyes.

It was long after daylight when I gave up. Exhausted, I dropped into the bed and fell into a troubled sleep full of horrible dreams. Still, my body refused to let me get up, as if it knew I had run through all my reserves, and finally the dreams stopped and I collapsed into a deep dark tunnel, where I stayed until night had fallen over the Quarter.

When I finally awoke, my head felt stuffed and logy. I had a hard time keeping my eyes open at first, as if they were reluctant to face the bitter reality I had to encounter the moment I stepped from the bed.

Instead, I lay in the bed and listed each and every contact I had made, searching for some forgotten resource, a course of action I hadn't contemplated yet.

I had run through every possibility in the book, and each one had been a dead end. Clever was right. She could be anywhere in the country, maybe even in the islands, for all I knew. I could search for the rest of my life, still miss her by as little as an inch, and never ever find her.

There was a favor I hadn't called in, yet.

I suppose it was inevitable that I would find myself, an hour later, in Dag D'Agostino's church. Neither was I surprised to find him there, despite the fact that it was after nine in the evening.

Dag doesn't have a lot shoring him up in his life, and Farley and I took a big part of what he did have away when we pushed him into AA a couple of years back. Like a lot of priests, Dag D'Agostino tended to deal with the unbearable pressure of shepherding by diving into the bottom of the occasional bottle of Jack Daniels. Several times, I had received calls from Petey or Grover or any of a number of other lowlifes out in the quarter, telling me that Dag was puking his guts out in some storm drain, and Farley and I would drag him back to the rectory and toss him into a cold shower. After the ninth or tenth time, he got tired of the routine, and accepted our invitation to drive him to a meeting.

Dag had been dry for several years. That didn't mean he couldn't blow it all at a moment's notice. I wasn't about to make his recovery any easier.

He was sitting in the front pew of his church, chugging on a can of Diet Pepsi, when I strode into the sanctuary. I jerked my head toward the confessional. He slapped the cushion next to him, gesturing for me to join him on the pew.

I thought about it for a second, then looked around the room. We were alone, so I took him up on his offer.

I sat next to him, and took a moment to breathe in the aroma of ancient wood, cheap incense, and the must of a century of penitent believers.

"I thought you'd show up here sooner or later," Dag said.

"What do you know?"

"More than you think."

"He's Catholic."

Dag just stared at me.

I nodded. Dag and I went back a long way, but he wasn't about to violate the sanctity of the confessional, not for me or anyone else. He took his sacred duty as just that, and I had never known him to divulge a confidence. It was one of the reasons he used to drink so much.

"I'm thinking about killing him," I said.

"Yeah. I figured."

"I didn't come here looking for permission."

"I know."

"Or absolution."

"I can't forgive an act you haven't committed yet."

"What about later?"

He stood and walked to his end of the pew, then to the altar. He hadn't been expecting guests this time of the evening. I suspect he had just been sitting in the sanctuary, his place of refuge, drinking in the solitude and peace and silence, when I barged in and stomped all over his serenity. He kissed the shawl and placed it around his tired, slumped shoulders, before walking back down and facing me from in front of the pew.

"You wanna take this into the box?" he said.

"No, Dag... Father. This will do just fine."

"You know the rules, Pat, just as well as I. All acts are forgiven, if you come to the Lord in contrition and a genuine desire to purify yourself. I am merely the conduit. I neither judge nor do I condemn. You're asking whether you could come to me after killing this man, and be cleansed of that sin. The answer is yes. Of course you can. In the eyes of the Lord you will be as newly born, and you know this perfectly. Why, then, are you here tonight?"

"She's all I have."

"There, you're wrong. You have much more. You have a stubborn tendency to ignore that."

"I promised her."

"That you'd kill this man?"

"That I wouldn't let her die."

He nodded, and ran a hand through his sparse, straggly, graying hair.

"That was foolish, Pat."

"Isn't that a little judgmental?"

"So I slipped a little. You don't have the power over life and death. When you promised to keep her alive, you forgot where that power really lies. It was presumptuous."

"So I'm being punished?"

"Don't be ridiculous. You have no more power over what's happening than you did at the blackjack table. You could have made all the promises there that you wanted, and the cards still would have gone bust. This is beyond your control. It always was."

"What do I do, Dag?"

He walked back around and sat next to me, his weight collapsing the cushion. He leaned back and put his arm around my shoulders, and I felt a strength in his grasp that I had not noticed before.

"Damned if I know," he said after several moments. "You sure can put yourself in some spots. Tell you what. Why don't we just sit here and think about it for a while?"

I left an hour later, no closer to a decision than I had been when I walked in.

None of my leads panned out.

Tommy Callahan called the next morning. He had made some inquiries. Nobody he'd contacted knew anything about a contract on Merlie Comineau.

"You want to tell me what's going on?" he said. "Maybe I can help some other way."

"I wish I could, Tommy. Maybe in a day or so."

Petey called next. He had come up dry, too.

I called Farley.

"Damnedest thing," Farley told me. "One of my old Marine buddies called me just an hour ago. Seems he was knockin' back a few with some of the old squad just last night, said they started talkin' about me, and decided to get in touch."

"Don't get coy with me right now," I growled. "Did you learn anything or not?"

"Nothing," he said. "If Evers has arranged for someone from the covert services to do a whack on Merlie, it's a beaucoup secret. I don't think he could do it, Pat. Fibbies don't have those sorts of connections."

"I'm running out of time, Farley."

"I got a clock, too. I got something worse, though. Seems your buddy Grosbard lawyered up during the night. His attorney has filed a writ of *habeus*, and the Chief has gotten wind of his story. I'm overdue for a first-rate ass-chewing."

"What are you saying?"

"I gotta move one way or the other in the next twelve hours."

"My time's up before then," I said.

"You think I don't know that?"

"Give me a few more hours, Farley."

"I can give you until five. After that, I'm taking over."

He hung up the phone.

By four that afternoon, I had run out of options. I could almost feel Clever, sitting in his dingy, musty home, chuckling over my dilemma. As the clock struck four, I sat in the bar, sipping on a Dixie, hating him more than I had hated any single person in my entire life.

I set down the bottle, and walked around the counter to the cash register. Without looking, I stuck my hand into the hollow underneath the cash drawer, and my fingers closed around the plastic grip of Shorty's .38 Police Special.

I had killed once already with this gun, when Barry Saunders cornered me in the bar several years earlier, waiting to kill me and make it look like a robbery. I could still remember the hours I lay on the beer-stained floor behind the bar after surprising him with Shorty's gun, as his life seeped out of him into the heart pine in front of the stage, from the two neat holes I'd drilled in his chest.

I pulled the pistol out and stared at it, the way it fit my hand. I could smell the sweetness of the gun oil, and my fingers caressed the cool metal of the body and the cylinder.

I walked back to the table and set the gun down on it, then sat down and stared at it some more.

I would be forgiven, I told myself, as I drank the beer.

Dag had said so. I had already known it, of course, but it had been a comfort to get independent corroboration.

I could drive over to Clever's house, walk in the door, stick the Police Special right up his nose and blow his fucking brains all the way down the hall, and absolution was a silly little confession away. Dag didn't have to approve, but he did have to forgive. No matter what Farley did, whether I had to spend the rest of my miserable days at Angola, or whether I had to take it on the lam to some foreign shore, or if I just decided to stick my head in the oven because I couldn't live with the guilt, Merlie would be alive and my tarnished soul would be intact.

What the hell, I reasoned.

No plan was perfect.

The most important factor was that I had made a promise. There had been no conditions affixed to it. Merlie hadn't demanded that I keep her alive *and* not kill anyone else in the process.

I reached out again, and laid my hand on the gun. It was cold and inert, but it seemed to pulsate under my hand, and I realized it was the thrum of my own quickening heartbeat that I felt, as I inched closer to a terrible conclusion.

My fingers closed on the pistol, and I picked it up. I held it up to the light, and for a second I marveled at the power it imparted – not the power of life or death, but the power to right a heinous wrong in a way the law never could. I had forsaken my own seminary training and my trust in a merciful and forgiving deity. What I felt now was more ancient, an Old Testament sort of cleansing, a wrathful and vengeful justice that was ever so more satisfying than waiting for the asswipe to meet his fate at the hands of an unknowable Almighty.

The spell was broken by the voice of Farley Nuckolls.

"Bad move, Gallegher."

I didn't look at him. Neither did I lower the gun.

"I don't see it that way," I said.

"You'd never get away with it."

"I don't give a damn about that. She'd be alive."

"You'd be dead, or as good as dead. You'd never be together again."

"That doesn't seem very important right now."

He walked over, and faced me as I held the Police Special up in the light. He reached out, and his own bony hand closed around my hammy one, around the weapon.

"I've already made too many compromises," he said.

"You don't know the meaning of the word."

"Don't I? Give me the gun. Now. Let it go."

He twisted his hand, and the pistol came away from my grasp. Maybe it was some secret thing they teach cops at the academy.

Maybe my hand hadn't been as convinced as I thought I was.

He set the gun back down on the tabletop.

"I have to go get him," Farley said. "The Chief won't wait until morning. I have to go get him tonight."

"Or?"

"Or it's my ass. He knows Grosbard didn't do it. He suspects I know who did. I've run out of time. I have to go get Clever tonight."

"And what then?" I asked. "You'll arrest him? Prosecute him? You know what the chance is that he'll be executed? You want to know just how many serial killers have sucked the green gas over the last ten years? He'll walk on this one, and Merlie will take the heat."

"I have to do it this way," he said. "I can't…"

But he stopped. At that moment, I realized he had been waging his own internal struggle just as I had. Something in him wanted to see Clever splattered, whether he could allow himself to say it or not.

"You *see* it," I said. "You *know* what has to be done."

"I…*can't!*" he said. "I won't. It's wrong, Gallegher. I know that Clever Evers killed those girls, and I know he needs to pay for it, but I won't do it the way you want, and I won't let you do it either."

I couldn't look at him. I needed a drink. I slid my chair away from the table, leaving the pistol lying there as the gulf between me and Farley Nuckolls, and I turned.

Shorty was standing at the bar. I hadn't heard him come in through the back door. He was holding the zippered bag with the till money, but his eyes were riveted on mine, and they were glazed over with tears.

"You son of a bitch," he said. "I took you in. I gave you this fuckin' job. I let you live upstairs. This is how you give it back? You hold out on me when you know Evers killed my Lucy?"

"Wait, Shorty..." I started.

"Like hell. How long you known about this? A week? Two weeks? You were walking around with this in your head, and that asshole is still breathing free air?"

"I couldn't do anything about it," I said.

"Shorty," Farley said, "He's right. Evers has Merlie hidden away somewhere, and if he's arrested he says he'll have her killed."

"I'm trying to find where he's taken her," I said. "As soon as I know where she is, I can arrange for protection, and we'll nail the bastard. You have my word on that."

"What, he's using her to keep you from killing him?"

"I told you," I said, "It's more complicated than that."

I looked at Farley for help. He just shrugged.

"This is your play, Gallegher. I'd just as soon waltz over and put the cuffs on Evers. You're the one who insists on waiting."

"Waiting!" Shorty spat. "Waiting for what? For him to kill another girl, rip her open and leave her bleeding on the sidewalk?"

"He gave me forty-eight hours," I said.

"What's he doing, writing his fuckin' memoirs? What's he need forty-eight hours for?"

"You don't understand..." I tried.

"Then you better fuckin' explain it to me, or start lookin' for another job and another place to flop!"

"He wants me to kill him!" I said, all the frustration and anger of the last day flooding out of me like molten lava. "He gave me two days to kill him, or he's going to have Merlie taken out. If he's arrested, she dies. If I don't kill him by eight o'clock tonight, Merlie dies. If I kill Evers, Farley says he's going to put me in Angola. Clever's backed me into a corner, and I'm damned if I can find a way out. I've spent the last forty hours trying to find where he's stashed Merlie. It's all dead ends. The guy planned for every move I've made."

"I told you, Gallegher," Farley said. "It's all a shuck. He's yankin' your chain. Lemme arrest him, and we'll sweat it out of him where she is."

"That's not good enough for me," I shouted, turning back to him. "Damn it, I'm fifty years old. How many years do I have left? How many shots do I have to find someone as right for me as Merlie? It would be different, maybe, if only he had her stashed away in that big house of his. I'd just paint the ceiling with him and get her out, and you could send him up to rot at Angola. It's different this time, man. I can't take chances this time. I can't count on being *that* lucky."

"I'm already doing you a favor I don't owe you," Farley said, tipping his Panama hat back at an even more improbable angle than usual. "What makes you think I even have to give a flyin' fuck about your problems? I got a stone serial killer in the palm of my hand, here. I can pick him up any time I want. It's been a two days since he confessed to you. You tried, man. You've done everything you can to find her. Why don't you leave it to me? I can arrest him without it ever making the papers. I can get him out of that house so quiet that his *dog* won't even know he's gone."

"And maybe he's arranged it so that he has to contact someone every hour to make sure he's at home, waiting for me to come after him..."

"Jesus, Gallegher, you're getting paranoid..."

"It's only paranoia if it's irrational. Clever's thought this out to the smallest decimal. He's accounted for every move I've made. What makes you think he hasn't already thought of the moves I haven't considered yet?"

"You're talkin' crazy, now," Farley said. "Ain't it true, Shorty? Is he talkin' crazy or what..."

We both stared at the bar.

Somehow, while we were arguing, Shorty had disappeared.

"Oh, bloody Christ," Farley wheezed. "He wouldn't..."

"Wouldn't what?" I said coldly.

"He knows who killed Lucy now."

"Yeah, he does."

Nuckolls turned toward me.

"You saw him leave. You acted crazy so I would be preoccupied with you, and you gave him time to get out of here."

"That would be the act of a coolly rational man, Farley. As you observed a minute ago, I'm out of control."

Nuckolls turned back to the bar and seemed to think for a minute.

"Get going," I said.

"What?"

"Get lost. Take a hike. You're too wrapped up in this Clever Evers mess. Surely you have some other crimes to work on. Something to keep you occupied for a couple of hours?"

"What are you saying?"

"I'm saying it's time to open the bar. Shorty and I have some work to do. It's our job. It's what we do. The customers will be showing up soon. Shorty and I have to work."

"But Shorty's not..." he stopped.

"Get lost," I said. "I'll keep an eye on Shorty. He's going to be just fine. Come on back in two or three hours. We'll buy you a beer."

"You're nuts," Farley said, pushing his chair away from the table. "Both of you."

"Hear that, Shorty?" I said, waving toward the empty bar. "He says we're nuts. Think we ought to get it in writing? Might help in court. Maybe he's right. Comes from lack of sleep, maybe."

"Or a guilty conscience."

"Get lost, Farley," I said again. "Go see a movie. Clear your head. Take a stroll down the Riverwalk. Visit a sick aunt. Do anything you want, you hear? Anything that gets your mind off this Clever Evers thing."

There was nothing left to say. Nuckolls got the message. No matter what happened, Shorty had an alibi for that evening, as long as there was nobody around to dispute it. He didn't like it one bit, and for a moment I thought he might slip the bracelets on me and haul me down to the Rampart Station for safekeeping until he could decide what to do.

Then, something seemed to click in his head. Maybe he realized that even if Shorty did something monumentally stupid, like maybe twisting Clever's head around a couple of times, there was nothing the law could likely do to him. Considering Shorty's grief and his state of mind, he'd probably be found incompetent to stand trial.

He shook his head, as if warding off a bad memory. He didn't say anything. He just started backing away, slowly, deliberately, never taking his eyes off my own, until he reached the shadowed doorway to the bar. Then he stepped out into the fading sunlight of the Quarter.

Despite my anxiety, I decided to work that night. Maybe I thought it would be some sort of tonic, getting up on the stage and making some sort of music.

Shorty returned to the bar about two hours after he left, without saying a word. He just walked into Holliday's, pulled on an apron, and set about opening the bar for the night.

Even as I dropped out of a badly rendered version of *Summertime*, and handed the break over to Sockeye Sam, I had trouble catching Shorty's eye. When, at last, he did look over my way, he just gave me this conspiratorial wink, and went back to pouring drinks.

Around eleven that night, Farley Nuckolls walked into the club. Even in the dim light, I could see the sallow, sunken bags under his eyes, and the slump in his shoulders seemed, if possible, even more pronounced as he took a seat at an empty table. Shorty walked out from behind the bar and set a cold one in front of him. Farley didn't protest, but neither did he look at him.

I settled the Conn band cornet into the stand next to my stool, and stepped off the stage to join Farley at the table. Within seconds, an Amstel appeared in front of me. Shorty never comps me the good stuff. I looked up at him, and he winked again.

It was getting creepy.

After Shorty returned to the bar, Farley looked up at me, and took a long draw from the bottle.

"Busy night," he said. "Hell of a night. Forty-eight hours was up at seven-thirty."

I nodded.

"I know," I said.

"At seven-thirty-five, I parked in front of Evers' house, with two cruisers. The front door was unlocked. We went in, and found Evers hanging in the bathroom. You ever seen anyone that's been hanged, Gallegher?"

"No."

"It's gruesome."

He drank almost half the bottle in a single pull.

"Was there a note?" I asked.

"No. Doesn't mean much, though. Half the suicides I've worked didn't bother to leave any parting words."

"You're calling it a suicide?"

"That's what it is. No sign of forced entry, no bruises on the body, no indications of a struggle. Just this dead, bloating, black guy on the end of a rope. Had some unusual ligature marks on his neck. It might be possible to infer soft strangulation, of course, but it also could have happened if the rope hadn't been tied tight enough."

We both, instinctively, looked over at Shorty, who was bringing two fresh brewskis to our table. His forearms were like wire-bound stovepipes. He picked up the empties and walked away, and I wondered how anything those arms did could be construed as '*soft*'.

"Coroner was satisfied that Evers did himself. That's all fine with me."

"Maybe he did," I said.

"You figure?"

"It's possible. One last joke on everyone. He wanted to play us all, and he did a great job of it. Maybe this last forty-eight hours was the crowning touch, making us all squirm when he really intended to take the noose all along."

"That going to help you sleep tonight?"

"I'll take what I can get," I said. "If it brings Merlie back, I'll sleep like a babe."

He didn't reply. I didn't get the impression, though, that he bought it.

"So, it's over," I said.

"No, Gallegher, it's not over. There's a lot more coming. Some of it's already started. About an hour after we got to Evers' house, a courier delivered a sealed letter to the Chief. It was from Evers. He told the whole story, just the way you told me. He cleared Grosbard, and took responsibility for the stripper killings. He described each of the killings, how he tracked that poor German kid, how he took the girls to secluded places and sliced them up, and how he led the police on for weeks.

"Half an hour later, another courier delivered a package to the hospital. Inside were instructions on how to access money Evers had set aside to pay for Grosbard's treatment and recovery. Grosbard received a letter with a cashiers check in it for a little over a hundred thousand, to compensate him for his '*trouble*'."

"Sounds like he was putting paid all his debts," I said.

"You haven't had any couriers in here tonight, have you?"

"No," I said, wistfully. "I think I know what my payoff is. I just haven't gotten it yet."

"Well, all in good time, I suppose."

He drained the second beer in a little less than a minute, then picked up his panama hat from the table and slid it back on his head.

"I'm leaving now," he said. "You like doing favors, right?"

I nodded somberly.

"Yeah, I've been on to you for some time. Well, I'm going to ask you for a favor, right here and now. I plan to go away for a few weeks. Got some vacation time piled up. Thought I might go somewhere warm, look at some curvy babes in bikinis for a while, drink some fruity shit from pineapple halves, that sort of thing."

"Sounds like a good idea."

"I should be returning sometime after Christmas, you see. Around the first of the year."

"Fresh starts. New beginnings."

"Or, maybe I won't come back at all. This whole affair has left a rotten taste in my mouth. It's made me do things I won't want to think about for a while. You know what I mean?"

I knew.

I had a whole life like that.

"I think I understand."

"Then, you'll also understand this favor I'm asking. If and when I do come back, I don't want to see you around for a long time. Maybe ever. I don't know what goes on in that dumb mick head of yours, Gallegher, but somehow I have a feeling my nightmares are sweet dreams compared to yours. Someday, I think maybe you're gonna get badly splattered. I don't want to be around to catch the shrapnel."

"Can't blame you for that," I said. "But I wouldn't count on it, Farley. I don't splatter easy."

"That's what I mean. That's the kind of stinkin' thinkin' that's gonna catch up with you one day."

I held out my hand.

"Goodbye, Farley," I said, "It's been fun. Maybe we'll do it again sometime."

He grasped my hand, with a vigor I would not have suspected.

"She'll show up," he said. "That's the way things work for you. You are one lucky son of a bitch."

"Everyone seems to think so."

"Watch your back," he said.

He turned, made a gun with his hand and shot at Shorty with it. Shorty grinned and winked at him, like there was some kind of understanding there.

Maybe there was.

Farley walked out of the bar, into the December fog.

I wouldn't see him again for a long, long time.

Shorty walked over and took his seat.

"I don't want to know," I said.

"Don't want to tell you."

"Yeah you do."

"You too."

"Bad idea."

"Maybe," Shorty observed. "He had no business breathing, after what he did."

"You know, the coroner can establish time of death pretty accurately, especially in the first couple of hours."

"Yeah, I think I saw that on a cop show."

"It sure would help my conscience if he found that Clever hanged himself before four o'clock."

Shorty leaned back in his seat, and scratched at the stubble under his chin.

"Seems to me you spend way too much time dealing with that conscience. I said he had no business breathing. Never said I helped him stop."

He got up and returned to the bar.

Shorty never mentioned Clever Evers' death again. He never told me whether he hanged Clever from the shower rod, or if he found him that way, or if he even went to Evers' house.

I never asked.

Maybe it's better that way.

EPILOGUE

My mind wasn't in the music. I couldn't concentrate, watching Shorty standing behind the bar, pouring shooters and beers with this beatific smile on his face. All I could think about was Merlie, sitting out there somewhere, completely unaware that she was either about to be rescued, or killed.

Finally, the music stopped coming. I gestured to Sockeye to carry on without me. I don't think he saw me. It really didn't matter. Musicians like Sockeye Sam tend to be driven by something internal that defies interruption.

"I'm blown out," I told Shorty, as I grabbed the Abita he put on the bar in front of me. "I'm going upstairs to crash. Let me know if I get any visitors."

He nodded, and turned immediately to serve a woman who had sidled up to the bar.

Going to my apartment might have been a mistake. As long as I was in the bar, surrounded by people, my natural inclination not to embarrass myself had kept me from breaking out in flopsweat and losing bladder control. Alone in my quarters, though, my anxiety began to overcome me, and I started to shake as I sat in my overstuffed recliner next to the window.

I don't know when it happened, but after a while the accumulated tension and emotional exhaustion caught up with me, and I dozed off.

The telephone rang around three in the morning. I jumped up, almost before my brain registered it, and grabbed the receiver.

"Yes!" I almost shouted.

"Um, is this Patrick Gallegher?"

"Yeah."

"Um, my name is Tony Graham. I'm a student at Loyola."

"Yeah, Tony. What do you have for me?"

"Well, I don't know, actually. Some guy hired me a few days ago, gave me two hundred dollars and an envelope. He told me to hold on to the envelope, and he would call me with instructions."

"Did he call?"

"Uh huh. He said I should open the envelope and follow the instructions inside."

"What did they say?"

"Well, there's your name and telephone number. The instructions said for me to call you, and to read this message. *I win. Thanks for the game. 1156 Admiral Sems Highway, Mobile, Alabama. Room 667.*"

"Wait a minute. Let me write that down."

He read it again, and I copied it onto a message pad on my table.

"What does it mean?" Graham asked.

"Good news, kid. Great news. Do me a favor, okay?"

"Sure. What?"

"Forget everything about this, understand? This never happened."

"Jeez, this is like some kind of spy movie."

"Kid, you'll never know. Thanks for the call."

It took me ten minutes to find out which hotel was at 1156 Admiral Sems Highway in Mobile. I called, asked for room 667.

The telephone rang twice, before someone picked it up.

"Hello?" Merlie said.

"It's me," I said.

There was a long pause.

"It's over?"

"Come on home, beautiful. There's no danger now. Or I can come get you. I can be there in a few hours. Will you wait for me?"

"I've been waiting for you for almost a week, already. What in hell has been going on down there?"

"It's a long story. I just want you to understand, though, that I kept my promise."

I thought I heard a sharp draw of breath on the other end, as if she were reading my mind.

"You didn't let me die."

"And I never will. Shall I drive up? I can leave right now."

We agreed that I would come to Mobile to get her. I would have a lot of time on the way to figure out what kind of story I would tell her. I couldn't be certain, yet, whether I would make Clever the villain or not.

It was a tough business, fighting monsters. In the short term, it seemed to work out, but over the long haul the monsters always seemed to win. They'd tormented Galen Crosby until he had no choice but to swallow the business end of his service nine, and they'd turned Clever Evers into one of their own. Perhaps, if I had kept at it long enough, they would have destroyed me too.

Or, perhaps, given my checkered history over the last ten years, they'd already done it.

All I knew was that, four hours away, languishing in a hotel room off the Admiral Sems Highway in Mobile Alabama, was an auburn-haired, amethyst-eyed babe who made this hardscrabble life worth waging, and I had to get to her.

I dashed to my bathroom, splashed some water on my face, and prepared to leave. Just before I turned off the bathroom light, I caught my face in the mirror. It was craggier and more wan than I seemed to recall, and I wondered if that came with the years or the mileage.

It didn't matter. I was on the way to pick up Merlie, who was safe again, and that made all the other stuff worth it. Life was about to return to normal, which was about all anyone could ask of it. I was happy, and content again. That was fine with me.

For I am, after all, one lucky son of a bitch.

ABOUT THE AUTHOR

Richard Helms is a forensic psychologist and a nationally recognized expert in the field of sex crimes. As the former president of the North Carolina Association for Management and Treatment of Sex Offenders, he has been in demand to present at various local, state, and national conferences on the typologies and assessment of sex offenders.

When not working in the courts of his home state or writing, Helms indulges his other passions, including gourmet cooking, amateur astronomy, building stringed musical instruments, and spending time with his family.

Helms lives in North Carolina with his lovely spouse Elaine, their two children Alex and Rachel, and four cats.

JUICY WATUSI is his eighth published novel.

THE AMADEUS LEGACY
(ISBN 0-595-21147-X)

Twelve years ago, Geoffrey Sterling helped depose an American president, but lost everything he held dear. After hiding from life for twelve years at a small Maryland college, he is assigned to interview the author of a tell-all book about the inner workings of international spy agencies. The author's house is bombed, and his dying words to Sterling, "AMADEUS", propel Sterling headlong onto the gameboard of international intrigue, as a major player. In order to stay alive, Sterling must discover the meaning of AMADEUS, battle the latest generation in a dynasty of assassins dating back to the martyrdom of Thomas a Becket, and forestall the realization of a four hundred year old prophecy which could spell the end of civilization across the entire world!

THE VALENTINE PROFILE
(ISBN 0-595-21154-2)

Charleston psychologist Mark Lovell considered Judge Matthew Valentine to be a good choice for the US Senate—until he found a psychiatric chart for the judge on a colleague's desk. The information in the chart suggested dark psychological problems that could make the potential Senator dangerous.

When Valentine commits suicide, after the information in the chart is revealed to the press, Lovell must discover whether the judge was actually murdered, and whether he might have played some unwitting part in an insidious plot to discredit and ultimately eliminate Valentine from the race.

At the heart of his search is the information he gathered from the psychiatric chart, which might now get him killed too! In order to stay alive, Lovell must uncover the surprising secret behind

The Valentine Profile!

NON-STOP SUSPENSE AND ACTION, AVAILABLE FROM RICHARD HELMS and MYSTERY AND SUSPENSE PRESS!

ORDER YOUR COPIES NOW !

Printed in the United States
6379